# ABOUT THE AUTHOR

When *USA Today* bestselling author Alissa Callen isn't writing, she plays traffic controller to four children, three dogs, two horses and one renegade cow who believes the grass is greener on the other side of the fence. After a childhood spent chasing sheep on the family farm, Alissa has always been drawn to remote areas and small towns, even when residing overseas. She is partial to autumn colours, snowy peaks and historic homesteads and will drive hours to see an open garden. Once a teacher and a counsellor, she remains interested in the life journeys that people take. She draws inspiration from the countryside around her, whether it be the brown snake at her back door or the resilience of bush communities in times of drought or flood. Her books are characteristically heartwarming, authentic and character driven. Alissa lives on a small slice of rural Australia in central western NSW.

**Also by Alissa Callen**

*The Long Paddock*
*The Red Dirt Road*
*The Round Yard*

# THE
# BOUNDARY
# FENCE

## ALISSA CALLEN

mira

First Published 2020
First Australian Paperback Edition 2020
ISBN 9781489269775

The Boundary Fence
© 2020 by Alissa Callen
Australian Copyright 2020
New Zealand Copyright 2020

This is a work of fiction. Names, characters, places, and incidents are either the
product of the author's imagination or are used fictitiously, and any resemblance to
actual persons, living or dead, business establishments, events, or locales is entirely
coincidental.

Published by
Mira
An imprint of Harlequin Enterprises (Australia) Pty Limited (ABN 47 001 180 918),
a subsidiary of HarperCollins Publishers Australia Pty Limited (ABN 36 009 913 517)
Level 13, 201 Elizabeth St
SYDNEY NSW 2000
AUSTRALIA

A catalogue record for this book is available from the National Library of Australia
www.librariesaustralia.nla.gov.au

Printed and bound in Australia by McPherson's Printing Group

FSC
www.fsc.org

MIX
Paper from
responsible sources
FSC® C001695

*To Luke*

# CHAPTER

# 1

Being a rural vet didn't get any more glamorous than this.

Ella Quinlivan carefully felt inside the Hereford cow sitting on the ground in front of her. When she'd confirmed the cow was not carrying a calf, she sat back on her heels and removed the orange plastic glove that covered her arm from her fingertips to her shoulder.

She cast a quick glance at the young farmer who was fresh home from his first year of agricultural college. It didn't matter where her hand had just been, or that she was covered in dirt and her face would be flushed from the summer heat, the lanky redhead's broad grin hadn't waned. Neither had his attention on the front of her shirt.

She slowly came to her feet. It was going to be one of those afternoons. 'You said Polly's been drooling?'

'She has.' The answer came from Sophie, the farmer's teenage sister, who appeared at her brother's side. A battered, oversized cream hat covered her auburn braid. 'Is it pesti?'

'It could be.' Ella assessed the water trough beside which the Hereford had positioned herself before she became too weak to stand. Pesti virus could be spread via water or animal fluids but she couldn't see any other cattle in either the cow's paddock or the adjacent one.

Sophie too scanned the paddocks that contained the sparse stubble of a past winter oats crop. 'There were some other cattle but Dad sent them to the fat sales last week.'

The young farmer said nothing as he let his younger sister do the talking. When Ella looked at him, he gave her a wink. She pushed the brim of her navy Woodlea vet cap higher and gave him her best I-am-way-too-old-for-you stare before focusing on the prone Hereford.

From previous visits Ella knew Polly had been a poddy calf and was now a much-loved family pet. She also knew the farm traded cattle so chances were there had been a pesti virus carrier in the herd that had been sold.

She bent down to press her stethoscope against Polly's russet side. This farm wasn't the only one lightening their stocking rate after the dry winter and spring. Despite the lack of rain the Hereford was in good condition.

She straightened. 'I'll send some blood off to confirm it's pesti and give Polly a shot.'

'Thanks.' Sophie's solemn expression dissolved into a relieved smile. She went to collect a green tub from off the nearby farm ute. When she returned she frowned across to where her brother still stood watching Ella. 'Oi, Joe, I need some help here.'

Ella masked a smile at Sophie's exasperated eye roll. The teenager reminded her of herself when she was young. Sophie took the health of her animals very seriously and had already asked Ella about what high school subjects she needed to study in order to become a vet.

Joe speared his sister with an impatient glance before sauntering off to help her fill the bucket from the trough. When he'd placed the bucket in reach of Polly, he strode back to Ella as she finished drawing a sample of blood.

She swiped at a fly. The action caused her honey-blonde ponytail to slide over her shoulder. The young farmer's grin broadened as he hooked his thumbs into his belt. She made a mental note to talk to Taylor at the hair salon about donating her hair to be made into another wig for cancer sufferers. Blondes, even natural ones, didn't always have more fun.

Sophie settled a second bucket filled with hay in front of Polly. The teenager stroked the Hereford's curly white forehead. 'We can set up a tarp to give her some shade.'

Ella nodded. 'Great idea. Joe, I'm sure you could weld up a quick frame?'

'Yeah—'

'Wonderful.' She walked towards the veterinary hospital ute before he could add anything else, like ask her what she was doing tonight. It was Friday and even before sunset the Royal Arms would be full of laughter and locals.

A fatigue that stemmed from more than the heat dragged at her feet. She no longer had the energy to deal with masculine attention. She might have been genetically blessed but having a pretty face hadn't been an asset when her brother died, her parents divorced or her father started a new family. She was so much more than how she looked.

She stopped herself from favouring her right leg. Ticking the so-called attractive box also hadn't stopped her world from caving in on that icy English lane.

She disposed of the used glove in the small bin on the back of the ute and the needles in the yellow sharps container. When footsteps approached, she took a second before facing Sophie and Joe.

'I'll give you a call,' she said, careful to not hold Joe's gaze for too long, 'as soon as I hear anything.'

Joe went to speak but then grunted as his sister's elbow jammed into his side.

'Thank you,' Sophie said, smile sweet. 'Don't worry about closing the gate. Joe can finally make himself useful.'

Ella gave the siblings a wave before driving away. In her rear-view mirror she saw Sophie turn to her older brother and waggle a finger at him. This time Ella didn't have to hide her smile. It was common knowledge that she wasn't interested in any kind of relationship. Even Edna Galloway, the notorious local matchmaker, left her alone. Sophie would make sure Joe received the same message loud and clear.

Ella took the first turn right to head to town. The silver-tipped leaves of the gum trees beside the road didn't sway. The blades of the windmills, for which Woodlea was renowned, didn't spin. The only movement in the thirsty landscape was the shimmer of heatwaves across the black bitumen.

She adjusted the air conditioner temperature and angled the vents so cold air rushed over her hot skin. Her tight headache didn't ease, so she took a sip from the water bottle beside her. Joe's interest shouldn't have bothered her. Usually she had no trouble ignoring unwanted attention.

She slowed as she entered the town limits. The emotional toll of helping out after the bushfires last month must still be having an impact. Despite all the animals she'd saved when she'd spent a fortnight out west, far too many had been lost. She had to be tired and that's why she was on edge. There couldn't be any other explanation.

At the mixed practice veterinary hospital she drove along the side lane to park near the stables. A bay thoroughbred whickered as she left the driver's seat. The sociable gelding had been chased by wild dogs into a barbed wire fence. After rubbing his glossy neck, she checked that the bandage on his front leg remained in place.

The drone of the cicadas followed her as she headed into the cool of the vet surgery. The clinic was closed, and with no overnight guests in the kennel room, the normally bustling building was quiet. She busied herself with restocking the vet vehicle and completing the day's paperwork. Smothering a yawn, she double-checked the details she'd typed onto Polly's computer file.

A country melody blared from her mobile. She slipped it free from her shirt pocket and saw Fliss's smiling face on the screen. Ella hesitated. The local doctor was a close friend, but through no fault of Fliss's things had become complicated since Ella had returned from helping out after the bushfires.

She answered the call before she could change her mind. 'Hi, Fliss.'

'Hi, stranger. Hope you weren't outside in this heat for too long today.'

'Only this afternoon.'

'How's life out of town? All settled in?'

Three weeks ago she'd moved to a small farm that had belonged to an elderly friend who'd needed the support of an aged care facility in Woodlea. Though Ella had purchased the property, she viewed herself more as a custodian of what had been Violet's childhood and family home. The sandstone cottage was still filled with many of Violet's possessions that Ella was slowly helping her sort through. Ella was now also the owner of two affectionate and inquisitive brown-and-white goats.

'Just about. I left Hewitt a message, but can you please pass on my thanks for the hay?'

'Of course. Speaking of Hewitt, he's pulled a muscle in his back so instead of going into the pub for dinner we're having a barbeque if you'd like to come?'

'Thanks, but I can't.' In the past she'd have been the first person there and the last to leave. 'I promised Violet I'd see her after work. We've got boxes to sort through.'

'No worries. I'll see you at Cressy's on Sunday then?'

Ella didn't miss the doubt in Fliss's words. It was only a matter of time before the perceptive and no-nonsense doctor asked her what was going on. Ella briefly closed her eyes. She couldn't hide forever even if Sunday wasn't Cressy's baby shower. 'I'll be there.'

'Wonderful. Give my love to Violet. See you soon.'

'Will do.'

Ella ended the call and stared at the now blank screen. She wasn't sure how she would explain to Fliss that being around pregnant Cressy was proving difficult. Ella had never hidden that she was happy on her own but seeing the growing swell of Cressy's stomach had awakened yearnings she hadn't expected.

She stared unseeingly at Polly's file. Yearnings that only reminded her of what she could have had, someone who loved her, a home and a family, if she hadn't made such foolish choices. She shut down the computer, ignoring the little voice that said there could be another reason why she'd avoided Fliss and Hewitt's barbeque.

Now in her personal four-wheel drive, she drove through town. Outside the white wrought-iron trimmed Royal Arms, a row of dusty cars had already congregated. With the season continuing to be tough, it was reassuring to see people finding a social outlet for their uncertainty and stress. Next Thursday she would be talking to local farmers about livestock nutrition in dry times. The free event would provide a further chance for people to connect and to chat.

At the final street before the road headed out of town, she turned and pulled up outside the manicured gardens of Woodlea Lodge. A sign on the fence indicated that bore water was in use and was why the small swathe of lawn appeared such a fresh green. Arms laden with a large box, she followed the paved path to unit four. She didn't get a chance to knock before the door swung open.

Violet stood in the doorway, leaning heavily on the floral walking stick Ella had gifted her. Though she was tiny and thin, the lift to the older woman's chin countered any impression of fragility. 'In you come, that box looks heavy.'

Ella followed Violet into the tidy two-bedroom self-care unit. 'It's fine. It's the last of the items from your sewing cupboard.'

'It shouldn't take long to go through then.' Violet tapped the table with her walking stick. 'I'm sure you have better things to do on a Friday night than visit me.'

Ella sat the box on the living room table. 'With the day I've had, the only place I'm going to after this is home.'

Violet patted her arm. 'I'd better put the kettle on.'

Ella knew not to offer to help. Independent Violet had made it clear the first time she'd visited her sandstone cottage for a cuppa that she didn't appreciate assistance.

Instead, Ella unpacked the jars of pins, buttons and packets of lace and quilting squares. Each visit she brought a new box of Violet's belongings. Some items would go back with Ella for safekeeping, others would go in a pile to be donated to the charity shop and another pile would be for Violet's fellow residents. Mrs Amos in unit eight loved vases while Mrs Lewis in unit three collected old teaspoons. Any spare books would go to the little street library outside the adventure playground or the community bookshelf at the Reedy Creek Hall.

As she took out the final item, a pink cotton shirt with a tear, she glanced into the kitchen where Violet was spooning tea into a teapot. She could only hope the shirt had belonged to Annette and not Libby.

The answer came in a rattle of china as Violet walked into the living room and stared at the shirt before lowering the empty teacup and saucer onto the table. Ella quickly moved out the closest chair for Violet to sink into.

Violet might want to talk about her sixteen-year-old daughter who had vanished from her bed one summer night or she might not. When Violet didn't speak, Ella gently squeezed her shoulder before going into the kitchen to collect the teapot, milk jug and second cup.

When she joined Violet at the table, the older woman moved the shirt to her left. 'Staying pile.' There was only a slight quiver in her voice.

Ella held up the jar of buttons.

'Mrs Poole's pile,' Violet said, voice stronger.

When they'd sorted through the items and finished the tea, Ella took out her phone. She scrolled through the pictures before showing Violet an image of two goats who had jumped onto an outdoor table so they could peer into the kitchen.

The goats, a mother and daughter called Cinnamon and Nutmeg, were how Ella had first met Violet. Cinnamon had been prone to mastitis when Nutmeg had been born.

The life returned to Violet's faded eyes. 'There's my girls.' She tenderly touched the screen. 'Thank you for looking after them so well. They look so happy.'

'I can drive you out to see them?'

'Thanks, maybe Sunday. I have bridge tomorrow.'

Ella nodded. Violet wasn't yet ready to return to her beloved family home. While she'd made new friends and had all of her needs catered for in the retirement village, the transition hadn't been easy.

'I'd best get going. It'll be dark soon and the two mischief-makers will be hungry.' She kissed Violet's papery cheek.

Violet clutched Ella's hand in wordless thanks. They both knew she wasn't going home just to feed Cinnamon and Nutmeg; she would also be turning on the veranda light. Just like it had for the past two decades, the single light beside the front door would shine into the night to show Libby the way home.

On the drive back to Ambleside, the emotions that all day had hovered close to the surface ached in Ella's chest. She knew all about having a person you loved go missing.

When her older brother hadn't returned from a coastal camping trip, it had taken an agonising day to piece together what had happened and another four hours for his body to be located at the bottom of a sandstone cliff. The friends he'd been partying with had assumed he'd disappeared to spend the night with a girl. The reality was that, drunk and disorientated, he'd wandered too close to the cliff and the edge had given way.

Even though her parents' marriage hadn't survived, her family at least had closure. Lloyd, Violet's husband, had passed away never knowing what had happened to his daughter. Now Violet was nearing the end of her life with no answers. If she could, she'd do everything possible to bring Violet some peace.

Ella sighed as she stopped at the front gate. She waited until the cloud of dust kicked up by the four-wheel drive's tyres settled before opening her door to collect the mail sticking out of her green mailbox. No wonder she was treating so many cows and calves for pinkeye. The dust wasn't just irritating human eyes.

With a pile of mail and a small parcel sitting on the passenger seat, she drove along the winding driveway to park in the carport that overlooked the paddocks. Shadows dappled the summer-gold hills and the sky would soon burst into vivid crimson and apricot life. A distant boundary fence gleamed in the setting sun. Higher than the surrounding fences, it had been purpose built to contain the bulky, unfamiliar brown shapes that grazed on the far side.

American bison in the Australian bush were an unusual sight and if things had been different she would have loved to have a tour of the next-door facilities. The town talk about customised yards had her intrigued, as too the stories from a colleague she'd stayed with on an overseas trip to Montana. But thanks to its owner, the new bison farm wouldn't ever be a place she'd be visiting unless for work.

She went to turn off the four-wheel drive's engine but stilled. A figure on a black-and-white pinto rode over the hill closest to the boundary fence. Even with the distance between them there was no doubt who the rider was. The width of the man's shoulders and the sure way he carried himself were things she'd been trying to forget.

*Look away.* Except she could no more look away than she could make it rain.

She'd underestimated the impression Saul Armstrong had made when they'd partnered each other in Cressy and Denham's bridal party last autumn. The first sight of him since he'd returned to Woodlea six weeks ago dried her mouth and unlocked memories she'd battled to repress. The rugged, masculine beauty of his face. The flash of his rare smile. The warmth of his touch at her waist as they'd danced their obligatory waltz. But most of all the empathy in his denim-blue gaze when she thought no one had witnessed her sadness.

A stark realisation followed the flood of recollections. It wasn't emotional exhaustion after the bushfires that was making her feel on edge. It wasn't Cressy being pregnant that had unleashed long-buried yearnings. The real reason she'd avoided hanging out with her friends was because their close-knit group had a new member. Saul.

She gripped the steering wheel until her knuckles whitened. She'd never wanted to be aware of a man again. She needed everything to go to plan and to run on time. Never again could her life spiral out of control. Never again could she allow her heart, or her emotions, to render herself vulnerable. For the past five years she'd remained numb and built an impenetrable armour. Then in one night Saul had decimated every defence she held.

He'd done the unthinkable. He'd awoken something deep inside and reminded her that not only could she still feel, but she was also a woman.

Saul Armstrong was expecting a Sunday visitor. He just hadn't anticipated he'd have two and that they'd be of the cloven-hoofed kind.

The *tip-tap* of hard hooves on the concrete shed floor warned him before something solid butted the back of his right leg. He straightened from where he was examining the tractor battery and turned to see a pair of brown-and-white goats looking very pleased with themselves.

Just as well his Australian shepherd, Duke, had raced to the front gate when wheels had rattled over the cattle grid. Otherwise his two unexpected guests wouldn't have been allowed this close to the farmhouse. But these were no feral goats that had wandered out of the bush. They wore red leather collars and he knew exactly where they'd come from. His jaw tightened. Next door.

He scanned the yard to make sure their new owner wasn't far behind—a blonde and long-legged owner he'd been bracing himself to see. He was sure Ella wouldn't remember him from Cressy and Denham's wedding, but he remembered her. She was a hard woman to forget, no matter how much he tried.

When he was sure it was only the goats paying him a visit he looked back at the pair. With their bright amber eyes and floppy, oversized ears they appeared angelic, until the smaller one lifted its head and gave an ear-splitting bleat that echoed throughout the workshop.

He chuckled and scratched between the goat's tiny horns. 'Just as well you don't live outside my bedroom window. I've already got guinea fowls who think dawn starts at three in the morning.'

The younger goat bleated again. The strangled sound gave way to the crunch of gravel beneath heavy tyres and Duke's excited barking. The Australian shepherd made it his mission to race every vehicle that entered Windermere. Except this time he abandoned the challenge to cut across the lawn towards the shed. As soon as he saw the goats, he slowed and lowered himself to the ground.

Saul whistled him to his side. While the earlier head-butt on his leg had been friendly, the way the larger goat was lining up Duke made it clear the Australian shepherd would come off second best.

Duke came over to lean against his legs and he rubbed behind his grey-and-white ears. 'Easy there. Remember that bighorn sheep you thought you'd stalk …'

A car door closed then Denham entered the shed. He grinned as he glanced between the goats and Duke, who continued to eyeball each other. 'I thought it was too good to be true I'd won today.'

Saul returned his grin. 'As usual Duke had you at the first bend.'

The smaller goat made a beeline for Denham and nudged his hand. Denham stroked her white nose. 'Wonder what Cressy would say if I brought home a goat? You're actually pretty cute.'

Saul kept his smile in place. He'd been exactly the same when Trish had been pregnant. He and Denham might have ridden bulls on the American pro-rodeo circuit but the prospect of fatherhood had revealed their softer sides. He'd bought Trish a white, fluffy puppy called FiFi that she'd returned to him in their divorce. FiFi had stayed behind in America and now lived with the daughter of a neighbouring rancher who'd been in need of a forever friend.

He made sure his reply sounded light. 'It wouldn't be Cressy I'd be concerned about, but Reggie.'

Reggie was a slab-shouldered mountain of a rodeo bull Cressy had raised from a calf. Around Cressy and her older sister, Fliss, Reggie was a carrot-obsessed gentle giant. But to everyone else he was grumpy, disapproving and intimidating.

'True. But I swear he's excited as much as we are about this baby. You should see the way he looks at Cressy's belly.'

Duke pressed closer against Saul's legs. The Australian shepherd sensed how hard he was working to hide his emotions. Any pregnancy talk only reopened the wounds of all that he'd lost.

To his relief Denham changed the subject. 'I have time if you want to check the fences to see how these two got in.'

Denham had dropped by to help start the tractor battery that had refused to kick into life even with a jump-start. Despite Saul saying he had everything sorted, Denham had insisted on calling around.

Amusement pushed back the darkness of the past. Denham's expression and voice had been just a little too eager. 'What was it that Cressy was having this afternoon?'

'A baby shower.'

'Which translates into a house full of women?'

'Not only that, but Edna will be there. She's taken on the role of being baby Rigby's unofficial grandmother and wants to have a talk about whether she needs to help out until we find our feet.'

He knew he shouldn't laugh at his best mate's expense but the sheer horror on Denham's face made him chuckle. He'd only met chatty and forceful Edna twice but that was enough to know having her around at such a time wasn't the best idea.

He slapped Denham's back. 'Let's take a long look at the fences. Then I'm sure we'll need a swim and a cold beer.'

They headed towards the side-by-side gator parked at the shed entrance and the goats followed. Duke trotted at Saul's boot heels, not taking his attention off their two visitors. When the goats went outside to the overgrown lawn beside the water tank, Duke hesitated before jumping onto the back of the gator.

Denham slid into the passenger seat. 'No need to work out where your tank's leaking.'

In the sea of parched brown the vivid green stood out like the bright red plume of a fox's tail in the snow. Saul took the driver's seat. 'I know. Otherwise I'd have been digging for hours.'

Knee-deep in grass, the goats would be content mowing his lawn while they found out how they'd breached the boundary fence.

He started the gator engine and followed the track that led past the substantial brick home and large shed that had once housed an indoor dressage arena. The property had been an equestrian centre and he'd made full use of the infrastructure to build his state-of-the-art bison facilities.

'It's hard to believe,' Denham said, looking around, 'you've only been here six weeks.'

Saul ignored the twinge on his right side from an old rodeo injury. His body hadn't appreciated working from dawn to dusk every day of those six weeks. 'I've had some help with the fences.'

'They're pretty impressive.'

Saul slowed the gator as they neared an open gateway. In the powdery dust there were tiny hoof prints. The goats had reached his house via this laneway.

'Yes, the fencing guys did a great job. Though I'm sure they thought I had heatstroke when I showed them the plans.'

'I can see why. There's enough wire here to run a fence to Sydney.'

Saul had made sure that the boundary fence was high as well as electrified by several wires. Then, with space for bison to fan out as they didn't like to travel in single file, he'd run a parallel fence to form a laneway. This too was taller than a regular fence and marked the edge of the various paddocks. He'd wanted a second boundary fence for the exact reason why he now had goats munching in his garden. One fence could be compromised. Two couldn't.

As they drove along the laneway, Ella's sandstone home, with its tin roof and neat country garden, came into full view. When he went for a ride in the cool evenings the breeze would carry the scent of water from the automatic lawn sprinklers.

Denham cast him a quick sideways look. 'Seen much of Ella?'

Saul kept his grip on the steering wheel relaxed. 'Not since your wedding.'

'I thought as much.' Denham frowned at the farmhouse. 'Cressy and Fliss are worried about her. It's always been Ella dragging them off to every possible social event, now they rarely see her.'

Saul only nodded. Denham knew him too well. He couldn't risk his old friend sensing he'd been thankful that the local vet had kept to herself since she'd moved in three weeks ago.

He resisted the urge to flex his shoulders. He was still coming to terms with the irony that the one person he was wary of seeing was his new neighbour. At Denham's wedding it wasn't Ella's blonde beauty that unnerved him as much as what she fought so hard to hide. He recognised untold anguish and suffering. He saw it in his reflection every morning. He also knew the strength and tenacity it took to present a facade of normalcy. Ella Quinlivan was special. She was also someone he needed to stay away from.

He'd come home to Australia and to Woodlea for a fresh start. He couldn't now have Ella hold up a mirror to the hurt he was determined to leave behind. Denham didn't even know the real story behind why his marriage had failed. Instinct told him that instead of helping each other, he and Ella would expose and compound each other's pain. Neither one would want the other knowing the reality of what lay beneath their hard-won control.

Denham pointed ahead. 'There's your problem.'

A section of the large gum tree on Ella's side of the fence had broken away and fallen on the wire. Today, the breeze that sucked all the moisture from their skin was hot and sedate, but yesterday it had been fierce and unrelenting, whipping up the dust and testing tree branches. While the solid and heavy limb hadn't crushed the fence completely, it had provided the perfect bridge for nimble-footed goats.

Denham's grin was gleeful. 'This will take a while.' He took his phone from the pocket of his navy work shirt. 'I'll text Cressy and also Ella to let her know we'll have to go through her place.'

Denham's prediction proved true. After returning to the work shed to jump-start the tractor off Saul's F-truck, driving the registered tractor along the road to Ella's front gate and dragging the branch away from the fence, the day's heat had peaked. By the time the fence again stood strong and tall, the afternoon shadows were casting long footprints across the undulating hills.

'Please tell me you have beer in that shed fridge of yours.' Denham passed his sleeve over his forehead, having just loaded the final piece of the firewood he'd cut into the gator.

Saul shook his head. Denham groaned. Saul whistled to Duke. 'Only in the house fridge under the air-con.'

'Now you're talking.'

But it wasn't until they'd opened the small gate at the bottom of the garden and led the goats to where they belonged that they were finally done. While they walked back across the narrow paddock that divided the two farms, Saul listened out for the sound of a vehicle. Ella would be home soon.

When he closed the garden gate behind them, he released a silent breath. It was inevitable that his and Ella's paths would cross but it would now be later rather than sooner. He'd continue to have time to prepare himself.

Cold air embraced him as he stepped through the back kitchen door. As much as his new farm looked inhabited with machinery in the shed, Cisco in the stables and bison in the paddocks, the house was still a work in progress. Tea chests sat stacked in the hallway and rooms lay empty. He sidestepped a pile of boxes on the way to the fridge. He was in no rush to unpack anything but the bare essentials. He hadn't come here to make a home. He'd come to make his dreams of breeding bison a reality.

He cracked open two beers to the sound of a large splash. Denham was already in the pool. He took a swig of icy beer before shrugging off his shirt so he could also take a swim. As for the dreams he'd once held that involved having a woman to grow old with and a family to love, they were now nothing more than the red dust that coated his boots.

# CHAPTER

## 2

The cicadas in the gum trees behind the vet surgery were already synchronised in a steady drone when Ella arrived for work early Monday. The breeze was a warm wash across her skin and the sky a cloudless cobalt blue. As hot as the summer days were, she loved the cool tranquillity of the quiet mornings. After she pottered in the garden, with a little weeding help from Cinnamon and Nutmeg, she'd take a walk before getting ready for work.

The injured thoroughbred was no longer at the stables to greet her. The bay gelding had been given the all-clear to return home on Saturday. She opened the surgery door to the welcome rush of chilled air, the smell of antiseptic and a chorus of loud barking. The stables might be empty but the kennel room was occupied by what sounded like at least three patients. Claire had been the on-call weekend vet and had been busy.

Ella bent to pat Oscar, the vet surgery cat, as he curled himself around her jean-clad legs. Next weekend the ginger cat would be keeping her company while she was on call. Having to work had given her the perfect excuse to not go to Dubbo with Fliss and Taylor. She hadn't missed Fliss's sideways glances at yesterday's baby shower. Even though she'd now realised Saul was behind her feeling so on edge, she still couldn't explain to Fliss, or anyone else, why she'd been distant.

She continued to scratch beneath Oscar's chin. His appreciative purr failed to lighten her thoughts. Any explanation, even a simple one, would only lead to a need for more explanations. No one fully knew her reasons for not being interested in a relationship. From day one she'd been careful to stick to the abbreviated version of her past, which was that she'd had her heart broken while working overseas. The strict hold she kept over her life meant that all the finer details, especially the pain and the guilt, remained locked away. Her brother was another part of her life that she never talked about. It was just easier to keep her emotions in order that way.

She straightened and walked along the hallway. At least now she knew Cressy's pregnancy wasn't the reason for her biological clock going haywire, she'd been able to enjoy the baby shower. As for her maternal yearnings, they'd just have to be content with cuddling Cressy and Denham's tiny bundle of cuteness when he or she arrived early winter.

Her steps light, she turned into the treatment room where she could hear Penny talking on the phone. The young brunette receptionist ended the call and gave her a sunny smile. 'Morning. Hope you had a big breakfast.'

Ella returned her smile. Penny's enthusiasm was infectious. 'What's up?'

'Let's just say ten minutes ago your job list was shorter by two cancelled appointments, but now … lucky you get to go out to the new bison farm everyone's talking about.'

She failed to stop herself from stiffening. A thick band wrapped around her chest and pulled tight. *Lucky* wasn't exactly a word she'd use to describe herself right now.

'I'm not sure it's the bison farm everyone's been talking about.'

Penny giggled. 'True. Sally keeps everyone up to date about when Saul comes into the café. I mean … have you seen him?'

If only she could have answered no and saved herself countless sleepless nights. 'Briefly at Cressy and Denham's wedding.'

'Do you think he's an Aussie or an American?'

She half turned towards where the keys for the vet vehicle hung on the wall. 'Aussie. He just sounds American sometimes because he's lived over there.'

'He doesn't wear a ring.'

Ella took hold of the keys. It had been the second thing she'd noticed about him. 'Neither does Denham when he's working on the farm.'

Penny's brow furrowed. 'If Saul did have someone, they'd have joined him by now.'

Ella only nodded. Even though she shouldn't have been thinking about Saul, she'd also wondered the same thing. What she wasn't going to share was her belief that he'd once had someone significant in his life. When Cressy and Denham had said their vows, a muscle had worked in the grim line of his jaw. She'd also seen him rub the spot where a ring would have been on his left hand. Twice.

Penny spoke again. 'I said you'd head out straight away. It sounds like one of his young bison needs her shoulder stitched.'

The surgery phone rang. Penny beamed a make-sure-you-tell-me-all-about-him smile before speaking into her headset. Ella gave her a quick wave before heading out into the heat.

Once in the vet ute she released a tense breath and started the engine.

*You've got this. He'll have no idea who you are.*

Her bravado lasted the drive out of town and until she crossed Windermere's cattle grid. Then, her big breakfast didn't prove an advantage. Between her full stomach and nerves, her midriff felt as though it were stuck on the spin cycle of her washing machine. She didn't know what concerned her more, Saul again seeing her vulnerable side or her personal life affecting her professionalism.

But when she spotted a grey-and-white dappled dog from out her left window, racing her along the driveway, a smile eased her strain. As a child, animals had always brought her joy, and they still did. The excited dog had to be an Australian shepherd, a breed that despite its name originated on ranches in the western states of America.

She lowered her tense shoulders as she negotiated a bend in the driveway. Everything would be okay. She might be out of her comfort zone dealing with her new neighbour but she'd soon be in work mode.

She parked near where the dog waited for her in what looked like a designated car park. A quick look around confirmed there wasn't any sign of Saul. She left the driver's seat and the Australian shepherd raced towards her, tail wagging. Both his eyes were a clear and bright blue. The last time she'd seen a dog of this breed, they'd had one blue and one brown eye.

A whistle cut through the air, causing the Australian shepherd to freeze and to sit an arm's length away from her. Boots crunched on gravel. She looked up at the man who stood behind the Australian shepherd and spoke before self-consciousness could render her breathless. 'Is it okay to pat him?'

Saul's eyes were hidden beneath dark sunglasses but his mouth tilted in a brief smile. 'Duke will be offended if you don't. He takes his welcoming role very seriously.'

Ella looked down at Duke who had wriggled forwards, desperate to say hello. It was either pat the sociable Australian shepherd or stare too long at his owner.

No wonder Penny and her friends were smitten. Even with his sunglasses and his cap brim pulled low, Saul's stubbled jaw and the indent in his chin left quite an impression. Add a deep voice and an accent that wasn't quite Australian but also not American, and he was the complete package. She hadn't dared let her attention leave his face. She didn't need to be reminded of how wide his shoulders were or how in shape the rest of him was.

She ruffled Duke's neck. 'Hello, gorgeous boy.' When the Australian shepherd leaned against her legs, getting as much of himself as close to her as possible, she couldn't help but laugh. 'You're a great welcoming committee.'

Conscious this wasn't a social call, she glanced at Saul who stood with his arms folded. Giving Duke a last pat, she stepped forwards and offered Saul her hand. 'I'm Ella.'

For a moment he didn't move. She had to be mistaken but she thought she saw his jaw clench.

Then, his calloused palm slid against hers. 'Saul. We met at Cressy and Denham's wedding.'

It didn't matter if she concentrated on giving his hand a firm shake or on the thought he was a client, the heat from his skin warmed her far more than the midsummer sun above them. She'd mull over later whether it was good or bad he remembered her. Right now all she could breathe in was his crisp woody scent. All she could feel was the gentle strength of his work-hardened grip.

She released his hand and tugged her own cap brim low. 'So where's this patient of mine?'

'Follow the track around to the right to the far end of the big shed. I'll meet you there.'

The brief drive and blast of air-conditioning gave her a chance to cool off and to collect herself. The worst was over. She'd met Saul again. She'd heard the husky timbre of his voice and felt the respect and care in his touch. She'd learned to sum up a man's character by the way he shook her hand.

It was now just another regular day as a rural vet. She glanced at a group of bison that lumbered close to the fence. Even if she was dealing with an animal she'd never dealt with before.

She pulled up alongside a gator parked in a narrow shed. The nearby equestrian complex had been converted into a bison handling centre with both external and internal yards. A small group of bison rested in the shade of a holding pen, while further inside Saul stood next to what looked like a narrow race. Just like when dealing with cattle, Saul would have brought the injured bison in with some companions to keep her calm.

She collected what she needed from the back of the ute before heading towards Saul. Duke bounded over to her. She gave him a quick pat before assessing her surroundings. The internal set of yards was high, with more curves than angles, and the central race had covered sides as well as a grid across the top. It wasn't only Cinnamon and Nutmeg who could jump. The attention to detail and the solidity of the yards reassured her that Saul took the safety of his stock, as well as himself, seriously.

She increased her pace. The quiet cluster of bison in the holding yard didn't fool her. Domesticated bison retained their wild instincts, which meant it was a priority to treat her patient as quickly and efficiently as possible. A *thwack* sounded as the injured bison kicked out at the side of the race.

Saul turned to greet her with a nod. He'd removed his cap and sunglasses. His dark hair was longer than she remembered and his eyes were a serious and muted blue. 'The injury's on her left flank. She's only a yearling so at the bottom of the pecking order.'

Moving closer to the race, he used unhurried movements and the relaxed tone of low-stress handling to move the bison forwards as he slid the gates shut behind her. He soon had her in the hydraulic squeeze chute and her head carefully caught in the headgate. Ella opened a drop-down chute panel to see what she was dealing with. The metallic scent of blood mingled with the smell of dust. There was no doubt the bison had been gored by the sharp tip of a horn.

The young bison's laboured breathing and lifting tail warned her before the animal struggled and tried to kick out. Even though the bison was immobilised, Ella took a step back. She'd witnessed enough accidents when people had become complacent and animals did the seemingly impossible. She'd also seen what happened when a latch on a cattle squeeze chute gave way.

Saul moved closer to her side. The action didn't fill her with reassurance. She hoped it wasn't a sign he didn't think she was able to cope. Chin angled, she moved forward to administer a light sedative in a vein in the bison's tail. While she waited for the drug to take effect she prepared what she needed to flush out the wound. Making every movement count, she examined, cleaned and stitched the flap of torn skin into place. She then gave the bison a tetanus shot as well as one of antibiotics. As the young bison had only been lightly sedated, she didn't need to inject any antidote.

After checking the bison for any other injuries and finding none, she nodded at Saul. 'She's good to go.'

He released the headgate and the bison made her slow way out of the chute.

'Thank you,' Saul said, his attention on the bison as she went over to the fence that separated her from the others. 'I can deal with the normal scrapes and cuts but that was way above my skill set.'

'It was a nasty tear.'

Now the bison had been treated there was nothing to distract her from her intense awareness of the man beside her. Her rapid pulse and dry mouth couldn't only be blamed on the heat. She made sure her expression didn't reveal her uncertainty. She had her fingers crossed the way she'd handled the bison's injury would reset any impression of weakness that Saul may have formed at the wedding. She couldn't afford him remembering the tears she'd fought to hold back when she'd been sure no one was looking.

When the silence lengthened, she made cheerful small talk. 'Bison are such fascinating animals. Their heads and shoulders are so large and powerful, but don't seem to match the rest of them.'

'I know what you mean. Their head and horns are their widest part, so if they can get their head through an opening, the rest will follow.'

'Unlike a certain goat. Cinnamon's head fits through the gap beside the vegetable garden gate but luckily her stomach stops her from getting any further no matter how hard she tries.'

She thought Saul was going to chuckle but instead a gone-too-soon smile shaped his mouth. 'How are they after their adventure?'

'Full of cheek. They were in the kitchen this morning when I came back from my walk. That will teach me to leave the screen door ajar. Thanks for bringing them home and for the firewood.'

'No worries.'

The conversation again lapsed, reminding her that Saul wasn't someone she should be making small talk with. He might remember her from the wedding but this didn't mean they were friends. She also had a full day of clients to see. Cressy and Fliss were always joking that her schedule ran as smoothly as the Swiss rail system.

She took a final look at the young bison who stood with her head lowered. The light sedative would soon wear off.

As if sensing her thoughts, Saul spoke. 'I'll keep an eye on her. I've got a small paddock she can go into by herself that will allow her the social contact she needs. I've also made some changes to her family group so the herd she'll go back into should be more tolerant.'

Ella's heart warmed. It wasn't only the way Saul had acted to protect the young bison that moved her, but also his tone. Husky and rich, it proved he cared about the welfare of his animals. It also suggested that behind his reserve, genuine compassion existed.

Feeling her self-control waver, she focused on gathering the equipment she'd used. Nothing won her over more than someone who loved animals as much as she did. Duke left the comfortable spot he'd been sleeping in beside the fence to come over for a farewell pat.

She risked a quick glance at Saul. 'Give me a call if you're worried about anything.'

'Will do.'

She hesitated. For some reason she was reluctant to leave. Maybe she needed a sign, or something, to indicate that she'd amended any poor opinion he may have held.

Then, he smiled. A full, real smile that lightened the solemn blue in his eyes and erased the grooves beside his mouth. 'Thanks again for your help.'

She gave a single nod before turning on her boot heels.

Nothing was guaranteed to provide a reality check faster than the white flash of a man's smile that made her senses melt and her heart hammer.

Thoughts of Ella continued to preoccupy Saul long after the dust had settled behind the veterinary hospital ute.

He'd stayed with the young bison to make sure she recovered from the sedation and then moved her into a paddock that shared two fences with what would be her new herd. But even when the bison no longer needed observing, all he could think about was Ella. So he'd cooled off with a swim and retreated to the kitchen to unpack boxes in a last ditch attempt to keep busy.

Duke lay asleep on his dog bed beneath the air conditioner, unconcerned that Saul was clanking cutlery as he put the knives he should have found weeks ago into a drawer.

When Penny had said Ella would soon be on her way, he realised his belief he'd see the vet later rather than sooner had been nothing but wishful thinking. He'd spent the time before she arrived making sure his self-control was bulletproof. When Duke had barked, signalling she was here, he'd squared his shoulders, convinced he was ready to see her. He was wrong.

He stared at the half-empty cutlery drawer. He still wasn't sure what had done the most damage. The memories Ella triggered or the new ones he was having trouble filing away. This time she might have been makeup free, her hair in a ponytail and wearing scuffed boots, but she'd still caused his breathing to stall. If that wasn't enough of a red flag, he'd never reacted to Trish in the same way. As for Ella's soft laughter when Duke had greeted her, it was a sweet sound that would haunt his dreams.

He emptied a packet of forks into the open drawer with another loud clatter. At the wedding Ella had been elegant and sophisticated but today he saw a down-to-earth woman who was so much more than a beauty who turned heads. She'd shaken his hand with the confidence of someone who knew her own mind. She'd dealt with an unfamiliar breed of animal with empathy and expertise. It was only when he'd clasped her hand, and again when she was about to leave, that he'd caught a flicker of wariness in her brown eyes.

The vulnerability had been fleeting but it had been enough to make him want to put her at ease. She'd obviously remembered him for all the wrong reasons. It also wasn't her fault he wasn't the easiest person to be around. Denham's favourite saying since he'd returned was 'mate, lighten up'. Except when he'd tried to, his smile seemed to have sent Ella running.

He ripped the tape off another box. As for the cold clutch of fear when the bison had kicked out at her, where had that come from? Even though the bison had been held securely, things could go wrong. He'd seen firsthand why squeeze chutes had a reputation for being jawbreakers with their protruding handles and moving parts. There was an old saying that a bison could kick you a second time before you'd even realised you'd been kicked.

Giving in to his restlessness, he abandoned the unpacked box and grabbed his F-truck keys from off the bench. It was bad enough that Ella's dignified strength had drawn him to her at the wedding and that holding her for their waltz had made his chest tighten with a need he'd never wanted to feel again. Today he could add that he respected and admired her as well. A combination that had no place in his plans for starting a new life at Windermere.

He glanced at Duke. The weather was too hot to ride Cisco, so he'd clear his head with a drive instead. 'An Aussie meat pie sounds pretty good right now.'

Duke leapt to his feet and dashed out the kitchen door.

Instead of lowering the tailgate of the F-truck for Duke to jump into, Saul opened the passenger door of the rear seat. Duke bounded in and Saul secured him in the dog harness.

After they'd passed Ella's sandstone cottage, he made a conscious effort to relax. He focused on the landscape that undulated in sun-bleached waves either side of the gravel road. Even in the short time he'd been in the district, new signs for water carting services had appeared on the way to town. Despite the lack of rain, the heat and the dust, there was no other place he'd rather be.

The Bell River Valley with its distant rugged ridge, its timbered plateaus and rich alluvial soil reminded him of where he'd grown up further north. His younger brother may have left the bush for the city but he'd never be content unless there was blue sky above him and space around him. When, as a teenager, his father had died and his mother had sold the family farm, he'd vowed to get back onto the land. And he had.

He sighed, the sound lost under the noise of the air-conditioning. Even if his first attempt had been in the Rocky Mountains of

Wyoming and saw him walk away with nothing but his dog, his horse and a gutful of regret.

For his second attempt he'd planned to return to the hills of his childhood. Except his mother was now buried beside his father and there was no family left. When he'd come to Cressy and Denham's wedding he'd stayed a few days to look around. It had only taken a casual comment by a guest about a local equestrian property proving hard to sell, an afternoon's inspection, a morning on his mobile and the property had been his.

He slowed as the WELCOME TO WOODLEA sign appeared out of the shimmering heat. He had to be crazy wanting something hot to eat on a day like today. But a pie and sauce was one thing he'd missed in his decade and a half overseas and the bakery did make a particularly tasty chunky beef pie. The drive had also served its purpose. His head had now emptied of all thoughts of Ella.

At the top of the hill he drove by the red brick local hospital that commanded panoramic views. He could only hope that by next spring the valley floor would be a carpet of yellow and green. For that to happen, much-needed rain had to fall before the winter oats, wheat and canola crops could be sown.

The road dipped, taking him past the historic stone church with its distinctive bell tower to the heart of the main street. Last autumn the streetscape had been yarn-bombed in wedding white, but now it was dressed in the restful hues of blue. Woollen creations were wrapped around benches, lampposts and tree trunks. The recent storms had only delivered wind and dust devils and the guerrilla knitters were doing what they could to lift town spirits.

He parked outside the bakery in the shade of a leafy plane tree. It was too hot to leave Duke inside the F-truck but he would be right in the trayback for the short time while he grabbed some pies to go. He'd then eat in the cool of the truck where Duke had his own bowl for his share.

The Australian shepherd hadn't even jumped out of the passenger seat when an exuberant voice sounded behind them. 'Well, hello there.'

He slowly turned. He hadn't been in town five minutes and Woodlea's social queen bee had tracked him down.

'Morning, Edna.'

With her styled grey hair, pearls and white linen dress, Edna Galloway hadn't made any wardrobe concessions to the blistering weather.

'I was only thinking I haven't seen you in town for a while.' Her smile stretched and he thought for a moment she might embrace him. He readied himself not to inhale. In the heat the strong scent of her perfume bordered on overpowering. 'But here you are. No doubt you're in for those pies you like?'

Was there anything Edna didn't know? He could only be thankful that his life had unravelled thousands of miles away.

'I'm making up for lost time.'

'It's our little secret I had one of their beef, bacon and cheese pies earlier. Dr Fliss says I have to watch my cholesterol but I've been so busy in the charity shop I'm sure I've walked the pie off as well as the caramel slice I had with my morning coffee.'

Saul masked a smile. Edna's heels were not made for walking.

She briefly glanced at Duke who sat quietly near Saul's boots. The Australian shepherd had met Edna when she'd visited the day they'd moved in and had quickly sensed she wasn't a dog person.

'Of course you have Duke with you.'

'I do.' Ever since he was a pup the Australian shepherd had been the one constant in his life. It was now very rare for them to be separated.

Edna continued to stare at Duke but made no move to pat him. 'I must say I'm surprised to see you both in town so early. Ella mustn't have spent long at your place. Duke looks fine so it must have been one of your bison she went out for.'

It took all of Saul's willpower to keep his expression deadpan. Denham joked that Edna had superpowers and right now he almost believed it. Edna lived on the other side of Woodlea, so she couldn't have passed Ella on the drive in. 'Yes, I had a bison who needed medical attention.'

Edna stayed silent, her gaze speculative.

Saul held her stare. There was a reason why, just like Denham, he had a world champion bull-rider belt buckle stashed in a box somewhere—he never gave in.

It was Edna who broke the silence. 'You know, seeing you has reminded me you haven't put your name down for our paddock-to-art fundraiser. I thought that the paddock between your place and Ella's would be perfect for a combined display.'

He resisted the urge to cross his arms. He'd heard about the hay bale challenge to raise money for the new windmill museum. He'd been too preoccupied with settling in his bison to give any design a second thought so had planned to give Denham a hand with his.

'It would be except I've missed the deadline to sign up. I'll let Ella know she's welcome to use my paddock.'

'Consider yourself signed up.' Edna's smile could only be described as smug. She half turned. 'Tell Ella as committee chairperson I'll also add her name to the list. I can't wait to see what the two of you come up with.'

'Sorry, no can do.' He kept his words quiet as he remembered the vulnerability tensing Ella's mouth. She wouldn't want to be thrown together with him on a project, no matter how worthy the cause, and she might have had her own reasons for not participating. 'By all means put my name down but it's Ella's call whether she wants to be involved or not.'

Edna faced him again. Denham had mentioned that Edna was the town's go-to person in a crisis and he could see why. Her smile didn't dim even when a cool hardness narrowed her gaze.

'Ella wouldn't hesitate to be involved. She has a big heart as well as an unflagging sense of community spirit. She's been busy and that's why she hasn't registered.'

Saul let his own steely gaze answer for him. He wasn't having Ella being railroaded.

Edna gave a lighthearted laugh that didn't fool him. When it came to getting her own way, Edna possessed an arsenal of ammunition. 'There's nothing disingenuous about my very practical *suggestion* of the two of you working together. Many neighbours are doing joint projects.'

He kinked a brow. Edna had as much subtlety as a rodeo bull at a chute gate.

This time her laughter was more genuine and her expression softened. 'Everyone knows Ella's content on her own. As much as I'd love to see her with the happily-ever-after she deserves I promised my dear Noel I wouldn't give her a helping hand. Ever since she saved his prize bull he thinks the world of her.'

Saul nodded and waited for where Edna was going with her apparent sincerity. He didn't need to wait long.

'So, I'll not do anything until you've spoken with Ella about your proposed joint project and *then* I'll sign her up.' She gave him an airy wave. 'I really must get back to work. The charity shop will soon have a rush. Enjoy your pies.'

He scraped a hand across his unshaven jaw as Edna left. His appetite had deserted him. So much for being free from thoughts of Ella. They'd now have to have a conversation about the hay bale challenge. Worst case scenario, for the benefit of the community she might decide to participate as well as share Edna's belief that it was a good idea to work together. Moving hay bales would require farm machinery she wouldn't have. Best case scenario, she'd have a valid reason for being unable to sign up.

If he was a lesser man he'd ignore Edna's directive, but his conscience had never allowed him to let others down. He'd always been a team player, even when it hadn't been in his best interests.

He sighed and looked at Duke who gave a soft whine. 'Yeah, buddy. I should have listened to Denham about never underestimating Edna. We've just been outplayed.'

# CHAPTER
## 3

'Don't give me those big hungry cat eyes, Oscar,' Ella said, stifling a yawn. The day that had started with seeing Saul's young bison was almost over. 'I saw Penny feed you dinner.'

Oscar gave a throaty purr before he padded across the front counter in the closed vet surgery to rub his head against her arm.

'Penny also snuck you an extra handful of food so you can schmooze me as much as you want but you're not having thirds.' She scratched under the cat's chin and his purrs grew louder. 'I've two phone calls to make before you're lord of your kingdom again.' The kennel room was free of overnight visitors so the cat would have the building all to himself.

The first client she needed to call was Sophie's parents. The teenager had sent a photo of the tarpaulin tied onto a metal frame that shaded the Hereford and had promised to let Ella know as soon as Polly was mobile.

As she dialled Sophie's home phone number, Oscar curled up on her lap. She stroked his neck while the answering machine picked up the call and she left a brief message. Even though it had been confirmed Polly had pesti, the Hereford should soon regain her appetite and once recovered would have lifelong immunity. Ella ended by wishing Sophie all the best in her upcoming chemistry assessment.

She shifted on the seat as fatigue turned into a dull ache in her lower back. She'd had to pull an oversized calf in the afternoon heat that had proved difficult.

One more call to go. She opened a new file on the computer but made no move to dial the listed number. She'd conducted follow-up phone calls countless times. Even if this one was to Saul it shouldn't be any different. But she just needed a moment.

She'd replayed that morning's visit many times and came to the same conclusion. There was no justification for feeling uneasy. She'd conducted herself in a competent and capable manner. Saul had also been a dream client. Helpful. Respectful. Appreciative.

She hadn't noticed she'd stopped patting Oscar until he batted her hand with his paw. It shouldn't matter that it had been impossible to tell from Saul's closed expression if he remembered they'd once waltzed around a wooden dancefloor beneath the soft glow of fairy lights. His indifference should have been welcome, even if a persistent niggle reminded her there hadn't been a flicker of interest in his eyes.

Oscar again swiped at her hand and she ran her fingers through his thick ginger fur. 'Wish me luck.'

She dialled Saul's mobile. She'd keep their conversation short and professional. But when Saul's deep voice rumbled in her ear and her stomach fluttered, all thoughts about how she wanted to sound fled. It became simply a matter of making sure she spoke in coherent sentences.

'Hi, Saul, Ella from Woodlea Vet Hospital here … just calling to see how your young bison was doing.'

'She's going well.'

'Great.' She paused. It would be too easy to end the conversation there. But she'd never taken the easy option even when she should have. 'She recovered okay from the sedation?'

'Yes and having no trouble moving now her shoulder's been stitched.'

'Wonderful. Give me a call if anything changes.'

She readied herself to lower the phone. Apart from her composure deserting her when his deep voice had strummed across her senses, she'd stuck to her game plan.

Except Saul wasn't following the same narrative. Their conversation wasn't over. 'I hope it's okay but I asked Denham for your number. I sent you a text about the hay bale challenge.'

She glanced through the side door at her brown leather tote that sat on a bench and contained her mobile. She hadn't checked it for a few hours.

This time when she stopped patting Oscar, the cat jumped off her lap in disgust.

She forced a smile to make sure her voice would come across as relaxed. 'We're neighbours and having each other's numbers is only sensible.' Needing a distraction, she wrote Saul's number from the file on a scrap of paper. 'Are you doing the challenge?'

'I am now.'

The wry edge to his words suggested he'd come into contact with someone who'd been on a mission to recruit people. 'Let me guess … you bumped into Edna.'

'Let's just say I turned around and there she was.'

'Edna has many talents.'

'So I'm discovering.'

She wasn't sure if it was amusement or another emotion that made his accent sound more Australian.

'Do you need hay? Hewitt dropped over some small lucerne bales the other day.'

'I'll keep that in mind. Tanner's delivering a load of round bales tomorrow. To be honest I don't know what size I'll need.' Saul paused and when he continued his voice had deepened. 'I just wanted to say that if you were interested we could do a combined design in the paddock close to the road.'

Surprise and suspicion held her silent. Whenever Edna was involved things were never as straightforward as they appeared. 'Thanks ... did Edna say anything about me entering?'

'The topic did come up.'

She briefly closed her eyes. So much for being safe from Edna's machinations. 'I really appreciate your offer but I was planning on helping Fliss and Hewitt and not entering myself.'

'All good.' It could have been relief lowering Saul's tone or his need to end the conversation. 'But if you change your mind let me know. Thanks for calling.'

'No worries. Bye.'

She ended the call and went to collect her mobile. Her frustrated sigh echoed in the quiet as she dialled Edna's number.

Thanks to her friendship with Noel, Edna's husband, she'd enjoyed an immunity from Edna's matchmaking. But with the number of single locals dwindling she had to be back on Edna's romance radar. There was no other explanation for why Edna would have mentioned her in a conversation with Saul. Call her cynical, but nothing Edna ever said, or did, was by chance.

When Edna's mobile went to voicemail, Ella didn't leave a message. The only way to deal with Edna was to talk to her in person. She wanted to make it clear Edna wasn't to meddle in her life. The last thing she needed was to be bulldozed together with Saul.

She shut down the computer, gave Oscar a pat and locked up. The cool of the air-conditioning gave way to the warmth of early evening and the fragrance of eucalyptus as she made her way to her four-wheel drive parked in the shade.

She heard the chug of a diesel engine before a graphite-grey Hilux pulled into the car park. The vehicle might be Mac Barton's but a glimmer of blonde hair through the dusty windscreen said it was Edna's daughter, Bethany, behind the wheel.

Bethany parked alongside Ella's four-wheel drive and got out. Usually dressed in jeans and a bright cotton farm shirt, today Bethany wore a white top and tailored black trousers. Tall and willowy, she resembled her quiet and reserved father.

'That was perfect timing,' Bethany said with a pretty smile. 'I was hoping to catch you.'

When Ella had first met Bethany she'd kept to herself and had spent as little time as possible in Woodlea. Ella could only guess how difficult it was to be known around town as Edna's daughter. But since she'd been with Mac, Bethany appeared more relaxed and comfortable in who she was and where she belonged. She'd recently started work as an exercise physiologist at the health collective that had opened to provide local access to much-needed specialists.

Ella returned her smile. 'Heading home?'

'Yes, after I do a quick grocery shop.' She hesitated. 'I've a favour to ask … you can say no. I mean I would.'

'That doesn't sound promising.'

'It's nothing bad, it just involves my mother.'

'Did you buy another pony?'

Last autumn Bethany had bought a black Shetland to distract her mother from her interest in Mac. The plan had been for Edna to be so sidetracked by then eligible bachelor Tanner training Skittles with Bethany she'd not realise her daughter had fallen for the son of a man Edna had been embroiled in a family feud with.

'Thankfully those days are over. Mac and Mum are great mates now.'

At Ella's dubious expression, Bethany laughed. 'Well, as much as they can be with Mum already having organised our engagement party when Mac and I haven't even set a date yet.'

'I heard talk about a three-piece orchestra coming up from Sydney.'

Bethany groaned. 'All we want is a quiet and simple get-together.'

'Everything will work out. Your dad will make sure of it.'

It was common knowledge that Bethany and her father were close. It was also a relief for many that even though Noel didn't say much, when he did even Edna listened.

'Actually that's why I'm here. Dad thinks very highly of you and it's no secret he's told Mum not to interfere in your life. You're the only person she leaves alone.'

Ella didn't miss the edge to Bethany's voice. Even as Edna's daughter she hadn't been spared from her mother's plotting.

'I think after today I might be back on her list.'

She didn't add any more. As much as her mother needed to know everything, Bethany never pried.

She touched Ella's arm. 'By tonight, you'll be off again. I'll make sure of it.'

'Thanks, but it's fine. I'll take care of it.'

Bethany nodded. 'It would be very handy if Mum went back to having as little to do with you as possible, because the favour I need to ask is that you'll be her surprise party co-coordinator.'

Ella's mouth fell open. It wasn't Bethany's request that shocked her but what she was planning. 'No one can keep a secret from Edna Galloway.'

'True but if anyone knows the way she thinks, I do.'

'Call me crazy but I'm in. I love a challenge. What do you want me to do?'

'I'll draft up a guest list if you can handle the invitations and RSVPs and be the contact person for the bookings.'

'Too easy.'

'Thank you.' Bethany turned with a smile. 'We can do this.'

'Yes, we can.'

On the drive home Ella made a mental list of all the people to be kept out of the birthday plan loop while she watched for kangaroos and wallabies grazing on the roadside verge. By the time she'd reached her front gate she'd come to the conclusion that two-thirds of the town would be a liability when it came to keeping the party a secret. Edna's social network had more threads than a spider's web.

She left the driver's seat to the sound of galahs chirping overhead. The pink blush of their feathers blended in with the sunset sweeping across the sky. It wasn't only humans who appreciated the cooler evening temperatures. If she had time she'd go for a walk to loosen the kinks in her stiff back.

Once the veranda front light shone out into the dusk, she went to feed Cinnamon and Nutmeg. When Nutmeg saw her with the food bucket she pirouetted and jumped from a block of wood onto the top of an old box and back again. Ella stopped to watch. No wonder the internet was full of cute clips of agile goats doing goat-parkour.

But as adorable as Nutmeg was, Ella's attention strayed towards the distant boundary fence. Thankfully there was no sight of Saul on his pinto. Today had brought more than enough contact. If Fliss and Hewitt didn't need help with their hay bale design she'd find someone else to work with. It was out of the question she join forces with Saul.

The way she'd reacted to him, both this morning and during their phone call, proved she'd been right to protect herself by avoiding him, even if her self-imposed isolation had come at a personal cost. He continued to threaten every barricade she'd constructed. Staying in control meant never letting a man affect her again.

Nutmeg's plaintive bleat had her walk forward to open the small gate into the goats' paddock. It was a certainty that she'd see Saul again and when she did she'd make sure he didn't glimpse the chink he'd witnessed in her defences at the wedding. No one could know the depths of her anguish or the desolation of her guilt at having caused emotional and physical pain to someone who had loved her and who had wanted to spend the rest of his life with her. Least of all Saul who harboured his own darkness and who might understand.

Compassion or support weren't on her list of things that she needed or wanted. Until Cressy and Denham's wedding she'd been doing more than okay on her own. Once Saul saw her as the together person that she was, and she'd worked out how to remain unaffected when around him, she'd be back to coping just fine.

She tipped chaff into Cinnamon and Nutmeg's feeders before checking their water. Then, making sure she didn't glance at the boundary fence, she retraced her steps along the mosaic stepping stones that dotted the garden. Every so often she stopped to pull out weeds. Even though there'd been no rain, between the water from the bore and the buckets she recycled from inside, the weeds thrived as much as the plants. Next trip to town she'd cut a bunch of the double-delight roses for Violet.

She stepped into the enclosed back veranda that was now a sunroom and, just like always, she took her time looking around. Violet had confirmed that the house had been searched multiple times after Libby had vanished and nothing had ever been found. But every time Ella packed a box to take to Violet, she checked cupboards for secret hiding places and ran her hands over and under shelves. Somewhere there had to be a clue as to why Libby disappeared.

A shadow above the external window frame caught Ella's eye. She dragged over an old church pew to give herself extra height. When she took a closer look, while a sandstone block was set a little further back, there was nothing in the small crevice at the top of the window frame but dust.

Resolve filled her as she returned the church pew to its spot against the wall. She had no idea what she was looking for but if there was anything in the farmhouse that would explain what had happened to sixteen-year-old Libby, she would find it. Violet's peace of mind depended on it.

'Where do you want this hay?' Tanner asked as he jumped out from the truck cabin.

'Shed to the left, thanks, mate.' Saul didn't bother to whistle to Duke as the Australian shepherd bolted towards Tanner. Duke and the horse trainer were firm friends. Saul too had connected with Tanner over their need for wide open spaces and both having spent time in the Rocky Mountains. Tanner's free-spirited palomino gelding was a mustang he'd brought back to Australia when he'd come home to go droving.

A young border collie leapt out of the truck cabin, a black patch over his right eye. He came over to Saul for a quick pat before he and Duke tore off to where a cluster of speckled guinea fowls were having a dust bath beneath a shade tree. When Duke and Patch approached, the guinea fowls made their displeasure known with loud chirps and squawks before flying up into the tree.

Tanner removed his Woodlea rodeo cap and shook his head before dragging his hand through his dark-blond hair. 'It's beyond me why those two would run around in this heat.'

Both watched as Duke and Patch disappeared into the garden.

'Tell me about it.' Saul rubbed at his gritty eyes. He didn't add that it wasn't the high afternoon temperature that drained him but a sleepless night. He'd paid a heavy price for seeing Ella yesterday. 'Let's get this hay unloaded, then we can cool off before fishing.'

'I like your thinking. By the way, Denham's sent you a special delivery.'

Tanner's wide grin warned Saul that whatever Denham had sent out wasn't the usual machinery parts.

Tanner returned with a box filled with what looked like white paper bags. The aroma of meat pies wafted over to him.

Saul groaned. Denham must have heard about his meeting with Edna outside the pie shop.

'At least your cousin's sense of humour means we're sorted for dinner,' he said, as Tanner handed him the box.

While Tanner went to park his truck near the shed, Saul put the pies inside. On his way out he texted Denham to see if he and Cressy wanted to come for dinner. Denham had sent out enough pies to feed the local rugby team.

Denham's quick reply was followed by a string of laughing emojis. *Sorry, in Dubbo. Edna would be free.*

Saul texted back an eye rolling emoji as he walked towards the machinery shed.

Tanner stood over near his truck talking on his mobile but there remained no sign of Duke or Patch. That morning he'd relocated a blue-tongue lizard Duke had discovered in the front garden. He could only hope the dogs didn't find any brown snakes. An emergency trip to visit Ella at the vet surgery wouldn't exactly be ideal right now.

He climbed into the tractor and fired up the engine. Even though he had spoken to Ella about the hay bale challenge, he couldn't seem to move on. As casual as her voice had sounded, he hadn't missed her strain when she'd said she wasn't doing the challenge on her own. He'd been right to not let Edna add her name to the list, but he didn't now need the distraction of wondering what her reasons had been.

He drove towards the truck and, using the tractor hay forks, lifted off the end round bale. For the past six weeks he'd had no trouble zeroing in on what needed to be done to get his bison farm operational. Today he'd been flat out deciding what to have for breakfast. He glanced at his bare ring finger. He had no time or emotional energy to be thinking about a woman and the pain she went to such great lengths to hide. He wasn't fitting the pieces of his broken life back together for a second time.

Once he'd unloaded the last round bale, he returned the tractor to the machinery shed. Quiet descended as the tractor engine rumbled to a stop. By now both dogs had appeared and were sitting in the shade of the hay shed. Tongues lolling, they stared at the curious bison who had come over to the fence.

Tanner nodded in the direction of the bison bull and five cows. 'Seeing them makes me feel like I'm back in Montana.'

'Same here. Some mornings when I look outside I still expect to see pine trees instead of eucalypts.'

Together they walked towards the bison. Beyond the paddock and meandering tree line of the Bell River stretched a distant rugged ridge. Neither had to say anything to know the other was thinking of the snowy peaks and golden aspen groves of the faraway mountains they'd once called home.

They stopped at the fence. Bison were unpredictable and it had been a priority these past weeks to build trust with each bull and cow. He was now able to handfeed this breeding group. The bull, Dakota, had a soft spot for apples.

Tanner spoke quietly as Dakota approached. 'I never thought I'd find anything that out-sized Reggie, but this guy's massive.'

Saul reached through the fence to rub the bull's curly wide forehead. A beard hung from beneath his jaw and wads of light-brown wool draped from his shoulders.

'Dakota here is a gentleman but the bull in the paddock to your left would make even Reggie look friendly.'

'Rather you than me when you work him in the yards. I've seen how high bison can jump. As for how quickly they can move ...'

The light in Tanner's blue eyes as he scanned the adjacent paddock for the temperamental bull confirmed he'd be over anytime Saul needed help. He wasn't the only cowboy drawn to working with the massive thunder beasts.

Saul moved to scratch a cow's neck. The first time he'd seen bison they'd been stampeding across the valley floor at the base of a Wyoming mountain range. He could still remember the feel of the ground shaking. Their power, their ruggedness and their disdain for order had all spoken to something within him. He'd gone from riding cantankerous rodeo bulls to working on a bison ranch and then to buying out the owner. He flipped the switch on his memories. He wasn't revisiting what had then followed.

Tanner nodded at a fluffy bison calf the colour of caramel who stayed close to his mother's side. 'He looks young for a summer calf?'

'He is. He came from a farm in Queensland where it's also been dry so the cows were joined late. He won't start turning a chocolate colour for at least another month.'

The first hurdle in making his dream to breed bison in Australia a reality had been to source stock. Bison couldn't be imported and there was only a limited number available for sale. He'd been patient and lucky. When a bison farm in Victoria had sold up he purchased their herd to add to the Queensland cows and bull. His last addition had been a bull from the Dubbo zoo to vary the bloodlines.

Saul gave the cow a final scratch and stepped back. The sun continued to burn through the thick cotton of his shirt but the shadows thrown by the bisons' humped shapes were lengthening.

He glanced at Tanner. 'Like to meet the herd who'll be giving Arrow a run for his money?'

'Sure would.'

They followed the dirt road past the yard complex to an extensive set of stables. Duke and Patch ran beside them, their brief rest having replenished their energy.

Behind the stables stood a rectangular outdoor dressage arena. Over a few beers at the Royal Arms one Friday night, he and Tanner had hatched a plan to make the sandy arena circular and to add a set of steel yards. It would be from here that Tanner would run his campdrafting courses using Saul's bison. Thanks to a bison's speed, stamina and ability to turn quickly, they were sought after as training animals for both campdrafting horses and riders. As soon as the fencing contractor finished his next job, he'd start on the arena modifications.

Cisco looked up from where he was grazing at the far side of his paddock. When he realised there was no food in sight, the pinto swished his tail and went back to eating.

Tanner chuckled. 'Well, I know where we are on Cisco's list of priorities.'

'That's Cisco for you.' The aloof and impatient gelding could never be described as needy. 'He's the only horse I know who thinks apples are overrated.'

They continued on to a paddock that was home to a group of bachelor bulls. When the bison saw him and Tanner, they pounded towards the fence. A cloud of red dust trailed behind them.

'Arrow's going to love drafting this lot,' Tanner said as the boisterous bulls slowed and two butted heads.

'I'm sure he will. Just as much as they're going to love outwitting him.'

Saul gave the still jostling bulls a once-over to make sure none had come off second best against a set of curved horns. When he was satisfied there were no injuries, he and Tanner returned to the farmhouse.

While Saul cut up cheese for fish bait, Tanner helped himself to two meat pies. When they returned outside, the stiff early evening breeze contained a hint of welcome coolness.

Tanner sighed with relief. 'Now this is more like it. I'm not so tempted to move to Antarctica.'

'Does Neve know of your plans?'

Tanner was in the middle of building his dream home on his new farm with the redheaded occupational therapist.

'She's so besotted with Dell's foal it's a no brainer, I'd be going on my own.'

Even though his words were said in jest, a seriousness tempered the laughter in his eyes. Tanner could no more leave Neve behind than he could wear polished city shoes instead of worn cowboy boots. Saul fought a wrench of loss. Once he'd loved a woman with the same soul-deep intensity.

After fishing rods and tackle boxes were loaded onto the farm ute and the two dogs had leapt onto the back, Saul drove to the machinery shed. He'd inherited an old silver tinny with the farm and this was the second time he and Tanner had taken it out on the river. Last trip Tanner had caught a Murray cod and in true fishing-story style its size grew with each telling.

With the boat trailer attached to the back of the ute, Saul took the track that ran along the boundary fence and would lead past the tree that had split in the wind storm. At the open double gates Tanner looked across the paddocks towards Ella's house but didn't make any comment. Saul too risked a look at the sandstone building illuminated in the waning light but he couldn't see any movement around the house or in the garden. Cinnamon and Nutmeg stood inside a small shed. Ella wasn't yet home.

The screech of cockatoos grew louder as a line of red river gums filled the horizon. The Bell River wound its way through Windermere and along the back boundary of Ella's farm. With the summer being so dry the river provided a crucial source of water for both stock and wildlife. A mob of kangaroos bounded away through the trees, while a hare sped into the shadows.

Saul made a quick stop at the river pumps. He left the ute to climb the ladder to the control box that sat on a steel platform above the flood line. From the elevated view he caught a glimpse of movement that could have been Ella's four-wheel drive pulling into her carport. When he'd switched the main pump to automatic, he and Tanner continued on to a flat section of the riverbank.

Once the tinny was in the water, the dogs onboard and the fishing gear stowed, Saul pull-started the outboard motor. He sat at the back of the boat and steered it towards the bend where Tanner had caught the good-sized Murray cod. The breeze increased to a brisk wind, stealing the heat from his skin and the tension from his shoulders. The faint scent of honey sweetened the air; somewhere on the riverbank there had to be a beehive in a tree hollow. He swapped a grin with Tanner.

They stopped to add bait to their hooks and to cast their lines. Time slowed as they waited for a bite. When there'd been nothing but a nibble, Saul headed the tinny closer to the riverbank that gave way to rounded pebbles and coarse river sand. Focused on the increasing tension on his line, he almost missed the flash of brown-and-white at the top of the bank. But he couldn't fail to hear an ear-piercing bleat.

He and Tanner reached for Duke and Patch at the same time to stop the pair from jumping into the water to give chase. The tinny rocked before both dogs settled.

The goat bleated again before a larger goat appeared.

'That answers Denham's question about Ella's goats finding another way to escape,' Tanner said, keeping a gentle hand on Patch who whined and quivered with excitement.

'I don't think they got out by themselves.' Saul kept his words light even though it felt as though a fishing line drew tight around his chest. 'Ella won't be far away.'

As resourceful as the two goats were, they would have needed to find their way through at least three fences to get to the river. One evening while riding, he'd seen Ella out walking with the goats and he guessed she was doing so again.

Pebbles clattered before the vet appeared at the top of the bank. Dressed in loose black running shorts and a fitted white tank top, she was all long legs, curves and tousled blonde hair. Saul's hold on Duke's collar loosened and the dog slipped away. It was only a sharp whistle that kept the Australian shepherd in the tinny.

Tanner grinned as Nutmeg again gave a strangled bleat. 'There goes the serenity.'

Saul only nodded. He was too busy reading Ella's reaction. After briefly stopping when she saw them, she waved and continued down the bank. The goats ran beside her before lowering their heads to drink at the water's edge.

'So this is the infamous Cinnamon and Nutmeg?' Tanner said as Patch wriggled, again making the tinny rock.

Ella flashed Tanner a warm smile. Her smile at Saul then didn't quite reach her eyes. 'How's my patient? Still doing well?' She barely waited for his nod before she refocused on Tanner. 'You know you've set the bar high with that fish you caught last week. Denham and Hewitt are determined to beat you.'

'Seeing as it was this big …' With one hand still on Patch, Tanner indicated a width that was almost double the size of the Murray cod that he'd caught and released. 'They'll have a hard time.'

The breeze tangled in Ella's hair and she brushed the windblown strands away from her cheek. 'Are you *sure* that's how big it was?'

Tanner's blue eyes twinkled. 'Give or take a few centimetres.'

Ella laughed but Saul's attention wasn't caught by the beauty of her animated face. The wind had caught in the front of her running shorts and lifted the light black fabric to reveal her smooth, toned thighs. Except high on her right leg the skin was puckered and raised in a white scar.

A scar that wasn't the result of a simple injury. A scar that spoke of trauma and suffering and strength.

Ella's hand clapped down on her shorts. He registered the shock on Tanner's face before Ella's wide defensive gaze met his.

A scar that was synonymous with secrets.

# CHAPTER
# 4

On any other trip to town, after spying Edna's white Land Cruiser in the main street, Ella would have taken the next turn and parked elsewhere. But for once Edna was someone she wanted to see.

Ella reverse-parked beside Edna's red dust–coated car. Every call to Edna's phone over the past few days had gone to voicemail. If she didn't know better she'd have thought the town busybody was avoiding her.

After slipping the vet mobile phone into her shirt pocket—it was Saturday and she was the weekend on-call vet—she collected a box from the back of her four-wheel drive. The charity shop closed in five minutes. She would have come earlier except a young boy and his mother had walked into the vet surgery with a sheep on a lead.

The black-faced dorper had been wandering past their house in town. The ewe was wearing a green collar and was friendly so had to be someone's pet. Ella had placed a post on the local missing animal social media page and until the sheep's owners realised she'd gone for a stroll, she was living it up in the vet stables.

With the box of items that Violet no longer wanted perched on her hip, Ella pushed open the door of the charity shop.

Sue greeted her with a smile from where she sat behind the counter. A vase beside the cash register was filled with fragrant pink roses that would have been from the retired librarian's much-loved garden. 'I was hoping to see you. Meredith said she didn't think you'd been in for a few days.'

Ella sat the heavy box on the smooth countertop. 'I've had this in my car since Tuesday.'

'You've been working too much.' Sue glanced at the phone in Ella's front pocket. 'And you're still working. At least next weekend is the hay bale challenge and the Friday after that the dessert night. Both will give you a chance to unwind.'

Ella thought hard. While she'd been out west after the bushfires she was certain Cressy had mentioned something about desserts at the old bluestone schoolhouse and buying tickets. 'I'm helping Cressy tomorrow on her hay design and I think I have a ticket for the dessert night.'

'Taylor said you all were going and it would be like old times.'

Before she'd bought Violet's farm, Ella had lived in town and her place had always been the get-ready venue before any big social event. Sue was Taylor's mother and had often saved the day with a needle and thread when an evening dress strap had broken or a heel had gone through the hem of a ball gown. But now, with Cressy married and Fliss engaged, their close-knit group wasn't as social anymore.

Ella banished a pang of loneliness and regret. The only reason why she was on her own and wasn't partnered up was because she'd made the decision not to marry Charles. She'd had everything, and more, within reach and yet she'd thrown it away because she'd been naive and uncertain. She had to live with the consequences, and the nightmare that had followed, even if she ended up being the only one without a significant other in their life.

Sue inclined her head towards the front window and Edna's car. 'Bethany mentioned you've been given a very special job.'

It wasn't unexpected that Sue knew about Edna's party. Sue could keep a secret and had known Edna since they were girls. 'A special and challenging job, so much so our code word for Edna's party is mission impossible.'

Sue laughed. 'Let me know when you have a venue sorted and I can help decorate.'

'Thank you. At the moment we're still trying to outsmart Edna and find a way to keep this all hush-hush.'

'Good luck.'

'We'll need it.'

With a cheery wave, Ella went back out into the heat. She still had a little time before she was due at Violet's for a late lunch, and she had a hunch exactly where Edna would be.

As she walked along the sunny main street she made sure her strides were even and that her right leg didn't lag. It was no coincidence that ever since her ill-fated evening walk earlier in the week she'd worn her biggest work shirts to cover her thighs. She resisted the urge to pull the hem of her pink shirt lower. Even though her scar was hidden beneath her jeans, she still felt the warm flush of self-consciousness.

Except for Neve, who she'd shared a glamping tent with at Cressy and Denham's wedding and who had glimpsed her in only a long T-shirt, no one knew of the physical evidence of her guilt. It had been thanks to having just met Saul that she'd been too distracted to wear leggings to sleep in. Otherwise she'd been so careful. Whenever she went swimming she wore shorts over her swimmers. When out walking in public she always wore knee-length lycra leggings. She'd never expected to see anyone in her loose-fitting shorts, especially Saul, when she'd taken the goats to the river to cool off.

A horn honked and she gave a brief wave as old Will passed by. But now her secret was out and the only thing she could do was brace herself for any fallout. Tanner was a close friend and if he mentioned what he'd seen she'd be comfortable giving him yet another sanitised version of her life story. She'd been injured while overseas. She was certain he'd never press for more details.

As for Saul, she could only hope the subject of her scar never came up. Whereas Tanner had appeared shocked, Saul's intense gaze had never left hers. Even with the distance between them she'd glimpsed unmistakable empathy. Somehow he knew of the pain that went far beyond the physical.

Her steps faltered. She couldn't have anyone see beneath the composure that every morning when she looked in the mirror she smoothed into place, let alone a man who didn't appear to have any scars of his own. But instinct told her they existed. Now that she could no longer avoid her new neighbour, it was critical she kept all contact to a minimum. She couldn't have him know that the vulnerability he'd glimpsed at the wedding wasn't just a one-off occurrence.

At the entrance of the Windmill Café she paused to allow her emotions to settle. To deal with Edna she needed to bring her A-game. She stood tall as she walked through the doorway. The scent of coffee and the sound of laughter welcomed her. Even with there being no farmers' markets on today, the café was busy.

Locals mingled with tourists and school-aged boys in cricket whites refuelled after their morning's match.

As she'd suspected, Edna sat at her regular table that overlooked the main street and offered a perfect view of inside the café. While others around her were on their phones or chatting, Edna sat with her hands folded, people-watching. Her beaming smile invited Ella over even before she patted the empty chair beside her.

'Isn't this a nice surprise,' Edna said, voice loud as Ella approached.

Ella only smiled. Edna would have seen her through the window. As Ella took a seat, she searched the older woman's face, hoping her remark had been innocent and not a sign that she already knew about her daughter's plans. But there didn't appear to be any knowing glint in Edna's eyes.

Edna's smile widened. 'Have you eaten? You're welcome to join Mrs Knox and myself for lunch.'

'Thank you but Violet's expecting me. I'll just stay for a quick chat.'

'I thought you were on your way to dear Violet's. I must say you're running late.'

Ella kept her smile in place. Not only did she never run late, she also hoped she wasn't so predictable. 'Yes, I had a stray animal turn up. You don't happen to know who owns a sheep that wears a green collar and leads better than half the dogs I know?'

'That must be Missy, one of Caroline's sheep.' Edna reached for her navy handbag to take out her phone. 'I'm surprised you haven't seen Caroline walking them in the park. They're so well behaved.' Edna touched the phone screen and then held up a photo of an elderly woman with two black-headed dorper sheep beside her. In the background was the colourful play equipment of the park beside the sportsground.

'Yes, that's the missing sheep, the ewe on the left.'

'It just so happens I know Caroline's number. She isn't a fan of the internet so wouldn't see any of those posts you young ones are always putting online.'

Ella stayed silent while Edna called Caroline. Even if Edna's enthusiasm for knowing everybody's business wasn't always appreciated, her extensive knowledge at times proved useful.

After ending the call, Edna returned her phone to her bag with an air of satisfaction. 'Caroline's so relieved. She'll come to the vet clinic in an hour to pick Missy up. I love it when things fall into place.'

'So do I.' Edna's gaze turned speculative and Ella spoke while she had the chance. 'I've been trying to contact you about the hay bale challenge … I haven't put my name down because I'm helping Cressy.'

'That's such a thoughtful idea. I'll add you to Cressy's entry form.'

Ella waited but Edna didn't say anything further. This was all too easy. She'd expected at the very least a comment about how the more entries there were the better. She'd also expected Saul's name to crop up.

'Edna, I believe you spoke to Saul about me entering. I hope this wasn't why he offered for us to work together. I don't need to remind you that I'm happy on my own.'

Edna flashed a conciliatory smile. 'Saul's new to town and as you're his neighbour I was just trying to help him settle in. That was all. I won't mention you to him again.'

That was as close as she'd ever heard the older woman come to apologising. What was she up to? 'Thank you.'

Edna patted her hand. 'Don't mention it.'

Ella went to push back her chair. It was subtle but what she could only describe as smugness shaped Edna's lips before she spoke again.

'I'm so glad you're helping Cressy. This hay bale challenge will not only lift spirits and raise money but it will also generate some very welcome publicity.' Edna leaned closer. 'I don't want to say too much but we have a television crew coming to talk to a select few about the inspiration behind their designs. People far and wide will be hearing about our lovely little town.'

Edna paused while she waved to someone behind Ella. When she continued her voice had lowered. 'I must say Mrs Knox has aged. The poor thing is beside herself over Harriet's new Dubbo boyfriend. Now, are you sure you won't have lunch with us?'

Ella had already come to her feet. 'I'm sure. Thanks for calling Caroline.'

'Anytime. Please say hello to Violet for me. She's been through *so* much.'

It wasn't until Ella turned away that she realised exactly what Edna had been up to. Edna's spiel about the publicity the hay bale challenge would generate hadn't been random small talk. What she'd really been saying was that the weekend could provide a unique opportunity to help ease Violet's pain. The media interest would be a perfect platform to raise public awareness about Libby's disappearance.

Ella withheld a sigh as she left the café. If she gave Edna the benefit of the doubt she simply had Violet's best interests at heart. But if that was all that was behind their conversation, why not just simply say the media attention might help find Libby?

She didn't realise that she was still frowning until she reached Violet's unit. When the door opened, compassion softened the older woman's expression. 'Had another one of those days?'

'Actually, it's been a great day. I had the cutest litter of red heeler puppies to vaccinate.'

Violet ushered her in with a smile. 'I'll put the kettle on and you can tell me all about them.'

While they enjoyed the fresh ham and salad rolls Violet had made, they went through the new box Ella had packed from the farmhouse. As Ella placed the items in their designated piles, her attention kept returning to a mat that lay on the floor near the window. She'd assumed it was there to protect the beige carpet whenever Violet sat on her walker to watch the birds in the garden. Now she wasn't so sure. Beneath the hem of the curtain she could see the round contours of a blue rubber shape.

When the final items, some unused exercise books, had been placed on the charity pile she again glanced at the blue object. She could have sworn it was a dog's chew toy. The vet surgery stocked a similar range.

Violet followed her gaze. 'That's Duke's. Mrs Lewis thought he might like it when he came to visit.'

Ella fought to conceal her shock. 'Duke ... as in Saul's Duke?'

'Yes. Saul's such a lovely young man. He came to introduce himself when he first moved in and now pops around for a cuppa.'

Ella only hoped Violet wasn't paying too much attention to her face. Her cheeks felt hot as if she'd been for a run in the midday heat. It had never occurred to her that Saul and Violet would have met. And by the look of the mat for Duke to lie on, he and Saul were frequent visitors. 'I don't know him very well but he does seem ... nice.'

There were many other adjectives she could use that she would never say out aloud. Gorgeous. Compelling. Off limits.

'He is.' Violet's shrewd grey gaze met Ella's. 'Is there anything you want to talk about? You seem a little distracted.'

The first reason she couldn't talk about, even more so now that she knew Violet and Saul were friends. The second reason was one she did need to mention.

She took Violet's thin hand. 'Apparently the hay bale challenge will bring all sorts of media to town. It might be an opportunity to talk about Libby.'

Violet stiffened. 'How so?'

'I haven't worked out the finer details but people will be interviewed about the inspiration behind their displays, so maybe I could do one in memory of Libby.'

Tears welled in Violet's eyes but her voice emerged steady. 'I've never given up hope … but so many years have passed. It's time we do talk about her again. It might be my last … chance.'

Ella gently squeezed her hand before reaching for the exercise book on the top of the donation pile and then delving to the bottom of her tote bag to find a pen.

Ella turned to the first blank page. 'What things did Libby like?'

Violet stared into the distance as treasured memories took her to another time and place. 'While Libby's friends were interested in boys and makeup, she still loved her dog, her horse and her art and craft. Lloyd and I kept waiting for the teenage hormones to kick in as they'd done with Annette. But she was never in any trouble.'

'What type of dog did Libby have?'

'A kelpie called Chip. Her horse was called Mrs Potts.'

'Are any of her friends still here?'

Violet shook her head. 'Fee was her main friend. They were always swapping books. I think Fee's a teacher in Sydney now. Her family left town years ago.'

'What about movies?'

'She loved Disney movies, which might sound childish but she was young at heart. She was also quiet and sensitive and hated any form of attention. Annette was the noisy and confident one.'

Violet's voice had thinned and her hand resting on the table trembled. Ella made a final note and closed the exercise book. Violet had talked enough for today and Ella didn't want stress to trigger an asthma attack. It had been when she'd been rushing to reach her inhaler that Violet had fallen and broken her hip.

'I'll let you know what idea I come up with.'

'Thank you.' The hope that shone from Violet's eyes renewed Ella's resolve to find the answers that the older woman needed. 'This might be it. Someone might know something.'

Ella kissed her cheek. 'I have everything crossed that someone will.'

She packed away the next lot of items that needed to go to the charity shop and with a smile at Violet and a quick glance at Duke's mat, she left.

Her thoughts raced, even though her steps were slow, as she walked along the concrete garden path towards her car. One of these days Edna wouldn't get her own way. But, on this occasion, she had yet again. Not only would Ella now be entering the hay bale challenge with her own project, but as much as it sent her nerves into a freefall, she was going to have to work with Saul.

There was no other flat space beside her house to construct a design except for his paddock that fronted the road. If she wanted to attract media interest she had to go big and Saul also had the machinery to move the heavy bales she'd need to achieve this. The question now was whether or not his offer to do a joint project had been genuine.

Ignoring the pitch in her stomach, she slid into the driver's seat. She was about to find out.

∾

The pool water muffled the volume of Duke's barking but not its message. Saul had company. Company he hadn't planned on having.

He came to the surface and swam over to where his shirt lay near the pool steps. He'd only stripped off his T-shirt as his old rugby shorts doubled as swimmers. But depending on who his visitor was, even then he could be far too exposed. He was due for another Edna house call. Not to mention Ella's goats might have come for a second visit. When he'd taken Cisco for a late evening ride yesterday, the goats had been in Ella's garden and walking along the lower fence line looking for a way in. If the goats were here, Ella might not be far behind, seeing as it was Saturday afternoon and she wouldn't be at work.

The grey T-shirt snagged on his wet hair as he reefed it over his head. Just as well he was supposed to be doing bookwork so wasn't dressed in his usual jeans and thick cotton work shirt. Trying to pull on wet jeans could have proved interesting.

Conscious that water dripped down the back of his neck and pooled at his feet, he dragged a hand through his wet hair. Whoever his visitor was they'd just have to take him as they found him. Duke's barking reached a crescendo, which made it more likely it wasn't Ella's goats but a vehicle that had driven up the driveway and now arrived.

Feet bare, he headed through the pool gate and around the side of the house. The silence warned him that his visitor was someone Duke was happy to see. He rounded the corner and was met with the sight of the Australian shepherd melting against Ella's legs. His steps slowed.

He'd spent the past four days blanking out thoughts of Ella by cramming his head full of farm plans and lists. Except at night there proved nothing he could do to get her out of his mind. If Tanner, a close mate, hadn't known about her scar, then he'd bet he wasn't privy to the other wounds she carried. He didn't know what haunted him the most—the physical pain she must have endured or the realisation that she carried the burden of her past alone. Generous, compassionate and warm-hearted, Ella deserved to have support in her life. Instead every day she faced her demons on her own.

She glanced up from where she patted Duke. Her brown gaze flickered over his damp grey T-shirt before she gave him a smile that was just a little too bright. 'Hi.'

'Hi.'

Unlike when he'd last seen her, she wore an oversized white top that covered her thighs and black leggings that stretched to her knees. Instead of making her look shapeless, the outfit revealed the length of her tanned legs and accentuated the curves that had filled out her dusky-pink bridesmaid dress. In her hand she carried a phone.

When she noticed his attention on her mobile, she held it up. 'I don't have any pockets and I'm on call this weekend.'

He nodded, resisting the urge to fold his arms. When Ella's direct gaze met with his, his light-headedness had little to do with the glare of the sun. Even though he was far from comfortable with seeing her, his body language couldn't communicate his uneasiness. It was still important to him that he put her at ease. He couldn't let his emotional baggage compound her vulnerability. She had enough to deal with.

'What can I do for you?'

He hadn't meant for his words to sound clipped but with every second his awareness of her intensified. The too-large neckline of her shirt revealed the fragile hollow of a collarbone and the satin-smooth texture of her tanned skin.

'I'd like to chat about Violet.'

'Come inside.' He led the way along the path, the pavers hot beneath his feet.

'Don't mind the mess,' he said, as he held the screen door open.

When she stepped through the doorway, he didn't immediately follow. As spacious as the farmhouse was, it would still feel too small when they were both inside. At the wedding he and Ella had been surrounded by people. When she'd helped with his young bison they'd been focused on a combined task. And down at the river Tanner had been with him. Now there was nothing to distract him from the intense pull of attraction but unpacked boxes.

'Tea, coffee or a cool drink?' he asked as they entered the open-plan kitchen.

'A glass of water would be great.'

Ella took a seat at the table he'd nodded towards and set her phone beside her. Duke went over to his favourite spot beneath the air conditioner and flopped onto his dog bed.

Ella gazed around at the box-cluttered kitchen. 'Call me strange but I quite like unpacking, if you need a hand.'

He didn't know if it was her unexpected kindness or that wariness again flittered across her face, but he opened the cupboard he'd just looked in only to find it empty again. He wasn't the only one needing something to do as a distraction. 'Actually, we might need to find the glasses.'

'Consider it done.'

She moved to the closest box and the sound of tape ripping filled the kitchen. She held up a small saucepan.

He rubbed at his chin. 'I was wondering where that was.'

Without waiting for any instructions she carried the box over to a large kitchen drawer and arranged the rest of the saucepans inside. He didn't make any comment. He was having a hard time maintaining the illusion he was relaxed. The subtle scent of cherry blossom was doing strange things to his pulse rate. He opened a box to his left and found a set of glasses. He wiped one with a clean tea towel, filled it with ice and chilled water and set it near her phone.

From over in the walk-in pantry she smiled her thanks. She'd already grouped the non-perishable items he'd bought in town that morning into neat rows. It was no surprise she liked unpacking, seeing as she liked things ordered and tidy.

He finished emptying the box of glasses. 'Is Violet okay?'

'She's still settling in but I think so.' Ella took a sip of water before ripping the tape off another box. 'Thanks for visiting her with Duke.'

'She's a lovely lady.'

'She said the same thing about you.' Ella paused, a white dinner plate in her hand. 'Has she mentioned anything about her youngest daughter Libby?'

'She has. I can't imagine the pain she's been through.'

'Me either.' Ella's expression remained serious. 'If it's still possible to do the hay bale challenge together, I'd like to do a design in memory of Libby to generate some publicity. Somebody somewhere has to know something.'

Saul didn't hesitate. Helping Violet overrode any reservations about working alongside Ella. 'Count me in.'

'Thanks.' Ella bent down to place the plate into a low cupboard and he lost sight of her expression.

This time when she unwrapped another plate she hugged it to her chest. 'Saul … I'm sure Denham would have wised you up about Edna. She loves to play matchmaker. I just want to put it on record that I'm happily single. We're working together to help Violet, that's all.'

'Denham did give me the heads up. Believe me when I say you're safe with me.' He fisted his left hand so he'd not be tempted to look at his bare ring finger. 'I've also no intention of being anything but single.'

For the first time a genuine smile curved her mouth. 'Edna won't want to hear that but I sure do.' Ella relaxed her tight grip on the plate. 'Any idea on what we should do for our design? Libby liked art, horses, kelpies, books and Disney movies.'

'I'll get my laptop. If you've got time, we could decide on something so we can start building asap.'

She nodded as she folded the empty box flat. 'I'll let Edna know what's happening. Cressy will be fine without my help. Denham has almost finished their hay bale caterpillar.'

Saul managed to keep his control in place until he left the kitchen. Then he scraped a hand over his face. To think he'd been dragging his heels getting stuck into his bookwork. Holed up in his office entering numbers into a spreadsheet would be a much better option right now. For any other single male, having Ella Quinlivan in their kitchen, let alone working with her on the hay bale challenge, would be at the top of their hell-yeah list. It was at the bottom of his.

Despite having cleared the air about neither of them looking for a relationship, it would be impossible to be around her and remain unaffected. It would take all of his willpower to ensure that no one, not even Denham, knew how much she'd gotten under his skin. He unplugged his laptop that had been charging while he'd taken a swim. When he returned to the kitchen Ella gave him a sunny smile that started a pounding at his temples.

He placed the laptop on the table, opened the lid and typed in his password before Ella could pay too much attention to his screensaver. Taken at his and Trish's wedding, it showed them sharing a tender kiss against a backdrop of snow-capped mountain peaks. He didn't keep the picture because of sentiment. His ex-wife was the first of two mistakes he'd made. He kept the picture as a reminder that he was never making such mistakes again.

Ella finished unpacking another box before pulling up a chair to his left. Thankfully she sat a careful distance away. His testosterone was still obsessed with how sweet she smelt and how gold flecks glowed in the rich brown of her irises.

'This might be a good place to start,' he said, as he typed into an internet search engine and the screen filled with clipart outlines of castles.

When Ella didn't comment he glanced at her. Instead of looking at the screen, she stared at him, her fine brows lifted. To answer her unspoken question he opened the pictures folder and clicked on an image. A little girl with a short dark bob wearing a mauve-and-white princess outfit grinned out at them.

'Meet my niece Rosie. She loves purple and anything to do with fairytales. I have been known to fit myself into her castle play tent.'

'Now that I'd like to see.'

He looked back at the computer. The laughter warming Ella's eyes shouldn't unlock something within his chest or make him feel relieved that she appeared more at ease in his company.

He pointed to a simple castle picture. 'This would be easy to build using large hay bales for the foundation and round ones for the turrets.'

'It would.' He thought she was going to reach over and type on the keyboard but then her hands clasped together. 'Can you put in a search for princess goats?'

He groaned. 'You're kidding?'

'Every Disney hay bale castle needs princesses.'

Shaking his head, he typed and images appeared of goats wearing princess hats, pink coats and tiaras. He had to admit the goats did look pretty adorable. Next trip to Sydney he'd have to remember to show Rosie.

'Violet will love it,' Ella said, a smile in her voice.

'So will the media.'

Before Ella could reply, her phone rang from where it sat on the table. She answered, carrying her water glass to the sink while she spoke to the person at the other end.

She ended the call, already halfway towards the door. 'Sorry, I'm needed at the surgery. Thanks again for doing a joint challenge. I'll see you early tomorrow so we can get started.'

After giving Duke a quick pat, she was gone, leaving behind an unpacked kitchen and a house that on the surface resembled a home.

Saul stared at the empty doorway. An intense silence pressed in around him, taunting him that he was alone and the reality was this house could never be a home. All hopes for a place to call his own, filled with the love and laughter of a family, had ended the day Trish gave birth to a baby boy.

# CHAPTER
## 5

For once it wasn't Ella's internal alarm that woke her but the steady chug of a tractor beyond her bedroom window.

Dragging her hair from her face, she checked the phone on her bedside table. Even though it was Sunday she was still the on-call vet. After confirming she hadn't missed any calls or texts, she slid out of bed and stretched.

Yesterday her back hadn't liked her hefting the heavy box of Saul's saucepans. She'd been so intent on doing something other than stare at how his wet grey T-shirt clung to every toned ridge, she'd ignored the twinge in her lower back. She really did like unpacking, it soothed her need for order, but she'd never before done it with such single-minded focus. Saul rattled her, mentally as well as physically, and she'd need to come up with a better coping strategy than ripping off box tape if she were to survive working with him today.

She put a slice of bread in the toaster before staring out the kitchen window. Thankfully Saul hadn't extended his high boundary fence all the way to the road, otherwise that would be her view instead of a regular low fence that ended in a small garden gate. Violet had mentioned that the family who lived next door before the equestrian owners had also had small girls, so the gate had been put in to allow the children to play at each other's houses.

The toast popped but she made no move to place it on her plate. Thanks to Saul's established garden she couldn't see much of his house, apart from a silver roofline, but she had no trouble seeing the tractor slashing the paddock that ran between the two farms. She still couldn't believe he'd arrived at the castle idea so quickly. It really was perfect. She'd been thinking along the lines of a kelpie and a kennel which would have been much more complex. She'd never have picked that not only was Saul in touch with his fairytale side but that his gruff voice could sound as tender as it did when he'd talked about his niece.

She wrapped her arms around her waist. She'd also had her suspicions confirmed that Saul had been married. She hadn't missed the romantic and beautiful wedding image that he had as his screensaver. Even though he didn't wear a ring and there were no other pictures anywhere, he must still care deeply about the woman in the photo. An emotion she didn't want to examine made her turn away from the window.

She spread butter and vegemite on her toast. Despite her visit to Saul achieving all that she'd wanted it to, she couldn't shake a growing sense of unease. His quiet reassurance that she would be safe with him should have her opening a bottle of champagne. She'd finally found a single man with no expectation of anything beyond friendship, but for some strange reason she didn't feel relieved.

She took a bite of toast before squaring her shoulders and switching on her laptop. Today wasn't about how out of control her feelings were, it was about helping Violet. She'd check her banner design, have a quick shower and then help Saul, as chances were she'd be called away for a sick or injured animal sometime today.

She brought up the graphic she'd created after dinner last night using a photo of a fresh-faced Libby in a purple shirt that Violet had said would be the best one to use. As no one in town made banners, Ella had texted around to see if anyone was heading to the larger centre of Dubbo. When no one was, she'd found an online design website. After creating a horizontal banner for the castle, as well as a freestanding display, she did a final proofread and then pressed submit. She made sure she ticked the express postage box.

Last night she'd also called Sue, who after years of making Taylor's dance costumes, was happy to design Cinnamon and Nutmeg their princess hats. Ella could only hope the goats wore their costumes instead of eating them.

Half an hour later, dressed in her usual work gear of jeans, boots and a cotton shirt embroidered with the vet hospital logo, she went to say good morning to the two goats. A magpie warbled in the early morning peace. Bees buzzed as they hovered around the water in the goats' trough. The tension ebbed from her stiff shoulders. Even when her fractured world had brought nothing but darkness, nature brought her solace.

She snapped a photo for Violet of Cinnamon appearing oblivious to a willie wagtail perched on her back before making her way to the small gate in the bottom of the garden. Silence now replaced the noise of the tractor as Saul walked over the area he'd slashed. When Duke raced towards her, Saul turned and lifted his arm in a casual wave.

She returned the greeting before Duke's warm weight squirmed against her legs.

'Good morning to you too,' she said with a laugh. Duke's unbridled affection never failed to make her smile.

Together they walked across the paddock to where Saul now ran a string line. She wasn't the only one who liked to do things properly. Even though he wore a loose royal blue shirt, as she drew near she had trouble looking away from where the cotton pulled tight across his biceps. Just as well Penny hadn't seen him dripping wet in his T-shirt yesterday as that's all she'd be talking about at work tomorrow.

Even though his sunglasses and low cap brim hid his expression, the flash of his brief grin was enough to trigger a flurry in her midriff. She returned his smile, striving for calm. She couldn't forget he'd seen her at her worst at the wedding and she couldn't now appear anything but composed. 'You started without me?'

'Violet's guinea fowls believe dawn begins three hours early.'

She laughed. 'I would offer to have them back but Violet said they were happy at your place.'

Saul bent to hammer a peg into the ground. 'Tell me again why they're camped out in my garden?'

Even though she'd lost sight of his face she had no trouble hearing the amusement in his words.

'Because with its lawn and big trees it's a guinea fowl's paradise.' She tickled behind Duke's ears. 'You think they should stay, don't you … they'll keep the snakes away.'

Saul straightened. 'Of course he does. Stalking guinea fowls is one of his top-ten things to do.' Then, as if conscious of all the work they had to do, or simply done with small talk, he nodded at the string line. 'This is the width of one large hay bale so now it will just be how high and wide we want the castle to be.'

'Big for impact but as we've only got today not so big it's a herculean task to build.'

Saul paced out a large space.

Ella stood silent, wishing she had something to do other than watch him. Saul moved with a lithe grace and economy of movement that when paired with his perceptiveness explained why he'd done so well on the American pro-rodeo circuit. He'd be able to sense what a bull was going to do and then have the physical attributes to handle whatever the bull threw at him.

'To here?' he asked over his shoulder.

'Yes.'

He hammered in another peg. Restless, she collected the roll of string and ran it over to the new peg.

'Okay.' Saul assessed the allocated space. 'We'll need about seventeen large bales, twelve round bales and about twenty-five small bales.'

Ella blinked. She might have letters from an honours degree after her name but there was no way she'd have been able to do such mathematical calculations in her head. She would be flat out remembering the dimensions of the hay bales let alone how many would fit into the space.

'Did you just work that all out or did you know from the design you mocked up and texted to me last night?'

'My younger brother's a number nerd.'

Ella stared at him. 'And you aren't.'

'I left school when our father died to help Mum.'

'That would have been an incredibly tough time.' When Saul only nodded, she asked, 'Your number-whizz brother, is he Rosie's father?'

'He is. There was only the two of us and we're now the only ones left.' Saul took a penknife out of his pocket and cut the string. 'How about you?'

Ella swallowed. She was glad Saul's attention was on tying the string ends. Besides Violet, she'd never mentioned her brother to even her close Woodlea friends. It had just been easier to not talk about her past and a way to guarantee that she'd always stay in control. But now it somehow felt fitting to mention Aiden. Saul wouldn't be the kind to ask questions.

'I had a younger brother too. As for my parents … my mother's ageing disgracefully on the Gold Coast while my father has a second family in Adelaide.'

Saul faced her. 'I'm sorry about your brother. Your family has also been through a lot.'

She was thankful that sunglasses hid his eyes, as the sympathy in his tone was enough to stir her grief. 'It was a long time ago now. Mum's happy living life to the full and Dad … he's busy raising four teenagers.'

She didn't add that her mother was too preoccupied with her friends to take any interest in what she was doing or that she only spoke to her father twice a year. Neither of her parents had known how serious she and Charles had been and why she'd left England when she'd planned to use her ancestry visa to stay long-term.

'Nathan only has one five-year-old so I can imagine how busy your father is.'

As if Saul shared her thoughts that now would be an appropriate time to talk about something less personal, he glanced at the tractor. 'If you like, you can use my farm ute for the smaller bales. I'll bring the larger ones down with the tractor.'

'Sounds like a plan. I'll get as much done as I can in case I get called in to work.' She paused. 'Actually … do we have enough hay? I've only got about ten small bales.'

'We do.' Saul turned towards the tractor and she fell into step beside him. 'My hay shed's full. I'll also have enough to cover this week of feeding while the castle's on display.'

When they reached the tractor, Ella went to keep walking. It wasn't far to the small gate that would give her access to Saul's garden.

'I'll give you a lift.' Saul climbed the tractor steps to open the door. 'There's something to be said for tractor air-conditioning.'

Ella hesitated but when Duke bounded up the steps and turned to look back as if to say hurry up, she followed. It would be rude to refuse. After she'd settled into the smaller tractor seat, the affectionate Australian shepherd rested his head on her knee.

Saul didn't glance at her from the main tractor seat as he fired up the engine.

She concentrated on patting Duke and not on the way sitting so close to Saul put her senses on high alert. All she could breathe in was his fresh woody scent that reminded her of strolling by the river after a shower of rain. All she could focus on was the width of his shoulders and the way his well-shaped hands rested on the steering wheel.

She forced herself to look out the dusty windscreen. She may as well have walked. The air-conditioning did little to strip the heat from her warm face.

Neither spoke while the tractor made its slow way through the gate and along the track to the hay shed. Once at the open-sided steel building, Saul went to turn off the ignition when his phone rang. The engine still running, he reached for his mobile in his shirt pocket.

'Saul Armstrong speaking.'

Ella didn't need to recognise the loud voice coming from the phone to know the caller was Edna. The way Saul put his sunglasses on his hat and rubbed at his forehead said it all.

'Hi, Edna. Yes, she is. I'll put you on speaker.'

Edna's greeting filled the tractor cabin. 'Good morning, Ella. How fortunate to find you with Saul.'

Ella didn't dare look at Saul as he held the phone between them. 'I'm guessing it will save you a call.'

'It will. I've a busy day.'

Saul spoke before Edna could continue. 'Edna, how did you get my number?'

'I've always had it.'

'Have you now.'

'Yes. You were so kind as to buy raffle tickets your first trip to town.'

Ella covered her mouth with her hand to mask her smile as Saul looked at the roof and slowly shook his head. He would have written his phone number on the tickets.

'What can we do for you, Edna?' he said, his tone curt.

'Well, now that you've asked … I'm after a *huge* favour.'

Saul's eyes narrowed. 'Is this to do with the hay bale challenge?'

'Of course. The Saturday night presentation was supposed to be at the rodeo ground but the wind has damaged the roof of the amenities block and it won't be fixed in time.'

Ella met Saul's gaze. They could only guess at what Edna's request would be. The blue of his shirt was reflected in his irises, making them appear more of a clear blue than dark denim.

Edna continued on. 'So our plan B is your paddock, Saul. The historical society will run the sausage sizzle, I've already organised portable bathrooms and a water truck. The television crew will also be able to use it as a base. What do you think?'

'No problem. It sounds like you've thought of everything.'

'I have. Now, Ella … I've organised for the television station and the newspaper to interview you first thing Saturday morning.'

'I'll be camera ready.'

'I hope so. Just don't wear anything too short. I know you have legs half the Woodlea ladies wish they had but you need to be taken seriously when you talk about dear Libby.'

This time it was Saul who grinned and Ella who looked skywards. 'You know I always dress appropriately and don't worry, I'll be taken seriously.'

'Of course. Cheerio, you two, you'd better get back to work.'

Silence filled the cabin. Saul's eyes met hers and in their depths she glimpsed unconcealed laughter. She wouldn't be able to look away even if Edna called again. For the first time she felt as though she were seeing the real Saul beneath his reserve.

'Edna's one of a kind,' he said, the corner of his mouth lifting in a half smile. Before his marriage ended she had no doubt he'd been a man who smiled often.

'As if I'd wear anything too short. For the record my dresses always pass the fingertip test.'

He turned off the tractor and opened the cabin door before sitting back in his seat. 'Which is?'

She came to her feet and once on the top step, where she could stand straight, she held her arm by her left side and wriggled her fingertips. 'Dresses always reach to here.'

Something indefinable flashed across his gaze before he plucked his sunglasses from off his hat and slipped them on. 'I'll remember that for when Rosie's a teenager.'

She thought his voice had deepened but then the phone in her shirt pocket rang. She walked down the tractor steps while listening to the details about a dog that had fallen off the back of a ute.

When she ended the call, she turned to see Saul had left the tractor. Duke lay at his feet while Saul rubbed the Australian shepherd's fluffy belly with the toe of his boot.

'Work calls,' she said. 'Sorry, this could take a while.'

'When you get back there should be something in the paddock that resembles a castle. Rosie wants photos and has already asked Nathan to send me a hurry-up text.'

Then, before she could analyse a strange pang of loss at having to leave Saul, Ella jogged the short distance home.

The day of the hay bale challenge started like any other. The morning chorus of the guinea fowls woke Saul far too early.

He jammed a pillow over his head before the thought fully registered that he had a fairytale castle in his paddock along with a white marquee. Duke padded over to the bed and prodded him with his wet nose. Between Violet's runaway guinea fowls and the Australian shepherd he didn't need an alarm clock.

He glanced at the luminous display of his obsolete clock and rolled over to pat Duke. 'Feel like a run?'

Duke dashed from the room. Saul pulled on some rugby shorts and a singlet top before following more slowly.

He'd padlocked the gate of the hay bale challenge paddock that opened onto the road to stop anyone who had any ideas about helping themselves to the equipment needed for today. Woodlea might be a close-knit community, but rural theft and trespassing were still a problem. Last week a local farmer had his quad bike stolen after he'd left it on a stock route when he'd gone to open a gate to let his cattle onto the long paddock. A youth had taken the four-wheeler to sell for drug money.

The first blush of dawn crept across the horizon as Saul jogged along the driveway, Duke running beside him. They crossed the cattle grid and continued along the side of the road. The cool of the early morning air splashed over his skin, chasing away any lingering lethargy.

It was only when they'd reached the crest of the hill that the castle came into sight. Two huge pink flags flapped against the rose-coloured sky. He stopped to use the elevated view to check that everything remained in place after the overnight winds.

A neat row of large hay bales formed the front castle wall, stacked round bales resembled turrets and small bales acted as battlements along the top. In the middle was a square arch and drawbridge he'd welded in Denham's man cave. Ella had then placed small bales in strategic spots around the left of the castle for Cinnamon and Nutmeg to climb and sit on.

A sense of pride and achievement crept through him. Rosie had given the construction a big tick and requested that he build her a smaller version when she came to visit. He glanced over to where the front veranda light gleamed from Ella's cottage. It was thanks to Ella that their design had been accomplished so quickly. When she'd returned from her work call-out, she'd shared his attention to detail and work ethic. She'd driven the tractor, scaled the hay walls and stayed until late. Their castle really was a work of art.

His gaze lingered on the sandstone cottage. Yesterday he'd learned something new about her. She'd suffered the loss of a younger sibling. And just like every other time Ella revealed a new layer of who she was, what he discovered only made it more impossible to stop thinking about her. The calm way she'd mentioned her brother had been at odds with her defensive stare over her scar. The two couldn't be connected, which meant she'd endured two traumatic events in her life.

Filled with a sudden need to move, he ran down the hill to the padlocked gate. Every visit with Ella made it harder to keep his distance. She made him feel emotions he'd vowed to never feel again and she awakened longings that stole his sleep.

He'd learned his lesson after giving her a ride in the tractor. They couldn't again be in a confined space. Having her near only magnified his awareness and tested his already tenuous self-restraint. It had taken all of his willpower to not stare at the curve of her soft mouth when they'd been on the phone with Edna. As hard as it was, for both of their sakes, he had to stay on his side of the boundary fence.

He stopped at the gate and unlocked the heavy chain. Sightseers had begun driving past late yesterday and would be out early today. He went to pick up a plastic bottle someone had thrown out of their car window when shoes pounded on the bitumen. Duke's tail wagged as Ella jogged down the hill past her cottage and towards them.

Just like on the day she came to talk about Violet, she wore black knee-length leggings and a white shirt that rose and fell with her accelerated breathing. And just as it had then, the unexpected sight of her left him feeling dazed and on edge. While they had forged a working companionship, he hadn't yet mastered the art of remaining relaxed around her.

'Morning.' Her greeting was both casual and contained. While she did appear more comfortable in his company, she continued to keep her guard in place. He was the only one having difficulty remembering their boundaries.

'Morning. You're out early.'

'I needed a little quiet time before today's mad rush.'

As she bent to pat Duke, her heavy honey-blonde ponytail slid over her shoulder. His grip tightened on the plastic bottle against the urge to run his fingers through the silken strands.

'If everything that Edna says is true there could be quite a crowd.'

'We can only hope … and also that someone knows something about Libby. Daniel at the police station is all set to take any calls. Are you still right to pick up Violet?'

'Yes, first thing. Did you get Edna's message that there's a magazine who would like to do a photoshoot?'

'I did. I also washed Cinnamon and Nutmeg last night and am hoping they haven't found any dirt to roll in.'

'Good luck with that. And in case I don't get another chance, thanks for all your help.'

He wasn't sure if colour flushed her cheeks or if it was just a rosy glow from her run. 'You're very welcome. I should be the one saying thank you after lobbing this on you at the last minute.'

'It's all been for a worthwhile cause.'

Then, before his regret that their working partnership was over could show on his face, he whistled to Duke and they jogged through the paddock, past the castle and home.

By the time he returned with Violet sitting beside him in his F-truck, cars were congregated in the paddock and lining the roadside. A dusty four-wheel drive sported the logo of a regional television station.

'Look at all of these people,' Violet said, gazing around.

'It's a bit busier than when I was here earlier.'

On their trip back from town they'd taken an hour to drive around the other displays. They'd seen everything from a red ute, a bride and groom and a teddy bear made out of hay bales as well as Cressy and Denham's caterpillar. There were more designs on the other side of town that if they had time they'd see on their way home. But wherever they'd been, while there had been people out of their cars looking, there hadn't been as many as there were here now.

He drove in through the gate to join the queue that had stopped on the track that led behind the castle to the parking area. He followed Violet's gaze as she stared out the side window. Draped across the right castle wall was a large banner featuring Libby's grinning face and the hotline number to call with any information.

He reached for Violet's hand, not surprised to feel it shaking.

Violet spoke quietly. 'Libby would be thirty-six this year and Annette would be thirty-eight.'

He squeezed her hand. 'Someone somewhere will know something,' he said, as the traffic crawled forwards.

Not only had Violet lost her youngest child, her older daughter had died from an aggressive melanoma before her thirty-fifth birthday. Annette had only had one child, a daughter, who was at university in Brisbane studying medicine. Violet said she'd last seen Gemma when she'd come to visit her in hospital after her fall, but she still called every weekend.

When he reached the SES parking volunteer directing the traffic, he stopped and lowered the window. He didn't know the young brunette but she seemed to know them.

'Morning, Saul. Morning, Violet.'

'Morning,' he said as Violet gave the girl a smile. 'Can I make a left turn to save Violet a walk?'

The brunette nodded, stepped back and waved them through. He drove behind the castle to where a temporary fence enclosed the left wall. It was here that Cinnamon and Nutmeg were making the most of their royal abode. He parked and helped Violet out so she could walk to the fence.

The goats, the ribbons in their pink conical princess hats rippling in the breeze, were further around the front of the castle being patted by tiny hands. As soon as Nutmeg saw Violet she gave her ear-splitting bleat and both goats bolted towards her.

Saul held Violet's arm to steady her as she greeted the goats. A surge of emotion held him silent. This was the first time Violet had seen the mother and daughter duo since she'd moved out.

Violet took her time to pat each goat before adjusting Cinnamon's hat. 'Off you two go, you've a little fan club waiting. I'll see you again soon.'

Violet watched the goats wander away before turning to survey the crowd. Her forehead furrowed in a concerned frown. Saul looked over to where the older woman was staring. Ella stood in a sleeveless, flowing white dress that brushed the tops of her brown cowgirl boots. Below the wide floppy brim of a brown felt hat designed for fashion and not the paddock, her long blonde hair fell down her back.

He too frowned. The man who stood too close to her wore a blue shirt, tie and dark pants. In his hand he had a microphone but he seemed more intent on making Ella laugh than on recording an interview. Not far away stood a cameraman who appeared hot, bothered and bored.

'This was a bad idea.' The tension vibrating in Violet's tone snapped his attention back to her.

'What was?'

Violet pointed a gnarled finger towards Ella and the reporter who finally appeared to be addressing the camera. 'Ella doing the talking is a bad idea.'

He searched Violet's strained face. 'I'm happy to do the talking?'

'Now they've seen her, they won't be interested in you.'

He laid a hand on his chest in mock offence in an attempt to make her smile.

Violet's lips barely moved. 'Don't worry, if it was a female reporter I'd send you out there quick smart. But over there, that man hovering in the background with the laptop bag, he's a reporter as well.' She turned towards the car. 'Please take me home. You need to get back here.' She stopped to clutch at his hand. 'Promise me you'll not let anyone catch Ella off guard … this was only ever meant to be about Libby.'

'I promise.'

After he helped Violet into her seat he looked back to where the reporter now held a microphone towards Ella. Whatever it was that he didn't know about Ella, Violet either knew or suspected it wasn't something the media needed to get hold of.

He made the trip to Violet's unit and back again in under forty minutes and returned to the sight of Ella sitting with the goats having her photo taken by yet another male. Just like earlier, Ella laughed at something the man said. But it wasn't flirtatious or contrived, she was just being her natural warm self.

He made his way from the car park to the back of the castle, a fresh water bottle in his hand. Once at the temporary fence, he vaulted over the wire and walked around the castle corner. Ella's photoshoot had ended but the grinning photographer continued to socialise instead of letting her leave.

Saul approached, gave the man what Denham called his go-ahead-make-my-day stare before taking Ella's hand and leading her behind the castle. If she was surprised at his action he didn't feel it in her loose clasp. It was only when they were out of sight that she slipped her hand from his. The loss of her touch kickstarted a deep need he'd long ago sworn to never feel again.

She stopped in the shade and took off her hat to fan her face. He passed her the water bottle.

'Thanks.' She took a sip of the chilled water. 'I didn't think he'd ever stop talking.'

'You must be getting tired of answering questions.'

'A little, but this is all for Libby so I don't mind. The questions haven't been too tricky.'

'Was that the last interview?'

'Yes, now there's just an afternoon shoot planned in front of the castle once the winners are announced.' The breeze carried the aroma of onions and sausages and she gazed over at the barbeque marquee. 'I'm starving.'

'I'll get you a steak sandwich if you want to stay here and have a break.'

Her smile would have made him climb to the top of the turret beside him if she'd asked. 'Thanks but it's fine. You can walk over with me though as it's like these city boys haven't ever met a girl in boots before.'

Once at the food marquee, Ella went to sit with Fliss and Tanner's fiancée Neve while he went to help Denham with the barbeque. If Denham noticed his preoccupation with keeping tabs on Ella, he didn't make any comment. Saul had made a promise to Violet and he wasn't going back on his word. He again checked that Ella was over talking to Fliss and Neve.

The lunchtime rush stretched into the early afternoon. He was on his second shift of flipping steaks when Edna took centre stage in front of the crowd. Preoccupied with the meaning behind Violet's concern for Ella, he didn't pay attention to Edna's welcome or the category winners of the hay bale competition. It wasn't until Denham slapped him on the back that he realised he and Ella had won the main prize.

Within five minutes Edna had him and Ella in front of the castle holding a blue rosette the size of a mini pony. In front of them was a sea of people snapping pictures on their phones. Not knowing where to look, he stared over their heads towards the distant ridge.

Denham's voice sounded. 'Saul … just smile, mate.'

So he did. Briefly. Beside him Ella didn't seem to be having any trouble being in the spotlight.

A woman holding a camera that sported a large zoom lens called for them to move closer together. Ella obliged, making sure the rosette remained centred in front of them.

He didn't know if it was the brush of Ella's side that reminded him of the intimacy he'd lost, or if it was all the phones aimed at him, but time rewound. He was once again back to having his life fall apart under a very public microscope. Back again to feeling cornered.

He hadn't realised he'd stiffened until, voice low, Ella asked, 'Everything okay?'

When he didn't reply, or move, her fingers sought his behind the oversized blue rosette.

He allowed their warmth and her silent message that she had his back to hold him in place until the final photograph was shot. Then, without a word to anyone, he stepped into the crowd, wove his way towards the small garden gate and headed home to feed his bison.

# CHAPTER
## 6

Who knew the men of Woodlea had such sweet tooths?

Ella drove past yet another ute sporting a bull bar and oversized light bar as she looked for a parking spot at the old schoolhouse. She'd expected the decadent dessert night to be well supported by the local women but that the majority of men would be off down the pub for pizza and beers. She was wrong.

She passed a poison ivy green ute that sported two sky-high aerials and had picnic race day stickers plastered across the back. She didn't recognise the vehicle and hoped it didn't belong to Sophie's brother, Joe. Sophie had texted that morning to let her know that Polly was on her feet and doing well. Three cars along Ella saw a spot with enough room to park her four-wheel drive.

Cressy, Fliss and Taylor were already here. Thanks to having to recover a swallowed hearing aid from a puppy she was running late. Luckily the puppy responded to the emetic, and his dinner came back up along with the hearing aid. Otherwise surgery would have been necessary.

She grabbed her brown leather tote bag and started the trek to the schoolhouse. According to old Will, who loved his history, the bluestone building lit up with a string of white festoon lights had replaced the original slab hut schoolhouse. It was also one of the few schoolhouses left that had been built as both a school and a teacher's residence.

The once vacant building would now be the home of the windmill museum that would also house other historic rural items of interest. The hay bale challenge last weekend had raised some much-needed funds and tonight the dessert event would raise even more. In a few weeks the final fundraiser of a beer night and bush dance would be held.

Concentrating on walking over the rough ground that even in wedges proved problematic, she didn't pay any attention to the cars around her. Then, the unmissable chrome front of an F-truck shone in the gloom. She stopped. She'd assumed Saul wouldn't be here. They'd exchanged a few texts over the week and he'd never mentioned going to the dessert night. But then again neither had she.

She stared at the glossy white bonnet of his F-truck. As for any face-to-face conversations, there'd been none. She hadn't seen him since he'd left the hay bale challenge. He hadn't needed any help dismantling the castle and had returned her small hay bales while she'd been at work. When she'd felt him tense while the crowd had been in a photo-frenzy, she'd snuck a sideways look. Not everyone was comfortable being the centre of attention. To anyone else he would have appeared like a celebrity with an unsmiling signature pose. But to her it was clear something was wrong.

The remote cast of his profile went far beyond someone simply being out of their social comfort zone. His body had been as rigid as cattle grid steel and when she'd linked her fingers with his they'd been winter cold. For a long second she'd thought he'd shift his hand away, but then his fingers curled around hers. She could only hope that her smile in the photos of that moment wouldn't reflect the relief that Saul thought enough of her to accept her support.

When he'd disappeared into the crowd she'd made to go after him but Edna had called her name. After the photographer had taken some extra shots and locals had congratulated her she'd headed for the garden gate. When she saw Denham and Tanner walking towards the farmhouse she hadn't followed. Saul would be in safe hands with mates who knew him far better than she did.

She looked around, thankful she was the only one in the car park. Edna would have a field day if she heard that Ella was caught lost in thought studying Saul's F-truck. She kept walking. She was supposed to be keeping her distance but now that everyone knew they'd worked together it would appear strange if she avoided him.

If she were honest a part of her also needed to make sure he was okay. It had to be because she needed closure. It just felt like last weekend was unfinished and she didn't like having loose threads. She could weave a tapestry from the ones left hanging after the way her relationship with Charles had ended. She pushed aside the ache of entrenched regret and continued through the car park.

The glow of the festoon lights guided her past a freestanding old-fashioned school bell around to where music and laughter sounded at the back of the building. The stifling heat of the day had given way to a temperate breeze. Sue gave her a wave from where she sat beside Denham's aunt Meredith. In front of both women sat plates filled with a large slice of fruit-topped pavlova.

Ella gazed around what had once been the school playground. Inside a small marquee, also draped with festoon lights, a local singer-songwriter strummed on her guitar. Her lilting country songs merged with the buzz of conversation that seemed louder at one end of the crowd. On the schoolhouse veranda refrigerated display cabinets housed a smorgasbord of sweet and fancy treats, while across the yard by the fence, food vans offered everything from waffle cones to paper-thin crepes. Her mouth watered. It was well past her dinner time.

After catching sight of Taylor's platinum-blonde bob at the far end of the grassed area she made her way through the picnic rugs and camp chairs. To her right, beside a cabinet full of a rainbow array of gelato, Saul stood talking to Penny and Sally. Penny's high-wattage grin said as much as the way Saul's body was half turned away from her. Penny was thrilled to be chatting to him. Saul just wanted to leave.

She hesitated. He could look after himself. Then another two girls joined them. When one ran her hand through her loose blonde hair and the other leaned forward just enough to show a valley of creamy cleavage, Ella detoured to her right. Saul had made it clear he wasn't interested in any relationship. She also knew how it felt to be subjected to unwanted attention, even if it was well-intentioned.

When she approached, Penny gave her an enthusiastic hug, indicating that there had been as much champagne consumed as sugar. 'You made it.'

'I did. But I'm not quite off-duty yet. I need to see Saul about his bison.' She smiled at the other three girls. 'Would you mind if we had a quick word?' Then, not waiting for an answer, she accompanied Saul over to a quiet veranda corner.

A smile relaxed his mouth, and there appeared no trace of the tension that she'd glimpsed last weekend. 'Did you really want to ask me about my young bison or were you just being my vet in floral armour?'

She tried and failed to keep her face from warming as his gaze swept over her fitted black dress decorated in pale pink peonies. But just like the other times when his attention focused on her, his eyes remained guarded. Again, his lack of awareness of her as a woman left her more empty than relieved. 'Both.'

*Wrong answer.* His resulting grin only intensified the heat in her cheeks.

For a split second he seemed to focus on her lips before he replied, but it had to have been a trick of the poor light. 'Your patient has made a full recovery and is enjoying being with her new herd.'

'That's great.'

As much as she wanted to talk to him about what happened at the hay bale challenge photoshoot, now wasn't the time. She caught a glimpse of Edna dressed in a vivid royal-blue dress as she moved from one group to another. Neither of them could afford for Edna to see them together.

She also needed some physical space between her and Saul. Tonight he wore a white T-shirt with jeans and for the first time since Cressy and Denham's wedding his lean jaw was clean-shaven. He also smelled as good as he looked. She took a firm hold on her tote bag in case her fingers heeded the urge to touch the smooth indent in his chin.

Penny's loud giggle sounded. The cluster of girls were now talking to Joe and the redhead looked more than comfortable in their company.

Ella took a small step away from Saul. 'I'd better keep moving. I think the coast is clear for you to make it back to Denham and Tanner in one piece.'

Saul's slow smile shouldn't have made her steps light as she continued over to where her friends sat on their picnic rug.

Cressy came to her feet to give her a hug. Instead of her usual boots and jeans she wore a loose denim dress. 'I was starting to think I'd have to pack a doggy bag and take it to the clinic.'

Ella returned her hug, careful of Cressy's neat baby bump that had grown since she'd seen her at the baby shower. 'I'm here now and starving.'

She settled on a spare spot on the rug. Taylor and Fliss lifted their champagne glasses in a welcome toast.

'It's great to see you,' Taylor said.

'Ditto,' Fliss said, clinking her glass with Taylor's.

Ella glanced over to where men were standing in groups at the quieter end of the yard. Like Cressy, many appeared to be drinking water or cans of soft drink.

'You know, it threw me,' she said, looking back at Taylor and Fliss's full champagne glasses. 'It just didn't seem to fit that there were so many men here but now I know why … for once they're on designated driver duty.'

Taylor grinned. 'They are. It was also their idea. Not that I have anyone to be my designated driver, mind you, but Hewitt very kindly said I can share him with Fliss.'

Taylor was trying to make her long-distance relationship work with a man she'd met while travelling in Ireland.

Ella laughed. 'I bet the boys were quick to offer to play chauffeur. They won't be wanting to drive on the beer night.' She smiled at

Cressy. 'I'll stick to drinking water with you. I haven't eaten since morning smoko.'

Fliss stood and offered a hand to pull Ella to her feet. 'We'll soon fix that.'

When Ella returned to the picnic rug she carried a plate laden with desserts from colourful macaroons and chocolate lava cake to mini cheesecakes. While she enjoyed her feast she sat back and relaxed as laughter and jokes surrounded her. It was so nice to be amongst her friends, even if every so often she snuck a glance over at the reason why she'd isolated herself in the first place.

Saul continued to stand with Tanner, Denham and now Hewitt. Deep in conversation, Saul showed no sign of being uncomfortable amongst the crowd. When she felt Fliss's gaze on her she made a point of checking her watch. Now that she was out socialising again she'd hoped Fliss would stop keeping a close eye on her. She took hold of her bag and stood.

'You're not going already?' Taylor said with a stern frown.

'Of course not. I promised to take Violet some desserts. I shouldn't be long.'

'We'll still be here,' Cressy said, rubbing her rounded stomach. 'I've got some more sugar cravings to satisfy.'

Fliss smiled. 'If you're not back, I'll text when we're going to the pub.'

'Thanks.'

Intent on getting a varied selection of desserts for Violet, Ella didn't realise Saul was standing beside her until she caught a familiar woody scent and a glimpse of white out of the corner of her eye. She turned to see him also holding takeaway boxes.

He looked at the ones she held. 'Great minds?'

'If those desserts are for Violet, then yes we're thinking the same thing.'

A smile warmed his eyes. 'I can take them if you want to stay?'

'Thanks but I haven't seen her for a few days.' She reached for the boxes he held. 'I can take yours though?'

As Penny giggled nearby, he shook his head and turned towards the exit. 'I think this amount of dessert needs two delivery people.'

Making sure it didn't look like she was leaving with Saul, she took a different pathway to the playground gate. Her heart did a funny little jump when she realised he stood beside the school bell waiting for her. She'd just assumed they'd make their own way to Violet's.

'Where are you parked?' he asked as they walked side by side into the shadowed car park. The only source of light was the pale wash of the moon overhead.

'At the very end.'

'We can take my truck?' It was just a subtle change in his tone but his Australian accent seemed more pronounced.

'I'd better drive myself. I might need to play chauffeur later.'

'No worries.'

Too busy trying to gauge whether his tone had again changed, she stumbled over the uneven gravel car park surface. Even though she quickly righted herself, Saul's arm had encircled her waist. She froze.

It seemed a lifetime ago that a man had held her. And another lifetime since she'd felt the strength inherent in a masculine touch. She swallowed. But what she'd never felt, or couldn't ever remember feeling, was the heat of her own response.

'All good?' he asked.

Barely breathing, she nodded as his arm lowered and he stepped away. As if on autopilot, she walked forwards. When they'd waltzed at the wedding, the warmth of his hand at her waist had made her senses yearn. Now the solid weight of his arm around her didn't only awaken her body but also her emotions. Emotions she refused to let sabotage her composure ever again. She'd never been so glad to see a vehicle than when the squared front of Saul's F-truck came into view.

'Here you are.' Even to her own ears her words sounded strained.

Except Saul made no move to stop when they reached his truck.

So she did. She wasn't having him walk her to her four-wheel drive. She'd need the time between now and arriving at Violet's to run some much-needed damage control.

She took her phone from out of her bag and activated the torch. 'I'll be right from here and won't be too far behind you.'

The shadows hid his expression, but not the quietness of his words. 'Okay then. See you at Violet's.'

To think he'd believed he'd emerge unscathed from seeing Ella again.

Saul unclipped his seatbelt and flexed his shoulders, which felt as though they'd been shaped from his bison-yard steel. Things between them couldn't have gone more wrong tonight than if he'd walked under a ladder on the way into the dessert event. He already needed to clear the air about what had happened at the hay bale challenge and now everything had become more complicated.

He again checked the rear-view mirror for Ella's car lights. He was parked outside Woodlea Lodge and waiting for her to arrive. But the only flicker of white light was from a car passing the lodge turn-off. He could go in and see Violet on his own but he'd never been a coward. His mother also hadn't raised him to be inconsiderate or impolite. As much as his tension ratcheted up a notch with every minute that passed, he'd stay where he was.

When Ella had tripped, it had been pure reflex that had him reach out to catch her. He would have done the same for anybody walking beside him. But the instant his arm looped around her waist and his hand settled into the curve of her hip, it had become all about the way only Ella could make him feel. Warm and soft, she'd briefly rested against him. The silkiness of her hair brushed his chin and her cherry blossom scent enveloped him. Then she'd stiffened and reality had kicked in with a vengeance.

He'd promised her she'd be safe with him. He'd promised himself that he would keep himself safe. Responding to her on any level beyond platonic friendship wasn't adhering to either of those promises. The lift of her chin and her insistence on continuing alone to her car flagged she too had been thrown by the contact between them.

It was now important in the short walk to Violet's door that he re-establish the boundaries of the companionship they'd formed on the hay bale weekend. Any awkwardness between them had to be erased. Neither needed to carry any more emotional weight than they already did.

Headlights gleamed in his rear-view mirror and he collected the boxes filled with Violet's desserts. He left the driver's seat and waited on the footpath for Ella to leave her vehicle. While the streetlight threw out a pool of white light, she kept to the shadows as she approached.

He kept his voice casual. 'I hope Violet's hungry.'

'So do I.' Ella's eyes didn't meet his for as long as they usually did. 'I also hope I haven't ruined any of the desserts from tripping over. I'm not game to look.'

'My sister-in-law makes a berry meringue smash,' he said, as he followed Ella through the garden gate. 'Rosie's the chief meringue smasher.'

Ella didn't glance at him when she replied. 'Odds are that's what I have in one of these boxes.'

They stopped at the unit door and when he went to knock Ella spoke in a low tone. 'I can't believe that after all the publicity the hotline hasn't received more leads.'

'I've been thinking the same thing. The two people who phoned in gave inaccurate descriptions of Libby. One also said she'd been taken from her bed, but this was impossible as the house had been locked, including her bedroom window.'

'Violet and Lloyd also had an aggressive blue heeler that wouldn't have let anyone in through the gate—'

The door swung open.

'I thought I heard cars pull up. Come in.' Violet's gaze brightened as she took in the dessert boxes. 'Shall I put the kettle on?'

Ella didn't hesitate. 'Yes please. I need a coffee otherwise I'll soon be in a sugar coma.'

He nodded. 'A coffee for me too would be great.'

While the kettle boiled Violet inspected the contents in each box. When Ella opened the pavlova box she glanced across at him with a smile. 'This one's … a smashed peach and passionfruit meringue.'

It shouldn't move him the way it did that things appeared to have returned to normal between them.

While they drank their coffee and Violet sampled some of the desserts, the conversation flowed. Ella updated Violet on what mischief Cinnamon and Nutmeg were up to. Nutmeg had worked out how to jump onto the outdoor kitchen window frame so she could look inside to see what Ella was doing. Saul shared stories about bison jumping fences with the agility of a pole-vaulter and swimming across icy rivers.

When Violet gave a small yawn, Ella met his gaze and began to clear the plates. After Violet heard Ella washing up the teacups and shooed her out of the kitchen, they said their goodbyes. As they walked along the garden path, Ella's phone chimed and then Saul's.

Ella checked her message. 'Fliss says everyone's heading to the Royal Arms.'

'Denham says the same.'

'Are you going?'

'Let's just say that if I don't I've been told that it will be my job to dissuade Edna from helping out when baby Rigby arrives.'

Ella's quiet laughter lasted until they reached their cars. 'I'll see you there.'

Ella left first and led the way to the local pub. Instead of driving along the main street, she took a side lane that ended in a row of vehicles illuminated by the streetlights. She pulled in beside a battered ute and Saul parked alongside her. Even with the wrought-iron clad pub being a block away, the music thumped through his truck windows with a boisterous beat.

'Just as well everyone's on a sugar high,' Ella said, when he joined her on the footpath.

They set off to join the stream of locals heading towards the two-storey building. Ahead a loved-up couple giggled as they strolled. Saul made sure he kept a careful distance away from Ella. He couldn't risk anything else going awry tonight let alone anyone thinking they were an item. He hadn't missed the curious looks when he and Ella had been talking at the dessert night.

When the couple stopped to kiss, Ella kept her eyes averted and increased her pace to walk around them.

Once at the pub, she turned to him. 'If you see Penny, be careful. Once she gets you on the dancefloor, it will be impossible to leave.'

'Thanks to my creaky old bull-rider bones, my dancing days are over.'

Ella's smile stayed with him as he followed her inside and worked his way through the crowd to where Denham sat at a table with Tanner, Hewitt and the local horse chiropractor, Hugh. He wasn't sure where Ella had headed but when he sat he thought he saw Fliss and Cressy on the other side of the packed pub.

Denham shouted a round of beers and talk turned to how dry the season was and when rain would fall. Penny had walked past and given him a smile but seemed content dancing with her friends and a group of young farmers which included the lanky redhead he recognised from earlier. Judging by some of the dance moves of the redhead and his friends, their alcohol consumption had now surpassed their sugar intake.

While Denham, Tanner and Hugh bantered about which of their utes was superior, Saul sat back and again looked for Ella. She now stood over at the bar talking with Cressy and Hugh's partner, dark-haired Sibylla. Her floral dress might pass the fingertip test and cover all the parts of her that a group of women nearby had on display, but the effect was far from conservative. The soft drape of the fabric caressed every soft curve and as for her long tanned legs, Edna was right. He'd seen at least half a dozen women glance at her with envy.

He looked away. As for the men, he'd lost count of the number who'd checked her out. Ella might say she was happy being single but there was a score of men here tonight who would be willing to change her mind. She appeared oblivious to any attention. She neither gazed around to catch a bold gaze nor responded to any wave or greeting other than with a casual smile. Her message was clear. She hadn't come tonight for anything other than to spend time with her friends.

He didn't realise that Hewitt had noticed where his attention had been until the pickup rider said quietly, 'You can almost hear the hearts breaking.'

Even as they watched, a man approached to buy Ella a drink until her smile friend-zoned him.

'The thing is …' Hewitt spoke again. 'That look Ella has of not being interested was one I had. And is one you have too.'

Saul didn't answer, only took a mouthful of beer. Hewitt had read him accurately.

Hewitt lowered his voice. 'There's nothing any of us would like better than to see Ella happy, so until then we all look out for her.'

Saul gazed at Ella as she laughed at something Sibylla and Cressy said. 'Ella deserves to be happy … but her reasons for wanting to stay single might never change.'

Hewitt touched his beer to Saul's. 'Fliss and I are proof that anything can happen.'

He hoped for Ella's sake there did come a time when she was willing to let someone into her life. She did deserve to find happiness. She had so much warmth and love to give. He could see it in the way she cared for Violet and whatever animal she came into contact with. He'd also glimpsed longing in her eyes as she'd stared at Rosie's photograph.

He drank from his beer to wash away the bitter taste in his mouth. As for him, the look he wore was a permanent one. He'd stick to building up his bison herd.

This time it was Denham who clinked his beer against everyone's glass. 'While we're toasting, I just want to thank Hewitt for taking over the wedding baton. You have no idea how glad I am to hand it to you.'

Tanner chuckled. 'I think we do. We've been the ones dragging you to the pub to de-stress.'

Hewitt turned to Tanner with a grin. 'I'm more than happy to pass it on.'

Tanner held up his hands. 'Whoa, Neve and I haven't finished our house. I can't even get my head around the difference between a loop and cut pile carpet let alone think about a wedding.'

The group's laughter rolled around Saul, banishing the memories of his own wedding day and making him thankful for the mateship he'd found since he moved to Woodlea.

Denham spoke again. 'So, Hewitt, any update on these secret squirrel wedding plans of yours?'

'At the top of Fliss's three page *pre-wedding* list it says to not talk about anything yet, even if Denham offers to buy me a beer.'

As everyone laughed, Saul again glanced at Ella. The young redhead had left the dancefloor and now, a beer in his hand, sauntered over to where Ella stood with Cressy and Sibylla.

He wasn't the only one to notice.

Hugh dipped his head towards the redhead. 'I haven't seen him around.'

Tanner answered. 'It's Joe Wilkes. He lives out past Edna but has been jackarooing up north and has just finished his first year of ag college.'

Denham pushed back his chair. 'He has a few beers on board and is missing Ella's signals. I'll set him straight.'

Saul came to his feet. 'I'll go. I owe her.'

Tanner nodded with a wink. 'I did see Ella run interference when Penny and Sally made a beeline for you.'

Saul headed to where Joe now stood too close to Ella. As he reached her side, Joe swayed and it was only Ella taking a quick step backwards that stopped her from having beer tipped over her front. Amber liquid splashed over the floor.

'Easy there, big fella.' Saul reached out to steady him.

Ella's smile appeared serene but when she glanced at Saul frustration tempered the light in her eyes.

'Saul,' she said, tone dry, 'meet Joe. Joe, meet Saul.'

'No way.' Joe swayed again. 'You're the bison dude.'

'Yeah, I'm the bison dude.'

'And the F-truck dude.'

For once he was glad he was a creature of habit. Since he'd driven F-trucks overseas, he'd bought one when he arrived home. Joe clearly liked his cars as much as he did long-legged and beautiful blonde vets. 'Yeah, I'm him too.'

'Does it have a ten-speed transmission?'

'It does.'

In his peripheral vision he saw Ella, Cressy and Sibylla swap glances before they edged away and disappeared into the crowd.

'I have a V8 AU Falcon.'

Joe went on to talk about the work he'd done on his ute. At the end of the conversation Saul made sure the young farmer held a bottle of water instead of a beer. He was on his way back to his table when Ella walked past on her own, her brown bag looped over her shoulder. She waved across at Denham's table but didn't stop to chat as she headed for the door.

Denham caught his eye and he nodded. He'd make sure Ella made it to her car.

He followed her outside. Crickets chirped in the stillness and the moonlight now glowed through a thin veil of clouds. It wasn't until she reached the bottom pub step that she turned to look at him. For a moment she stared and then waited for him to reach her side.

She cast him a quick glance as they walked. 'Thanks for helping out with Joe.'

'To be honest I was more worried about him. I've seen you manhandle a hay bale.'

A brief smile tilted her lips. 'I was close to giving him the look I reserve for badly behaved Angus bulls.'

'I might need you to use that look on one of my bison.'

She laughed softly. 'I'd like to learn more about working with them; if you ever need help let me know.'

'I will.' He paused. 'Ella … I owe you an apology.'

Her steps slowed as she searched his face. 'What for?'

'For running out on you at the hay bale challenge.'

'You didn't run out … the day was over.'

'We both know I did. I want to explain.'

'You don't need to. Really.'

He hadn't realised they'd stopped walking until she faced him. In the glow of the streetlight her eyes were large and her expression serious.

'I do. We both put it on record that we have no plans to be anything but single. My short explanation is … I got married. I got divorced.'

'I can see why you don't want another relationship.'

'The slightly less short version is when my marriage ended it did so in a very … public way. Trish and I were the talk of our small town.'

'Ahh.'

'Crowds normally don't bother me. I saw more than my fair share on the rodeo circuit. I just hadn't realised that when my marriage disintegrated, how trapped I felt until all those people were in front of me.'

Her touch on his arm was as light as the night breeze. 'I understand.'

They started walking again.

He felt her attention on him before she asked, 'Do you still feel trapped?'

'I feel free.'

But even as he said the words he knew they were a lie. After what Trish's duplicity and deceit had cost him, he'd never be free to trust, or to love, another woman again.

# CHAPTER

# 7

The next time she had the brilliant idea of going for a mid-morning jog, even if thick clouds covered the sun, she needed to think again.

Ella climbed the veranda steps of her cottage and bent to rest her elbows on her knees. Breathing laboured and her skin slick, she waited for the dizziness to pass. The only time to go for a run was in the early morning or late evening.

At least she'd come home to a cool house. She'd flicked on the evaporative air conditioner before she'd left as she only used a fan in her bedroom at night. As noisy as the air conditioner was, it kept the original section of the sandstone cottage a comfortable temperature as well as the renovated back extension. There was nowhere else she would be spending the rest of her Saturday morning than inside. When she headed to town for the last hair appointment before lunch, Taylor's hair salon would be nice and refrigerated.

Still gasping for air, she unlocked the front door. She'd have a shower and dust Libby's room. Violet had kept it as it was and Ella wanted it to look perfect for whenever Violet was ready to visit.

Instead of a draught of chilled air hitting her, the hallway possessed the same clammy feel as outside. She quickly shut the front door to keep the hot breeze out. An ominous silence filled the cottage as she headed for the air conditioner control panel on the wall outside the kitchen. No longer did a hum and a rattle sound from the roof. She flicked the switch on and off. Nothing.

She grabbed her phone from off the kitchen bench. As she dialled she held open the fridge door, savouring the wash of cold air. Her trusty electrician Roy would soon have the air conditioner humming again.

After several rings a voice answered. Except it wasn't Roy's gravelly tone. 'Woodlea Electrical, Sharon speaking.'

'Hi, Sharon, it's Ella.'

Sharon was Roy's wife who Ella knew from when she'd treated her young Maltese terrier for mites.

'Hi, Ella, it's been a while.'

'It has. I hope Snuff's well. I know it's a Saturday but I have an air conditioner that's decided it's been overworked and needs a break.'

Sharon laughed but her amusement gave way to an apology. 'I'm so sorry, Ella, but Roy and I are in Dubbo … at the hospital. A certain person thought it would be quicker to fall off the ladder and break his leg than to climb down.'

'That doesn't sound good. Does Roy need surgery?'

'He's in there now.'

'Wish him well for me and I'll pop around when you're back.'

'Give Nick a call otherwise there's a new guy … I took down his details from the community noticeboard … it's here in my bag somewhere. Okay, his name's Doug Jones and his number is …'

Ella shut the fridge door and wrote the number Sharon read out onto the back of an envelope. 'Thanks. Hope Roy's home soon.'

She poured a glass of iced water before ringing the second electrician. When the phone rang out she left a message before calling the new person. He picked up straight away.

'Hi.'

'Is that Doug Jones? I'm after someone to fix my air conditioner.'

'Yup. That's me. Where are you?'

'Ambleside, on the left, twenty minutes after the turn onto Woolpack Road. I know it's Saturday …'

'Give me an hour.'

Relief quickened Ella's words. 'Thanks so much.'

As she ended the call she had a thought that not only did he sound young but perhaps there was a reason why he wasn't busy in the peak of summer, especially when the town was down one electrician. Her doubts fled as she went for a shower.

Hair wet, and with a raspberry yoghurt iceblock in her hand, she went out to sit on the shaded front veranda where there was a semblance of a breeze. She had everything crossed that this Doug Jones not only turned up but was on time.

She settled in a white wicker rocking chair and looked out over the garden. The standard iceberg roses that lined the front fence were in full bloom as was the cerise-pink crepe myrtle tucked into the corner beside the veranda. A blue wren perched on the mosaic bird bath that Libby had made out of broken china and tiles to match the mosaic stepping stones scattered throughout the garden. Ella had made sure that when Violet moved into town two of Libby's handmade stepping stones, as well as a smaller birdbath, had gone with her.

The lavender hedge that ran along the side fence perfumed the air with its sweet fragrance. Even though she knew she shouldn't, her gaze lifted from the delicate purple spikes to where a corrugated iron roof gleamed amongst the established trees of Saul's garden. This week they'd texted each other, though the texts had been infrequent and solely about Violet. In a quiet moment she'd find herself checking for new messages. As much as she didn't want to admit it, she missed his dry humour that had made her smile while they'd built the castle.

When yoghurt dripped on her wrist she realised she was doing more thinking than eating. As short as Saul's explanation of why she would be safe with him had been, the pain that had edged his low words spoke of the anguish associated with the longer version. The wedding photo on his computer suggested he was the aggrieved party in what could only have been a brutal break-up.

She finished her iceblock, which was now in danger of sliding off the stick and into her lap. No good would come of her wondering about Saul's story; he already affected her far more than he should. The way she'd reacted to his touch was more than enough of a warning. She'd wanted closure about why he'd left the hay bale challenge, now she had it. She'd seen him the past two weekends so this weekend needed to be two Saul-free days. It was the only way she'd restore order to her emotions and her life.

An engine sounded before a Hilux drove through the front gate and parked behind her four-wheel drive. Things looked promising. Doug Jones had arrived when he said he would. She walked around the house and through the back garden to meet him. Thankfully as he left the driver's seat he appeared older than he sounded.

'Morning,' he said, chewing gum and making no attempt to hide that he was checking her out. His attention lingered on her bare legs below the cuffs of her denim shorts before settling on her loose, still damp hair.

She stopped a good distance away, her hopes falling that the new guy would prove to be even half as reliable as Roy.

'Morning.' Her tone was as cool as the ice melting in her water glass beside the rocking chair. 'The aircon's turned off inside and the unit's this way.'

She waved for him to precede her. Even if she was wearing an oversized green work shirt she wasn't having him inspect the back of her as thoroughly as he had the front. She didn't make small talk when they stopped and he stared up at the square unit perched on the rooftop.

'I'll leave you to it,' she said, before heading inside to collect the book she'd been reading from off her bedside table. As she returned to her seat on the veranda, clunking sounded as the electrician clamoured around on the tin roof.

Two chapters later Doug Jones appeared at the veranda front steps, no longer chewing gum. Sweat dripped down his cheeks and the front of his faded red shirt was wet around the neck. But as hot and uncomfortable as he looked, the open interest in his gaze hadn't waned.

After he'd come inside to look at the control panel, she poured him a glass of cold water. As she added ice, a familiar hum and rattle sounded overhead.

'Thank you,' she said, smiling with relief as she passed him the glass.

He sculled the water before answering. 'It was an easy fix. I'll drop an invoice round Monday.'

She kept her smile in place as she took the empty glass he handed her like she was his personal assistant. She resisted the urge to wrinkle her nose. Whatever antiperspirant he used hadn't held its own against the heat. 'I'll be at work so just pop it in the mailbox.'

'I can call around *anytime*.'

She spoke before she could roll her eyes. 'Putting the invoice in the letterbox will be fine.' Her words were as firm as her gaze was steady. He was the first to look away.

'Righto.'

She walked with him to the front door. 'Thanks again.'

'Are you sur—'

She raised her brows.

He stopped, then said over his shoulder, 'See ya.'

She shut the door with a sigh. That was the first and last time Doug Jones would fix anything for her. He may have got the job done but his customer service was far from professional. She dragged hair from off her face. It could have been worse. The air conditioner might have needed to be replaced or she could have had to call on a certain neighbour for help.

After she was sure Doug had left, she went outside to pick the mauve roses that possessed a strong aromatic fragrance. By the time she'd changed into a red fit-and-flare dress, the cottage smelled like a perfume shop. She didn't usually dress up to go to town but for some reason after thinking far too much about Saul this week, it seemed important to remind herself how liberating it was to be on her own.

As a London lawyer Charles had liked her to look a certain way so that she fit in with his city friends. He'd bought her a wardrobe of high end clothes for when she'd have a weekend off from her locum position with a Cotswold vet practice. As much as she loved her wax cotton jacket and gumboots, they hadn't been acceptable attire in Charles's sartorial opinion. She grabbed her bag and headed past her well-worn gumboots that had pride of place in the shoe box at the back door. Nowadays she wore what she wanted, when she wanted, and wasn't fulfilling anyone's expectations but her own.

Taylor didn't miss her wardrobe choice when she arrived in town and walked into the empty hair salon. 'You're looking very glam. Is there something you're not telling me … like you have a hot date?'

'The only hot thing in my life was my house this morning when I had no aircon.'

Taylor's eyes sparkled. 'You know I live in hope there will be other hot things.'

Ella laughed. Taylor was an incurable romantic and her light teasing wasn't ever meant to cause any pain. If Ella did ever have a hot, or even lukewarm, date, Taylor would be the first person to sit her down to make sure she was doing the right thing. 'You'll be waiting a while. Besides, you only want me to go on a date so you can do my hair.'

'True. You're a hairdresser's dream.' Taylor's expression sobered. 'Are you sure you want to do this?'

Ella ran her hands through her thick hair that had grown extra long since she'd been too busy to have a trim. 'Off with the lot.'

'Well then, let's get started.'

Ella sat in the chair Taylor indicated and was soon cloaked in a synthetic black cape.

Taylor parted her hair in the middle, twisted small sections and pinned them into place with large clips. 'You know people pay a fortune to have natural highlights like these.'

'They're all thanks to our Aussie sun.'

In the mirror she saw her smile fade as she remembered how dark her hair had become when she'd been away from the Australian summer. Charles had booked her into a fancy London hair salon to have it lightened. At the time she'd thought it was sweet of him as she'd been too busy to think about her appearance. Now her older self wasn't so sure his intentions had been so unselfish.

Taylor's fingers stilled as she secured a small ponytail with a rubber band. 'Second thoughts?'

She went to shake her head, then spoke instead. 'Not at all.'

Taylor sectioned Ella's hair into another three ponytails. After wrapping bands in regular intervals along their length, she measured them to make sure they met the requirements of the hair donation charity. From when she'd donated her hair last time Ella already knew she ticked the chemical-free box.

Taylor picked up her scissors with a gleeful grin. 'Ready?'

Ella tried not to smile. 'Usually you wear that expression when you're chasing Fliss around with a can of hairspray ... but yes, I'm ready.'

Taylor cut above the top elastic band on each ponytail. With every snip shorter sections of hair fell around Ella's face to brush her collarbones. With each ponytail that Taylor carefully laid on the trolley beside her, she felt lighter, and not just because her heavy hair didn't now fall down her back.

She didn't consider herself a blonde bombshell, but for those of the opposite sex who were tempted to think of her that way, the label now wouldn't fit. For whatever reason, short blonde hair didn't seem to hold the same sex appeal on her. If she now met up with Doug Jones she was confident he wouldn't give her a second glance.

Taylor's expression turned serious as she styled what was left of Ella's hair. 'You know this won't change a thing. You'll never be invisible.'

'It made a difference last time.'

Taylor simply shook her head.

With her hair falling in bouncy waves around her face, she blew Taylor a farewell kiss before walking out into the bright sunshine. She slipped on her sunglasses. *Short hair, don't care.* A new hairstyle deserved to be celebrated with one of the Windmill Café's famous brownies. She'd buy two and pop around to see Violet.

She'd only covered half a block before her name was called in almost a wail. 'Ella Quinlivan … what have you done?'

She slowly turned to face Edna who power-walked towards her. Whatever it was, she had no idea. 'Nothing? Why?'

Edna stopped, puffing slightly. 'Your beautiful hair …'

Ella touched the soft, short waves. 'I donated hair to be made into another wig.'

'That's a very selfless gesture but you did that when you first arrived in town.'

'There's no rule that says I can't do it again.'

Edna's gaze sharpened.

Ella resisted squirming. She didn't envy Bethany growing up with a mother whose stare quite possibly had the ability to see everything a person wanted to hide.

She spoke again. 'It's also summer, we're in a heatwave, and this style will be cooler.'

Edna's expression softened. 'You're far too sensible to have had your hair cut for any other reason. The wig charity is a very worthy cause.'

To her surprise Edna wasn't in the mood to chat further. 'Now, I'd better keep moving. Bethany's in town somewhere.' As Edna turned, she gave Ella a stern look. 'I know poor Roy's out of action and you had an emergency but you should have called me to check out that new electrician. I'm glad he did what he was supposed to but a word to the wise, a reliable source has told me that he sets up shop and when something goes wrong he leaves town.'

Ella kept her expression from changing. How was it that Edna knew everything that went on around town? 'Thanks for the heads up.'

After Edna turned to leave, Ella sent Bethany a text. If why she was in town had anything to do with her mother's surprise party she couldn't have Edna track her down.

Bethany texted a reply thanking her for the warning. She had been looking at possible party venues but was now leaving. She'd call her later as she'd drawn a blank at finding somewhere suitable. Almost everywhere had a connection to her mother.

After finishing her small grocery shop, Ella drove home. She kept running her fingers through her shortened hair. She'd forgotten how it felt not to have long hair. Edna was partly right—there was the additional reason of wanting to go under the masculine radar, but that was it. There simply wasn't any further reason for her having had her hair cut.

When she pulled into the carport and turned off the engine, she held her breath until she heard the air conditioner making its usual din. Doug Jones might not have been the best choice but apart from his lack of professionalism he'd done what he'd come out to do.

She unlocked the back door. A rush of cold air failed to greet her. *Not again.* She closed her eyes only to immediately open them. Was that running water?

She lowered the grocery bags to the wooden floor and sped towards where the sound was coming from, which seemed to be the living room. She came to a sudden stop at the doorway. The room directly under the air conditioner unit had turned into a water feature. Water coursed through the air conditioner vents, down the wall and onto the floor before running through the sliding door into the hallway.

A tension headache throbbed between her temples as she raced to the control panel to switch the air conditioner off. There was no way she was calling Doug Jones. He wasn't setting foot on Ambleside again. When she'd calmed down she'd give him some constructive feedback. She was done with ineptitude.

What she needed was a ladder. Whatever this new problem was it involved water so it should be obvious where the flow was coming from. Surely there would be a video on the internet to show her how to turn off the water and fix the leak? She scooped her phone out of her bag before self-preservation could overrule her common sense. First she had a call to make. The closest person with a ladder was Saul.

'You have such a tough life,' Saul said to Duke as the Australian shepherd rolled onto his back so the kitchen air conditioner could cool his belly.

Duke responded with a brief wag of his tail. Saul smiled. Anything more and it would have been too much of an effort.

Saul lifted his arms above his head and stretched as he walked over to check his phone charging on the bench. He finally had his quarterly business activity statement done and dusted. The rest of the weekend would now be about working outside—a place he'd much rather be, even in this heat.

He checked his messages. Denham had asked him over for a cold beer with the boys but after the past two busy weekends he'd reached his threshold of being social. He'd replied saying he was having a quiet Saturday night in. The truth was that disclosing to Ella about his failed marriage had left him feeling on edge and he needed space.

He scrolled through the rest of his messages, only giving them a brief glance. Despite his best intentions, he'd allowed Ella to sneak under his guard. Even telling her about the shortened version of his divorce was still more than he'd told anyone besides his brother. Instead of talking about what had happened proving cathartic, reliving his past only reawakened memories he didn't need to revisit.

His fresh start didn't involve allowing emotions to sidetrack him. Even if every meeting with Ella revealed a new layer of who she was and made him feel things he'd vowed to never feel again. That would teach him to go off script. He needed to get back to focusing on his bison and not on his distracting new neighbour.

He was spooning coffee into a mug when his phone rang. Thinking it was Denham calling to talk him around to coming over, he didn't pay much attention to the caller ID until he'd lifted the phone halfway to his ear. Then he caught the name on the screen. Ella.

'Hi, everything okay?' he asked, making no move towards the electric kettle as it flicked off. She'd only ever texted before.

'Can I please borrow your extension ladder?'

'Sure. I can bring it around in my truck.'

'Do you also have a tool box handy? I only have a few things here.'

'There's one in my ute … what's the problem?'

'Half my rainwater tank's in my living room.'

'I'm on my way.'

He ended the call and Duke, sensing life was about to get more interesting, jumped to his feet.

When they arrived at Ella's, Nutmeg greeted them from the goat paddock with her blood-curdling bleat. While Duke raced off to see the two goats, Saul unloaded the ladder and tool box. Arms full, he turned to head over to the cottage. Except his boots remained anchored in place.

He'd ridden rank bulls no one could ride. He'd wrangled bison no one could handle. But the sight of Ella walking towards him in a red dress, her hair cropped and tousled, threw him. All air left his lungs. All thoughts fled except for the ones that involved sliding his hands through her now shortened hair. He forced himself to remember where he was and what he was supposed to be doing. He moved away from his truck.

'That was fast,' she said, stopping before him on the path. 'I didn't even have time to get changed.'

He lost the battle to not stare. Her new hairstyle framed her face, accentuating her large brown eyes, high cheekbones and the soft curve of her mouth. He broke eye contact to study the roof. 'So, you either have a burst pipe, a roof leak or something's up with your air conditioner.'

Duke joined them and she bent down to give him his compulsory pat. 'As my face is no doubt the colour of my dress, let's go with option C.'

He didn't dare glance at her dress, which only emphasised the feminine indent of her waist and reminded him of how right it felt to have his arm wrapped around her. 'How about I turn the water off, then we can see what we're dealing with. There's a box of towels in my truck if you need them.'

'Thanks. I can go up on the roof, though.' The breeze caught in the skirt of her dress. She placed a hand on her right thigh to hold the fabric in place but not before he caught a glimpse of smooth tanned skin. 'On second thought it will be quicker if you turn off the water. I'll keep mopping.'

She walked towards his truck, her hand making sure her dress wouldn't again balloon upwards. Duke followed as she lifted out the box of towels.

Saul used the short walk to the side of the house to slow the thumping of his heart. When it came to Ella, it wasn't only feelings that unnerved him. He'd never felt such an intense physical pull before, even towards Trish.

He settled the ladder against the side of the cottage and focused on the job at hand. Thanks to the temperamental evaporative air conditioner he'd grown up with, he located the water valve and turned it off. He also identified what the water issue was. The clamp on the hose supplying the water hadn't been secured properly. The pipe had come loose and instead of water going into the unit, it poured into the cottage's roofing space. He hoped the insulation, lights and wall gyprock weren't going to suffer any serious damage.

He climbed down the ladder, found what tools he needed from the tool box and returned to the roof to reattach the pipe. Once he made sure the clamp held firm, he went in search of Ella.

He knocked at the back screen door, not wanting to assume he could waltz inside.

Ella's voice sounded. 'Come in.'

He walked through the covered-in back veranda, through a homely kitchen and into what had to be a living room. He'd thought Ella's home would be highly organised and it was. There was zero clutter or mess. A polished dark wood fireplace gleamed from behind where two red chairs and a lounge had been pushed to the side. A thin stream ran down the white walls and across the polished floorboards.

Ella stuck her head through the doorway that led to a small hallway. She'd changed into mid-length denim shorts and a navy tank top and her feet were bare. 'Whatever you did, the water's stopping.'

'The hose had come loose.'

'You wouldn't believe I had someone fix the aircon this morning.'

'I wouldn't be using whoever it was again.' He lifted a plastic tub filled with the soaked charcoal-grey towels he'd brought with him. At least now when his sister-in-law asked if he'd used her housewarming gift he could say he had. 'Laundry is …?'

'Two doors past the kitchen.'

After he'd carried three more loads of towels to the laundry, the cottage floors were dry.

Ella stood and rubbed at her lower back. 'I need caffeine or sugar before we turn on the aircon and might have another waterfall to mop up.'

Once in the kitchen she poured two glasses of orange juice into tall glasses and handed him one.

'Thanks,' he said, making sure their hands didn't touch.

She opened the freezer at the top of the fridge and took out a container of salted caramel ice cream. 'I've been saving this for a special occasion. I think having the house water-free qualifies.'

She spooned ice cream into two white bowls before carrying them across to the kitchen table. He collected her juice glass and placed it beside her before sitting in a chair across from her. Crunching sounded as Ella snuck Duke a plain biscuit.

He ate a mouthful of the cold ice cream. He was unsure whether or not he should comment about her hair. Thanks to Trish he knew there was a fine line when it came to commenting on a woman's appearance—he either said not enough or too much. He decided on the less is more approach.

'Your hair will be cooler in this heat.'

'It sure is. I should have donated it a month ago.'

His spoon stilled halfway to his mouth. 'Was that for a charity like Kids With Wigs?'

'It was.' Her eyes searched his.

He rested his spoon in the bowl. 'Rosie, my niece, had a rough start. Her acute lymphoblastic leukaemia is now in remission.'

Ella stopped eating. 'Poor little possum. I can't even imagine what she's been through, as well as her parents.'

'I flew home whenever I could. Nathan and Amy are now expecting their second child and I've never seen them happier.'

He resumed eating and made a point of finishing his ice cream. The cottage kitchen felt more claustrophobic than cosy. As happy as he was for his brother and Amy, he was still working on coming to terms with their pregnancy news. First there would be Denham and Cressy's baby, and then his newborn niece or nephew. He wasn't sure yet how he'd cope being around either of them.

He came to his feet and carried the empty bowls over to the sink. 'I'll get back on the roof.'

While he restored the water supply to the air conditioner and checked that the hose clamp remained in place, Ella fed Cinnamon and Nutmeg.

From the bottom of the ladder he soon heard Ella call out, 'Shall I turn it on?'

He crossed to the roof edge and looked down. 'That would be great.'

It wasn't long until the air conditioner kicked into life. The clamp around the hose held. He waited another five minutes and when nothing changed he headed inside.

In the kitchen he held up a hand to the ceiling vent. A welcome gust of cool air washed over his palm. Movement sounded in the living room and he went to help Ella shift the red lounge back into place.

'Everything's working fine,' he said, looking away from the toned strength of her arms and the way her navy tank top pulled tight across her chest.

'I should have called you this morning.'

They moved the final red chair into place beside the sofa.

He glanced up at the ceiling, which didn't look to have suffered any obvious water damage. 'At least with all this heat everything will soon dry out.'

She went over to the half-open sliding door that separated the old and new sections of the cottage. 'So far this seems to be the only thing not right. I can't get it to close.'

He went and pushed the door, but it only moved a fraction. 'The water could have run into the cavity. I'll take a look.'

After finding the right-sized screwdriver in his tool box, he removed the strip of wood covering the top metal door track. He then unscrewed the two rollers that attached the door to the track and lifted the wooden door free.

'There's nothing wrong here,' he said, casting an eye over the door edges.

Ella didn't appear to hear him. Instead she was on her knees, her arm stuck into the cavity as if reaching for something. She sat back and slowly pulled out what looked like a concertinaed book. Attached to the corner was a piece of fishing line with a flat bead secured to its end.

Her wide eyes met his before she carried the book over to the living room coffee table and carefully laid it across the top. 'This could be Libby's or Annette's.'

He studied the book. 'When dry it would have been the perfect thickness to sit inside the cavity and still allow the door to slide in and out.'

Ella touched the glossy bead. 'All anyone would have had to do was feel inside, find this and pull the book out.' She clasped her hands together. 'I'm not sure if I'm game to open it. What if there's something in here that will only cause Violet more pain?'

'There could also be something that gives her some answers.'

'You're right.' Ella leaned forward and carefully peeled back the wet cardboard cover.

The book was a sketchbook and on the first page was a hand-drawn pencil sketch of a dog with a signature below.

'It's Libby's.' Ella's voice was little more than a whisper.

She turned the next fragile page, making sure the wet paper didn't tear. This time the drawing was of a horse and the title read *Mrs Potts*. Again Libby's name was printed underneath.

'She did love her animals just like Violet described,' Ella said, her voice still hushed.

With every turn of the page the water damage lessened and the pages grew less translucent. After three more drawings of farm animals, a cluster of pages had been torn out. The next drawing appeared to be a self-portrait but it was only half-finished. The following image was of a youth on a motorbike, then two more of the same boy with a fishing rod and kicking a football.

She rubbed at her arms. 'I have goosebumps.'

Saul nodded. The early drawings had been sketched with light strokes, whereas these last ones were dark as though they were drawn with a desperate intensity.

Ella smoothed open the book to the page of the final drawing. Silent, they stared.

This sketch was again of the same youth but it was a close-up impression of his face. Libby had been a talented artist. The portrait looked realistic, and the level of detail would have required a considerable amount of time to complete. It wasn't the quality of the drawing that had him and Ella look at each other. The words didn't need to be verbalised that they needed to see Violet.

This middle section of the book had been untouched by water except for a narrow section at the bottom. But the image was water-damaged. Blurring the fine pencilled lines were smudges that could only have come from the tracks of tears.

# CHAPTER

## 8

The drive to Violet's had never felt so long.

Ella snuck a sideways glance at the man sitting beside her, his attention on the road. Saul's relaxed hold on the steering wheel didn't match the clenched line of his jaw. His thoughts were churning as much as hers were.

She looked through the windscreen at the growing shadows. She'd turned on the veranda light in case they weren't back before dark. It seemed an indulgence to take two vehicles, so when Saul offered to drive after he'd dropped Duke home, she'd agreed. All her reasons for staying away from him seemed trivial in the face of what they needed to talk to Violet about.

The sketchbook could either raise Violet's hopes, cause her unnecessary pain or prove a dead end. Even if she couldn't think of a credible reason, there might be a simple explanation for the tear-soaked picture drawn with such care.

She glanced at Saul again. 'Do we need a game plan?'

He gave her a half smile. 'No, unless you'd like one?'

She hesitated. The answer was yes. Ever since she'd lost her brother and then her parents had divorced, she preferred to have a plan. It was only after she'd returned from England and fought to put her life back together that they'd become a necessity. She didn't cope well with uncertainty or the unexpected. But there was something about Saul's understated self-assurance that had her shake her head.

As grave and withdrawn as he could be, she'd seen the warmth and empathy with which he treated Violet. Saul would be able to handle whatever happened once they showed Violet Libby's sketchbook. This gave her the confidence that she would cope too. She swallowed. Even if she didn't have her usual game plan as a safety net.

Whenever she drove into town she kept watch for any new yarn-bombing but this time she didn't glance at the streetscape. The amount of dusty cars they'd passed on the roads said Woodlea was in for a busy Saturday night. She could only hope they weren't about to ruin Violet's quiet evening. She'd already suffered enough.

Saul parked outside Woodlea Lodge and looked across at her as he unclipped his seatbelt. 'Everything will be okay. Violet's made of sterner stuff.'

'She is.' Realising that her hands were shaking where they held the black plastic folder containing the sketchbook, she lowered the folder to her lap.

'Ella?' His tone was low.

The trembling of her fingers transferred to her knees. Now it was her turn to provide an explanation. Otherwise her over-the-top reaction at having to talk to Violet would undo all the hard work she'd done proving to Saul that the weakness he'd witnessed at the wedding was an aberration. She was nothing but in control.

She spoke without looking at him as the memory flooded back of her mother collapsing on the floor holding Aiden's shirt. 'My brother went missing before he was found … My parents didn't cope well then, or ever again. Anything of his, however small, was always a trigger.'

The warm clasp of Saul's fingers on hers steadied her tremors. 'I don't know of a single parent who would deal well with the loss of a child. I'll talk to Violet if you like?'

There was a bleakness to his tone at odds with the steady hold of his hand.

'Thank you, but I'm not backing out now.'

He nodded and his hand left hers. She turned to undo her seatbelt to hide how even his light touch had stripped off yet another layer of her armour. There'd been so much care and empathy in the way he'd comforted her.

They walked to Violet's door in silence. Ella was about to whisper something when the door swung open.

'I always know the sound of your truck, Saul. How lovely you're here too, Ella. Doesn't your hair look smart?'

Ella tucked the short strands brushing her cheek behind her ear. Since finding the sketchbook she'd forgotten about her earlier visit to Taylor.

Violet looked between the two of them and then at the folder Ella held. 'You have something to tell me, haven't you?'

Saul nodded.

Violet's smile didn't waver even though it shone a little less bright. 'Well then, I'd better put the kettle on.'

When the teapot was sitting on the table in front of them, and steam curled from their teacups, Ella turned to Violet. 'I had a little air-conditioning drama this afternoon, which is nothing to worry about, but in the clean-up we found this in the sliding door cavity.'

She carefully took the sketchbook out of the folder.

Violet didn't move or take her attention from off the book. 'It was in where the sliding door goes?'

Ella nodded.

'It has to be Libby's,' Violet said, her words barely audible.

'It is.' Saul's confirmation emerged calm and quiet. 'But you don't have to look at it now.'

Violet sat a little straighter before reaching out to rest her shaking fingers on the sketchbook. She slowly slid it closer. 'I want to.'

Ella swapped a glance with Saul as Violet opened the cover. Violet covered her mouth with an unsteady hand but continued to turn the pages. When she reached the one of the young man on the motorbike her hand lowered and she frowned. Without a word she left the table and hobbled to a sideboard. When she slid out a heavy photograph album Saul went to help her carry it to the table.

She flicked through the pages and then opened the album to a young man who stood beside a red-and-white motorbike with his arm around a teenage girl with long brown hair. From the photos Violet had displayed in silver frames, Ella knew the girl was Libby's older sister, Annette. Even though Libby was shorter and fine-boned, the girls could have been twins with their similar colouring and heart-shaped faces.

Violet tapped the photo, her mouth hard. 'That's Jeb. The only good thing he ever did was give me my granddaughter.' She glanced at the sketchbook. 'Are there more of him?'

Ella answered. 'There are.'

Violet took her time to look at each drawing and when she came to the last sketch smudged by Libby's tears, her shoulders bowed. She'd come to the same conclusion Ella and Saul had. Libby had harboured feelings for the boy in the picture.

Violet rubbed at her temple. 'All this time I thought Libby disliked Jeb as much as Lloyd and I did. He was always giving her a hard time about being a baby and not wearing makeup or having a boyfriend.'

'What was his story?' Saul's question had a taut edge to it.

'He didn't have a father and his mother worked two jobs to make sure he had everything he wanted. Annette lost all sense when around him.' Violet's sigh was long and shuddering. 'The sleep we missed when she wouldn't come home. The fights we'd have over her being grounded … and as for her drinking …' Violet closed her eyes. 'You can guess the rest. It wasn't long after we lost Libby that one morning Annette felt too unwell to eat breakfast. Gemma arrived nine months later.'

Saul voiced the question Ella was about to ask. 'Did Jeb stick around?'

'Until Gem was one. Annette never finished school and they'd gone to Queensland where he'd found work in a mine. When he lost their savings gambling in the pub she took Gem and went to Brisbane to my sister. Jeb refused to follow. Eventually Annette reconnected with an old school friend from here, who'd been a lovely boy, and they were married. He's the only father Gem can remember.'

Ella stared at the photograph and the arrogant expression on Jeb's good-looking young face. To a shy and sensitive girl like Libby who didn't have much experience with boys, she'd have not viewed Jeb in the same way that Violet and Lloyd had. She'd have only seen the picture Annette would have painted of how cool he was and the fun and grown-up things they were doing. 'Where is he now?'

'It's anyone's guess. Gemma didn't even hear from him when Annette died. Annette once said he'd started another family and still lived in Queensland.'

Ella chose her words carefully. 'Would you like me to try and find him?'

Violet didn't hesitate. 'Yes. I'm certain Gemma doesn't know where he is. His last name is Irvine. I want to know exactly what was going on between him and my Libby.'

Ella finished her tea and across the table saw Saul do the same. Violet's voice had sounded thin and tired. It was time to leave.

After the table was cleared, Ella kissed Violet's cheek. The older woman always shooed her out before she could wash the teacups and for once she didn't feel guilty about leaving. The familiar task of washing up would give Violet something to do while she processed today's news. 'I'll let you know as soon as I discover anything.'

'Thank you.'

Saul gave Violet a gentle hug. 'Duke and I will see you soon.'

The drive home started off in silence, then Saul spoke, his tone grim. 'If Jeb hasn't learned a lesson or two about how to treat people he'll be getting one from me.'

'From you and me both. Do you think he has anything to do with Libby's disappearance?'

'My gut tells me he does.'

'Mine too. The sketchbook was hidden so well, there's far more to the Libby and Jeb story.'

When silence settled between them, she sent Fliss a quick text before stifling a yawn.

Saul glanced at her. 'It's been a big day.'

She looked outside to where darkness pressed against the windows and lights glittered in the distance from an oncoming car. 'I'm looking forward to tomorrow being boring and uneventful.'

Saul's chuckle was low and deep and she wished she could see his face in the poor light. He needed to laugh more often.

Her phone chimed and she read the text. 'Fliss will help me look for Jeb online tomorrow. She knows all the tricks from when she was searching for the missing branch of her family tree.'

'Let me know what you find.'

She nodded, now glad that the gloom masked her expression just as much as it did Saul's. The injured bison and the hay bale challenge had provided a common goal for the two of them to work towards. Just when she should be having some Saul-free time, their quest to help Violet now brought them together again.

Her hold tightened on her phone. She'd be lying if she said this didn't make her feel relieved, as much as it terrified her. The cracks in her defences were already showing. Saul knew more about her past than the whole of Woodlea. Tonight she'd then had further proof of his empathy and compassion and that beneath his reserve existed a good heart.

When Saul pulled up outside the carport, she sent him her practised smile that gave no hint of her emotions. 'Thanks for the lift. Fingers crossed we'll know more about Jeb tomorrow.'

'For Violet's and Libby's sake, I hope so.'

The memory of his gone-too-soon grin remained with her long after the sound of his car tyres faded and the cottage grew silent and dark.

∝

By the time Fliss arrived at mid-morning the next day, Ella had done a quick internet search for any information about Jeb Irvine. Even though she was lucky his surname hadn't been a common one like Smith, he didn't appear to have any social media accounts or online footprint. He was going to be a hard man to track down.

When the doorbell rang she made a note in the notebook that sat beside her laptop before going to check the thermostat on the air conditioner control panel. So far the air conditioner was behaving itself and keeping the cottage lovely and cool. She'd left a terse message on Doug Jones's phone and didn't expect him to call her back.

She met Fliss at the back door.

'Morning.' Fliss greeted her with a hug. 'Your hair looks fabulous.'

'Thanks. I haven't even looked in a mirror today let alone done anything with it.'

Ella led the way into the kitchen. 'Cuppa?'

'I'd love one.' Fliss handed her a container filled with a single layer of raspberry muffins. 'There were more but Hewitt's such a sucker for Molly's I'm-having-puppies look that he sneaks her food even when my back's not turned.'

'I can't wait until Molly's puppies arrive and you and Hewitt have to bring them in to see me.'

It was heartwarming to see focused and driven Fliss relaxed and comfortable amongst disorder and mess.

Fliss groaned but her hazel eyes were alight with laughter. 'It will be chaos just like last time. I'm still looking for my missing boot.'

As Ella went to put the kettle on and to find a plate for the muffins, Fliss sat at the table and opened the laptop she'd brought with her.

Instead of typing in the password to unlock the computer, Fliss studied Ella. 'It's not only your shorter hair that looks good— you do too. When you came back from the bushfires, you looked exhausted.'

'I felt like I'd aged ten years.'

Sympathy softened Fliss's mouth. 'It would have been a challenging time. You also work far too hard.'

Ella smiled and leaned back against the kitchen bench while the kettle boiled. 'Like someone else I know.'

Fliss returned her smile but her expression grew serious. 'It was great to see you at the dessert night. I've missed you. We've all missed you.'

'I know, I'm sorry I've been keeping to myself. I just had some things to work through but everything's okay now.' She ignored the memory of Saul's denim-blue eyes that crinkled at the corners when his mouth curved in a full smile.

'I'm here anytime you need to talk.'

'Thank you. Likewise.'

The whistle of the kettle sounded and Ella turned to reach for the container holding the English breakfast tea bags. She could only hope Fliss thought the things that she'd needed to process were a result of being emotionally and physically drained from work and not anything to do with Saul. She hadn't missed the way, before Cressy and Denham's wedding ceremony, Fliss had been so focused on the two of them that Taylor had been able to apply some sneaky hairspray to Fliss's sleek bun.

After she'd spooned hot chocolate into Fliss's mug, she glanced at the local doctor. Fliss's attention had remained on her.

'How are the wedding plans coming along?' Ella asked, as a diversion. Not that she expected Fliss to give her an in-depth answer.

Fliss was keeping everything secret. When things were in place, and she was ready to say more, Ella had no doubt the plans would be spectacular. The rustic country wedding she'd planned for Cressy had run like clockwork and had been a perfect reflection of who Cressy and Denham were. So far all anyone knew about Fliss and Hewitt's wedding was that it would be in summer, as Cressy was to be maid of honour, and Fliss and Hewitt wanted to give baby Rigby time to grow.

Fliss's eyes twinkled. 'They're going well and much better than your Edna party plans.'

'Tell me about it.' Ella set Fliss's hot chocolate and her tea beside the plate of muffins on the table. 'As Edna basically organises every town social event it's impossible to think of a way to put one on without her knowing.' Ella took her seat and as she looked across at Fliss she lifted a brow. 'Unless … we combine it with something that's already on?'

'Can you imagine having our wedding with Edna's birthday party?' Fliss laughed so much she dabbed at the corner of her eyes with a serviette. 'Apart from the fact she'd scare away my groom, I wouldn't put it past her to think we only got married to provide a smokescreen for her birthday celebrations.'

Ella too laughed so hard she had to press a hand to her chest. She'd deeply missed Fliss and it was so enjoyable to be sharing a laugh with her again.

Still chuckling, Fliss typed on her keyboard. She glanced at the notebook and the checklist Ella had made about where she'd so far looked for information about Jeb. 'Okay, so nothing's come up from a general or social media search. Let's see if there's anything on the phone record database.'

Fliss angled her laptop screen so Ella could see and took a sip of her hot chocolate while the results loaded. There were no hits.

Fliss's brow furrowed. 'This man's a ghost. Let's try Jebediah and if that fails we'll tweak the spelling. I wonder if Irvine doesn't have an *E*.'

This time when Fliss did a general search the screen filled with information. 'Now we're talking.' She clicked on the first link.

Ella leaned in closer to scan the newspaper that publicly listed the names of drink and drug drivers convicted in a local Queensland court. 'Well, we now know he lived in Bundaberg and blew high range and lost his licence for fourteen months, and that his middle name is Arthur.'

Fliss opened another link. 'Three years later he was again convicted of drink-driving.' She sighed. 'Maybe I've been around emergency departments for too long but I have a bad feeling about why Jeb has no social media presence.'

She typed in his three names and this time Fliss didn't have to click on the link as the brief description contained all the information they needed. Fliss's hunch had been right. Jeb had died six years ago when his car had left the road and hit a tree.

Fliss brought up the full article from a small-town newspaper. Alcohol was suspected to be involved as he'd been driving home from the pub. He'd left behind a partner as well as a son and daughter.

Ella sat back in her chair. Sadness filled her for Jeb's second family; Gemma, who had two half-siblings she never knew; and for Violet. There could now be no answers about Libby. Despite all of their hopes, the sketchbook had proved nothing but a dead end after all.

Unlike the previous time his new neighbour had visited, this time Saul knew Ella was about to arrive. She'd texted while he'd been out spot spraying Bathurst burrs to ask him if he was busy and if she could come around. The heads up gave him a chance to make sure his restraint was as rock solid as it could be.

He parked the gator in the shed. Duke jumped down and together they walked across the yard to the farmhouse. Ella wouldn't be far away. If she needed to see him he assumed she'd found out something about Jeb Irvine and it hadn't been positive.

Last night, after seeing Violet's anguish and Ella's deep concern, his own emotions had refused to settle. He'd stared at the white expanse of his bedroom ceiling well past midnight. As for the distress on Ella's face when she'd mentioned her brother, he was thankful they'd had the bulk of the F-truck console between them as otherwise he would have held her close. As it was, covering her unsteady fingers with his only intensified his deep need to comfort her. He took off his cap and speared a hand through his hair. A need that had no place in his plans to get his bison farm operational or in his making sure that his second chance stayed on track.

He made a detour by the water tank to check the new fitting was holding as the grass remained green on the left side. Everything appeared to be in order. A guinea fowl ruckus sounded from within the front garden and he looked around to check where Duke was.

When the agitated screeches intensified, he called Duke over and tied him outside his kennel. If the guinea fowls had cornered a snake, he didn't want Duke anywhere nearby. As a child he'd seen firsthand the potency of a brown snake's venom and the speed with which it could kill a neighbour's kelpie.

He didn't need to walk far into the garden to know his hunch had been correct. Heads bobbing, the guinea fowls stood in a semi-circle around an eastern brown snake. When the snake moved towards the circle opening, two guinea fowls flapped into the air. With harsh and loud shrieks, the flock herded the snake out of the garden and towards the slashed paddock. As soon as the eastern brown disappeared beneath the wire, the guinea fowls ran up and down the fence line.

Duke's frenzied barking alerted Saul to Ella's arrival. By the time he'd walked around to the front of the house, Ella had left her four-wheel drive and was patting Duke. She again wore denim shorts and this time a fitted white top that left her toned arms bare. The hot breeze tousled her shorter hair.

She greeted him with a smile. 'I missed having my welcoming committee race me from the front gate.'

'You were right about guinea fowls not liking snakes.'

Ella's smile ebbed. 'Claire's treating a Jack Russell for a snake bite as we speak.' Ella ruffled Duke's neck. 'You be nice to those guinea fowls, okay? They'll keep you in one piece.'

When she looked back at him, he dipped his head towards the house. 'Shall we chat inside?'

'No need. You'll have things to do. I just wanted to let you know Jeb Irvine didn't appear to learn any life lessons. He died six years ago in a car crash on the way home from the pub.'

'That's no good … for him or for Violet. Would you like me to come with you to tell her?'

'She already knows. She called while Fliss was still there. When I said I would head over to see her, she said that whatever we'd discovered I could tell her there and then.'

'That's Violet. How did she take the news?'

'She went quiet. When I then told her Gemma had a half-brother and sister, she ended the call so she could ring Gemma.'

'So, we're back to square one.'

'We are, but now I know about Jeb, I'll keep an eye out for anything at the house that might connect him with Libby.'

'It can help looking at things through fresh eyes.'

As he spoke he glanced away to stare into the garden. Looking at things in a new light could also cost you everything and everyone you loved.

The guinea fowls now rested in the shade of a tree, so he moved to unclip Duke's chain. The snake would be long gone.

Duke took about two steps before flopping at Ella's feet and with a groan rolled over for her to scratch his belly.

She laughed as she used the toe of her black slip-on shoe to rub his belly. 'Duke, you do know your ancestors were all tough working dogs?'

'He will be soon, we're about to check the bison.'

Ella's head lifted and interest sparked in her gaze.

He spoke without thinking. 'You're welcome to come.'

There was only a slight hesitation before she replied. 'I'd really like that. I'll grab my hat.'

Even before she turned towards her four-wheel drive his jaw hardened. Strides long, he went inside to cut up apples for the bison. If he could he'd have retracted his words. He was a fool to prolong the time he spent with Ella.

The thought echoed in his head as she sat beside him in the narrow gator. Unlike in the truck, or even the tractor, they were so close he only had to move his elbow a little and their arms would touch. The subtle scent of cherry blossom clung to her tanned skin.

Her cap and dark sunglasses concealed her expression but her mouth appeared relaxed as she gazed around. She smiled when Duke hung his head over her shoulder from where he sat behind her.

Saul made a conscious effort to keep his tone casual as he initiated small talk. 'Aircon working okay?'

'It is, thanks to you.' She briefly glanced at him. 'Do you know what that electrician said when he returned my call?'

'Going by how you sound, something you didn't want to hear.'

'He was glad I changed my mind about not seeing him again.'

Saul almost felt sorry for the man. If Ella's words were half as fierce as her frown he would have copped an earful. 'I take it he wished he hadn't said such a thing?'

'Put it this way … he won't be calling again.'

The conversation stopped as a herd of six bison thundered towards them. He wasn't sure if Ella drew a quick breath but when she took off her sunglasses to see the bison better he caught awe in her eyes. 'No wonder they're called thunder beasts. It's a wall of moving bison.'

'Yes, they don't like moving in single file.'

The bison stopped at the fence and he left the gator to walk over. Ella and Duke followed. The cows in this herd were all accepting of humans; it was the bull at the back who wasn't so trusting. He eyed them with a belligerent and hostile stare.

Ella looked over at him. 'I never thought I'd see a bull more intimidating than Reggie, but this fellow isn't happy to see us.'

Saul passed Ella several pieces of apple. 'Hercules has mellowed. You should have seen the dents in the truck when he arrived.'

He stepped forwards and through the fence fed two of the cows and rubbed their curly brown foreheads. Ella stood beside him and fed apples to the others. She scratched the nose of any cow who was in reach.

Once Saul had checked over the bison in this herd they drove to a second breeding group two paddocks over. They again fed the bison apples and, unlike Hercules the bull, Dakota was pleased to see them.

On their way back they passed the stables and Cisco's shady paddock. When Ella turned to look at the gelding, Saul stopped the gator.

'What's his name?' she asked as she reached into the bucket that contained the last piece of apple.

'Cisco, but he doesn't like apples.'

'Seriously?'

'Or carrots.'

Ella left her seat. 'I have to see this. A horse that doesn't like treats.'

Saul followed and joined her at the fence. 'If we're lucky, he'll look at us.'

Cisco swished his black tail before lifting his head from where he grazed near a cluster of gum trees. He stared at them. Then he picked his way through the clumps of grass over to Ella.

Saul silenced a groan. He didn't need any reminder of Ella's appeal. Duke was already besotted and now even his aloof quarter horse found Ella irresistible.

The vet held out the apple on her flattened hand. While Cisco dropped his nose close to the apple, he didn't eat the fruit. Instead he took a step closer and sniffed Ella's hair.

'You don't like apples but I bet you like neck rubs.'

She smoothed his glossy black-and-white neck and the gelding gave a contented sigh.

Ella cast Saul a quick glance. 'Where did he come from?'

'Up north. Denham found him for me. I've also got a young mare coming next week who Tanner thinks will be good to work bison with.' He paused. He'd already taxed his self-control by showing Ella around, he now couldn't stretch it further by creating another opportunity to be around her. But there was something about the longing in her expression as she stroked Cisco's shoulder that silenced his reservations. 'When Amber's here, maybe we could go for a ride?'

'I'd love that. I'm planning on getting a horse. I just haven't had time.'

He only nodded as he didn't trust that his reply would sound casual. This was how Ella should be. Shoulders relaxed and smile content. Whatever the trauma was that caused her scar and the shadows in her eyes, he could only hope that one day it would fully free her from its grasp.

Feeling the hold on his feelings slip, he returned to the gator. He hadn't come here to become emotionally entangled with anyone. If he didn't start staying on his side of the boundary fence, he was in danger of breaking every vow he'd made on the day he discovered his marriage, and his future, had been built on a lie.

# CHAPTER
# 9

What had she missed?

Ella turned at the doorway to take a last look at Libby's freshly dusted bedroom. Her second job for the weekend was completed. But despite looking through Libby's things and checking under the furniture, she'd found nothing that connected the teenager to her older sister's boyfriend. She'd also been through Annette's room next door and had come up empty-handed.

Ella again scanned Libby's bedroom. Everything was just as the sixteen-year-old had left it. Horse books filled the bookshelves and half-finished art projects sat in clear plastic containers on her desk. A black-and-white doona cover was matched with a pair of white cushions. Sitting in front of the cushions was a large soft toy of a border collie.

She tucked the dusting cloth beneath her arm and slid her phone out of her shorts pocket. Another week had passed with only a handful of texts from Saul, and when he had messaged they'd all been about Violet. If it wasn't enough of a bad habit that she regularly checked her phone for a new text, when she turned on the veranda light at night she'd stare across at his farmhouse and wonder what he was doing. As hard as she fought, she was losing the battle to keep him at bay.

Last weekend mightn't have turned out to be Saul-free but there was no reason why this one couldn't be. Except a persistent and irrational part of her wanted to see him. She needed to hear his deep voice, see his slow smile and glimpse the emotion in his eyes when he spoke about his bison. When he was around them, his reserve fell away.

She stared at her phone. As aware as she was of Saul, he remained oblivious to her. Both of them weren't in the market for a relationship, and she should be thankful she wasn't fending off his attention. But as much as she had donated her hair to help others, she had also done it to become invisible. Except when it came to Saul, this was increasingly becoming the last thing she wanted to be.

She rubbed at the scar on her leg. If she had any sense she'd put her mobile away, but this wasn't about her. Saul was right—fresh eyes could prove invaluable. She'd been through Libby's room numerous times, but she might be missing something. For Violet's sake, Saul needed to take a look. He'd view things from a different perspective and she knew from when they'd built the hay bale castle that he had an eye for detail.

She sent him a quick text.

*Found nothing in Libby's room. Might be worth you taking a look?*

She went into the kitchen to check on the banana bread. Cressy was having her over for lunch and to help choose nursery furniture. Since the dessert night, the soon-to-be mother craved anything sweet. She'd just tugged off her oven mitts when her phone chimed from over on the kitchen table.

*Good idea. After lunch?*

She stepped away from her mobile. For her own sense of self-worth she couldn't reply straight away. When it came to Saul she had to exercise more restraint. She turned off the oven and loaded the dishwasher before sending an answer.

*Late afternoon? Will text when back from Cressy's.*

Saul's thumbs-up reply was instant. She quashed her happiness that he'd been waiting for her message. After rereading their conversation she put her mobile into her tote bag. She wasn't checking it again or thinking about seeing Saul that afternoon; she had a lunch to get ready for.

Right on schedule, Ella crossed over Glenmore's cattle grid. She lifted the sun visor so she had an unobscured view of the horizon. The pristine blue sky had turned a dull pewter-grey and the temperature had dropped, but no sheets of distant rain fell. All that would arrive with the approaching storm front would be more winds that whipped up the dust into twirling red spirals.

Through the trees she glimpsed the historic homestead with its four distinct chimneys and wraparound veranda. It seemed a lifetime ago since Cressy and Denham's wedding had been held in the paddock overlooking the river. The bridal party had used the homestead to get ready and her partner was to be Denham's rodeo friend who hadn't yet arrived as storms had delayed his flight from San Francisco.

She'd heard Saul before she saw him. Taylor had been doing her hair when a deep voice with American inflections had rumbled outside the living room door. Then Denham had brought Saul in. Weary and stubbled, his shoulders had filled the doorway. All she could do was stare at the cleft in his chin and the strong line of his jaw and remember to nod when Denham introduced her.

When Saul's dark-blue eyes had met hers it was as though the laughter and bustle around her faded. In his intense gaze she'd glimpsed an integrity and a strength that went beyond the physical. The man she was to accompany all night had the power to breach the defences she'd so carefully constructed. Even knowing this, she hadn't been able to break eye contact. Then, the real world had returned with a vengeance.

She'd had no idea that Taylor had even spoken to her, let alone what she'd said, until the hairdresser stopped blow-drying her hair to look at her. Embarrassed and shaken, she'd somehow thought of something witty to say before the noise of the blow-dryer again enveloped her. She'd spent the rest of the night not looking at Saul unless she had to. Even if she'd remained acutely aware of everything he said or did.

She slowed to take the sharp corner in Glenmore's driveway. Her throat ached as more memories broke free. The bridal waltz, where Denham and Cressy had gazed deep into each other's eyes, had been her undoing. Charles had once looked at her with such love. Young and foolish, she hadn't realised the value of what she'd had or that her choices would have inflicted so much damage.

After she'd danced a brief waltz with Saul, she'd sought solace in the shadows behind the reception marquee. There in the darkness and solitude, she'd wrapped her arms around her chest and her silent despair and guilt had slipped over her cheeks.

In hindsight she should never have turned when Saul said her name. She should have ignored him. But there was something in his grave and husky tone, as if he shared her anguish, that made her swing around. They'd simply stared at each other. She still didn't know what it was in her expression that caused him to give her a solemn nod and return to the other wedding guests, but it was the outcome she'd wanted and needed.

Ella hadn't realised she'd arrived and parked at Cressy's garden gate until a white cockatoo landed on her bull bar. She blinked and refocused on the present. The cockatoo peering through the windscreen wasn't a wild bird but one Cressy had nursed back to health when he'd been young. He now refused to leave and was more of a watchdog than Cressy and Denham's dogs, Tippy and Juno.

When she left the car, Kevin flew onto her shoulder. She scratched his yellow crest. 'That's the spot,' the cockatoo squawked, angling his head into her touch.

A grey-muzzled kelpie made her unhurried way across the lawn. Ella watched how the old kelpie moved. The arthritis needles seemed to be making a difference. On her last vet visit, Tippy had also had a session on a vibrating therapy mat to help with her mobility.

With Kevin still perched on her shoulder, she bent to pat the tail-wagging kelpie. 'Nice to see you too, Miss Tippy. Where's that hyper Juno? Out with Denham?'

Juno was part kelpie and part prize-winning show poodle and was as fluffy as he was active.

Kevin left Ella's shoulder and flew to the top of a nearby cedar tree to keep watch for further visitors.

Footsteps sounded as Cressy walked along the path. While the green garden around her held its own against the heat, the plants filling the beds were sparse and immature. It wasn't that long ago that Cressy's farm had experienced a pocket drought and had received no rain while those around her had. She'd since put another large tank off the shed and Denham had organised for a bore to be drilled. The swimming pool had been refilled and the garden beds replanted.

'Where's that baby belly gone?' Ella said as she hugged her. With an oversized purple cotton shirt, it was hard to see Cressy's baby bump.

Cressy turned sideways and smoothed her shirt over her stomach. 'Baby Rigby's here, don't you worry.' She stilled, then reached for Ella's hand. 'See.' She pressed Ella's palm against the side of her stomach. Ella felt movement as a tiny foot kicked out against her hand.

'Cressy … that's incredible.'

'I know.'

Ella felt another kick. Every maternal yearning she'd ever had coursed through her. She had no doubt that one day she too wanted to be a mother. The only thing of uncertainty was whether or not it would ever happen.

She lifted her hand and avoided Cressy's gaze as she turned to collect the container on the front seat of her four-wheel drive. 'I baked you and baby Rigby some banana bread.'

'You must have read my mind. That's just what I feel like.' Cressy looped her arm with Ella's. 'It's so lovely you're here.'

'It is.'

Ella meant it. Cressy was the first friend she'd made when, pale and broken, she'd moved to Woodlea to start a new job and a new life.

As if sharing her thoughts, Cressy glanced at her hair and squeezed her arm. 'I really like your hair short. It reminds me of when you first came to town.'

'Edna wasn't a fan but I like it this length too. It's much quicker to wash.'

'I bet it is.' Cressy let go of her arm as they walked up the veranda steps. 'As for Edna, she'll get used to it. Just like she will the idea that Meredith will be the one helping out when baby Rigby arrives.'

Ella walked through the door that Cressy held open. Meredith was Denham's aunt and would be unobtrusive as well as helpful. 'She didn't take the news well?'

'It was more like she really wanted to help. I think she's so desperate for grandchildren she just wants to be involved.'

'All I can say is poor Bethany and Mac.'

Cressy laughed as they entered the large kitchen that formed the heart of the sprawling homestead. 'I won't tell Bethany quite yet that Edna has a cupboard full of baby items.'

Ella went over to where some tomatoes sat on the chopping board beside a bowl of green leafy salad. She didn't need to ask if she could help, they were always doing things for each other.

'Is Denham in for lunch?' she said, slicing a tomato.

Cressy shook her head as she took a frittata out of the fridge. 'It's just us and Reggie.' She nodded out the oversized kitchen window.

Ella moved to look through the window. A grey mountain of a bull stood beneath the shade of a box tree. 'Isn't he supposed to be with Denham's rodeo cattle?'

'He is, but you know what he's like. He jumps fences like a showjumper. He does go back to see them but this past week he's mostly been here near the house.'

Ella glanced to where Cressy rubbed her belly as the baby again kicked. 'He's just being protective.'

'Poor Reggie. He's going to be standing under that tree for months. I'm not due until winter.'

Ella glanced at the chopped carrots in a bowl that weren't for the salad. 'If there was ever a bull not to feel sorry for, it's Reggie. Between his daily carrot delivery and being able to go wherever he wants, he's perfectly happy.'

'I hope so. He's such a gentle soul.'

Ella laughed. 'I'm not sure that's how everyone would describe him. He sure did make the boys work hard to pass the Reggie test.'

Cressy and Fliss had labelled the feeding of carrots to the unfriendly bull as the Reggie test. If any male didn't pass then they weren't yet man enough for a relationship.

Cressy joined in with her laughter. 'There's no doubt he's an accurate judge of character.' Cressy looked as though she was going to say something more but then stopped.

With the salad completed, they sat at the table to enjoy lunch. The conversation went from baby names and the upcoming beer night and bush dance to possible smokescreen events for Edna's party and then to Ella's air-conditioning saga.

'Just think if your living room hadn't flooded you'd have never found Libby's book,' Cressy said, before taking a second serving of salad.

'True. The other electrician, Nick, finally got back to me and he had a look in the roof and confirmed there was no serious damage.'

'Just as well Saul had a ladder because by the time you'd driven out here or to Fliss's to get one, it could have been much worse.'

Ella nodded and focused on cutting another piece of frittata. Cressy wouldn't miss any reaction, however small, to the mention of Saul's name. 'Saul knew what he was doing and turned the water off far quicker than I would have.'

Cressy stopped eating to look across at Ella. 'I'm glad you two are looking out for each other. Denham's quite concerned about him.'

Ella continued the conversation, even though Saul should be the last person she was talking about. 'He seems to be settling in okay, even if his house isn't yet fully unpacked.'

Cressy frowned. 'Still?'

Ella nodded.

Cressy looked down at her belly. 'I'm trying to give him space … otherwise I'd be over helping him.'

Ella stilled. 'Space? He's mentioned he's divorced.'

'He is. If Saul's told you about his divorce that's encouraging as he must see you as a friend.'

'We cleared the air early on about not being interested in anything but friendship.'

'That's also a positive. Denham says Saul isn't opening up, even to him. At least he's talking to you, except he wouldn't be saying much.' Cressy paused. 'It might be helpful for you to know that Saul isn't just dealing with his marriage ending … he also lost his son.'

Ella's thoughts whirled, making words impossible to find. No wonder Saul displayed such compassion and understanding towards Violet; he knew all about losing a child.

Cressy kept talking, voice quiet. 'The old Saul was always smiling and joking around. He was so excited to be a dad and would send Denham ultrasound pictures.'

Ella placed her knife and fork together on her plate even though she hadn't finished her lunch. She'd lost her appetite. The reason behind Saul's gravity and reserve was even more heartbreaking than she could have imagined.

'Does Denham know what happened?'

'No, all Saul says is that his marriage ended the day he lost his son. Denham has pictures of Saul holding Caleb when he was born but then they stopped. It was only when Denham called after not hearing from him that he learned Saul had sold his bison ranch and was coming home. Alone.'

Duke was almost beside himself. Not only did the Australian shepherd have Tanner's blue ute to race as he drove into Windermere, but also a horse trailer with two horses inside. On the back of Tanner's ute, Patch barked as if it had been years since he'd last seen Duke instead of weeks.

Saul shook his head. The Australian shepherd was a grey blur as he streaked through the driveway trees. At least with the cool change he didn't need to be as concerned about Duke getting heatstroke.

He headed for the gator so he could meet Tanner at the stables. Not that Duke would mind having to see Ella. He hadn't realised what Duke did outside of an early evening. When he'd thought he was off looking for rabbits, he was sitting at the corner of the side garden close to the road. When Ella drove into her driveway after work, he'd run along the fence line until he reached the garden gate. He would then wait and it was only when Ella went inside that he wandered off to explore.

Saul glanced across the boundary fence towards Ella's garden before sliding into the gator seat. Wherever she was this Saturday morning he hoped she was enjoying herself. Just as well she'd said to come over to look at Libby's room later this afternoon. The delay gave him more time to compose himself. Duke hadn't been the only one missing her this past week. He couldn't walk into his kitchen, or now drive around his farm, without memories of her sabotaging his concentration. He was lucky he didn't burn his kitchen down two nights ago while cooking a steak for dinner.

He headed along the road that led past the bison handling shed to the stables. The fencing contractor had spent the week enlarging the outside dressage area and building a set of bison-friendly yards. Tanner wasn't only delivering his new buckskin mare, he was also bringing his mustang Arrow to try out the new campdrafting arena.

The horse trainer left his ute with a wide grin. 'How great is this cool weather?'

'Now all we need is rain.' Saul scanned the gun-metal grey sky.

Tanner's expression sobered. 'I passed the water truck on the way here. People are running out of water.'

'I know how low my tanks are getting.'

Mock-growling sounded from beside them and they turned to see Patch and Duke wrestling in the red dust.

Tanner shook his head. 'Those two. Now all we need is Juno and we'd have the three most hyper dogs in Woodlea.' A hard hoof hit steel. 'And that would be the most impatient horse in Woodlea.'

'I don't know,' Saul said as they headed for the back of the horse float. 'Denham's Bandit isn't the most chill of horses.'

'You can say that again. He's one bad-tempered bronco.'

Once Tanner had unloaded his restless palomino, Saul climbed the ramp to lead out a buckskin mare. As she gazed around, he rubbed her golden neck. It wasn't hard to see where the buckskin got her name. Her smooth coat was the colour of rich amber. From over in his paddock Cisco gave a loud whinny which Tanner's Arrow answered.

The horse trainer looked between the two geldings as Cisco galloped towards the fence. 'That's a first. Cisco's being social.'

'Actually, it's the second time. Ella was here last weekend and he couldn't get close enough to her.'

'That doesn't surprise me. It's why Ella's so good at what she does. Her magic works on animals just as much as single men.' He threw Saul a quick glance. 'Present company excluded.'

He nodded, hoping it didn't show on his face just how much her charms did work on him. 'I wasn't sure if there'd be a local vet who could handle a bison emergency so I'm very appreciative of her magic touch. Especially if we ever have to deal with Hercules.'

'Ella treated Reggie when he had a run-in with a car of teenage trespassers, so she'll be fine with that surly bison of yours.'

The conversation ended as Saul led Amber into her new stables. While the mare pulled hay out of the hay net, he gave her a light brush. Every so often she'd fling her head high to see what was going on outside, but otherwise she remained calm.

Leather creaked before Tanner appeared riding Arrow. 'Thanks for setting up the pegs in the arena. I'll warm up Arrow and then we'll see how speedy those bison of yours are.'

When he was sure Amber was settled, Saul headed into the arena. He waved across to where Tanner was riding around the perimeter before he headed for the group of bison waiting in the shade-covered yards.

Tanner and Arrow joined him at the new steel gate. He swung the gate open so they could enter the pen that held the bachelor bison. From when they were weaners the bulls had been specifically trained for campdrafting. Arrow's nostrils flared in excitement and sweat darkened his coat even before they cut out a bison from the camp and blocked him twice from returning to the others. After a final turn and block, Saul opened the gate.

The bison bolted out with Arrow close behind him. The young bull showed no fear or aggression at being separated from his herd. Instead he twisted and spun with speed and agility to outmanoeuvre Arrow. Saul couldn't help but smile. Tanner and Arrow were champion campdrafters but right now the bull wasn't intending to do any neat figure of eights around the pegs.

Once the course was finally completed, the bison thundered between the two end pegs and back into the yards. Saul closed the gate and the bison headed to where the rest of his herd were gathered in the adjacent yard.

When Tanner rode over, the horse trainer's grin couldn't get any broader. 'They're so much faster than cattle and the way they can spin …'

'Not even a horse can turn ninety degrees when flat out. These guys will go fast for experienced riders and slower for novices, so you've just had the high-speed bison experience.'

Tanner didn't seem to move in the saddle before Arrow swung around ready to draft another bison around the course.

Saul grinned as he opened the bison pen gate. He knew what he'd be doing until Arrow tired or ran out of bison to cut out.

As the afternoon shadows deepened, Saul kept a close watch on his phone in case Ella texted to let him know she was home. It wasn't until the bison had been returned to their paddock and Tanner was hosing Arrow down in the wash bay that her text arrived.

*Sorry. Spent longer at Cressy's. Home now.*

*Tanner's still here. Be there soon.*

Unlike that morning, her reply was almost immediate. *Tell Tanner hi and he'd better get his glitter on.*

Laughter loosened the tightness of his chest. Ella's quick wit never failed to make him feel lighter. Tanner had already said he couldn't stay for a cold beer as Neve was having the two little cowgirls she sometimes babysat over for a sleepover and Tanner was on barbeque duty. The one time Saul had seen both girls they'd been covered in glitter after they'd painted the hooves of Neve's pony and donkey in pink hoof polish.

When Tanner came up beside him, he must have still been smiling as the horse trainer gave him a questioning look. He showed him Ella's message.

Tanner took hold of the phone to message a reply.

*Tanner here—glitter's on and playlist of snowman movie soundtrack downloaded.*

Tanner handed him his phone with a chuckle. Ella's reply had been a string of crying laughter, sparkle and snowmen emojis.

Saul waved Tanner off. When they couldn't see Patch or Tanner's ute anymore, Duke whined. Saul ruffled the top of his head. 'It's all right, buddy. Seeing Ella will soon cheer you up.'

As Saul predicted, when the Australian shepherd worked out where they were driving to, he again whined but in excitement. Once out of the F-truck, he made a beeline for Cinnamon and Nutmeg while Saul walked over to the back cottage door.

Ella greeted him with a smile that wasn't quite as sunny as usual. 'Thanks for coming over.'

'No worries.' He searched her face. Even her voice sounded subdued.

'Duke with you?' she asked, her gaze sliding away as she looked over his shoulder.

He didn't need to answer as the Australian shepherd bolted towards them, jumping over the mosaic stepping stones.

Ella's laughter contained its usual warmth as she tickled behind Duke's ears.

She straightened and turned to lead the way inside. When Saul signalled for Duke to stay in the garden, she glanced back. 'Duke's welcome inside.'

They both followed Ella through the kitchen and living room to the newer extension. At the second door on the left, Ella stopped. Expression serious, she opened the door.

Saul didn't immediately walk into Libby's bedroom. Once he'd had a good look around, there'd be no reason to stay. It could then be another week, or longer, until he saw Ella again. It suddenly seemed important that they even have just a few minutes of small talk. If Ella's week had been tough it might account for the return of her tension.

'So the room's just how Libby left it?' he asked.

'It is. Everything seems normal for a teenager and for what we know about Libby. I just can't shake the feeling that I could be missing something.'

'It always pays to listen to your gut. How's Cressy?'

'Really well. We looked at ...' She paused as if suddenly uncertain about what to say. 'A few things she needed help with choosing online.'

It wasn't just a feeling that something wasn't right, it was a certainty as Ella's lips pressed together as if to stop herself from saying something. 'Okay. Let's see what secrets there are in here.'

She held up her hands with her fingers crossed. 'Duke and I'll be in the kitchen if you need us.'

For the next half hour he went through everything in Libby's room, careful to return everything to its exact position. The room appeared just how Ella had described it. A straightforward representation of Libby. Then he examined the items on her wooden bedside table.

He left Libby's bedroom and walked into the kitchen. The aroma of freshly baked carrot cake filled the small and tidy space. Over on the bench, Ella was mixing icing in a bowl with a wooden spoon. Duke sat beside her watching her every move.

Ella glanced at his empty hands, disappointment creasing her forehead. 'You didn't find anything either.'

'Actually … I did.'

Glass clunked on the pale stone bench as she abandoned the mixing bowl. 'You did?' As she rushed across the small kitchen, he had the impression she was going to hug him. Then she stopped an arm's length away, her eyes a rich and vibrant brown.

He nodded, losing the fight to stop himself from smiling at her excitement. 'It's on the bedside table.'

He followed her into Libby's bedroom. They stared at the collection of items on the narrow wooden table beside her bed. A black desk lamp stood next to a small box with a decorative lid, a pink water bottle, a horse book and a brush with a hairband twisted around the end.

'It's either the book or the box,' Ella said, her words quiet.

'Take a closer look at the box.'

Ella picked up the small wooden box with the handcrafted lid. 'I did look at this. Libby obviously made it and mosaicked the top. Inside there's just some odds and ends.'

The lid featured what looked like small round silver tiles printed with a fish design. The tiles had then been set in white grout and covered with a clear layer of glossy lacquer. Saul took his house keys from out of his pocket and tapped a tile. Instead of sounding solid, the sound emerged as tinny.

Ella's eyes rounded. She held the box up for a closer look. 'These aren't tiles.' She tapped one with her fingernail.

'No, they're beer bottle tops. See the marlin, it's still used on a beer label today.'

Ella frowned. 'Violet believed Libby didn't drink.'

'A teenage girl might drink this beer but it's more like a beer Jeb would have drunk.'

Ella went to sit on the single bed. She carefully tipped out what was inside the box. Saul took a seat on the other side of the tiny pile of items.

Ella looked across at him. 'Hypothetically … Libby had a crush on Jeb so she collected his beer bottle tops to decorate the lid on this box. Which means everything inside could then be more Jeb mementos.'

Saul picked up a small yellow clip with a black number on it. 'Libby was a farm girl and this is a cattle ear tag, so perfectly explainable but …'

'But they can be worn on hats. In the picture of Jeb fishing he wore a wide-brimmed hat.'

Ella picked up an item which was a cream hair ribbon with pink and green flowers. 'Maybe this was worn when something significant happened between her and Jeb.'

Saul held up a small lead ball with a hole through it before placing it back in the box. 'This isn't a bead, it's a fishing sinker … Jeb's fishing sinker.'

'It also was probably Jeb's fishing line tied to her sketchbook.'

Ella returned a plastic white golf tee to the box. 'I've never heard Violet mention anything about Lloyd playing golf, so again this could be Jeb's.'

Saul examined the final item which was an old Manly rugby league footy card. 'Again there's a high chance this is Jeb's. There isn't any other footy memorabilia anywhere.'

Ella released a deep breath. 'Violet will be able to confirm whether these could be a connection to Jeb. Not that this will really help because he's not around anymore.'

'I can come with you to see her?'

'Thanks, but this time it's something I need to do by myself.' She hesitated then reached out to touch his arm. 'Thank you. Your new eyes were invaluable.'

He didn't know if it was the brief warmth of her touch or the gratitude in her face, but the room felt airless and far too small. He came to his feet. 'You're welcome.' Even to his own ears his reply sounded stiff.

She too stood. This time when she looked at him there wasn't any caution, just an unaccountable sadness. 'I'll let you know how I get on.'

He turned away before being in Libby's room not only revealed the teenager's secrets, but his own.

# CHAPTER
# 10

So much for her Sunday morning to-do list. Ella sighed and ripped a page out of her notebook on which she'd planned to write down everything she needed to get done by mid-afternoon. She couldn't even think of two things. She crumpled up the paper.

It was only breakfast but already her thoughts were consumed by Saul. Her ability to focus was zero. She couldn't stop thinking about him losing his son. Just like how looking at Libby's box with fresh eyes had revealed an unexpected truth. So did looking at Saul.

She'd known, from both his words and his reserve, that his broken marriage had left scars and they ran deep. But now she saw how much his anguish was embedded in who he was and how he acted. It was as though he had lost a part of himself.

From day one he'd breached her defences and made her feel and it was time to put up a white flag. As much as she'd tried to run, the end result was inevitable. She was emotionally connected to him. She'd dedicated her life to healing animals and utilised any opportunity to help her friends and the Woodlea community. She shouldn't now shy away from looking out for someone just because they made her heart beat too fast or they continued to be no good for her peace of mind.

Cressy had been right to tell her about Saul's son. When he'd come over yesterday afternoon to look at Libby's room she'd been able to explain why she was late without any reference to having helped Cressy decide on nursery furniture. There would be future occasions where she could shield him from anything that might prove painful.

She started a new list. At the top she wrote *See Saul*. Perhaps if she did this first, then she would be able to get on with the rest of her day.

Last night when she'd visited Violet, the older woman had confirmed their suspicions. The only common denominator between the objects in the box was that they all could have belonged to Jeb. As much as the discovery had upset Violet, the knowledge Libby had undoubtedly possessed feelings for Jeb had given her a renewed sense of purpose.

Violet had kept Libby's handmade box and this week would go through her photograph albums to look for more clues. Violet had then asked if she could come out next Saturday to return the box to Libby's room. Ella had answered with a hug. It meant so much that Violet was ready to see her family home again.

Ella left her seat, put her empty breakfast plate on the sink and went to change into her usual fuss-free weekend outfit of mid-length denim shorts and a tank top. Then, grabbing her keys and the container filled with the carrot cake she'd baked yesterday, she headed out the door. She didn't need to text Saul she was coming over. When she'd arrived home last night, she'd sent a quick message to let him know she'd drop around today to fill him in.

She glanced at the container she carried. As for the cake, she'd meant to give it to him yesterday. When she'd been at Cressy's at afternoon smoko Denham had said that carrot cake was Saul's favourite. It was just a cake, and a casual gesture from one neighbour to another, but for her it was something practical she could do to help him. It felt important that he knew she was there for him.

When she drove along the driveway, instead of racing her, Duke appeared on her right. As she stopped at her usual spot near the fence, her phone chimed. Saul had seen her and had texted to let her know he was at the stables. She followed the road around to where he was lunging a buckskin mare in the sandy arena. Duke ran ahead, every so often looking over his shoulder as if to make sure she was behind him.

When she'd left her four-wheel drive to give Duke a pat, Saul sent her a nod. The buckskin cantered around him for another circle before he slowed her to a trot, then a walk and brought her in to him. He led her over to the arena fence.

Eyes bright and ears forward, the mare extended her nose towards Ella.

'Hello, beautiful girl,' she said as she ran her hand over the buckskin's forehead. 'What's your name?'

'Amber,' Saul said with a brief smile. Today he wore sunglasses and a cap pulled low that hid his expression and drew her attention to the stubbled line of his jaw. She had trouble looking away. He had such a beautifully shaped mouth.

A whinny sounded from the paddock to their left where Cisco paced up and down the fence line.

Saul looked between Ella and the pinto gelding. 'I'm taking Amber down to the river, if you'd like to ride Cisco. We can talk about Violet on the way.'

Ella couldn't hide her delight or her smile. Her last ride had been with Cressy before she'd headed out west to help after the bushfires. 'Give me five minutes to throw on some jeans.'

'There's no rush.'

'I meant to give you a carrot cake yesterday … shall I drop it off on the way past?'

He didn't immediately answer, but then he smiled and this time it lingered. 'Thanks.'

When Ella took the cake inside Saul's farmhouse she was surprised there were no longer boxes lining the wide hallway. He had unpacked. As she walked past the living room a cluster of photos sat on a sideboard. Her steps slowed. The pictures all appeared to be of Rosie and her parents. His strength humbled her. His sister-in-law's pregnancy would have to be a difficult time and yet he'd sounded genuinely happy for her and his brother.

After she left the cake on the kitchen bench, she went home to change into jeans, boots and a blue long-sleeved shirt. Just as well the milder temperatures continued and today would provide a further respite from the extreme heat. Otherwise the idea of having a mid-morning ride would have been insanity. As it was, the feeling grew that while she and Saul were easing into a comfortable friendship, spending time with him, even to offer support, could also be considered a form of madness.

When she returned to the stables, Cisco was saddled and tied next to Amber at a low rail. The gelding turned his head as she approached and she patted his black-and-white neck before adjusting the length of her stirrups. She breathed in the familiar smell of leather and horses. Such scents were a beloved memory from her childhood and of a time when her world had been complete. She'd grown up on a small coastal farm and riding horses along the beach had been a favourite family activity.

Saul emerged from the stables with Duke beside him. 'All set?'

She nodded before unclipping Cisco and swinging into the saddle.

The horses' hooves crunched on gravel as they followed the road past the farmhouse to the laneway that ran alongside the boundary fence. The double gates were open and Duke raced ahead. Inquisitive bison lumbered over to watch them pass. The scent of eucalyptus tinged the breeze and a trio of pink-and-grey galahs landed on the concrete edges of a nearby water trough. They dipped their beaks into the clear water.

Ella relaxed into the saddle. The sun warmed her back and Cisco had a soft mouth and a smooth and comfortable gait. Saul too appeared at ease as he rode alongside her.

'Your text said Violet was okay?' he asked, after a sideways glance.

'As much as she can be. She's coming for lunch next Sunday and I was wondering if you'd like to come too?'

'I would. It could be difficult for her to see her old home.'

'That's what I was thinking.'

Once through the laneway, the paddocks rolled into an alluvial plateau that once would have been irrigated lucerne flats. A line of trees ahead marked the winding course of the river. White gleamed as cockatoos flittered in and out of the treetops.

'I'm not sure what's noisier, cockatoos or guinea fowls,' Saul said, the corner of his mouth lifting in a grin.

Ella was spared a reply when cockatoos flew overhead, their screeches raucous and loud.

The heat on her shoulders was soon replaced by the cool of shade as they wound their way through the ancient red river gums. Their thick, swirled trunks stretched into smooth slim branches that swayed over the water.

Saul whistled for Duke to stay near as a wild duck and her ducklings slid into the river shallows. Duke glanced at the ducks but his interest remained on something further along the bank. When his loose-limbed gait became a low-to-the-ground stalk, Saul whistled again and the Australian shepherd returned to his side.

'Call me paranoid,' Ella said, scanning the coarse river sand, 'but I keep imagining snakes everywhere.'

They rounded the bend and brought their horses to a sudden stop. Lying close to the water's edge was a lifeless kangaroo. Saul spoke to Duke in a low voice so he wouldn't dart forwards. From the injuries to the kangaroo's shoulder, it looked as though she'd been hit by a car or a truck on the road that ran past the two farms. She'd then made it to the peace and tranquillity of the river.

Ella slid from the saddle. Rigor mortis hadn't set in yet. If the kangaroo had a joey and it had survived it could still be alive inside the mother's pouch. Saul leaned over to take hold of Cisco's reins. He knew without her having to say anything what she needed to do.

She took her time to feel inside the kangaroo's pouch. If there was a joey, she only hoped it wasn't furless and attached to the mother's teat. She stilled as her fingers encountered soft fur and tiny bones and sinews that quivered at her touch. She turned to nod at Saul.

Movement sounded as the horses walked a short distance. Then Saul's footsteps approached. Intent on determining where the joey's small mouth was, she didn't realise he'd shrugged off his shirt until she saw the flash of cobalt-blue from the corner of her eye.

Once she removed the joey it needed to be cocooned and kept warm. Saul's shirt would be perfect and the only practical thing they had, unless she volunteered her own shirt. When she was sure the joey wasn't attached to his mother, she carefully eased him out and into the shirt Saul had formed into a makeshift pouch.

She straightened and held the shirt-wrapped joey close. The action was as much to allow the joey to feel her heartbeat as to provide a barrier between her and Saul. As much as her hormones were happy to travel back with a half-naked Saul, her self-preservation wasn't so ecstatic. It had already proved impossible to delete memories of him in his grey T-shirt, wet and with his dark hair tousled.

He stood still and silent, his arms by his side and his work-honed torso dappled by shade. Not wanting to be caught staring, or for her reaction to be televised across her face, she focused on a scar that curved over his left hip.

'Bison horn?'

'Mountain lion.'

Her attention flew to his face but his sunglasses shielded his eyes. 'They don't usually bother humans but a young male didn't appreciate me helping his elk-calf dinner out of a fence.'

'Were you both okay?'

'He jumped me from behind. But once I knew he was there everything was fine. I had bear spray in my coat pocket.'

Ella looked at the scar again. She knew how long physical wounds could take to heal. It was the mental ones she was still dealing with. 'I'm not so sure snakes are that bad after all.'

Saul smiled and strode over to the horses where he'd secured their reins to a fallen tree. Ella took a long moment to follow. Saul standing in front of her had been a work of masculine art. But

Saul moving with corded muscles rippling beneath smooth, tanned skin made her head feel light.

When he turned to see where she was, she walked faster and handed him the bundled joey. Once in Cisco's saddle she looked down. Her heart clenched. The careful way Saul cradled the joey would have been how he'd once held his son.

'I can take him now.'

Saul passed her the bundled shirt, but not before a muscle worked in his cheek. He swung into the saddle. 'I'll come back in the farm ute and move the kangaroo before the wild dogs get to her.'

'I'll call Sue. She's our local injured wildlife carer and will have the right milk. It's not a very well-known fact that kangaroos are lactose intolerant.'

Realising she was talking too much, she bit the inside of her cheek. Nothing screamed out-of-control more than incessant rambling. The sooner Saul had a shirt on the better. She risked another sideways glance but this time at his face. Just like at the hay bale challenge when they'd stood side by side being photographed, his profile was a carved immobile line. Holding the joey had unsettled him.

She swallowed as her own emotions stirred. Baking Saul a cake wasn't what he really needed. It was friendship and unconditional support. He'd taken a risk and disclosed that his failed marriage was the reason behind him not wanting a relationship. She had opened up about her brother, but was yet to explain why she too only wanted friendship. She needed to return Saul's trust and to show him that he was just as safe with her as she was with him.

She steadied her breathing before she spoke. 'Saul ...'

Something in her voice must have warned him that what she was going to say wasn't more waffle. He turned to look at her.

She spoke before her nerve failed her. 'I owe you an explanation.'

'No, you don't.' He didn't pretend not to know what she was talking about.

'It's only fair. Plus, just like you said, I want to.'

He slowly nodded.

She stared at a point on the track between Cisco's black-and-white ears. 'The short version of why I prefer being on my own is that when I was working in England, I met someone. It was serious. We broke up.'

She sensed rather than saw Saul search her face from behind his dark sunglasses. He stayed silent, allowing her to talk.

Still not looking at him, she continued. 'The slightly longer version is that I made … an error in judgement that didn't just hurt me but also Charles.'

She hadn't realised she'd adjusted her hold on the joey so she could rub her right thigh until Saul looked at her hand.

'Ella … I don't need to know details, but what I do know is that you're a decent and honourable person. You would have made what you thought was the best decision at the time.'

She cuddled the joey closer. She needed his warmth as much as he needed hers. Saul's faith and belief in her made her throat ache. She'd doubted herself for so long. But as much as she had thought she'd made the right decision, life had proved otherwise.

The yarn-bombers had been busy. Saul left the cool of the saddlery where he'd picked up some summer rugs for Amber and Cisco and walked along the main street to his F-truck. Whereas last town visit the bench in front of the craft shop had been bare, the wood was now covered in various shades of blue wool. He snapped a photo on his phone for Rosie.

He left the two rugs in his truck and crossed the street. Edna's white Land Cruiser was parked outside the café. It might have been three days since he and Ella had found the joey and she'd told him a little more of her story but his emotions were still raw. He wouldn't have the patience to deal with Edna this morning.

Ella's disclosure had communicated that she was now comfortable around him. The knowledge touched a frozen part of him that he thought would never feel again. Ella's trust was a precious gift. It was also an honour he felt unworthy of. The safe friendship he'd promised her increasingly felt like an empty promise. She was so beautiful, both inside and out, and the lines between keeping his distance and responding to her were now blurred.

As hard as he fought to hide his attraction, the more time he spent with her the more his self-control weakened. The day they'd ridden to the river, his sunglasses hadn't only stopped the glare. They'd also hidden what had to be in his eyes whenever he looked at her. When she'd told him the short version of what had happened in England, he'd had to stop himself from leaning over and kissing away her pain. Today was Wednesday and he now had until Violet's visit on Sunday to work on making sure that Ella's trust in him wasn't misplaced.

A horn honked and he lifted an arm to wave as Hewitt drove by with some wood in the back of his black Hilux. He and Fliss must have another DIY project on the go. He'd seen photos of the neglected bluestone Bundara farmhouse and outbuildings before Hewitt and Fliss had brought the property back to life.

He continued along the main street. Beside him the broad leaves of the plane trees rustled as a hot breeze barrelled by. From the clothing shop that sold everything from felt hats to woollen work socks, he found some more half-button cotton shirts. Since moving to town he'd shopped locally to support the small-town businesses as much as possible. He added some rugby shorts before making his way to the counter to pay. When he stepped outside he made sure Edna was nowhere in sight.

He had a few more jobs to do before meeting Denham at the bakery for a quick lunch. Duke had stayed at Violet's and would be making the most of being spoiled. Mrs Poole had dropped him off another dog toy and Saul had spied a bag of dog treats on Violet's kitchen bench.

After visiting the post office to collect a parcel too big for his roadside mailbox, he returned to his F-truck. Edna sat in the shade on the blue yarn-bombed bench. He silenced a groan as she stood and walked towards him with a satisfied grin. 'Saul, you're just the man I wanted to see.'

'Hello, Edna. How's your day going?'

The more questions he asked, the less he'd have to answer.

'Very well, thank you. Duke at Violet's?'

Saul placed his parcel and bags in his truck. 'He is. What can I do for you?'

'You sound like a man on a mission.'

He held her gaze. Unlike when he'd met her in town and the topic of the hay bale challenge had come up, she wasn't getting the better of him a second time. 'I am.'

Edna spoke in a cheery tone as though he had all the time in the world to stand in the heat and chat. 'That was such a nice thing you did helping Ella with the joey. Sue said it's going well.'

'Ella didn't need any help. She had everything under control.'

The subtle softening of Edna's stare told him he'd given her the answer she'd wanted. He'd yet again walked into whatever trap she'd set. A trap he suspected had been to see if he was still looking out for Ella. He ground his teeth. Edna couldn't know just how much that was true and how much such a realisation kept him up at night. He changed tack.

'I believe you have a birthday coming up?'

Edna's hand lifted to flutter over her chest. 'I do.' She leaned in a little closer. 'It's a *significant* birthday and usually *significant* birthdays have a *significant* party.'

Ella had mentioned the trouble Bethany was having organising her mother's surprise party. 'Do they?'

Her gaze pinned his. 'Yes.'

'Well then, I hope you have a happy birthday and an enjoyable party.'

'It goes without saying you'd be invited to any celebration.' She gave a coy smile. 'Whenever it is on.'

He kept his expression deadpan. 'Just let me know the date. I'll be there. Now, I'd better go as I'm meeting Denham.'

Saul didn't miss the twist of Edna's lips before he turned away. He didn't envy Bethany the job of keeping her mother's party a secret. Edna had to suspect something was being planned.

'You're looking very pleased with yourself,' Denham said as Saul entered the bakery and took a seat at a round table to the left of the bread counter. His stomach rumbled. The busy bakery smelled of fresh bread and hearty meat pies.

'It's not every day you can walk away from a conversation with Edna knowing something she doesn't.'

Denham chuckled. 'It's going to be a long month until her birthday. I take it she was fishing for party information from you too.'

'Yep. And it'll be a miracle if her party is a surprise.'

Denham nodded as he slid a magazine and a white envelope towards him. 'Here's the magazine with the article about bison meat I was telling you about. I also ran into Daniel from the police station and he asked if you could give this letter to Ella. It arrived this morning and apparently she's out of town all day. He didn't want to leave it in her mailbox. Even though it's addressed to her, it would have something to do with Libby.'

Saul glanced at the plain white envelope that lay facedown on the magazine. 'I'll drop it round tonight. Let's hope there's something in it that's helpful.'

'I hear you. It's a good thing what you and Ella are doing for Violet.'

Saul nodded as he pushed back his chair. Denham's blue gaze had just been a little too intent. He might have succeeded in hiding how unsettled Ella made him feel from Edna but he didn't stand a chance when it came to Denham.

'I'm so hungry, your four-pie record could be in trouble,' he said, coming to his feet.

They both headed to the counter where they ordered.

He made sure the conversation didn't return to Ella while they tucked into their plate of pies. Both had ordered two and then went back for a third.

When their plates were empty, Denham rubbed his stomach. 'My four-pie record isn't in danger even from me. In my defence I had finished harvest when I ate that many.'

Saul leaned back in his chair. 'I'm busted too.'

Denham drained his coffee mug. 'Great, because I volunteered you to help move furniture at the old schoolhouse.'

'What's that got to do with me being too full to move?'

Denham stood and slapped his back. 'You're just like Bandit and not as edgy after food.'

Saul stood. 'I'm not edgy and neither is that horse of yours. He's just bad-tempered.'

Denham only smirked. 'Trust me, you would be edgy after meeting the other volunteers if I hadn't fed you first.'

Saul headed to his F-truck and then, after a quick call into Woodlea Rural for some salt-lick blocks, drove across town to the bluestone schoolhouse. Denham hadn't elaborated on who else would be helping to prepare the building for the windmill museum. Tanner's blue ute indicated he was there but he didn't recognise any of the other dusty vehicles.

Before Saul entered the school gates he checked his phone. He'd sent Ella a text that he had a letter for her but she hadn't yet replied. He stared at his phone screen. He shouldn't be so conscious that this was the first week since the hay bale challenge that they'd reached the midweek mark without having communicated with each other. He switched his phone to silent and returned it to his jeans pocket.

He walked past the school bell and into the building. Voices sounded from the rooms to his left. He stepped into what would have once been a classroom.

Denham greeted him with a grin and Tanner with a nod from where they carried a cupboard. Mac Barton gave him a wave as he stacked chairs. Three older men turned to stare at him. The shorter of the gentlemen approached. Despite the liveliness of his eyes, his snow-white hair and the deep lines on his face spoke of a life that hadn't always been kind.

'Good to see you again, Saul,' the man said, offering him his hand.

Saul shook his hand. Old Will had walked Cressy down the aisle as her parents had been killed in a car crash years ago in Tasmania. 'Good to see you too.'

'Let me introduce you to Clive and Noel.'

Saul followed old Will over to the two men. Neither smiled.

Craggy and weathered, with discreet hearing aids, the tall man on the right's expression could only be described as a glower. But it was the gentleman on the left whose thoughts were indecipherable that Saul focused on. It was always the quiet ones you would be a fool to underestimate.

Old Will made the introductions. 'Clive, Saul. Saul, Clive Barton.'

So the man on the right was Mac and Finn's father. Saul had heard he was difficult to deal with. Saul met the power of Clive's handshake with the right amount of resistance. Anything less and Clive's first impression wouldn't be favourable. Clive's faded gaze glinted but he remained unsmiling.

Old Will spoke again. 'Noel, Saul. Saul, Noel Galloway.'

Saul concealed his surprise. The dignified man on the left was Edna's husband. He'd never met a more polar opposite couple. This time he made sure his handshake didn't overpower the other man's grip. Noel's impassive expression didn't change.

'So you're the American with the bison?' Clive's tone was as hard and unyielding as his handshake.

'I am, except I'm more of a tomato sauce than a ketchup guy. I grew up around Tamworth.'

Clive's gruff bark was what he guessed passed as a chuckle. 'I hope you're as strong as you look, because we've got truckloads of stuff to move.'

Then, not waiting for a reply, he strode out the side door to wherever the furniture was being loaded.

Noel's cool grey gaze locked with Saul's. 'I've been hearing your name mentioned with Ella's.'

He remembered Edna's words that her husband thought the world of Ella and this had made her exempt from Edna's usual attention.

'We're neighbours and have been helping each other out.'

'You'll never find a more talented or hardworking vet.'

He nodded. 'Ella's treated one of my bison.'

'My wife's the social one … I don't take any interest in anything that happens in town … unless it's to do with Ella.'

Saul kept his tone mild. 'I'm an old bull rider with no time to do anything but run his bison farm.'

Noel didn't answer, just studied him from beneath grey brows.

Boots sounded on the wooden floorboards as Denham and Tanner returned.

Denham sent him a long look. 'I thought you were supposed to be helping?'

Saul nodded to Noel before he left to help Denham lift a table. At Denham's serious glance, Saul gave him a brief grin to let him know everything was fine. Clive and Noel hadn't exactly rolled out the red carpet but he was still in one piece.

It took an hour until the schoolhouse was finally cleared. The removed furniture was being split between the Woodlea town hall and the nearby small corrugated iron hall at Reedy Creek. A second set of volunteers were on hand to help unload the truck at each destination so Saul said his goodbyes with Denham.

After promising Denham he'd visit his shed for a cold beer soon, Saul left. He stopped at the main street florist shop before driving to Violet's to collect Duke. There still hadn't been any reply to his text from Ella. Wherever she was working, the phone signal had to be poor.

He parked outside Woodlea Lodge and reached for the bunch of sweet-smelling flowers on the seat beside him. Except he didn't pick up the bouquet. He'd moved Denham's magazine and Ella's letter onto the floor and on the drive through town the glossy magazine had slid off the letter to reveal the front of the envelope.

He bent to pick up the letter. The typed label was addressed to *A Quinlivan, c/o Woodlea Police Station.* The incorrect initial wasn't the reason why he dragged a hand around the back of his neck. If the letter had been a response to the hay bale callout for information it could have been easy to get Ella's name wrong.

His jaw tightened. He didn't believe in coincidences. He also knew how the internet could make the world a small place. Violet had been right to worry about Ella being the face of Libby's publicity campaign. He stared at the stamp in the top right-hand corner. Ella had mentioned the United Kingdom when she'd shared more about her past. Now a letter had arrived with a stamp that bore the profile of the Queen of England.

# CHAPTER
## 11

Ella loved her job.

She stood on the front steps of the vet surgery and waved as members of her puppy preschool class headed home. Tonight it had been a cuteness overload. There'd been a fluffy border collie, a gangling Great Dane, a mini Jack Russell and a labrador the colour of chocolate.

Hattie, a student at the local Reedy Creek school, turned to give her a final wave. The tiny Jack Russell she carried was already asleep in her arms.

To the left of the path, in the middle of what had once been a green lawn but was now crisp yellow grass, stood a replica red fire hydrant positioned for dogs to lift their legs on. The Great Dane pulled his little owner over so he could sniff around the base.

When everyone had finally reached their cars, Ella went back inside.

'Oscar, you can come out now.'

The ginger cat had disappeared the moment the first puppy had bounded through the door. She smothered a yawn and tidied up the surgery waiting room where the puppy manners class had been held. Just as well she'd put the veranda light on a timer as it would be dark before she got home.

Oscar appeared from behind the counter and wrapped himself around her legs.

'I wondered where you'd been hiding.'

As she bent to scratch beneath his chin, her lower back protested. It had been a busy day pregnancy-testing cows out of town. While she'd returned in plenty of time for the puppy class, she still felt as though she'd cut it a little too fine. She'd only briefly been able to check her messages. If she was honest she'd only really been looking for one from Saul. To her relief he'd texted to let her know that a letter for her had arrived at the police station.

She straightened and went to switch off the air conditioner and the lights. She didn't regret telling him about her past last Sunday; it had felt like the right thing to do. He'd also made her feel comfortable. He hadn't asked her any questions or pushed for more information. His faith in her, and the way he'd called her a decent and honourable person, continued to make her feel warm and fluttery inside. She'd spent so long being content with her own company, she shouldn't now feel as though something was missing in her life just because she'd barely heard from him.

Steps purposeful, she locked the back surgery door and headed for her four-wheel drive. When Saul dropped her letter around tonight she'd return his washed and ironed shirt that sat on her kitchen table and keep everything casual between them. Even in an unguarded moment, she was a fool to wish that what lay between them was anything but friendship. Their connection had been forged on neither wanting anything more.

As she left the town limits she caught up to the small blue cattle truck of a local livestock carrier. The truck was driving slowly and between the oncoming traffic and road bends, it proved impossible to pass. By the time she'd turned into her front gate an inky darkness had stolen across the sky. In the gloom the bright rays of the veranda light illuminated the front façade of the sandstone cottage. She could only hope that whatever was in the letter would bring Libby home or Violet some answers.

After checking on Cinnamon and Nutmeg, she reheated the previous night's leftovers and readied herself for Saul's visit. She didn't have long to wait. Car lights flickered past her living room window before Duke barked.

She greeted them at the back door. The first thing she noticed was that Saul's hair was shower-damp. The second was that grooves again bracketed his mouth. The gravity she'd first associated with him had returned.

'Would you like to come in?' she asked, not realising she was holding her breath until he nodded. She wasn't sure if he was in a social frame of mind.

He and Duke followed her into the kitchen.

'Coffee?' she asked as she turned to face him.

'If you're having one.'

She wasn't going to, but she would now. She wasn't letting Saul rush off. Something troubled him, plus it was the first time she'd seen him all week. She'd be lying if she didn't admit that having him near made her realise how much she'd missed him.

She went to collect two mugs from the cupboard as Duke settled himself beside her kitchen chair. Saul placed the letter on the table before helping her with the coffees. If she didn't know better she'd have said he needed something to do.

As much as she appreciated his help, she wished he'd simply sat at the table. In the small kitchen there was no escaping his fresh clean scent or the way the soft cotton of his black T-shirt hugged his torso.

She finally took her seat opposite him at the table. Except now she had no choice but to look at him. She broke the silence, hoping her voice wasn't as breathless as she felt. 'I've been trying to think what information the letter might contain about Libby.'

'Ella …' The low, deep way he said her name confirmed that something wasn't right. His expression was too grave. His gaze too intent. 'This isn't about Libby.'

'There's nothing else it could be … unless …'

She hadn't realised he'd placed the letter facedown until he slid it over to her. She flipped over the envelope and frowned. She didn't need to see the United Kingdom stamp to know who it was from. She lifted her hand away from the envelope. The letter was addressed to *A Quinlivan*.

She'd stopped being Arabella the moment she'd boarded the plane home to Australia. Charles had moved on with his life. She'd thought he'd forgotten all about her, let alone about the unfinished business between them. She glanced up.

Saul's dark gaze hadn't left her. 'You look like you know who it's from.'

She ran a hand through her hair. 'Charles. The hay bale publicity must have made it to London.'

Saul didn't answer, only took out his phone. He typed something and then held up the screen. A simple internet search of her name flooded the screen with pictures and links to their hay bale castle.

Saul searched her face before he pushed back his chair. 'I'll leave you to read your letter.'

She hadn't realised she'd grabbed his hand until she felt the heat of his skin beneath her fingertips. 'Please stay. I'd appreciate the company.'

Saul being there would help keep her emotions in order. Just like when she'd had no plan at Violet's, she'd draw strength from his calm and steady presence. He'd also not ask her any unwanted questions.

When he glanced at where her hand gripped his, she let go. He settled back into his chair.

She ripped open the envelope and unfolded the letter. She shouldn't be surprised to see the impersonal letterhead of Charles's London lawyer's firm. Her attention focused on the illegible flourish at the end. At least he'd signed it. That had to count for something.

She started at the beginning.

*Dear Arabella,*

*You are a hard person to find. All these years I've been looking for the wrong person in the wrong place. I see you go by your shortened name now.*

*I'll keep this brief. Sophie and I have two daughters. Fatherhood has made me reconsider some of my past actions and hence the reason for this letter.*

*The accident wasn't your fault. I hope you don't still believe it is but I fear that could still be the case. You always took your responsibilities very seriously. I need to set the record straight about my intentions that night as well as my relationship with Sophie.*

*Arabella, I wasn't intending to ask you to be my wife. I had considered your reservations and could see their merit. I was instead intending to talk to you about us going our separate ways because, as you said, we did come from different worlds. I'm not proud of never revealing this in the aftermath of what happened but I believe you'll forgive me if I wasn't thinking straight.*

*As for Sophie, the truth is we didn't reconnect when she came to visit me in hospital. I'd met her three months before at a London fundraiser.*

*All of this might come as a shock, or might now be inconsequential, but I wanted to set the record straight. I did love you. You just didn't love me in the same way. I was right to set you free.*

*Yours,*

*Charles*

Ella stared at the final paragraph before reading it again. She wasn't sure what she'd expected to feel as she read the letter but she'd never have expected to have a moment of intense clarity. Charles had put into words what she'd never admitted to herself. She hadn't loved him in the same way.

All these years she'd put their relationship on a pedestal and envisioned the perfect future they would have had if she hadn't been so young and foolish. It was as though the fog of memories and heavy emotion had lifted and she could finally think clearly. The reality was their relationship had been far from a fairytale.

Without meeting Saul's eyes, she slid the letter over to him. 'I'd like to know what you think.'

While Saul read the letter, she leaned down to stroke Duke's soft grey-and-white back. 'You'd never have liked Charles. He hated dogs.'

Once he'd finished reading, Saul laid the letter on the table. 'Let me guess … Charles didn't like you getting your hands dirty being a vet.'

'I just thought he was set in his ways since he was older. And I was naive … I thought he'd eventually accept me for who I was and be okay about waiting until I was ready to settle down.'

'That's not being naive. Any relationship should be about give and take. As for Charles wanting to set the record straight, this letter's more about clearing his conscience.'

'We didn't part on the best of terms. The day he announced he was with Sophie, I flew home. I was devastated that he hadn't told me we were over, let alone that he'd moved on.'

'You're right. Duke wouldn't have liked him.'

Her fingers shook as shock kicked in along with self-doubt, guilt and anger. She'd maintained a constant vigil beside Charles's bed while he was in a coma. She'd visited every day afterwards, even when some days to walk had been agony. All that time he'd already been with Sophie. No wonder her perfume had lingered in his hospital room. As for his response that he was tired and had to sleep when she'd asked if anything was going on between them, he'd had a chance to be honest with her and he hadn't.

The kitchen walls closed in around her. She came to her feet, needing air and to move. She had some more boxes to pack for Violet.

Saul too stood. 'Ella?'

She gave a laugh that even to her own ears sounded hollow. 'You know what else he didn't like … my shortened name.'

Saul slid his hands into his jeans pockets before he answered. 'Charles wasn't the right man for you.'

'He mightn't have set me free when I left, but this letter does, even if it was written to serve his own interests.' The tremor in her fingers spread and she wrapped her arms around her chest to stop herself from shaking. 'What will take me a little while to process is that everything I thought to be true wasn't. And why couldn't I see that?'

'Because you look for the decency in people.'

'Which is nothing but a liability.' She bit her lip as her voice wavered.

She'd lost almost five years holding on to a dream she should have let go. She'd held on so hard to the perfect version of her relationship when the reality was she and Charles weren't good together. So much for being in control of her life.

Saul's arm lifted and he smoothed the hair that had fallen on her cheek behind her ear. His touch barely brushed her skin but the care in his gesture only reminded her of how, when broken and adrift, Charles hadn't even held her hand. Her foolishness extended far beyond not trusting her instincts about him and Sophie.

She didn't make a sound or move, but Saul must have sensed her composure crumbling. His arms enfolded her and he drew her to him. Surprise held her still and then she relaxed, resting her head in the curve in his neck. She fit against him in a way she never had with Charles. Emotion formed a tight wedge in her chest but she refused to let her vision blur. She'd cried enough for what she'd thought she'd lost. She wasn't shedding another tear.

Saul's hand came up to clasp her nape to hold her closer. He smelled of soap and sun-dried cotton. He felt warm, solid, real and safe. The unsteadiness of her knees now had nothing to do with Charles's letter and everything to do with the man holding her. She could spend forever in his arms and it still wouldn't be enough.

It wasn't just her hormones but also her feelings that wanted to renegotiate their friendship agreement.

She stiffened and edged away. The irony was that the one man who didn't find her attractive was the one man she was drawn to. But as his arms fell away from around her, in his eyes she caught a flicker, a glint, of something that could only be described as need. Even though the spark disappeared as quickly as it appeared, relief rushed through her. She'd never been so happy to know that a man was aware of her. Saul wasn't as immune as he appeared.

She took a step backwards. 'Thank you. I'm feeling less overwhelmed now.'

She rubbed her hands over her jeans, feeling the outline of her scar through the denim. She'd spoken the truth. Her feelings regarding the letter were subsiding. Except it was the emotions associated with the man standing grave and silent in front of her that were making a mockery of her composure. She needed the conversation to end before she said or did something they'd both regret. Saul hadn't yet asked about the accident and she couldn't take the risk that he might. Not even Violet knew all the details.

To prove she'd pulled herself together, she sat at the table and took a sip of her coffee.

He too resumed his seat. 'You know where I am if you need to talk.'

'Thank you.'

'Charles wasn't only not right for you, Ella, he simply didn't deserve you.'

She took another mouthful of coffee to hide that the sincerity in his words touched her as though he'd again held her close. It meant so much that he believed she deserved better than Charles.

When she replied, self-preservation kept her voice light. Saul couldn't know how much his support moved her. 'Which is exactly what I'll be saying in my one and only reply.'

Could the afternoon drag any slower? Saul rubbed at his tight forehead as he waited for the kettle to boil for his coffee.

It was only the day after Ella had received Charles's letter but it felt like an eternity since he'd held her. He'd barely slept before the guinea fowls had woken him. And now his thoughts continued to race like a bison bolting out of a squeeze chute.

Not only had he initiated physical contact, his restraint had cracked wide open. The feel of Ella's silken hair tangled around his fingers and her soft breaths feathering over his skin had tipped his common sense over the edge. Her dignified strength and her ability to find humour amidst her distress had stripped away the rest of his willpower.

When she'd slipped out of his arms he'd been powerless to repress how much she affected him. He could only hope she hadn't read too much into what his expression would have revealed. If she had, it was critical he reinforce the message that she was safe with him. Now, more than ever, she needed a friend.

Realising the kettle had clicked off, he turned to pour boiling water into his mug. He'd been so emotionally invested in making sure she was okay, he'd rendered himself vulnerable. Her anguish at finding out that things hadn't been what they seemed had only magnified his own pain of having made a similar discovery. His instincts had been spot on. He and Ella were no good for each other. But it was too late to retreat, he couldn't desert her when she needed his friendship.

While last night appeared to bring closure about her relationship with Charles, Ella had said herself she now had some things to work through. He also didn't miss the way she hadn't made any reference to the accident or her error in judgement that had resulted in her scar. There was still a longer version of her past that she wasn't yet comfortable sharing.

He returned the kettle to its base and glanced over to where his phone lay on the bench. He couldn't give in to the need to message her. He'd already called that morning before she'd left for work. She'd sounded tired but otherwise her tone had been buoyant and words cheerful. He also hadn't picked up on any awkwardness or regret about talking to him or accepting the comfort he'd offered.

He sighed and went to cut a small slice of carrot cake from the piece he'd earlier taken out of the freezer and thawed. What he should be doing with this Ella-free time was working out how to guarantee his self-restraint wouldn't splinter again. For the rest of the afternoon he'd concentrate on farm work and hope that when he wasn't thinking about Ella, his subconscious would repair his focus.

He put the sliver of cake in Duke's dog bowl. Duke wolfed it down and looked at him for more. When he didn't move, the Australian shepherd padded across to the bench to fix his bright blue stare on the remaining piece.

He cut Duke another tiny portion. 'Just as well this is the last of Ella's cake, otherwise we'd have to start jogging twice a day.'

Saul finished what was left of the slice and savoured the final mouthful. Carrot cake had always been a favourite as it reminded him of laughter-filled birthdays. His mother had used a recipe that had been handed down through her family.

He carried his plate and coffee mug over to the bench. The water troughs had been cleaned and the gator pressure washed so the next thing was to move the water tank that had blown over the fence from the small hobby farm on his western side.

He'd sent through a photo to the city-based owner, who only used the farm as a weekender, and he agreed the tank was irreparable. The almost new corrugated iron tank had been empty and not tied down. In the recent wild winds the tank had rolled down the hill, over the boundary fence and had come to a stop against a gum tree. Thankfully there hadn't been any bison nearby.

By the time he'd used the tractor to drag the tank to the front paddock ready for a local waste management company to collect it for recycling, the sky was more orange than blue. The cool change had been superseded by another heatwave and while the sun had lowered, the temperature hadn't followed suit. After he'd fed the horses and bison, he headed inside to swap his jeans for rugby shorts and his everyday boots for an old pair. Instead of cooling off like he usually did in the pool, he'd take Cisco and Amber for an early evening swim in the river.

Riding Cisco bareback, he led Amber past the sheds towards the laneway. Duke briefly disappeared into the garden to run along the fence line when Ella arrived home. Saul resisted the urge to text to see how her day had been. Not thinking about her for the afternoon had granted him some mental white space, even if he felt far from confident his control was again watertight.

Instead of following the boundary fence that separated his place from Ella's, they rode along a track that took them through the centre of Windermere and to a sandy-banked section of the river. He'd swum Cisco in the slow-flowing water before and the gelding's ears pricked forward when he realised where they were heading.

Saul smiled. He'd finally found something the pinto enjoyed besides seeing Ella.

Once at the river, Cisco and Amber didn't baulk as they walked into the water. Duke splashed beside them. When the flow deepened, Saul lengthened the lead rope to allow Amber space so she would avoid being kicked when Cisco needed to swim. By the time they'd crossed the river and pebbles again clattered beneath the horses' hooves, the cold water had stripped the heat from their skin. Amber bent to lick the shallows that rippled around her feet. The buckskin enjoyed cooling off as much as Cisco did.

They swam back across to the small sandy beach. Instead of returning home the way they'd come, they took the scenic route through the shade of the red river gums. A kookaburra cackled to signal he wasn't impressed they were passing through his territory.

Feeling the wet cotton on his back dry in the hot wind, Saul headed the horses towards a section of the river where they could take a final swim before the ride home. They'd rounded the bend when a familiar strangled goat bleat caused a nearby flock of galahs to take flight.

Ahead of them, Nutmeg ran along the trunk of a fallen branch that had been dropped by a gum tree to conserve water. Beside the river edge Ella's running shoes sat side by side while she floated on her back in the shallows. Cinnamon stood on the bank, chewing her cud. When Nutmeg caught sight of the horses, she bleated again and leapt to the ground.

Ella sat up and smoothed wet hair from off her face before giving Saul a wave. He stopped Cisco and Amber and whistled to Duke. Cinnamon had swung around to face the Australian shepherd and watched him, head lowered. If Duke took another step closer he'd find out just how hard her horns were.

As Ella waded out of the river, rivulets ran over the tanned skin of her bare arms and legs. He didn't miss the way she made sure the hem of her shorts was pulled low enough to cover her scar or how her wet tank top and running shorts clung like a second skin.

Duke sped towards her. After giving the Australian shepherd his usual affectionate greeting and collecting her shoes, Ella walked over to the horses. Unlike when they'd last surprised each other at the river, this time Ella's smile reached her eyes. 'Fancy meeting you here.'

He returned her smile. 'What are the odds?'

'In weather like this, there's no better place to be.' She bent to pull on her socks. 'The horses look like they enjoyed their swim.'

'They did.' Despite her relaxed appearance, fatigue stole the colour from her cheeks. 'Day went well?'

She struggled to pull a shoe over her wet sock. 'It did. I also made it to the post office to send Charles his letter.' She looked down to tie her shoelace. 'I feel like I have my life back. But as liberating as it feels, it might take a little while to get used to.'

'It'll feel normal again soon.' He kept his tone casual. All he wanted to do was kiss away the weariness tensing her mouth. 'Like a ride back?'

She glanced over to where Cinnamon and Nutmeg wandered along the path home, happy with their own company. 'That would be great. I'm not sure where my energy's gone.'

Saul slid off Cisco. He'd swap to riding Amber as the mare only wore a headcollar, while Cisco had on a bridle.

The pinto whickered as Ella went over to stroke the gelding's nose. 'It's you and me again, buddy.' Her gaze flickered to Saul. 'I might need a leg-up.'

Saul draped Amber's lead rope over her neck. The mare wouldn't go anywhere while he helped Ella onto the gelding's back.

'All set?' he asked, making sure his expression didn't reflect how aware he was of her. No matter how strong his willpower he couldn't blank out the way Ella's hair dried in loose curls and perfumed the air with the fragrance of cherry blossoms.

She nodded as she gathered the reins in her left hand and faced Cisco. He grasped her bent right leg and hoisted her upwards. She left the ground. Then, suddenly her right leg straightened and body stiffened. He let go of her knee and took a step back as she slid to the ground.

She carefully turned, chin angled. 'I think I'd better walk.'

Her grim hold on the hem of her shorts told him all he needed to know. She was worried that when she was riding her shorts wouldn't cover her scar.

'Ella … it's okay.' He kept his voice low as he lifted the front of his shirt to expose his own scar. 'I have one too, remember.'

She didn't glance at him but stared over his shoulder as if in another time and place.

He touched her arm. Her skin felt cold beneath his fingertips. 'You can ride on my left if that makes you feel more comfortable?'

Still, she didn't respond. With Charles's letter she'd been open and communicative. Now, she had withdrawn into a place where she was inaccessible.

If he couldn't reach her with words there was another way that he could. He closed the distance between them, placed a hand on her waist and cupped the back of her head with his other hand. For a moment she didn't respond and then she looked at him. Her eyes were so large and so bleak, without thought he pressed a kiss on her forehead. When she leaned into him, his lips trailed along her temple. Wherever she'd been, she was coming back to him.

When her arms slid around his neck and she turned her face up to his, he realised the enormity of his error. What had started out as a way to offer reassurance had turned into another assault upon his senses. He hadn't had enough time to reinstate his boundaries.

Even as the thought formed he had to move away, Ella's hold around his neck tightened. Her eyes met his. No longer dull, gold glowed amongst the brown as she gazed at him with a steadfast intensity. Her message was clear. Comfort wasn't what she wanted. Then there were no more thoughts, only urgency and need as he dipped his head and covered her mouth with his.

Nothing could have prepared him for kissing Ella. Her sweetness and warmth moved him in ways that went beyond the physical. She filled the lonely and dark void within him with laughter and warmth. Emotions he'd banished and refused to acknowledge flared into life. Being with Ella made him feel complete in a way he'd never felt with Trish.

He deepened the kiss, feeling every brush of her bare skin and every press of her wet curves. Her hands slid into his hair as if she too couldn't get close enough. His hands found the satin smooth dip of her lower back. A lifetime of having her soft and responsive in his arms would be too short.

Breathing ragged, they drew apart. She smiled before she lowered her arms from around his neck. He forced himself not to keep hold of her as she eased herself away.

Her fingers sought his and their unsteadiness matched the jackhammer pounding in his chest. 'Let's try that leg-up again.'

He only nodded. Her strength and courage made speaking impossible. This time when she bent her leg and he hoisted her upwards, she settled onto the gelding's back. Shoulders squared, she made no move to tug her shorts over her scar.

Before he could turn away, she touched his jaw and bent to brush her mouth across his. 'Thank you.'

Then she straightened and collected Cisco's reins as though their kiss hadn't just severed every bond of friendship that had existed between them.

# CHAPTER
## 12

'There's something different about you,' Bethany said as she examined Ella across the small table in the Windmill Café.

'It's just my hair.'

Bethany didn't say anything, just looked at Ella over the top of her coffee mug.

'You know I'm starting to feel like it's Edna watching me.'

'Sorry. You just look different … and it's a good different.'

Ella broke off a piece of shortbread. 'Thanks … I think.'

Loud laughter sounded to their left where a group of teenagers congregated over milkshakes. Otherwise the café was only half full as the Saturday sport and market rush had subsided. More importantly, Edna wasn't at her usual table or even in town. She'd gone to Dubbo with Mrs Knox on an emergency mission. Mrs Knox's daughter Harriet had moved in with her new boyfriend of two months. The boyfriend apparently had a hipster man bun, which had sent conservative Mrs Knox into even more of a flap.

Bethany touched her phone screen and showed Ella a list of places she'd checked off as being an unsuitable, or compromised, venue to hold her mother's party. The list was almost the length of the screen. 'I don't know what alphabet letter we're up to but it would have to be plan Z.'

Ella smiled to ease the despondency in Bethany's words. 'All we need is one plan and if it's our twenty-sixth it doesn't matter. We will find somewhere, even if we have to commandeer Denham's man cave. It's probably the only place big enough.'

'Denham's shed … now there's an idea. I had thought of the shearing shed on Mac's farm but it would need a lot of work, plus it isn't big enough.' She looked back at her phone screen. 'If you think this is long you should see the guest list.'

'I can only imagine. It's not an exaggeration to say Edna knows everyone in town.'

'The other thing we have to work out is how we get Mum there without her suspecting a thing.'

Ella broke off more of her shortbread. 'This might seem like mission impossible but we'll find a way.'

'I hope so and soon as time's running out.' Bethany's phone vibrated as a text came through. She read the message before sitting her mobile beside her coffee mug. 'Dad says hi and to call in anytime you're driving past.'

'I will. It's been a while.'

'Before I forget, Mum also said to tell you that Caroline's sheep has gone missing again.'

'Did she know we were meeting up after work?'

Bethany's brow furrowed. 'No. Maybe she said *if* I see you.'

'Knowing your mother, she said when. Is there any way she could know what we're planning?'

Bethany shook her blonde head. 'When I looked into venues I told a little white lie saying I was sussing out engagement party places.'

Bethany's phone vibrated again as another text came in. 'That's strange … it's Mac's dad. He wants us to meet him at the old schoolhouse when we're done.'

'Clive Barton wants to see us?'

When she'd treated one of his cows for grass tetany, he'd used more grunts than words.

'He never wants to see anybody.' Bethany gazed around the café and then looked out the large window that faced the main street. 'Call me paranoid but my mother mustn't be the only one with a sneaky spy network. Mac doesn't even know where I am.'

Ella too looked out the window. 'Clive probably just saw us walk in together.'

'Maybe. Since he's let the boys have more responsibility in running the farm and has become involved in the museum project, he's always in town.'

Ella finished her coffee. 'I'll meet you at the schoolhouse. I'll have a quick look around for Missy.'

As she settled into the driver's seat she slid the cover off the sun visor mirror. Did she really look different?

The reflection that stared back at her looked the same as how she'd looked before her river meeting with Saul. But Bethany was right. She did seem different. No longer did sadness cloud her gaze, instead her eyes sparkled. As for her mouth, even when she was sure she wasn't smiling, like now, the corners of her lips tilted.

Just as well Edna was out of town. She'd not rest until she'd discovered the reason behind Ella's new lightness. Not only was such a reason off limits, her kiss with Saul wasn't for public consumption, so too were the reasons why she didn't always look this way. She slid the mirror cover shut and started the four-wheel drive engine. Not all of her demons had been appeased by Charles's letter. A part of her life remained vulnerable to any inquisition from Edna.

Ella took the road that would lead to the park nestled beside the local sportsground. If she hadn't glimpsed the need in Saul's eyes in her kitchen, she'd never have had the courage to go after what she wanted. It was the raw emotion that had darkened his gaze after their kiss that had given her the strength to ride home with, for the first time, her scar visible to the world. Despite all he'd been through, Saul had been willing to take a risk and to lower his guard. He'd allowed her in.

As for their kiss, if she'd needed any further proof Charles hadn't been the right man for her, she'd found it. There was no comparison between the potency of her reaction to Saul and her lukewarm response to Charles. She'd go weeks without travelling to London to see him. Already she was craving Saul's touch and it hadn't been three days. It also mattered more than it should that he shared the intensity of the attraction between them.

She sighed as she stopped to wave as an elderly man walked his cattle dog across the road. Mr Ross and Lacey were frequent visitors to the vet clinic as Lacey had canine diabetes.

But as heady as her and Saul's kiss had been, it was a one-off. Her reasons for only wanting friendship might no longer exist but nothing had changed in Saul's world. He'd been supportive and understanding when she'd needed a friend. His touch and kiss might also have revealed his emotions when he'd held her close, but by the end of their ride home his profile had again settled into familiar remote lines.

While her hormones lamented his retreat, her head knew it was a natural reaction. The scars left by his failed marriage and the loss of his son were yet to heal. She had some things herself to process, one of which was Charles's cheating. Instead of listening to her intuition, she'd placed her faith in a man she should have seen through. She had to work out how that had happened, so she'd never make the same mistake. As much as she wanted to feel the strength of Saul's arms around her, they needed to rewind their connection back to an uncomplicated and platonic friendship.

She took a left turn. As she drove, she scanned the roadside for a sheep wearing a green collar, but all she could see was Mrs Smith's tabby cat as he walked along the footpath, his tail in the air. Monty had also been a patient when a bite on his back from a scuffle with a neighbouring cat had turned into an abscess.

When she'd reached the colourful play equipment of the park and had driven around the white-picket fence of the sportsground, there was still no sign of Missy. Keeping a close eye out for the sheep, she continued on to the bluestone schoolhouse on the outskirts of town.

When she arrived, Bethany's white sedan was parked outside along with what she assumed to be Clive's dusty Hilux. Not sure of what she would be walking into, she tucked her pink work shirt into her jeans. Clive was notoriously difficult but the word around town was that he had mellowed since finally getting hearing aids and spending his days now tinkering on trucks and windmills in his shed.

She walked into the cool of the bluestone schoolhouse. Her boots rang on the wooden floorboards and echoed in the hallway where once hundreds of little feet would have trodden.

'Ella,' Bethany's voice sounded, 'in here.'

She walked into what had been a classroom to see Bethany and Clive standing by the front window.

Bethany smiled. 'Clive found the missing sheep. Missy was wandering along the lane outside the lolly shop.'

'Too bad she has a home, I was looking forward to having lamb chops for dinner,' Clive said, tone gruff.

Only half sure that he was joking, Ella's eyes must have narrowed because he scowled at her. 'I don't eat people's pets.'

Ella held his gaze. 'Just as well. Where's Missy now?'

'Back home. Edna gave me Caroline's number.'

Bethany arched a fine brow. 'Yes, it's no surprise Clive has my mother on speed dial.'

Ella's lips twitched at both Bethany's expression and dry tone. She wasn't sure Bethany's soon-to-be father-in-law was used to people taking him to task.

Clive and Edna had been embroiled in a family feud for years until they'd decided to become co-conspirators and bring Bethany and Mac together. Their meddling had almost cost Bethany and Mac their relationship.

Bethany glanced at Ella. 'Which is just as well as Clive here has *volunteered* …' Clive grunted. 'To keep tabs on my mother and let us know if she's onto us. Which is the least he can do after all the grief he and Mum caused.'

Clive's glower deepened.

'But …' By now Bethany was smiling. 'He also has come up with the answer we've been looking for, so all is forgiven.'

Ella gave up trying to hide her own smile. Clive looked as if he was about to be dragged off to Dubbo on a two-day shopping spree. 'I can't wait to hear this.'

Bethany glanced at Clive. 'I'll let you explain.'

Clive folded his arms. 'There's a spare room here that could be set up for Edna's party the night of the museum opening. For once your mother isn't involved in any of the organising.'

'Clive,' Ella said, meeting Bethany's excited grey gaze. 'You're a genius. Edna will think she's coming for the opening and meanwhile the whole town will be here to celebrate her birthday, too.'

'He is.' Bethany moved forwards to kiss his weathered cheek. 'Thank you.'

For once a smile thawed the hardness in his eyes.

Bethany turned to Ella. 'Let's check the room out to see what we'll need.'

She nodded. 'Thanks, Clive. It really is a brilliant idea.'

He gave her his version of a smile.

She went to follow Bethany when he spoke again. 'I met that new neighbour of yours.'

She slowly turned. 'Did you?'

'He says he grew up in Australia?'

'I think Denham said it was around Tamworth.'

'Well, let's hope he starts talking like he's from there again. I couldn't catch half of what he said with that accent of his.' Clive unfolded his arms. 'Just as well he's as strong as he looks. Finn will be after him for the next rugby season.'

Finn was Mac's twin brother and he took his rugby very seriously. 'I'm sure he will be.'

Then, before Clive could see any colour in her cheeks, she turned to leave. She knew just how strong Saul was. He'd hoisted her onto Cisco's back as though she weighed little more than Nutmeg. She also knew just how good it felt to be anchored against those hard-packed muscles of his.

Bethany gave her a quick look as she entered the middle room of the schoolhouse.

'This is perfect,' she said, walking away to inspect the space and to give her face time to cool.

'It is.' Bethany snapped some pictures on her phone before giving Ella a high five. 'Mission impossible just became mission possible.'

'Now we just have to keep all of this a secret from a person who always knows what's happening.'

Bethany nodded as her phone rang. 'Hi, Mum,' she said with a wide-eyed look at Ella. 'Where am I? I'm with Ella. I passed on the message about Caroline's sheep but she's been found and has been returned. How bad is the man bun?'

Bethany was right. She did know how her mother thought and was able to steer the conversation away from any incriminating topics. She'd had many years of practice diverting her mother's attention.

Ella took some photos of the room's layout for Sue who would be helping to decorate before giving Bethany a wave goodbye and heading outside. Bethany had earlier mentioned she had an after-lunch meeting with a local cake maker who could be trusted to keep the party hush hush.

Once inside her four-wheel drive, she didn't move to start the engine. Instead she searched for her phone in her tote bag.

For the first time since the hay bale challenge she and Saul hadn't texted each other for an entire week. She'd been trying to give him the space that his silence suggested he needed. But tomorrow Violet would be coming to see Libby's room and Saul would be joining her and Violet for Sunday lunch. Apart from the fact she was missing him, it would be wise to clear the air. Violet didn't need to be in the middle of any awkwardness.

She sent a carefully worded text.

*Hope you had a good week. Still right for lunch?*

She reread the text, hoping it set a friendly tone and established that she had no regrets over their kiss, even if she couldn't stop reliving the moment when his mouth had claimed hers.

She clipped on her seatbelt when a reply whooshed in.

*Week good thanks. Made a quick trip to visit Rosie. See you and Violet tomorrow.*

She frowned as she typed. In the bush neighbours looked out for each other. She and Saul were also friends and yet he hadn't asked her to take care of his farm or told her he was going to Sydney.

*Next trip I'll be happy to feed animals and check water for you.*

*Thanks. Denham had it covered.*

She sent a thumbs up and stared at her phone even though she didn't expect an answer. Unease filtered through her, followed by a tide of uncertainty. Even after what had happened at the river and Saul's need to retreat, she had hoped that their friendship would have counted for something. If she'd been going away she would have felt comfortable asking him to feed Cinnamon and Nutmeg and to check that the timer turned the veranda light on each night. Duke also liked her and would have enjoyed hanging out at her place.

She started the ignition. The contentment that had cocooned her since Wednesday fell away. She'd misread her relationship with Charles; could she now be misreading the strength of the connection she thought she shared with Saul? Or did his silence and need for space signal that even friendship was no longer on the table?

⚭

'Thanks for looking after the troops and for having Duke to stay,' Saul said to Denham, lifting his shoulder to hold his mobile in place while he closed the laneway double gates.

'Anytime. How's your brother?'

'Home from hospital and doing what he's told by Nurse Rosie.'

Denham's chuckle was drowned out by the early morning call of a magpie balancing on the boundary fence. 'He's a wise man.'

Saul returned to the gator where Duke sat in the passenger seat. 'I'm not quite sure that's what Amy's calling him. She can't believe that when he fell he put his hands in the air to save his laptop, not to break his fall.'

'Are you sure the two of you are brothers?'

Saul laughed as he headed the gator towards home. He'd lost count of the amount of times he'd hit the dirt of a rodeo arena. Even after having a gymnastic coach perfect his landings, he'd still experienced his fair share of broken bones.

'Let's just say I had lots of tips for Nathan on how to deal with a broken leg.' His tone sobered. 'Sorry again for the short notice. I know you had a busy week.'

Saul had been over at Denham's Thursday morning helping him with his rodeo cattle when Amy had called saying she was taking Nathan to the emergency department. Within ten minutes he'd booked a lunchtime flight from Dubbo to Sydney and was on his way home to throw clothes into a bag.

Denham had volunteered to look after Windermere. Duke had spent the past two days at Glenmore wrestling Juno and stalking Cressy's Rhode Island Red chickens. Meanwhile Saul had been watching princess movies with Rosie and learning just how a fussy five-year-old liked her breakfast. Who knew toast could come in so many shades of gold?

'You don't have to apologise. We're mates.'

He hadn't missed the concern in Denham's tone or the looks he'd cast him as they'd drafted his cattle last Thursday. Apart from Denham needing a second pair of hands, the other reason why he'd been over helping was that since kissing Ella he'd been restless and unable to settle.

'We are.' He chose his words carefully. 'I'm still working through a few things. But I'll be ready for that cold beer in your shed soon.'

'I hope so.' Denham paused. 'If those things are new things you might need that beer sooner rather than later.'

Saul parked the gator in the shed before he replied. As vigilant as Saul had been to conceal his emotions when around Ella, Denham had seen through his pretence. 'It is a … new thing.'

'I thought so. To be honest, it's not just a new thing, it's also a good thing.'

Saul rubbed at his forehead. 'Not from where I'm sitting.'

'Trust me. It is.'

'Tell me it's not obvious.' Saul didn't try to strip the tension from his words. He ruffled Duke's neck as the Australian shepherd burrowed his head under his arm.

'Only to me.' When Saul didn't answer, Denham spoke again. 'You just need time, and there's plenty of that. So just go with the flow.'

Saul briefly closed his eyes as his senses remembered the feel of Ella moulded against him and the softness of her lips. 'That's easier said than done.'

Denham chuckled. 'Just as well there's a beer night coming up. It's not just one cold beer you sound like you need.'

'I thought there was dancing as well?'

'There is but I don't know of anyone, expect for Finn Barton, who'll be inside with the girls.'

He'd seen Finn busting some of his signature moves on the dancefloor at the Royal Arms. 'Does Cressy know you're planning to boycott the dancing part?'

'If she did I'd be sleeping outside with Tippy and Juno.'

Saul left the gator with a smile. 'You'd better leave space for Tanner and Hewitt in that doghouse of yours. I take it they're not planning on dancing either?'

'I reckon you could fit a few swags in those empty rooms of yours.'

Saul laughed. 'I could. I can't wait to see the girls' faces when they realise your plan. Hewitt's a braver man than I am. Fliss isn't to be messed with.' His tone sobered. 'Thanks again ... for everything.'

'Anytime. Just relax, okay?'

'I'll see what I can do.'

He ended the call. The reality was he couldn't relax. If he did, the first thing he'd do was pick up from where he and Ella had left off at the river.

He glanced over at the boundary fence as he and Duke walked towards the farmhouse. When he'd driven past Ella's cottage on his way to Dubbo he'd almost used his phone's voice-to-text function to send her a message. But as the cottage receded in his rear-view mirror, he'd hadn't followed through. If he needed some space to process their kiss and the way she made him feel, she would too.

On their ride home from the river, every so often Ella had made small talk but otherwise silence had settled between them. As much as she appeared to not regret what had happened between them, with each stride that Amber took, his own regret grew. He'd crossed a line he shouldn't have even been in sight of.

Even though Ella had made it clear she'd wanted him to kiss her, doing so had been the worst thing he could have done, for both of them. Along with feeling vulnerable over her scar, she would still be dealing with Charles's revelations. Just like he'd said to Denham, he still had his own issues to work through. It was coming up to two years since Caleb was born.

As for the attraction that had exploded between them, there was no going back or pretending that it wouldn't continue to simmer. But as neither he nor Ella were in a position to start something, and the last thing he'd want to do was hurt her, they had to find a way to make their now complicated friendship work.

He looked at his watch. There was just enough time to call into her place before he was due to pick up Violet. Even though the texts he'd received from Ella yesterday after he'd landed in Dubbo hadn't flagged anything was wrong, he wanted to make sure. He also needed to prove to himself, and maybe to her, that they could co-exist as friends without chemistry again blindsiding them.

He sent Ella a quick message to say he'd call in on the way to town to collect Violet.

When he arrived Ella was in the back garden weeding around the mosaic stepping stones. As he left his F-truck she straightened and rubbed at her lower back before walking over. She wore black shorts with a loose pink shirt as well as her navy Woodlea vet cap and sunglasses. Even dressed in her gardening clothes, she stirred his senses. She was so beautiful. As usual Duke swooned against her legs while she patted him.

She briefly glanced up. 'Does Duke want to stay with me?'

Even though her tone was friendly, there was a new tension around her mouth. He was certain that behind her sunglasses wariness tempered the gold in her eyes. He cursed his weakness. He should never have kissed her. Things were not okay between them.

'He'd love to. Then Violet won't have him breathing down her neck from the back seat.'

As he'd hoped, a brief smile lifted the corners of her lips. 'How's Rosie?'

'A little shaken up with her dad being in hospital. I used Tanner's tip and downloaded a playlist from that snowman movie every girl under six seems to be obsessed with.'

Her brow creased. 'Is your brother all right?'

'He will be when he doesn't have to wear an orthopaedic boot.'

'I hope for his sake that happens soon.'

Saul nodded. Ella's hand rubbed at her thigh in a gesture he wasn't sure she even knew she was doing.

She stared at him before she spoke. 'It goes without saying that anytime you're away I can look after your place.'

'I was at Denham's when I took Amy's call and wasn't sure if you were the on-call vet this weekend.' He paused. 'I also figured you might have seen enough of me.'

'Saul … what happened at the river … it doesn't have to cause any awkwardness. You helped me at a time when I needed someone. But we both know friendship's the only option for either of us, so I hope that's still on offer?'

He took a moment to answer. The need to tug her close and kiss her in a way that wasn't part of any friendship agreement made his chest burn. 'Of course it is. If you ever need someone again, you know where I am.'

'I do,' she said, voice soft.

He turned away before she could see how much of a battle it was to keep his hands by his side.

When he returned with Violet there wasn't a weed in sight and Cinnamon and Nutmeg were in the garden making the most of being out of their paddock. When he parked in the carport they ran over to the wooden fence like any farm dog would have.

Violet laughed from where she sat beside him. 'They haven't changed a bit.'

Saul helped her out and through the small gate where she stopped to greet the two goats milling around her. Nutmeg's excited bleating caused a pair of cockatoos to screech as they vacated the jacaranda tree.

Violet waved him on with her walking stick. 'Off you go. I'll be here a while.'

He reached the sunroom door as Ella and Duke walked through. Ella now wore a knee-length white dress that left her arms bare and hugged every feminine curve.

Expression solemn, she gazed over to where Violet lavished attention on the goats. 'We have to find out what happened to Libby.'

He held up Violet's bag that contained Libby's handmade box. 'Violet brought some photographs so let's hope something in one of them proves useful.'

As Violet made her slow way along the path, she'd stop to look at something in the garden. Saul stood in silence as he watched. He wasn't sure why Ella didn't speak but his excuse was that seeing Violet in her beloved home made his chest ache. Her perpetual smile seemed to lift years off her tiny frame.

When Violet reached the steps, he helped her inside. Her smile widened as she gazed around. Polished wooden floorboards gleamed and pink roses filled crystal vases.

'Shall I put the kettle on?' Ella asked when they reached the kitchen that smelled of fresh baking.

Violet shook her head and reached for the bag Saul carried. 'Not yet, dear. I need to return the box to Libby.'

As they walked through the living room her attention focused on the hallway doorway where her youngest daughter's sketchbook had been found. After a brief pause, she continued through to Libby's room, lowered herself to sit on the bed and patted the spot beside her. Ella sat. Saul remained at the doorway. Behind him, Duke made himself at home on the hallway floor.

Violet took out an envelope from her bag. 'These are some photographs of Libby with her hair tied back from around the time Annette was with Jeb. My eyes aren't what they used to be so I'm not sure what ribbon she has on.'

When Violet passed Ella Libby's handmade box, Ella opened the lid to take out the cream and floral ribbon. She laid it on the bed next to the pile of photos. When she glanced at him, Saul entered the room to look through the pictures she handed him.

In many photographs it was obvious that Libby's hair was in a ponytail but it wasn't clear how her hair had been tied back. In one where she was laughing at Violet, he could see the ribbon, but it was pink.

Ella stared at a photo and then placed it on the bed beside the ribbon. Then she skimmed through her pile and placed three more photos of Libby wearing a green dress on the bed. 'I can't see a ribbon, but look at this dress—it's the same colour as the green in the ribbon.'

Violet touched the closest photo. 'This was taken on Libby's sixteenth birthday. She hadn't wanted a party but we went shopping for a new outfit and we cooked lasagne for dinner, her favourite. We would have bought a ribbon to match her dress.' Violet looked around the small room, her gaze intent. 'There will be a framed family photo of all of us from that night.'

Saul moved to where a cluster of photographs sat on a bookshelf. He'd examined them closely on his last visit. He placed a wooden frame containing the family photo in Violet's hands.

Violet's fragile finger traced Libby's face and then Annette's. She looked out the doorway. 'I think Annette had a photo of just the two of them.'

Ella came to her feet. 'She does, on the corkboard hanging on her wall.'

She left and returned with a board covered in overlapping photographs. Many were of Annette and Jeb but several were of her and Libby, especially when they were little.

Saul scanned the photographs but couldn't see anything useful until he removed the photo of the sisters taken on Libby's birthday. Right on the edge that had been covered by another photo, where Libby turned to grin at her sister, there was a glimpse of a cream ribbon with pink and green flowers.

They all stared at the picture before Saul placed it on the bed beside the ribbon. 'Something significant with Jeb happened the night of her sixteenth birthday,' he said.

He knew Ella shared his unease about what that could have been when she gave him an intent look before reaching for Violet's hand. 'How long after her birthday did Libby disappear?'

Violet's forehead furrowed as she calculated the timeframe. 'Seven weeks.'

Ella again glanced at him before her quiet reply sounded. 'Violet … is it possible Libby might have been pregnant?'

# CHAPTER
# 13

'Am I in the wrong house?' Fliss asked as she walked into Ella's untidy kitchen carrying a container filled with cupcakes. 'Your benches look like you've been cooking for a cast of thousands.'

Ella groaned and went to run a hand through her hair until she remembered her fingers were covered in pink icing. 'I know, there's so much mess, and I'm going to be late.'

Penny had organised a cupcake day in the vet surgery with all monies raised going to a local dog rescue association.

Fliss placed the cupcake container on the kitchen table and opened the empty dishwasher. 'We can talk while I pack.'

'Thank you.' Ella lowered her tense shoulders and peered through the clear plastic of Fliss's container at the pretty silver-themed cupcakes. 'These look great.'

Fliss put a mixing bowl in the dishwasher. 'Between Hewitt and Miss Molly I'm lucky there's any left.'

Ella placed the now finished pink cupcakes in a nearby container. 'I take it nothing new about Libby turned up online?'

After Saul had driven Violet back to town yesterday, she'd called Fliss to give her an update. Fliss had volunteered to do an internet search to see if she could find out anything about Libby having had a baby.

'Just like the police, I found no record anywhere of either a Libby Mayer or an Elizabeth Mayer having given birth. I also looked at adoption records.'

Fliss's grim expression as she placed the last of the items in the dishwasher said there could be many medical explanations for why there was no proof Libby's baby—if she had indeed been pregnant—had made it to full term.

Ella shared her sober thoughts as she closed the dishwasher door and switched it on.

'How's Violet?' Fliss asked, words subdued as she filled the sink with soapy water.

'She's devastated that if Libby was pregnant why she didn't feel she could tell her and Lloyd.' Ella took a clean tea towel from out of the drawer to wipe the cupcake tray Fliss soon sat in the drying rack. 'They would have helped her raise the baby just like they did with Gemma.'

'I'll see her on my way home. What does Saul think?'

Ella hoped that Fliss's stare lingered out of concern for Violet and not because she'd mentioned Saul's name. She took extra care wiping the next tray. 'Like me he thinks it's the missing piece of the puzzle.'

'You and Saul make a great team. Violet's lucky to have you both helping her.'

Ella ignored Fliss's comment. At the moment Saul was the bane of her life. He was the reason why she'd slept in and was now running late and had a chaotic kitchen. 'I just wish we could do more. The only things to make Violet smile lately are a visit from Duke and the news that Gemma's coming to stay next week.'

'It might be a long shot but Jeb's new partner might know something about him having had another child besides Gemma.'

Ella wiped the final cupcake tray. 'Logic tells me that if Libby did have a baby, he mustn't have known about it, as not only did he stay in town, he kept going out with Annette. When she fell pregnant he stuck around, even if it wasn't for long.'

Water gurgled as the sink emptied. Fliss dried her hands on Ella's tea towel. 'I'll see if I can track his new partner down.'

'That would be great.' Ella touched her chin and grimaced when she realised she had sticky icing on her face.

Fliss answered her unspoken question with a smile. 'It's also in your hair.' She gave her a quick hug. 'I'll leave you to get ready. You've still plenty of time.' At the doorway she turned. 'Say hi to Saul for me. We really should have another barbeque, it seems like ages since the dessert night.'

Ella kept her smile in place until she waved Fliss off from the back door. Then she turned and headed for the shower. She had precisely ten minutes to get clean, dressed and on the road.

Hair still wet, she made it out her front gate in nine minutes. The containers of cupcakes were piled high on her passenger seat. It was only when she passed the rusted forty-four-gallon drum letterbox of the farm down the road that was currently home to a swarm of bees that she relaxed. Despite her morning chaos she was now running on time.

As for Fliss's suggestion that they have another barbeque, Ella was back to not wanting to go if Saul was going to be there. Even though they were a team when it came to looking out for Violet and they'd confirmed that they were still on the same friendship page, she needed to keep all contact to a minimum.

Saul's explanation about why Denham had looked after Windermere had shone a spotlight on the instability of her emotions. It wasn't like her to take things personally but that was how she'd reacted. Instead of giving him the benefit of the doubt, she'd overthought why he hadn't asked her.

Embarrassment merged with uncertainty. When her brother had gone missing, and again when her parents hadn't coped either alone or together, she'd worked hard to maintain an even keel. She'd done the same in the aftermath of what had happened on that narrow English lane. While all those around her were on an emotional roller-coaster, she'd stayed on the ground. But since Saul had come into her life, she felt as though she'd too been spinning and it scared her.

She sat straighter in her seat as she stared through the dusty windscreen at the heat mirage that blurred the black bitumen. Before she could think about relaxing back into their friendship she had to restore order. It was the only way she knew to truly keep herself safe. And to achieve this she had to renew the battle to keep her distance. Physical distance would be impossible to maintain, but when she was with Saul from now on she'd keep her emotional defences firmly in place.

She walked into the vet surgery, which no longer smelled of antiseptic but of all things sweet and creamy. Penny had set up a table on the far side of the waiting room and strung pink and lime bunting around the walls. The table centrepiece featured a white-tiered cupcake stand filled with as many rosebuds as cupcakes. On either side, more stands were laden with a rainbow array of cakes.

Penny greeted her with an excited smile. 'How cool does this all look? I've had people dropping cakes around since lunchtime yesterday.'

'It looks amazing.' Ella handed her the containers of cupcakes. 'These fancy ones are from Fliss and these not-so-fancy ones are from me.'

Penny lifted the corner container lid of Ella's cupcakes and took a deep breath. 'They smell divine. What are they?'

'Somewhere under all that icing they're red velvet.' Ella glanced at the clock. Her first client would soon arrive. 'So, what have you got for me today?'

Penny ran her through the day's list and she busied herself getting ready.

After she'd seen two patients and had a five-minute break, she snuck an elegant white cupcake dusted with gold glitter. She'd put her money for whatever cakes she ate in the donation box at the end of the day. After a session with a client about the needs of her elderly dog who had Cushing's disease, she selected another cupcake. By lunch, the stands were beginning to empty.

Penny had a twinkle in her eye as she came for a chat while Ella ate her salad sandwich. 'I just had a run of tradies on their lunch break. Sue's been in too and said to tell you the joey's going well.' Penny's grin broadened. 'And guess who just left?'

Ella shook her head even though she knew the answer.

Penny leaned in closer. 'Saul … and he had his dog with him. I've never seen that shade of blue eyes before.'

'Duke or Saul?'

Ella instantly regretted her question. Penny didn't need to know that she'd noticed the colour of Saul's eyes.

'Both. Duke's are such a bright blue but Saul's are so dark and—'

Ella spoke before Penny put into words just how compelling and dreamy they were. 'Were they just in for cupcakes or did Duke need an appointment?'

'Just cupcakes. Saul bought a whole container.' Penny blushed. 'He didn't rush off, either. We had a chat.'

Ella nodded, her sandwich feeling like a leaden weight in her stomach. One day Saul would be ready for something other than friendship and lighthearted Penny was exactly who he needed to bring laughter back into his life. 'He's a nice guy.'

'Sally says she's sure he has a kid but is now divorced and that's why he's moved here alone.'

Ella stilled. Saul had only been comfortable telling her a bit about his past and that hadn't included his son. Even Denham didn't know all the details. 'What makes her say that?'

'He was in for a coffee the other day and this little kid apparently ran over to him and wanted to be picked up. The mother was horrified, at her son, not Saul, and when she was apologising he apparently said it was okay and that he was used to kids.'

Ella relaxed. Saul would have been talking about his niece, Rosie. 'You don't have to have your own child to know what kids can be like. He might be a godfather, an uncle or even have a friend with a little one.'

Penny frowned. 'That's true. Sal and I didn't think of that.'

Ella didn't answer as she drank from her water bottle. She had to perform a caesarean this afternoon to deliver a very round Pekinese's five puppies and it was time to get back to work.

When the tiny puppies had arrived safely and she'd seen the last of her afternoon clients, Ella headed out to the waiting room. The rumbling in her stomach made her attention zero in on the cupcake table. Except the tiered stands were empty.

'Please tell me there's a cupcake left somewhere?' she said as she glanced across to where Penny sat at the computer on the counter.

Penny looked up and seemed to be making some sort of gesture to Ella's left. When a familiar exuberant voice said her name she knew what Penny had been trying to tell her. She slowly turned.

Edna stood over near the leads and collars that were hanging on the wall. Preoccupied with looking for cupcakes, Ella had only registered that the room's chairs were empty and not that the waiting room remained occupied.

Edna gave her a satisfied smile as she walked over and held out an open cake box filled with cupcakes. 'Here … Penny very kindly gave me all that she had left. I'm sure I can spare one.'

Penny gave her a look that said she hadn't been kind at all, she'd had no choice. Ella selected a vanilla butterfly cupcake. 'Thank you.'

Edna watched her as she tucked in. 'Just as well I stayed to look for a new lead for Prinnie.'

'I second that. This cupcake's exactly what I needed.'

'I meant that you're someone I wanted to see.'

Ella silenced her groan and made sure she finished her cake before replying. 'I'm the weekend on-call vet but can still help out at the bush dance when I'm there.'

'You're not on my to-help list, but I hope you'll still come. Maybe it's just your new hair, but you're looking rather rundown. You need to have some fun.'

From the corner of her eye, Ella caught Penny's smirk.

Ella folded her arms. Her sugar hit hadn't fully kicked in yet to guarantee a zen-like calm. 'I've never felt better.'

Edna's stare remained sceptical. 'At least you won't be seeing that new electrician there … the last I heard he was headed to Victoria.'

Ella only nodded. Edna always dispensed with the unimportant things before focusing on what she really wanted to discuss. Whatever the topic was, it would either be about Saul or her upcoming birthday. In either case, Ella needed to shut down the conversation before it turned into an interrogation.

Edna touched Ella's arm. 'It's so lovely you and my daughter have been spending time together.'

'We do have more chances to catch up now Bethany's working in town.' Ella paused, for dramatic effect and not because she didn't know what to say. Edna wasn't the only one who could have an agenda. 'You're not keeping tabs on me, are you?'

'I wouldn't *dream* of doing such a thing.'

'Of course not. I was only saying to Bethany the other day that I really need to drop around and see Noel.'

Ella's gaze narrowed. 'Were you now?'

'Yes.'

Ella only said the one word but it was enough. It was common knowledge that since she'd helped Noel with his prize bull she enjoyed the unique privilege of being insulated from his wife's plotting. Edna couldn't have Noel know that she was becoming a little too interested in Ella's life.

Edna closed the lid of the cake box. 'Well, that's all I wanted to talk to you about … Doug Jones leaving town.'

'Thanks for letting me know, and for the cupcake,' Ella said, as Edna turned and with a brief wave left the surgery.

Penny walked out from behind the counter. 'I've never seen Edna move so fast. What was that all about?'

'Maybe she thought I'd eat all her cupcakes.'

Penny laughed but her attention remained on Edna as she power walked past the red fire hydrant.

Ella moved to collect the tiered cupcake stands before Penny could ask any more questions or revisit their lunchtime conversation. It was all right for Penny to be smitten with Saul, but for her, from now on as much as she could she needed to remind herself he was strictly off limits.

'Duke, don't even think about stalking Hercules.' Saul whistled as the Australian shepherd, body low and attention on the surly bison, took a slow step closer.

A taut wire fence might stand between them but Hercules didn't look like he was in a sociable mood. His tail stood straight up, his nostrils flared and his eyes were black with belligerence.

Duke took a last look at the bison bull before racing over to Saul's side as he headed towards the stables. It was only early morning but the cicadas were in full song. It was going to be another scorcher.

He flexed his shoulders beneath the sun-warmed cotton. Today an unfamiliar fragrance clung to his shirt. Whatever detergent Ella had washed his shirt in after they'd used it to cocoon the joey was a brand he didn't use. The strong scent wasn't unpleasant but it made it impossible to push thoughts of Ella out of his mind. While he usually associated her with the subtle perfume of cherry blossoms, her shirts too smelt like the one he now wore.

He scraped a hand over his stubbled chin. It was bad enough that the cupcakes filling his freezer also reminded him of her. Just as well when he and Duke had called into the vet clinic last Monday, Penny had been distracted by patting Duke. Otherwise she wouldn't have missed the way he'd kept an eye out for Ella. When the consulting room door had opened as a patient left, he'd briefly seen her typing on a computer.

Three days had since passed and apart from a few texts about Libby they hadn't seen each other. This was exactly what he needed—time and a chance to refocus. Except Ella was still the last thing he thought of at night and the first thing when he woke.

Duke's ears pricked forward before he dashed off towards the front gate. The Australian shepherd had heard Hugh drive over the cattle grid.

Yesterday afternoon Saul had noticed Amber wasn't as willing to lift her left front hoof as her other feet. As the buckskin's tenderness seemed to be coming from her shoulder and could be a chiropractic issue, he'd called Hugh instead of Ella.

When he reached the undercover bison yards that now held Amber and Cisco, Hugh's white Hilux appeared. Duke ran to greet him as he parked and left his vehicle. Even though they hadn't met before, Duke's tail wagged with delight. Just like when Saul had been introduced to Hugh at the pub, Duke sensed the quietly spoken horse chiropractor was a man to have on your side.

When Hugh joined Saul at the yards, he half turned to look at the bison herd that Saul had moved into their new rotational grazing paddock. Dakota and the cows were congregated beneath a nearby shady tree. Hugh's gaze lingered on the shoulders of the bison bull. 'There's a set of scapulas I don't see every day.'

'Let's hope you never need to take a closer look. As much as Dakota's a gentleman, I'm not sure how he'd handle you getting up close and personal with him.'

Hugh chuckled as he entered the yard. 'My risk-taking days are over. Between Dr Fliss reading me the riot act over my last two concussions and Sibylla and Riley keeping a close eye on me, the most dangerous thing I do nowadays is say no to Jelly Bean when she wants to come inside.'

Riley was Hugh's space-obsessed son who Hugh had raised alone before Sibylla had come into their lives. Even just spending five minutes with the father and son was enough to know of their deep bond.

Saul grinned to hide a tug of loss. 'I'm yet to meet a more determined pony than Jelly.'

'What she lacks in size, she sure does make up for in attitude.' As he spoke he watched Amber as she turned her head to look at him. 'That near side shoulder looks tight.' Hugh untied the mare's lead and draped it over her neck.

'I thought so.' Saul stepped away to give Hugh space to work. The sensible buckskin wouldn't move even though she was untied. He looked over at Cisco who was yet to stand still. The restless pinto moved from side to side as much as his lead would allow him.

Hugh patted Amber's neck, speaking softly so the mare became used to his touch. His hands moved to her poll and along the sides of her jaw feeling the bones beneath her golden coat. As Hugh ran his hands down her neck and left shoulder, he kept his attention on her eyes. When she fussed to indicate that was where the problem was, he concentrated on a spot between her neck and shoulder. With unhurried movements, he turned her head and pulled her left leg forward to release the tension in her shoulder.

This time when he smoothed his hand over the area that had been tender, she didn't react. He again trailed his hand down her left leg. The mare shifted her weight and allowed him to pick up her hoof without any hesitation.

Saul moved forwards to pat Amber. 'That feels better, doesn't it?'

The mare nuzzled his arm.

Hugh looked across to where Cisco now pawed the ground. Even though the pinto didn't appear to be uncomfortable anywhere, Saul had mentioned to Hugh he'd like him checked over. 'If Cisco digs that hole any deeper he'll find water.'

Saul retied Amber to the blue baling twine looped around the steel bar before walking over to the irritated pinto. 'Let's just say patience isn't one of his virtues.'

'He and Denham's Bandit would be a great match.'

Saul held the lead rope while Hugh took his time to move his hands over the gelding. He concentrated on a spot between the gelding's black-and-white ears. After Cisco tossed his head several times, Hugh smoothed his neck. 'See, that wasn't so bad.' He glanced at Saul. 'His poll was out but otherwise he's fine.'

Hugh gave Cisco a final pat before Saul walked him to his Hilux.

'Will I see you at the beer night?' Hugh said as he opened his ute door.

'I told Denham I'd go. Hopefully we won't be the only ones. Just as well the committee put beer on with the bush dance, otherwise I think Woodlea's male population would be underrepresented.'

Hugh chuckled. 'You wouldn't believe how many calls I've had about sore backs in the last week.'

Hugh mainly treated horses but was still a registered human chiropractor.

Saul grinned. 'With a few beers on board I'm sure people will make a miraculous recovery until dancing's involved.'

Hugh gave him a wave as he drove away. Powdery dust lifted and draped the driveway in fine red clouds. The long-term forecast didn't fill him with hope that rain would arrive soon. As dry as it was here, out west things were even more critical.

Ground cover was at a minimum, leaving topsoil exposed and stock hungry. Farmers were hand feeding and cutting kurrajong branches as well as trucking in water. Herds were also out travelling on the long paddock or grazing on the roadside verges. Along with other locals, he'd pledged a hay donation to the hay runners who'd be soon passing through town in a convoy of trucks.

He returned the horses to their paddock. Before Cisco sauntered away, the pinto swished his tail and sent him a glare as if to question why he'd left the paddock in the first place if that was all they'd been going to do. Amber gave him a soft-eyed look before she followed the gelding.

Saul headed towards the farmhouse. He'd cool off with a swim and morning smoko. Duke ambled beside him. When they passed Hercules's paddock, Duke again lowered himself to the ground as he eyeballed the bull who hadn't moved from where he'd stood earlier.

This time, instead of whistling, Saul touched the top of Duke's head to keep him still. His attention didn't leave Hercules. Whereas earlier cows had surrounded him, he now stood in isolation, his stance hunched and stiff as he struggled to breathe. Even as Saul watched, Hercules gave a strangled cough, saliva slipping from his mouth.

Saul took his phone out of his shirt pocket and called the Woodlea Vet Hospital number he'd stored in his contacts when he'd arrived in town. At the time he'd hoped he'd never have a need for a vet, and if he had, that it wouldn't be Ella. Nearly three months later and nothing had changed. Even though they'd cleared the air about their kiss, and he was determined to stay within the boundaries of their friendship, when around Ella his best intentions never failed to vanish.

'Woodlea Vet Hospital. Penny speaking.' Penny's voice sounded bright and chirpy.

'Hi, Penny, Saul from Windermere here. I've another bison that needs looking at if any of the vets are free. The bull appears to have something stuck in his throat.'

'Let me check who's available.'

Murmured talking sounded. 'Ella can come out now.'

'Thank you.'

He ended the call. Right now seeing Ella was the least of his worries. He had to get Hercules and his herd into the yards and in a low stress way that didn't increase the bull's surliness. He headed for the tractor that still had the hay forks attached. As he approached a black-and-white peewee perched on the side mirror took a final look at his reflection before flying away. With a bale of hay positioned on the front, Saul drove into the laneway. The bison herd surged forwards looking for food.

Saul opened the gate and slowly made his way in the direction of where he wanted the herd to go. The cows followed, with Hercules trailing behind. Saul unloaded the hay into the steel hay feeder positioned in the largest yard. While the cows helped themselves to their early dinner, the bull stood by himself, his neck extended and breathing laboured.

Saul checked his watch. Until Duke raced off to the front gate to let him know Ella was there, there was no point moving Hercules into the smaller yards. The less time the bull was contained the better.

Saul had only just finished sliding the central race gates open when Duke bolted towards the cattle grid. Ella would soon arrive.

Working carefully, Saul moved Hercules and some of the quietest cows through the series of smaller yards to the round pen that fed into the narrow race. He gave Ella a brief nod as she came over to the fence. She'd approached from behind so as not to spook the herd. Dressed in her usual Woodlea vet cap, pink work shirt, jeans and boots, her expression was serious as she returned his nod.

Two cows headed into the round pen but at the last minute Hercules baulked. He threw himself at the side fence in an attempt to jump over. Steel rattled and dust tainted the air. Saul's chest pounded. Logic told him that he'd planned the yards with the utmost detail. Hercules would not breach the fence. But his fear argued if he did, he'd be in the same yard as Ella. He hadn't processed that he'd moved to the fence ready to scale the steel until he felt the solidity of metal beneath his hand.

The cows behind Hercules moved forwards, encouraging the bull to walk through with them. Saul followed and slid the race doors shut at regular intervals to prevent the bison from moving backwards. He then walked along the chute opening the side panels to let the bison cows out. There was no mistaking which portion of the race Hercules occupied. Metal rattled as he bucked and kicked. Saul opened the sliding gates to allow the bull to charge forwards. When the bull's feet scuffed the rubber floor of the end chute he caught the bison's head in the headgate and body in the hydraulic squeeze.

Saul moved to swing open the crash gate to allow Ella access to Hercules's head. The harsh rasp of Hercules's breathing was the only sound as Ella joined him. She gave Saul the briefest of glances before opening the drop-down side panel to administer a sedative into the bison bull's tail.

She'd just finished when Hercules shifted and went to kick out. Even though Ella's hand was halfway out of the chute, the bull trapped her fingers between his bulk and the metal. Saul moved quickly. He used his body weight to push against the bison so Ella could slip her fingers free.

He spun around, his hand reaching for her waist while his other one cupped her elbow as she held her fingers flat. For a moment her pain-darkened eyes met this and she swayed towards him. Then she stiffened, took a step back and shook her fingers.

'I haven't jammed my fingers since I was a kid. That will teach me to be so slow.'

Saul didn't reply, just studied her. There was a tightness to her mouth that if he was a betting man he'd say wasn't caused by pain.

She bent to collect the syringe that had fallen at her feet and he lost sight of her expression. 'Let's get Hercules sorted and out of here. Did you notice anything wrong with him before he had trouble breathing?'

'Nothing. The drooling and coughing started no more than an hour ago.'

Ella bent to examine the bison's mouth and nose. The sedative had quietened Hercules's agitation, but Ella's movements remained efficient and methodical.

She opened the bison's mouth. 'Okay, Hercules, let's see if you've got anything stuck in here. Fingers crossed if you have, it's in your throat and not your oesophagus.'

Saul folded his arms to hide the unsteadiness of his hands. Ella appeared to not have suffered any serious harm but he hadn't recovered so quickly. His temples hammered as his blood pressure refused to subside. He'd seen enough ranch hands with digits missing thanks to farm accidents. Seeing Ella's fingers caught in the chute reawakened the cold fear he'd felt the day the young bison had attempted to kick her.

He uncrossed his arm to ruffle Duke's head as he leaned against his legs.

Ella carefully pulled her gloved hand from out of Hercules's mouth and held up a dark chunk of wood. The bull now breathed normally. 'As far as foreign objects go, this would never have fit down Hercules's throat.'

She checked inside Hercules's mouth again before straightening to remove her glove. 'As soon as the sedative wears off he'll be back to his usual charming self.'

Saul released Hercules. The bull charged out of the chute and then, movements stiff and slow, made his way over to where the cows stood in the adjacent yard.

When Saul turned, Ella had already collected the items she'd used.

'How's the hand?' he asked, wishing her cap brim wasn't quite so low so he could see her eyes.

'All good.' She gave Duke a pat. 'I'd better head back. I think every dog in Woodlea has been booked in to see me today.'

He slid his hands deep into his jeans pockets. He had to respect she had a busy day even if he wanted to keep her talking. He accompanied her over to the vet ute.

After she'd closed the back canopy she looked across at him. 'See you Saturday?'

'You will.'

He hoped his reply didn't sound hoarse. She might be standing beside him but she suddenly seemed so far away. His fingers ached to slide through the heavy silk of her hair and his skin yearned for the warmth of her touch.

He glanced at her hand. 'Stay away from cranky bison for the rest of the day.'

'That's a given.'

Long after the dust had settled he stared down the driveway. Duke sat silent beside him, also looking in the direction Ella had taken. Today she'd been in professional mode. He wouldn't have expected anything less. Yet again she'd dealt with a bison emergency with a competence and expertise that he was grateful for. Hercules had been an intimidating and unpredictable patient and even after her hand had been trapped, she hadn't lost her composure.

His jaw locked. But he had. There was no reason why Ella treating him as a client and as a friend should leave him feeling uneasy and hollow. There was no justification for the restlessness that left him feeling as though something he didn't even know he was searching for had slipped out of reach.

# CHAPTER
## 14

'To past memories and the creation of new ones,' Fliss said, making a toast with her champagne flute filled with sparkling water.

As glasses clinked, contentment relaxed Ella far more than any bottle of bubbly. She'd missed the feeling of female camaraderie. In the bedrooms of her small house in town they'd donned ball gowns and race-day outfits, drunk champagne and dipped strawberries in chocolate. Now her friends were in her new home and dressed in western shirts, jeans and their best boots for the beer night and bush dance.

She touched glasses with Cressy who too was drinking sparkling water. For the next charity ball in spring there would be a tiny addition to their close-knit group.

Ella turned to clink glasses with Neve and Sibylla and then with Freya and Bethany. The past year had brought precious new friendships and already new memories were being made. She pushed aside the thought that apart from Taylor, who technically wasn't single, she was the only one there tonight who remained on her own.

Taylor raised her crystal flute filled with champagne. She wasn't on designated driver duty. 'To Ella having many more get-togethers here.'

Glasses again clinked and smiles shared.

'Does anyone know what time the boys are supposed to be getting there?' Neve asked as she dipped a cracker in homemade pesto. 'Tanner was very vague.'

The boys were all at the Royal Arms and those not driving were catching a shuttle bus to the showground.

Sibylla smiled. 'I bet he was. They make me laugh. As if we don't know they think dancing ranks right up there with trying on wedding suits.'

Freya, the teacher from the Reedy Creek school, nodded. 'Drew wouldn't give me a time, either. I'm sure they think they can quietly slip into the crowd and we won't know they're there.'

'Don't worry,' Bethany said, words merry. 'I have a plan that will guarantee the boys will get on the dancefloor.'

Ella smiled. 'I wonder who that sounds like?'

'My mother … but she actually is my plan.'

Fliss laughed. 'I like it already.'

'Whatever it is, it's brilliant.' Taylor lifted her glass in a salute to Bethany.

'It's simple really,' Bethany said, looking around the room. 'The boys can either dance with us … or my mother.'

Cressy's eyes rounded. 'Edna dances?'

Bethany nodded. 'That's how she met my dad.'

Taylor shook her head. 'You learn something new every day.'

Bethany's smile widened. 'The boys are all too well-mannered to say no when Mum asks them to dance.'

Fliss refilled her sparkling water. 'I'd love to see their faces.'

Sibylla giggled. 'Tanner will be beside himself. He still swears Edna has a GPS tracker on his ute as she always knows when he's in town.'

Ella took a sip of her sparkling water and checked the phone sitting on the arm of her red chair. There would be no champagne for her even if she wasn't anyone's designated driver. She was the on-call weekend vet.

Her attention lingered on the blank screen as laughter swirled around her. She could add to the conversation about the boys all secretly being a little terrified of Edna. Saul also would be too polite to refuse Edna's request to dance even if he felt that she scrutinised his every move. A tug of loneliness detracted from her happiness. Even though she'd seen him when she'd treated Hercules, the depth with which she missed him had intensified this past week.

As much as her self-preservation argued she was doing the right thing by keeping things low-key between them, she hadn't been able to stop staring at his farmhouse when she switched on the veranda light or avoid the memory of Saul holding her like she belonged in his arms. She might now be free from Charles, but she was far from at peace. As illogical as it seemed, the only time she truly felt whole was when around Saul.

Feeling eyes on her, she looked up and caught both Fliss and Cressy studying her. She gave her best smile before she came to her feet and reached for the cheese platter to pass around. 'Eat up. We'd better get going otherwise the boys will beat us there.'

When she took the empty glasses into the kitchen, she didn't miss Fliss and Cressy sharing a look before Cressy followed her. Ella mentally braced herself. She was now comfortable talking about Charles but when she did she wanted to have her feelings for Saul under control as otherwise Cressy would sense she wasn't as settled as she should be.

Except as Cressy busied herself with wiping down the kitchen bench their chatter revolved around nursery colour schemes. It wasn't until Cressy turned to face her that Ella knew their conversation was about to turn serious.

'You look beautiful tonight and it's not just the way you've blow-dried your hair.' Cressy blinked as she paused. 'I'll keep this short as these pregnancy hormones make me so emotional I'll only end up crying. Something's changed with you and Fliss and I were worried it wasn't for the better, but now we hope it is.'

Ella concentrated on nodding and not glancing out the kitchen window in the direction of the boundary fence. 'Yes, something's changed. The jury's still out though on whether it's for the better.'

'If this helps, I was going to tell you when you were over for lunch, but a certain person passed the Reggie test. In fact it wasn't even a test. Reggie walked over to Saul even when he didn't have any carrots. Denham's still shaking his head that Reggie never accepted him so readily. As for how long Reggie took to accept carrots from Tanner ...'

Cressy's message was clear that not only did Saul have Reggie's approval, he also had hers and Fliss's. 'A certain person ... inspires trust. It's just that while things may have changed for me ... they haven't for him.'

A smile brought out the green in Cressy's hazel eyes. 'Denham suspects they have.'

Ella couldn't stem the telltale heat flooding her cheeks. The urgency and possessiveness in Saul's touch had communicated he hadn't exactly been thinking about his ex-wife when kissing Ella. 'Suspecting is good … but to be honest it's not really enough … for both of us.'

'It wouldn't be.' Cressy moved forward to give her a hug. 'But it's a start.'

Cressy's words echoed in Ella's head as the group drove in convoy to the showground on the other side of town. As much as a part of her wished Saul might see her as something more than a friend, the pain that continued to etch grooves beside his mouth said he was still a long way off being ready for anything more than what they had.

Ahead of her the brake lights on Fliss's four-wheel drive flashed red as she slowed to enter the venue for the beer night and bush dance. Once through the showground gates, Ella turned to her right to park near the exit so she would have no trouble leaving should there be an animal emergency. Here in town, she'd be closer to the vet surgery than if she'd been at home.

By the time she'd walked through the car park to join the others, red dust coated her boots and the overhead sky appeared as though it had been painted in pinks and gold by a gentle hand. It wouldn't be long before the outdoor lights draped between the gum trees emitted a cheerful glow.

To the left of the corrugated iron show pavilion the flags and banners of independent breweries and cider makers flapped in the breeze. So far the only noise was of the crowd but soon the bush band would crank up in the pavilion. Her gaze swept over the clusters of men holding their plastic cups filled with beer or cider. Not that much of the male-dominated crowd would be keen to head inside.

She waved as she caught sight of Sophie with a group of other teenage cowgirls who hovered outside the pavilion entrance. All held water bottles while they ate small tubs of ice cream. Sophie cast her a bright grin. At least someone had come for the bush dance.

Ella scanned the crowd. She was almost certain Saul and the others weren't there. Then, she caught sight of a familiar dark head and pair of broad shoulders. The boys had arrived and had tucked themselves away at the far corner of the beer stalls.

Ella met up with Fliss, Cressy and Bethany outside a food van that filled the air with the aroma of spiced meat. Taylor and Neve were already in the line queuing for nachos and burritos. When a fiddle sounded from within the pavilion, cheers sounded. All around Ella men remained silent and seemed to stand in a closer huddle.

'Girls … there you are.' Edna's exuberant voice called above the music.

She bustled over from where she'd been talking to Mrs Knox. Instead of her usual tailored town clothes, Edna wore a long denim skirt, a white linen shirt with her pearls and a fancy pair of hand-stitched red boots.

Bethany whispered to Ella. 'I didn't know Mum owned a pair of boots.'

Edna air-kissed everyone and when it was Ella's turn she also squeezed her arm. 'I know you're working but remember to have some fun.'

The older woman surveyed the group. 'Right. Let's get these men of yours onto the dancefloor. Once they go, others will follow.'

She marched through the crowd.

Cressy grinned. 'I've got to see this.'

They followed Edna and then stopped a discreet distance away, keeping a group of men between them and where Denham, Tanner, Finn and Saul stood. Except when Ella glanced across at Saul he'd half turned and looked straight at her. For a moment their eyes held. When he smiled Ella couldn't stop a flare of happiness or her own smile.

By now Edna had reached the boys. Neve laughed as they exchanged alarmed looks. Edna's exact words were indistinguishable but when she spoke to Denham his expression of horror caused Cressy to grin. 'This is priceless. Look ... he's looking around so he can say he's about to head inside with me.'

Cressy walked over and the relief on Denham's face as he put his arm around her shoulders and headed to the pavilion was indeed priceless.

Edna only had to turn to Tanner and he strode away in search of Neve. The group quickly disbanded as the others followed to find partners so they wouldn't have to dance with Edna.

With a satisfied smile, Edna went to stand beside Noel as he talked to Clive and old Will.

Ella didn't realise Saul stood behind her until she heard his amused words. 'Well played.'

Ella turned, her heart light. Saul seeking her out shouldn't make her feel so happy. 'Who knew that dancing with Edna would prove so terrifying?'

'For the record, I would have danced with her.'

The laughter in Saul's eyes made it hard to keep her breathing even. 'That's what they'll all be saying tomorrow to save face.'

Saul chuckled before he stared over her shoulder and offered her his arm. 'Unless you want to dance with Joe, it might be an idea to follow the others.'

Without hesitation, she curled her hand around the muscled strength of his forearm. Tonight he wore a crisp blue-and-white checked shirt she hadn't seen before. She breathed in his fresh woody scent as she strolled beside him. She kept her hand in place until they neared the historic pavilion. When she lowered her arm she didn't miss Saul's sideways glance.

The once quiet pavilion pulsed with energy and life. Round white lanterns hung from wooden beams, casting light over the musicians who filled the makeshift stage and the groups of dancers. Boots thumped on the wooden floor and hands clapped as couples wove in and out amongst each other.

Ella swallowed as her feet dragged. The reality was that in avoiding Joe she had literally put herself in Saul's hands. It had been years since she'd been bush dancing and she'd forgotten how tactile it was. Penny gave her a broad smile from where she linked arms with a young man Ella didn't recognise.

Fliss and Hewitt moved to create a space between them and Cressy and Denham. Ella had no choice but to follow Saul and to take her place next to him. To her relief the music stopped. Keeping her head high, she told herself to smile and that she'd only be in his arms for a few minutes before she moved on to her next partner.

Then the bush band started to play again and she realised it was a swing waltz that was a set dance and didn't require any partner swapping. If Saul was uncomfortable at their close proximity, it didn't show as he took her hands and guided her through the directions called over the microphone. He caught her eye and when he gave her a quick smile, she forced herself to relax.

The joy on the faces around her proved infectious. The stress associated with the lack of rain seemed to have lifted, giving people a brief respite. Laughter merged with the upbeat tempo of the music.

Even the boys, as much as they'd resisted the idea of dancing, were enjoying themselves. Hewitt grinned while whatever Denham said to Cressy caused her to laugh so much she missed a step.

The song ended. Saul released her hands and stood an arm's distance away. Needing something to focus on other than wanting to again feel his touch, she checked her phone to make sure she hadn't missed any work calls before the next song started. This time the set was a progressive barn dance and all too soon Saul twirled her and she moved on to the next partner in the circle.

As she danced with Hewitt she tried not to notice how well Saul moved and how much his smile altered the serious lines of his face. After another twirl she was on to a new partner. In some cases the next twirl couldn't come soon enough. When Joe's idea of personal space didn't match hers, her pointed stare had him move further away.

After dancing with Denham she was back to where she'd started in the circle. Numerous masculine hands had held hers and rested at her waist but when Saul's arms reached for her it was as though she'd come home. Throat tight, she placed one hand on his shoulder and her other in his. When his fingers closed over hers with such care, she couldn't stop herself from shaking. Dancing with Saul was so much more than a physical connection. His touch stripped her bare and triggered emotions that refused to remain orderly.

Staring at a fixed point on his chin, she willed herself to complete the required moves. As if from a distance, the music stopped. Saul's arms lowered and she felt the loss of their warmth and protection as though he'd pushed her away.

She gave what she hoped passed as a regular smile and then, calling herself a coward, she slid her phone out of her pocket and walked away as if she had a message to listen to.

Once away from the busy beer and cider stalls she abandoned any pretence of listening to her voicemail and returned the phone to her shirt pocket. The further she walked into the car park, the more the music faded and the brighter the stars gleamed above her. She inhaled the soothing scent of eucalyptus and forced her tense shoulders to lower. The charade was over. She had to stop pretending.

From the beginning Saul had affected her like no man ever had and she'd never been able to regroup. As much as he made her feel as though her world was spinning, he also gave her the strength to not always have a plan. Edna had been right; there'd been another reason why she'd had her hair cut. She'd been subconsciously testing him.

She'd wanted him to treat her differently when she wasn't so glamorous. She'd wanted a reason to find fault with him. It would be the only way to stop the disintegration of her defences. Instead he'd treated her the same regardless of how she looked. He'd proved he valued her friendship, and who she was as a person, more than her outward appearance. And by doing so the damage he'd done had been immeasurable.

She reached the vet ute and leaned against its solidity, her hands fisting as her eyes closed. What she'd felt for Charles had been a young and naive infatuation. What she felt for Saul was intense, agonising and soul deep. It was an emotion that if she didn't recognise and accept she'd have no hope of controlling.

Her breath emerged as a ragged sigh. As if from a long distance away her mobile rang.

She loved him.

Saul didn't wait for any signal from Denham that he should go after Ella. To anyone else nothing would have appeared to be wrong. Her smile contained its usual serenity and she was the on-call vet so it made sense that she might have to up and leave. But he knew better.

When he'd first clasped her hands, her tension had been unmistakable. Then as the song had progressed the tilt to her chin had lowered and the stiffness of her spine had eased. He'd kept a close eye on her as she'd progressed around the barn dance circle, especially when she'd danced with Joe, but she'd seemed to remain comfortable. It was only when she'd returned to him that tension had again vibrated through her.

The conclusion was unmistakable. Out of all the men here tonight he was the one who still made her feel wary. As much as he believed they'd cleared the air between them, the truth was they hadn't. The thought that he still unsettled her unleashed his emotions and locked his jaw. She was supposed to feel safe with him. Strides long, he headed out of the pavilion. He'd cleared the brick entrance when a figure stepped in front of him.

He stopped and met Noel's cool grey stare. Noel didn't speak, just took a swallow of his coffee.

Saul folded his arms. There was no point denying his intention was to follow Ella.

'Give her five minutes,' Noel said, voice low and firm. 'If Ella had to leave because of work you won't hold her up. If she didn't ... give her some space.'

'I'll wait for three.'

Noel simply took another mouthful of coffee. His attention never left Saul's face. A tense silence lengthened between them. As talkative as Edna was, Noel could say nothing but still communicate as effectively as his wife.

His eyes glinted. 'If you state the obvious and say that my wife talks more than I do, it's back to five minutes.'

Saul allowed himself a brief smile. 'Three minutes is up.'

Noel didn't move. 'Ella's like a daughter to me. I won't have her hurt.'

'As I said before, I'm an old bull rider with a bison farm to run.'

Noel held his gaze before stepping aside. 'For an old bull rider you sure walk fast.'

Saul nodded before continuing on his way. When he'd bought his cupcakes, Penny had mentioned that Ella was the on-call vet this weekend. So he'd kept watch for when she arrived in the vet hospital vehicle and parked near the exit.

Once away from the beer and cider festivities, the glow of the portable lights illuminated his way through the rows of cars. The flash from a phone and Ella's quiet voice then had him detour to his left. As he drew near Ella ended her call and slipped her phone into her shirt pocket before facing him.

She appeared to smile, but even in the gloom the strain tensing her face was unmissable. 'My dancing night's over. I've a pony to see.'

'I've called it a night too.'

She reached for the door handle, signalling she had to get going. He thrust his hands into his jeans pockets and silenced his need to make sure she was okay. Even though her words had emerged flat, it wasn't appropriate to engage her in conversation when there was an animal who needed her.

She slowly turned back to him. 'Can I ask a favour?'

'Of course.'

'Where I'm going is on your way home. Hilda's son and husband have cattle out on the stock routes so she's alone. Her pony's been unwell for a long time and she's made the decision she doesn't want him to suffer anymore.'

'I can come and hold him.'

'Thank you … Hilda's upset enough as it is. It's the farm on the left with the silver milk can for a mailbox.'

'I'll be right behind you.'

He headed to his F-truck before the emotion deepening his words would be apparent on his face. Not even the darkness would conceal his relief that Ella felt she could call on him.

He caught up to her on the outskirts of town and followed her tail-lights to the turn-off to Hilda's farm. An elderly lady waited for them at the bottom of the sensor-lit garden, a torch in her hand. Grief already etched her face into haggard, worn lines.

After Ella made a brief introduction, Hilda turned on her torch and they walked over to a paddock where a thin, white pony stood with his head down. The rattle as he drew breath echoed in the still night air.

Without being asked, Saul jogged back to his truck and drove it closer so his light bar would provide some light. Hilda buried her face in the pony's mane while she said her final goodbye. He stayed by his truck while Ella collected what she needed to euthanise the old pony from the back of the vet ute.

When Hilda was ready, she left the paddock. Without looking at either him or Ella, shoulders shaking, she retraced her slow steps to her farmhouse.

Ella sighed as he followed her through the paddock gate. 'We've kept Buffy comfortable for as long as we can. He's been going so well, but Hilda's right … it's time.'

When they reached the ill pony, he didn't flicker an ear or attempt to lift his head.

Ella placed the tarpaulin she carried on the ground and clipped a lead onto the pony's headcollar. She passed Saul the lead, stroked Buffy's nose and then, expression solemn, inserted the first of the two needles she held. As the sedative and then the barbiturates took effect, Saul smoothed the pony's neck until he relaxed and slowly sank to the ground as if in a deep sleep.

Ella spoke quietly. 'I'll leave a message for Denham. Hopefully he'll be free to bury him tomorrow. Otherwise, Tanner might be able to.'

Saul glanced over at the two sheds on the edge of the pool of light. He'd earlier noticed a backhoe in the second one. 'I can do it now.'

'Really? It's late.'

'I'd rather Hilda didn't have to come out in the morning and see Buffy like this, even if he will be covered by a tarp.'

Ella didn't immediately reply and when she did her voice was husky. 'Thank you. That will mean a lot to Hilda. I'll take her his headcollar and see if she'd like him buried now.'

It didn't take long for Ella to return. Keys glinted in her hands. 'Hilda's very grateful. She asked if you could please put him to rest between the two old gums. That was his favourite place.'

'No problem.'

He waited for Ella to hand him the keys. Instead she stared at him before stepping forward to brush her lips over his cheek. 'Your wife was a fool to ever let you go.'

Before he could respond, she pressed the keys into his hand, turned and disappeared into the darkness. The engine of the vet ute sounded before she drove away.

Once the red gleam of tail-lights had faded, he climbed into the backhoe and set about digging. The bone-dry ground was as hard and intractable as concrete. The clash of steel against dirt echoed his thoughts.

Trish wasn't the fool; he was. He should never have rushed into marriage or mistaken convenience for a deep connection. He should have heeded the signs that Trish wasn't the person he thought she was. Hindsight made for a cold and lonely companion even if it now helped him put his failed marriage into perspective. Unconditional love was just another term for being taken for a ride by someone you trusted.

He glanced along the road Ella had driven out on. As for who else was a fool, it was Charles. If there was anyone that should never have been let go, it was Ella.

His mobile rang from inside his pocket and he put it on speaker.

'What are you doing?' Denham's voice questioned. 'You sound like you're on a tractor?'

'Backhoe. I'm in Hilda's paddock.'

'That's a shame. Buffy was a cracker of a pony. Ella still there?'

'No.' Saul paused as loud laughter erupted in the background. 'How's those dancing boots of yours holding up?'

Denham groaned. 'Edna even talks when she dosidoes.' Cressy's voice sounded before Denham spoke again. 'We're heading back in. Talk to you tomorrow.'

Saul ended the call. As much as Denham had resisted having to dance, let alone partnering Edna, the smile in his voice confirmed he was having a good time.

Steel again warred with stubborn dirt and he focused on what he needed to do. After Buffy had been laid to rest, he returned the backhoe to the shed and tucked the keys away on the front doorstep. Despite the fatigue aching behind his eyes, as he drove home his thoughts refused to slow.

He couldn't shake the unease that Ella wasn't comfortable in his company. Despite her parting kiss and comment he couldn't erase the memory of how rigid she'd been when they'd danced. He hadn't imagined the connection between them. Only last weekend she'd been responsive and relaxed in his arms. They'd both also been comfortable about disclosing elements of their past as well as working together. Now it was as though their friendship hadn't existed. And he missed it.

He passed a hand around the back of his neck. If he was honest, he missed more than just the easy companionship he believed they'd shared. He missed Ella's laughter and her quick wit. He missed her smile that brought out the gold in her eyes. He missed her warmth and generosity that never failed to make the day a little brighter. He also missed having her fitted against him and kissing her until they both couldn't breathe.

He crested the hill and her sandstone cottage appeared to his left. The light from her front veranda spilled into the night. He slowed, his hold tightening on the steering wheel. Tonight the soft beams weren't just calling to Libby to come home. They were also beckoning to him. In the darkness of his world, Ella had become the light.

As much as she'd distracted him and as much as he'd fought to keep her at arm's length, she'd brought him back to life. The fear he'd experienced when she could have been injured while working with his bison wasn't the only intense emotion to have broken through his control. He also felt contentment and need, but most of all love. He'd vowed to never feel such things again but for the first time they felt natural and right. Gone were the doubts and whispers he'd put down to normal relationship jitters. When he was with Ella nothing else mattered.

Mouth dry, he looked away from the veranda light. But admitting how much Ella meant to him wasn't going to address the return of her wariness. As much as he loved her, friendship remained the only thing on offer. There were still parts of each other's lives that they weren't yet ready to divulge. Neither of them were truly free.

# CHAPTER
## 15

Ella shifted the basket she balanced on her hip into a more comfortable position as she took the long way round to the hills hoist clothesline in the back garden. A loud buzzing in the Chinese elm suggested that the swarm of bees from down the road had left the mailbox and found a new home.

While she hung up the load of washing, the sun warmed the bare skin of her arms and brought out the aroma of lavender from the purple garden border beside her. It felt strange to be wearing casual clothes on a Wednesday, let alone be doing her weekend chores, but she'd taken the day off. She stilled as a bee hovered close by.

She went back to hanging out her clothes. The first official reason for the day off was because Fliss, who was in Dubbo for secret wedding business, was collecting Violet's granddaughter from the airport. Fliss would take Gemma to see Violet before dropping her at Ella's where she'd stay until Friday. The second official reason was that next weekend was the museum opening and Edna's surprise party and Ella had to finalise the guest list.

She rested the empty basket on her hip as she retraced her steps through the cool and green garden. As for the unofficial reason, for the past five weekends she'd seen Saul and would do so again this Saturday. After the high emotion of last weekend, she needed a day to regroup.

The core of tension that occupied her midriff after she'd acknowledged what she felt for him hadn't eased. Somehow she had to find a way to act as though nothing had changed between them the night of the bush dance. As for when he'd helped her with Buffy, emotions raw and hovering far too close to the surface, she was lucky it was his cheek she'd kissed and not his mouth. She was also grateful she hadn't said more than she had. She ran a restless hand through her loose hair. She never wanted to feel so out of control around him again.

Once inside she checked the guest bedroom and headed to the kitchen to take the feta and spinach quiche out of the oven. Tyres crunched on the driveway. She walked past the boxes piled at the back door of the sunroom. Violet still didn't feel like sorting through any more boxes. Hopefully Gemma's visit would restore her high spirits.

A tall brunette left the passenger seat of Fliss's four-wheel drive. Gemma's heart-shaped face reminded Ella of the photographs she'd seen of Annette and Libby. But as hard as she looked she couldn't see any resemblance to Jeb. Perhaps it was from him that Gemma had inherited her height.

Ella crossed the lawn to meet her. Gemma's quick smile was warm as she gave Ella a hug. 'It's so lovely to finally meet you.'

Ella returned her embrace. 'Violet's told me so much about you.'

'Thanks so much for looking out for Oma and for having me to stay.'

'It's my pleasure.'

Fliss joined them and handed Gemma her duffle bag with a smile. 'Your bag's a little lighter now.'

Gemma nodded, her expression turning serious. 'I hope Oma liked her presents. I would have come sooner if I realised how frail she's become. She always tells me she's fine.'

Ella and Fliss swapped glances. Gemma was studying medicine and it was just like Violet to not want to distract her granddaughter from her studies.

Fliss tucked her arm in Gemma's. 'You're here now.'

As they entered the farmhouse Gemma looked around, her gaze soft. 'I always loved coming here as a child, and so did Mum.'

A lump in her throat, Ella led the way through the cottage. She could only imagine Violet and Lloyd's joy whenever Gemma and Annette had come to stay. Despite the loss of Libby, they'd remained a close and loving family.

She opened the door to the guest room. 'In the boxes are some of your mum's things that Violet thought you might like.'

'Thank you.' Gemma didn't enter the room but instead turned to look through the open doorway behind her. Sadness turned the corners of her mouth down as she studied Libby's untouched bedroom. 'My Aunt Libby mightn't have been here with us but I felt as though she was. Oma always sat a place at the dinner table for her.'

Ella answered with a single nod. When her brother had gone missing she'd stopped eating at the dining room table as she couldn't bear to see his chair empty. He'd always sat opposite her, and even when young, there'd been a mischievous glint in his brown eyes. As much as Ella had been bookish, conservative and serious, he'd been outgoing, loud and a risk-taker.

She swallowed as precious memories caused loss to burn behind her eyelids. Aiden's energy and enthusiasm had always catapulted her out of her comfort zone even when she'd been determined to remain there. He was the reason why she could snowboard as well as ski, why she had a small scar on her arm from falling out of a tree and why she'd disregarded her parents' wishes for her to study law and had become a vet. He'd always told her that the real killer of dreams wasn't failure, but doubt.

Needing to keep busy, she left Gemma to settle in and headed to the kitchen where she could hear the kettle boiling. Fliss was making herself at home.

She paused at the doorway to take a deep and silent breath. When she walked through, Fliss gave her a long look before making Ella her tea just how she liked it. When Gemma went outside to visit Cinnamon and Nutmeg, Ella sliced the oven-warm quiche while Fliss added the last touches to a green salad.

They sat around the small kitchen table and enjoyed their home-cooked lunch while they talked about Gemma's university life in Brisbane. It wasn't until their plates were empty and the kettle again bubbled that the conversation turned to Libby.

Gemma took a sip of her water before looking between Ella and Fliss. 'Do you really think Libby was pregnant?'

Fliss nodded, while Ella spoke. 'We have no proof, just a hunch and circumstantial evidence.'

'And you think Jeb was the father.'

'We do.' Ella studied Gemma as her restless fingers tapped on the table. 'Do you know something?'

Gemma's fingers stilled before she looked up. 'I'm not sure it's relevant but it involves Jeb, so it might be.' She paused to chew on her lip. 'I told Mum I wouldn't tell Oma, she'd already felt she'd disappointed her enough, but … she never really knew who my father was.'

Fliss and Ella remained silent to allow Gemma to talk.

'Mum had grown tired of Jeb's partying so they were on a break, even though he hadn't taken her seriously when she said they needed time apart. I think it was after some sort of family dinner that he called drunk and threatened to come round. So she snuck out to see him. For some reason Libby went with her. When they got to his place his mother was at work and Jeb was passed out on the floor. They couldn't move him so Mum asked a school friend to help. Libby left and Mum walked out with the friend. They were sitting in his car talking, and the way Mum describes it she never planned for anything to happen, but she'd had the biggest crush on this guy. She said it was only the one time and he'd used protection so when she found out she was pregnant, she assumed the baby was Jeb's.'

Gemma looked between the two of them, her serene smile at odds with what she'd just told them.

'Your mum's assumption was wrong, wasn't it?' Fliss said quietly.

Gemma nodded. 'The school friend from that night is Simon, who Mum married. When Mum left Jeb, Simon was there for her and after a long-distance relationship, he moved to Brisbane. A year after Mum died, Simon and I did a DNA test. He's my father.'

'That's such a lovely ending,' Fliss said, eyes overbright.

Ella thought hard. 'When's your birthday, Gemma?'

Gemma answered with a date that was roughly nine months after Libby went missing.

Ella looked over at Fliss. 'That family dinner must have been Libby's sixteenth birthday celebration.'

'It would have to be.' Fliss pushed back her chair and came to her feet to collect their empty plates. 'And I don't think Libby went home.'

Ella also stood to help clear the table. 'I don't, either. She would have been concerned about Jeb. He also wasn't technically her sister's boyfriend anymore.'

Gemma spoke, expression contemplative. 'I'm actually sure she didn't go home. Mum wasn't proud of the fact she went back to Jeb but she really thought I was his. Mum also could never understand why, but he'd always believed they'd gotten back together that night.'

Fliss returned to her seat with a box of the fancy donuts she'd bought in Dubbo. 'Because the person he thought he was making up with wasn't Annette but Libby.'

'Exactly.' Ella sat a teapot covered in a bright red-and-pink tea cosy beside the donuts. Her excitement buzzed and thoughts raced. Maybe this was the missing piece of the Libby puzzle. 'This also explains why Libby could have been pregnant. I wonder ... Violet said it wasn't long after Libby disappeared that they discovered your mum was expecting. Maybe Libby knew earlier and that was why she felt she had no choice but to leave. Not only would Jeb have not treated her any differently, as he'd thought she'd been Annette, but Violet and Lloyd would now have had two pregnant daughters.'

Fliss offered Gemma a donut. 'Not only that, Jeb appeared to be the father of both babies. They would have been the talk of the town.'

'They would have.' Gemma placed a donut on her plate. 'But Aunt Libby would have known deep in her heart that her baby would have been accepted and loved by Oma and Opa. If

Aunt Libby was alive … she'd have come home by now. I'm sure of it.'

Ella leaned over to squeeze Gemma's shoulder before pouring everyone their tea.

Fliss added milk to her mug. 'I didn't say anything to Violet earlier, but through social media I've found Jeb's wife. Except if Jeb was too drunk to know it was Libby he'd slept with, he'd have no idea she was pregnant let alone have mentioned to a new partner he might have another child.'

While they drank their tea and ate the donuts, a sombre silence settled over them.

Fliss looked over the top of her floral china mug at Ella. 'I'll dig a little deeper into the birth and adoption records. Maybe Libby used a different name. At least we have a more specific timeframe for when her baby could have been born. Then this friend in Sydney Violet mentioned … Fee, wasn't it? That's another possible angle.'

Gemma reached out to touch both of their hands. 'Thank you … for all that you're doing for Oma.'

Not realising what she was doing, Ella looked out the kitchen window towards Saul's paddocks. It was only Fliss's sideways glance that made her aware that she not only hadn't answered Gemma but she was staring at the boundary fence.

She focused back on Gemma and spoke quickly. 'You're very welcome. I'm sure Violet's mentioned Saul … he's also been helping to piece everything together.'

'I'm looking forward to meeting him and his dog Duke.'

Ella refilled Gemma's mug before asking what she would like to do while in town. Now was an opportune time to change the topic before Fliss studied her any more or her cheeks could become any warmer.

When they'd finished their tea, Fliss left to return to Bundara and Gemma went to her room to rest. Ella washed the dishes and once the kitchen was spotless, she found herself standing near where her phone lay on the kitchen bench. She needed to let Saul know about the latest development. Last week she would have gone to see him but after admitting to herself that she loved him it would be better if she called. If she couldn't remain composed when mentioning his name, she had no hope when she talked to him face to face. Before she could overthink things, she dialled his number.

He answered after two rings.

'Hi, Ella, everything okay?'

The concern deepening his voice stole her breath. The warmth and care in his tone hit her deep inside with the accuracy of a slingshot. It would take far longer than one day to regroup.

She cleared her throat. 'I'm fine. I've got the day off. Gemma's here and I just wanted to pass on some new information.'

Even knowing she was babbling wasn't enough to silence her. She worried the inside of her cheek to stop herself from talking.

'How's Gemma?' Saul asked. 'Did she have a good flight?'

'She did.' Then, making sure she stuck to the facts, she relayed the news they'd learned over lunch.

'So Jeb was basically too drunk to tell the difference between a shy sixteen-year-old and her older sister.' Censure roughened Saul's words.

'That's what it looks like. Violet has always said Libby seemed herself before she disappeared so whatever happened with Jeb hadn't been unsettling. Violet also said Libby had been quiet and engrossed in a book the week prior to her leaving but this wasn't unusual.'

'That fits with her having discovered she was pregnant. Maybe she'd also started to feel unwell.'

'It does. Fliss is going to do some more internet digging, while I'll see if I can find Libby's old school friend.'

'Let me know if you need help with anything.'

'Will do.' She mentally crossed her fingers at the white lie. Until she was confident she could hide how she felt she would be flying solo as much as she could.

'How's mission impossible going?'

'My afternoon job is to wrangle the guest list. Bethany's implemented our ace card by taking Mrs Knox into her confidence, saying she's planning a get-together for a select few on Edna's actual birthday. Needless to say within ten minutes Mrs Knox passed on the details to Edna. So if Edna discovers any party plans, she'll assume they're for the smaller gathering.'

Saul's low chuckle resulted in a ripple of goosebumps across her arms. His laughter was a sound she'd never get tired of hearing. One day she hoped he'd have more of a reason to laugh. 'I didn't think keeping a secret from Edna could be done, but you and Bethany might just pull this off.'

'Here's hoping.' Feeling her composure unravel faster than a ball of Violet's knitting wool, she kept speaking. 'I'd better let you get back to whatever you were doing.'

'Thanks ...' It was just her wishful thinking that a note of regret edged his reply. 'I've got a load of gypsum being delivered.'

'See you Saturday?' The words slipped out before she could hold them back.

'You will. I'm looking forward to seeing Edna's face.'

'Me too.'

Ella ended the call. She stared at the black screen and then, shoulders squared, went to switch on her laptop. The more she focused on what she needed to do the less she'd heed the deep longings that wished there wasn't a high boundary fence separating them.

'That's a job well done,' Saul said as he and Duke walked away from the machinery shed where they'd unhooked the spreader trailer from the tractor. For the past two days they'd spread a fine white cloud of gypsum to improve soil structure and water drainage.

The Australian shepherd looked up at him and Saul ruffled his head. Duke had been his constant companion even when he'd spent hours in the tractor.

Guinea fowls squabbled from somewhere in the front garden and Duke darted away. Saul shook his head. Duke's obsession with the speckled birds was only rivalled by his fascination with Ella. Saul scraped a hand across his stubbled chin. It was a fixation he shared. He kept watch for when Duke ran along the fence to welcome her home and then again for when she'd flick on the front veranda light.

Hearing Ella's voice on the phone last Wednesday hadn't come close to being enough. As much as he knew he shouldn't, he was counting down the days until the museum opening tomorrow. Not that he'd be spending much time with her at the event. As well as Ella being busy with Edna's party, he needed to be careful about how much contact they had. Loving Ella meant fulfilling his promise to keep her safe, even if that meant concealing every emotion he'd acknowledged last weekend.

A stiff late-afternoon breeze tugged at the brim of his cap. Thankfully he'd spread the last of the gypsum before the wind picked up. They were in for a blistering weekend that would only deliver more heat, no matter how many rain dances from local businesses were doing the rounds on social media. He stared at the horizon that wasn't as crisp a line as usual. Dust had blown in from out west and now cast a dull, blurred haze.

Duke hadn't reappeared, so he headed for the cool of the hay shed. He needed to finalise the number of bales he was donating to the hay convoy. As he calculated how many large bales formed the hay wall in front of him, Duke returned to his side for a pat. Tongue lolling, the Australian shepherd headed deeper into the shed in search of mice.

Saul counted the hay bales again. He'd lost count when he'd been distracted wondering if Ella would be more relaxed around him next time he saw her. After this weekend, the run of town social functions would be over. Fliss had mentioned a possible barbeque, so unless he bumped into Ella in town or at the river, or Cinnamon and Nutmeg escaped again, he would probably see her there. He was mid-count when Duke yelped and his high-pitched bark echoed throughout the shed.

Saul moved quickly. Such a bark was either one of excitement or pain. Despite the day's heat, a chill feathered over his skin. It also wasn't Duke's usual response to finding a mouse or a bird.

At first it wasn't obvious what Duke had cornered against the shed wall. Then the unmistakable shape of a brown snake, its small head flattened, reared up from amongst the scattered hay. Heart hammering, he killed his instinctive response to whistle Duke away. It would only take a second of Duke being distracted and the snake could strike.

Duke's fluffy tail wagged as he continued to bark. The Australian shepherd had no idea of the danger he was in. If he was a different type of breed, like a Jack Russell, he'd have been intent on killing the snake, but he only wanted to play. Saul fisted his hands. There was nothing he could do except stay still. Any movement might divert Duke's attention. All he could hope for was that Duke would lose interest and let the snake go.

After what seemed like an eternity, the snake lowered itself to the ground. Duke stopped barking and retreated a few steps. The snake slithered through the gap now left between Duke and the corrugated iron wall. Hay rustled and burnished skin rippled as the snake headed for the open side of the shed.

When Duke went to follow, Saul gave him the command to stay. It wasn't blood that transported a snake's venom through a victim's body but the lymphatic system. The only way to stem such a flow was immobility. As he jogged over to the Australian shepherd, he glanced at his watch so he'd be able to keep track of time. He couldn't remember taking his phone out of his shirt pocket but suddenly it was in his hand. If that yelp had signalled that Duke had been bitten, every second became precious. They had at least a twenty-five-minute drive to the vet surgery.

He dialled the vet clinic. Penny answered with her usual cheery tone, but as soon as Saul said Duke could have been bitten by a brown snake she was all business. 'Bring him straight in. Ella can run some blood clotting tests.'

Saul didn't answer. Duke had slumped to the ground.

'Saul? You still there?'

'I am.' His voice was nothing but a hoarse rasp as he closed the distance between him and Duke. 'There's no doubt he's been bitten.'

He wedged his phone between his shoulder and ear before putting his arms around Duke. This time there was silence from Penny before Ella's serious voice sounded. 'Saul, how long has it been and was it definitely a brown?'

'Five minutes, and yes, a brown.'

'We'll be ready whenever you can get here.'

Saul didn't bother saying goodbye. He hefted Duke into his arms. The Australian shepherd didn't even wriggle. As fast as he could he headed to his F-truck.

The entire drive to town Saul kept his hand on Duke. Every spasm and contortion as the venom took effect carved off another sliver of hope. This was all his fault. If he hadn't been distracted thinking about Ella he would have taken more notice of where Duke was. His fingers dug into the thick softness of Duke's grey-and-white coat. He couldn't lose him. He was far more than just his best mate.

He pulled up outside the vet hospital. Duke didn't even lift his head. With the Australian shepherd limp in his arms, he raced up the path. Ella held the door open and a male vet nurse he didn't recognise took Duke from him. Ella gave him a quick look and he thought she might have squeezed his arm but then they disappeared through the door into the treatment room.

Hands in his hair, he stared at the closed door.

Footsteps sounded before Penny said softly beside him, 'Ella's the best. She'll do everything she can.'

He lowered his arms. His surroundings were now coming into focus. To his left sat a little girl in pigtails with a pug puppy sleeping on her lap. Her round eyes stared at him. On his other side sat an elderly woman who had a tabby cat in a carrier at her feet. Sympathy creased her lined face. The four walls closed in on him.

He glanced at Penny. 'Thank you for dropping everything and fitting him in. I'll be … in my truck.'

Steps leaden, he headed outside and past the red fire hydrant Duke always stopped to lift his leg on. When he reached his F-truck, instead of sitting inside he walked to the shade cast by a plane tree yarn-bombed in blue. He took out his phone and dialled his brother. Except it wasn't Nathan who answered.

'Hi, Uncle Saully.'

He took a moment before answering. He couldn't have Rosie sense his anguish. 'Hi, Rosie Posie.'

The five-year-old giggled as she always did when he called her his pet name. 'Are you coming to see us? Mum said Dad's bored and not a very good patient.'

'Maybe you could come and visit?'

'Yes please.' Rosie's enthusiasm failed to lift the heaviness that weighed upon his shoulders. 'I can see Duke and your bison calf, and we can make my princess castle. I also can see Ella.'

The mention of Ella's name diverted his thoughts from the very real possibility Duke might not be around. 'Ella or her goats?'

'All of them. Dad says you talk about her a lot. She must be nice.'

He briefly closed his eyes. Thanks to Rosie's illness and being bedridden, she didn't miss much, especially when it came to what others were discussing. As for his brother, Saul had no idea he'd picked up on how much he mentioned Ella. It was usually numbers Nathan remembered, not names.

'She is.'

Rosie gave a dramatic sigh. 'Dad says I have to hand the phone to him now.'

A smile broke through Saul's fears. He could almost feel the tightness of the hug she always gave him. 'Bye, Rosie Posie. See you soon.'

Nathan's voice replaced his daughter's. 'I'm not a bad patient but I would like to get this boot off.' His tone sobered. 'You don't normally call during the day.'

Saul swallowed. 'Duke's been bitten by a snake.'

'That's rough. I hope he makes it.'

His brother's simple but heartfelt response was exactly what he needed. He was only just keeping his emotions in order. 'Me too.'

'There's always a bed here for you if you need it.'

Talk then turned to what Rosie had been up to at preschool and Nathan's latest garden project fail. Saul didn't do much of the speaking but the conversation had the desired effect. Time passed.

When the front door of the surgery opened and Ella walked down the steps, he'd headed towards her even before he'd ended his call. When they met near the red fire hydrant he folded his arms to hide the unsteadiness of his hands. He couldn't read anything from Ella's closed expression other than that she appeared tired.

Her gaze searched his. 'Duke's okay. He had a lethal dose of venom and needed two vials of antivenin but his vital signs are now stable. He's on fluids so will need to stay overnight.'

'Thank you.'

He didn't care that his reply emerged deep and husky.

'Saul ...' She stopped and slid her hands into her jeans pockets as if rethinking what she was about to say. 'You're very welcome. You getting him into town so quickly was critical.' She took a step away. 'I'd best get back inside but I'll call in tonight with an update if you'd like.'

'I'd appreciate it.'

Then she was gone and all he was left with was the memory of the intensity of her brown eyes and a feeling of profound relief and gratitude. Duke had survived.

By the time darkness lay beyond the kitchen windows and the doorbell rang, fatigue blunted Saul's emotions. He padded along the hallway on bare feet. He'd been for a gruelling run and taken a long, hot shower to defuse his tension but still the chime of the melodic doorbell grated on his nerves. This was the first time it had been used. Normally Duke's barking signalled he had company.

He stopped at the door but didn't reach for the handle. His earlier strain had been understandable but now Duke was okay he couldn't allow Ella to see how gutted he still was. He couldn't have her know why Duke meant so much to him.

Chest tight, he opened the door.

'Hey,' Ella said, the sensor light teasing out glimmers of gold in her loose hair.

He stepped away from the doorway and the yearning to have her warmth thaw the coldness inside him. 'Come in.'

Neither spoke until they'd entered the kitchen.

'Coffee?' he asked, needing something to say and do.

She sat in what had become her usual chair at the table. 'I'd better not as otherwise I'll be awake until midnight.'

'Decaf tea?'

'Perfect.'

After he'd added milk to her tea, he made himself a strong coffee. Without Duke with him, he wouldn't be getting any sleep anyway so would catch up on some bookwork.

Ella studied him over the rim of her mug. 'The good news is Duke's on track to come home tomorrow morning. The bad news is that you'll have to keep him quiet for at least two weeks.'

'No problem.'

He clenched his teeth as he failed to achieve the casual tone he'd been aiming for.

'Duke's muscles might be sore and he'll have to be watched for any antivenin serum sickness.'

This time Saul only nodded. He couldn't trust his words would be any less raw or tense.

'Saul … these things happen. It's not your fault.'

His only answer was to stare into his coffee.

Metal dragged as Ella moved her chair around to his side of the table. She sat close enough so she could curl her hand around his forearm resting on the table. Her cherry blossom scent wrapped around him.

'Duke might be okay but you're not. Talk to me.'

Still not looking at her, he shook his head. His shoulders felt as rigid as the pale stone on the kitchen benchtops.

Ella's only response was to move her chair closer before her fingertips brushed the edge of his jaw. 'You're safe with me … remember.'

It wasn't her words that proved his undoing, but the echo of hurt and of something else that remained indefinable. She'd allowed him to help her when she'd been vulnerable and concerned about her scar, and here he was blocking her out. Through letting him in, her message had been that she could trust him. His message in return now was that she didn't belong in his life. Which was in no way the truth.

'It's a long story …' he said, in a rasping voice that didn't sound like his own.

'I've got nowhere else to be.'

The sincerity in her answer lifted his gaze to hers and unlocked the emotions he hadn't revealed to anyone but his brother.

'After I retired from bull riding I went to work on a bison ranch in Wyoming. The rancher, Adam, was a widower but he had a daughter ...'

'Trish.'

He nodded. 'Maybe it was expectations, convenience, or we really did have something, but we were married in the local small-town church. I bought into the ranch and ran it full time. An old bull-riding mate, Jamie, dealt with the marketing side. One summer Trish fell pregnant ... we were so excited ... then she miscarried. It took a while but she fell pregnant again and Caleb was born.' Saul paused to find the right words. 'Seeing him arrive, cutting his cord and feeling his heart beat against mine were things I can never really describe.'

When his pause stretched into silence, Ella rubbed his forearm. After a moment, he spoke again. 'Caleb was three days old and Trish's hormones were making her feel like she couldn't cope, so I took him to a room across the hospital hallway and held him while he settled. Not wanting to move in case I woke him, I read through his paperwork that had been on the shelf below his crib. From my own injuries, and from Rosie being sick, I had a basic understanding of blood types. When I saw Caleb's blood type I realised ... he couldn't be my son.'

'Oh ... Saul.' Ella pressed a kiss to the place on his jaw where her fingers had touched.

'I went to see Trish. Jamie was holding her hand. The guilt on their faces when they noticed me standing at the doorway said it all. Not only had I made the mistake of trusting my wife, I'd also trusted a friend. We made it to the car park. Things remained civil until Jamie said he never wanted to be a father and that I had to stay with Trish as he didn't want the commitment that came with having a child. I decked him. The images snapped on nearby phones became favourite fodder for the local newspaper and social media. Then all the talk started …'

Ella again touched her lips to his jaw and this time didn't draw so far away. She stayed silent, letting him continue.

'I could handle Trish not loving me … but losing Caleb … I holed myself up at the ranch and did nothing but work. One night Adam came home with a rescue puppy. I was sitting on the porch, staring at nothing, and this warm bundle of energy landed in my lap, wriggled up to my face and licked my nose.'

Ella smiled. 'Duke.'

'He filled the emptiness in my arms.'

'And Trish and Caleb?'

'I made sure Jamie fulfilled his responsibilities. He bought out my share of the ranch and on Caleb's first birthday married Trish. Adam sends me photos of Caleb and lets me know how he's doing. He's a great little kid.'

'I'm sure he is.' The warmth of Ella's hand on his forearm slid upwards to encircle his biceps as she leaned in closer. 'I'm guessing the only time you and Duke have been apart was when he had to go into quarantine to enter Australia.'

'That's right.'

'I'll stay if you want, so you're not alone tonight. I can sleep on the couch.'

As the intensity of his emotions receded, it was as though a switch flicked on. He became acutely aware of just how near Ella was, of the full curve of her bottom lip, of the way her attention dipped to his mouth. He also became aware of the peace that had replaced the weight of his loss. Sharing his story with Ella, trusting her with his past, had been what he'd needed to truly set him free.

Her eyes again met his. In the golden-brown depths he saw the shimmer of his own need and longings. She no more wanted to stick to their friendship agreement than he did. Neither had to say the words that if they took this step, there'd be no going back. He turned his head to brush his mouth over hers and to give her a chance to move away. She didn't.

They stared at each other, their breaths already uneven.

'Saul Armstrong,' she whispered, closing the distance between them, 'if you expect me to sleep on the couch, I'm telling Rosie her uncle needs some serious lessons in how to treat a princess.'

# CHAPTER
## 16

Ella awoke to a strip of pale light above an unfamiliar bedroom blind, the subdued hum of an air conditioner and the warmth of an arm looped around her waist.

Still drugged with sleep, she felt around to make sure that a sheet covered her scar. When her fingers encountered smooth cotton instead of marked skin, she relaxed. She eased her head back a little on the pillow to look at the man sleeping beside her. In the dim light Saul's masculine face was all shadowed angles and stubbled lines. For the first time since she'd met him, he looked peaceful.

She swallowed as emotions swirled in her stomach and caused her throat to constrict. If she hadn't already fallen for him, after the night they'd shared she'd be head over heels. She'd never known a man's touch could communicate so much tenderness, need and honesty. He hadn't just physically beguiled her senses, he'd touched her soul.

She fought a wave of panic that prickled over her skin. She could do this. She could embrace how Saul made her feel even if her emotions proved overwhelming. She wasn't sure what communicated to Saul that she was awake but his eyes flew open and his hand drew small circles on her back as if to calm her. The intensity of his gaze suggested he hadn't been asleep at all.

As fixed as his expression was, his smile was slow and relaxed. 'Morning, princess.'

'Morning.' She matched his light tone, even as she knew he must feel the tension tightening her muscles.

His hand moved to brush her tousled hair from off her face. His fingertips lingered on her cheek. 'Ella … this can be exactly what you want it to be.'

She thought hard. As much as she loved him, her doubts wouldn't be silenced. It was too soon to rush into anything serious or risky. They both could still have things to work through. The fact that she felt so emotional confirmed she certainly did. A platonic friendship wouldn't now be possible, they could no more suppress their chemistry than they could avoid each other, which left one other alternative.

She rested her hand on his chest and drew strength from the even rise and fall of his breathing. 'Friends … with benefits?'

For a long second his eyes turned serious and then he smiled a lopsided grin. 'That works for me.'

She couldn't help but return his smile. A lightness replaced the heaviness within her chest. 'Actually, that had better be friends with *secret* benefits.'

His low chuckle had her reaching for him. The sound of his laughter never failed to stir her senses.

'Absolutely,' he said, as he turned towards her and she entwined her arms around his neck. 'Noel's already warned me off twice.'

Whatever she was going to say fled her head as his mouth moved over hers.

Her next conscious thoughts were that the strip of light above the bedroom blind was now daylight bright and that all hell had broken loose outside Saul's window. She prised herself away from where she'd slept curled against him.

'Those guinea fowls are so coming back to you,' Saul said, his voice muffled with sleep.

This time when her drowsiness receded emotions didn't blindside her. She simply felt … happy. She laughed and planted a kiss on the smooth tanned skin of his shoulder. 'Good luck getting them out of your trees.'

She looked around and to her relief saw that her dress lay within reach on the floor. There was a huge difference between Saul catching a fleeting glimpse of her scar compared to allowing him an unobstructed view. As she went to slip from Saul's bed, his hand caught hers. His dark gaze scanned her face. 'Everything okay?'

She leaned over and let her kiss answer for her. 'I'll head home and get ready for work. See you about ten.'

When it came time for Saul to collect Duke from the vet clinic, Ella made sure she was busy. Penny never missed a thing. While it was normal for Ella to show her feelings, she wouldn't be able to hide how much Saul and Duke's reunion affected her. Even the thought of them seeing each other made her eyes mist.

She gave Saul a wave when he entered the surgery and then disappeared into the treatment room to finish her phone call. She made it back to reception just in time to see Saul leave with a tail-wagging Duke. In Saul's hands were Duke's medication and a blue-and-white folder containing Duke's aftercare notes. Even knowing that she shouldn't, she watched through the window while Duke stopped to lift his leg on the red fire hydrant. Saul's grin flashed white.

Penny came to her side. 'If that's not a sight to bring tears to your eyes, I don't know what is.'

'It never gets old seeing animals recover.' She headed for the computer behind the counter, hoping her cheeks weren't an incriminating pink. In this case it wasn't just her patient she was glad to see was in a better place today.

Penny stayed by the window as Saul held the F-truck door open for Duke to jump into the back seat. 'Saul's expression yesterday when he carried Duke just about broke my heart. It was as though he'd already lost him.'

Ella hoped her nod appeared casual as she read through a client's file. 'Have we had any blood results back yet from Mr Wright's poodle?'

Penny came to look over her shoulder at the computer screen. 'No, not yet. You know …' Ella glanced at Penny who now stared at her. 'The person who deserves Saul the most … is you.'

Ella fought to keep her expression from changing. 'Me?'

Penny arched a brow. 'No offence, but you're not getting any younger.'

Ella couldn't contain a burst of laughter. To Penny she probably did appear positively ancient. 'I'm not that long in the tooth. I've still got plenty of years ahead of me.'

Penny's stare didn't waver or her eyebrow lower. 'Maybe, but it isn't every day that a man like Saul comes along.'

Ella blinked as Penny sent her a you-know-I'm-right look before she moved away to talk into her headset as a call came in.

Penny's words replayed in her head as she drove home after seeing the last of her Saturday morning patients. As much as Penny was right, she'd made the correct and safe decision to keep things simple and lighthearted between her and Saul. She bit the inside of her cheek. Even if a persistent niggle reminded her that this was the man she loved and that she should be holding on to him with both hands. Life had already proven that it had the power to snatch away those who were precious to her.

She slowed to turn into her front gate and pressed stop on any further thoughts of Saul. In less than three hours she had a surprise party to pull together. After checking on the goats and finding Nutmeg had put her small front leg through the side handle of a food tub, she went inside to take a shower and swap her work clothes for town clothes.

Dressed in the red dress she'd worn the day she'd had her hair cut, she stilled as she caught her reflection in the wardrobe mirror. It wasn't her quick frown that had her swing away and riffle through the dresses hanging beside her but the glow she'd glimpsed in her eyes. They usually looked more brown than gold.

Bethany had already once remarked that she looked different and it hadn't been due to her haircut. She couldn't now risk the entire town seeing anything that publicised there could be something going on between her and Saul. She flicked through the dresses to the very end where tags swung off a teal-green dress. She'd wear something no one had seen before to mask anything else that could appear different.

After a quick stop in the main street to collect two clusters of white and gold helium balloons, she arrived at the old schoolhouse that now sported a museum sign out the front. Amongst the handful of cars in the car park there was no sign of Edna's Land Cruiser, even though Noel's farm Hilux was parked in the shade of a pepper tree. Bethany had conspired with Taylor to give Edna a late hairdresser appointment to ensure her mother didn't turn up to the museum opening early.

Ella parked beside Tanner's blue ute. She was just about to remove the sheet she'd used to conceal the balloons when her phone chimed. The message was from Bethany and contained multiple exclamation marks.

*Can you believe it!!! Mum's here!!!*

*No way. How?*

*She discovered Taylor had a cancellation so turned up an hour early. Taylor took as long as she could …*

*Where is she now?*

*Don't know. I'm stuck in the party room. She thinks I'm at work.*

*I'm here too. Edna will think I'm helping out … I'll text when the coast is clear.*

Intent on typing her reply to Bethany, Ella didn't realise she wasn't alone until someone tapped on her driver's side window. She jumped and looked up to see Edna staring in at her. She slipped her phone into her tote bag and made sure the large bag blocked the covered balloons from Edna's view. She could only hope a renegade balloon didn't suddenly bounce free.

She lowered the window. 'Afternoon, Edna.'

'Afternoon.' Edna's attention zeroed in on her face.

Ella kept her smile in place and stayed silent. At least if Edna was focused on her she wouldn't notice the bag of presents on the floor of her passenger seat.

'Is that a new dress?' Edna asked, expression speculative.

'It is. You're here early. Have you come to help?'

It was common knowledge that the museum and its opening was something Clive, Noel and old Will had handled on their own. In the history of Woodlea she wasn't sure there had ever been a project that Edna, her mother or her grandmother hadn't played a role in organising.

'No, I just … had some spare time.'

If Ella didn't know better she would have almost said Edna looked a little lost at having nothing to do.

'Could I ask a favour? I meant to pick up some extra milk—'

'Consider it done. Full cream, skim, lactose-free and soy?'

'Yes, please.' She only hoped that whoever was bringing the milk for the tea and coffee table hadn't already bought a fridge full. 'Thank you.'

Edna turned with an airy wave.

While Ella waited for Edna to leave in Noel's ute, she texted Bethany that they had a small window of opportunity. She then sent a blanket group text asking that if anyone was in town could they please run interference by keeping Edna talking in the grocery store.

The first reply was from Saul. Contentment filled her at both the speed of his reply as well as his message.

*Walking there now. Hope you had a good morning. Guinea fowls glad to see Duke.*

She sent a quick reply of a crying laughter emoji and at the last minute added a blowing kiss that she then deleted. Technically friends with benefits didn't involve romance or displays of affection, even if she couldn't stop smiling.

Bethany greeted her with a hug as she walked into the designated party room. Sue and Bethany had been busy. Gold swirls hung from the ceiling while gold organza runners topped crisp white tablecloths. On the far table a two-tiered birthday cake with pink flowers took pride of place. Ella arranged the white and gold balloons on either side of the cake before adding the bag of presents to the large pile assembled on the nearby table.

Bethany caught a small square box as it toppled off one side. 'I know Mum's a handful but I can't believe how many people dropped off gifts to my office and genuinely wished her a happy birthday.'

'As much as Edna terrifies us, we really would be lost without her.' Ella paused as a text came through from Saul. 'That would have to be the quickest grocery shop ever. Apparently your mother didn't want to chat and is on her way back.'

They had just enough time to put the final touches in place and for Bethany to slip out the back door when Edna's loud voice sounded in the main room. Ella went to meet her.

Once the milk was in the fridge of what had been the second classroom, and tonight would be the dining room for the museum opening, Ella made sure Edna kept busy. The plan was to surprise her before the official ribbon cutting as otherwise no one would relax. Even Clive appeared nervous, his scowl deepening every time Edna marched past the closed door of the party room. It was just like Edna to open the handle and sneak a peek at what lay inside.

To everyone's relief, the main classroom holding the museum displays soon filled as well as the school playground that was now home to a collection of restored windmills. The bare tables in the dining room became laden with food as people dropped off the salads and desserts that would accompany the barbeque.

Ella caught sight of Saul over near a display cabinet of old shearing handpieces talking to Fliss, Cressy, Denham and Hewitt.

Before she had a chance to catch Saul's eye, Noel gave her a small wave. It was the signal she'd been waiting for. Bethany had taken Mrs Knox into the party room and forbidden her to text or call Edna and spoil the surprise.

Edna appeared deep in conversation with Clive and oblivious to the crowd quietly drifting out of the room. As Noel went to join Edna, Ella moved to the closest glass cabinet, pretending to read the information plaque. She was in position to distract Edna if she went to walk into the hallway.

When Saul strode by and gave her a wink, she couldn't stop a rush of longing. Her skin remembered every slow and sensual sweep of his hands last night and her heart remembered every tender and lingering kiss.

The room had almost emptied when Edna glanced around. 'Where's everyone gone?'

Noel took her arm. 'There's going to be a demonstration of a working windmill on outside.'

Not wanting to appear obvious, Ella waited until Noel and Edna went by before following them.

When Noel and Edna reached the closed party room door, Noel stopped. 'There's something in here you might like to see first.'

He opened the door to darkness. Then the lights came on and a chorus of voices erupted in a boisterous 'happy birthday'.

Edna gasped and Ella glimpsed genuine surprise, joy and a sheen of tears before Edna placed an unsteady hand on her chest.

Bethany stood in the front of the beaming crowd, an oversized bunch of roses filling her arms. Beside her was her older brother, Rodger, who'd made it back from their property out west and who held a magnum of champagne.

For once Edna was speechless. All she could do was keep shaking her head. As Bethany hugged her mother, she gave Ella a thumbs up. Against the odds, they'd pulled off the impossible.

Ella smiled as wellwishers surged around the guest of honour.

It was one for the record books. Edna Galloway hadn't been privy to everything that had been happening in small town Woodlea.

It took all of Saul's willpower to concentrate on the conversation flowing around him while plates were emptied and beers consumed.

Over to his left Edna held court, surrounded by people wishing her a happy birthday. While across from him, after news of Duke's snake bite had dominated the conversation, Denham was now fishing for wedding plan details from Hewitt while Tanner chuckled at another Jelly Bean story from Hugh.

Saul nodded every so often. He'd shot several glances to where Ella sat with Fliss, Cressy and Neve and had missed half of both conversations. Tonight Ella was radiant. He wasn't sure if it was the colour of the blue-green dress that made her skin look flawless and brought out the honey-blonde highlights in her hair, or just that he was so hooked she could have been wearing scrubs and he wouldn't have been able to look away.

As he snuck another glance, he saw he wasn't the only one finding her irresistible. Her dress might pass the fingertip test but the silky material would have to reach the floor to completely hide the shapely length of her tanned legs. At least Joe hadn't put in an appearance. While many looks were being cast her way, no one had approached to bother her. If they did, he already knew he'd have a hard time remaining in his seat.

The reality was that he had no claim on Ella. They were worlds away from being a couple. Her tension when she'd woken in his bed that morning, the way she'd checked her scar was covered and her need to label what they had as friends with benefits all reinforced he had to tread carefully. She wasn't ready for more than what she offered.

The dreams he'd thought he'd lost, of someone to grow old with and of having a family, may now have flickered into life but he couldn't lose Ella by rushing things. It wasn't yet possible to speak the words that for the first time he knew to be true. What he'd felt for Trish didn't compare to the depths or intensity of his love for Ella.

Tanner again laughed and Saul refocused on the group around him. He made a conscious decision to not look at Ella. Any more sideways glances and their secret benefits wouldn't be so secret. He tuned in to Hewitt and Denham's conversation. Hewitt was still resisting Denham's efforts to find out what Fliss had planned for their wedding.

'As much as I'd like to say more, Fliss has all but made me sign an official wedding secrets act,' Hewitt said with a grin.

Denham's attention never left Hewitt as he finished his steak. 'Something's up. I can feel it in my bones.'

'All you feel are your bones complaining that you didn't listen to the medical advice I gave you,' Fliss said as she joined them. Hewitt moved over on the bench and they shared a smile as she sat and he put an arm around her.

Saul chuckled. He'd been on the American pro-rodeo circuit with Denham at the time he'd been running from his demons and Fliss had been trying to keep him in one piece. 'I remember those phone calls. Is it too late to say that they usually took place when Denham was already out the hospital door pretending he was still inside.'

Fliss's no-nonsense stare pinned her soon-to-be brother-in-law. 'No, it's not.'

Denham's grin turned sheepish. 'I didn't lie ... I just might have been a little economical about saying where I actually was.'

Fliss glanced at Saul. 'If you were with him, there'd have at least been one voice of reason.'

Saul grinned at the compliment. 'Thank you.'

Denham raised his eyebrows in mock outrage. 'Hang on. At least I went to hospital. The only time Saul voluntarily set foot in there was to pick me up.'

This time Saul felt the full force of Fliss's intent hazel gaze. He shifted in his seat hoping Fliss didn't hear the creak of his own bones complaining. 'I did go ... I just don't ever remember how I got there.'

Fliss glanced between the two of them. 'You two ... if either of you ever turn up in my emergency department I'm keeping you for at least a week.'

Denham and Saul didn't join in with the surrounding laughter, instead they exchanged a look that said they'd rather dance with Edna.

When the conversation moved on, Saul came to his feet. The talk about hospitals made him yearn for fresh air. The last time he'd been inside a hushed sterile corridor was when Caleb had been born. But while the memory still pained him, it didn't cause him the sadness it once had. One day he now felt he would be able to return to Wyoming to see him and Adam.

Denham also stood. They took their paper plates over to the row of recycling bins before swapping the classroom for the floodlit playground. Clusters of people were congregated around the restored windmills so they headed to a far corner where a windmill stood in a pool of light with no one else around.

Saul studied the neat circle of blades that was such an iconic image of rural life. While living in Wyoming, whenever he'd seen a windmill it had always reminded him of home.

When he felt Denham's attention on him he rubbed at his jaw. 'You haven't stared at me so much since I said I was marrying Trish.'

'Just like then I'm trying to work out what's really going on with you.'

'I didn't think there was anything going on back then, but now I have no idea where my head was at. Marrying Trish was a big mistake.'

'For the record, Trish would never have made you happy. Everything was always about her.'

'I used to make excuses … she lost her mother so young, she's never had to think about anyone else … but I ran out of reasons.' Then, after only a short pause, he told Denham what had happened between Trish and Jamie and how the baby he'd loved hadn't been his son.

Denham remained silent until the end, when he clasped Saul's shoulder. 'I can't imagine what you've been through. Cressy won't mind me telling you … we're having a girl and every time I feel her kick it makes my knees go weak. I already love her with all that I have and if anything happened to her or Cressy …'

Saul nodded as Denham cleared his throat. His own throat felt raw. 'For a couple of tough bull riders, who knew we'd be such emotional wrecks.'

'I thought Cressy was the only one whose emotions were supposed to be all over the place.' Denham stopped to frown. 'Speaking of bull riders, Jamie was always bad news. He came from old money and didn't think he had to get his hands dirty like the rest of us.'

'He has to now.'

Silence fell between them as they studied the windmill. Saul again sensed Denham staring at him before his low voice sounded. 'It was great to see you looking relaxed over dinner.'

While Denham hadn't said Ella's name, Saul knew exactly what Denham meant. He hadn't only looked relaxed, but also distracted.

'That new thing we spoke about … while it now does feel like a good thing, I'm not so sure it is for everyone involved.'

'It is a good thing, for both of you. And like any good thing it will be worth the wait.'

Before Saul could reply, a text came in on his phone. He answered Ella's message asking if he was still there. Her reply was instant and queried whether he'd like to come and see Violet. Gemma had flown home yesterday so Ella wanted to check in on her.

Two more texts and they'd arranged for Ella to message when she was leaving. He'd then meet her in the car park. The entire time he typed, Denham smirked.

When he was finished, Denham gave his back a hearty slap. 'I think my days of telling you to lighten up are over.'

Saul only shook his head as together they returned inside. Edna's birthday cake had been cut and as Ella approached to hand him and Denham a piece he made sure he didn't hold her gaze for too long. Her fingers brushed his as she passed him his plate. She then went to collect more slices to offer around.

Saul and Denham drifted over to sit with Finn, Bethany and Mac near the tea and coffee table. The conversation soon turned to the upcoming rugby season. Finn's tall tales about his rugby field exploits ensured that their laughter never faded. When Saul's phone vibrated in his pocket, he slipped it free. Ella had texted that she was leaving. He waited a few minutes before saying his goodbyes.

He hadn't made it halfway along the hallway when boots sounded behind him. He turned to see Noel.

'Still walking fast, I see,' the older man said, tone mild.

Saul slowed. 'Not fast enough for some.'

Noel's lips twitched but he didn't smile as he looked past him in the direction Ella would have taken.

'Noel … I promised Ella she'd always be safe with me.'

Noel's cool gaze assessed him. 'Did you now?'

'I did.'

'For an old bull rider with a bison farm to run you don't only walk fast you also know the right things to say.' Noel gave him a nod. 'You'd better get moving then, she'll be waiting. Tell Ella to bring you out sometime. I'd like to hear about this bison farm of yours.'

As the older man turned away, a smile warmed his eyes.

Saul continued on outside and past the school bell that had been yarn-bombed in crocheted blue squares. Blonde hair glimmered from over near the first row of cars as headlights lit up the car park. When Ella saw him she pointed in the direction of Violet's. He gave her a wave to say he understood she'd meet him there. Unlike the previous time they'd been in the car park together, tonight it wasn't at all private.

He waited in his F-truck until he was sure she'd reached her four-wheel drive before driving away. Once at Violet's he didn't have long to wait. Ella arrived and parked behind him where the glow from the streetlight dimmed.

He left the driver's seat and hadn't taken more than three strides before Ella was in his arms. He kissed her like it had been twelve days and not twelve hours since he'd held her. She kissed him back as though he'd been on her mind for every minute of those twelve hours.

When they broke apart, speaking was impossible. He rested his forehead on hers and waited for the harshness of their breathing to ease. But even when he had caught his breath, he stayed silent. Telling Ella how much he'd missed her, let alone how much he loved her, wasn't an option.

She pulled away with a smile before smoothing her hair into place. 'There's a reason why I only wore a light lipstick tonight.'

He stole another kiss that only meant she needed to run a hand over her hair for a second time. Then, fingers linked, they walked along the garden path. It was only after he'd knocked on Violet's door that she slipped her hand free and took a step away.

The door slowly swung open. 'Hello there, you two.' Violet stepped away from the door, leaning on her walking stick. 'I'll put the kettle on and you can tell me about the party and museum opening.' She turned, her eyes twinkling. 'And a tip for the future … when cars pull up outside and there's a delay until a door knock there's usually only one explanation.'

Ella's soft laugh didn't contain any embarrassment. 'I'll remember that for when I have teenagers.'

Saul didn't immediately follow as Ella walked inside. Her comment gave him hope she did see herself with someone one day.

While Violet and Ella were busy in the kitchen, he collected the latest boxes that Violet had sorted through and that needed to go to Ella's car. When she handed him the keys she gave him a quick kiss when Violet's back was turned.

Once they were all seated at the small table, Saul reassured Violet that Duke was doing well before Ella filled Violet in on Edna's surprise and what rural items were in the windmill museum. Behind her thick glasses, Violet's gaze drew dreamy when she reminisced about the open cab tractor her father used to drive.

Whenever mention was made of Libby, Violet's expression possessed a new serenity. She appeared to be making peace with the information they'd discovered and the answers, as painful as they'd been, as to why Libby had left. The questions she'd had about what had happened to her youngest child no longer seemed to overwhelm her.

Conscious of Violet becoming tired, Saul carried their empty teacups into the kitchen. He washed them before Violet could notice.

When he returned to the living room, Ella sent him a quick look. 'Violet has something to tell us.'

Violet nodded but waited until he was seated before speaking. 'It's time … to let Libby go.'

The surprise widening Ella's eyes would have to mirror his own.

Ella leaned forward to take her hand. 'Violet?'

'If Libby were still alive, she'd have come home. And if there was a child … Libby would have made sure that they too would have found their way back to us.' Violet's words emerged subdued but strong. 'Please pack up Libby's room just like you have the rest of the house.'

When Ella went to speak, it was Violet who patted her hand. 'Ambleside is your home now and you need to make it yours.'

Violet glanced at Saul and in the intensity of her gaze he saw sadness and pain, but also contentment. He nodded as he read her unspoken message. She cared for Ella just like she was her own daughter and Violet was trusting him with Ella's heart.

'If you're sure?' Ella's low question had Violet look at her again.

'I am, sweetheart. You need space for all those teenagers.'

Violet's smile and light tone appeared to reassure Ella. She nodded as she settled back in her chair. 'Next trip to town I'll pick up some more boxes.'

After they both promised to see Violet soon, he followed Ella out into the warm night.

When she turned to him, he pulled her close and kissed her temple. 'Are you okay about Violet's decision?'

'I'm just a little stunned. But if what we discovered about why Libby left has given Violet closure then that's more than we could have hoped for.'

Hand in hand, they strolled along the path. Crickets chirped from the manicured lawn kept green by bore water, while overhead the moon was now surrounded by faint pinpricks of starlight.

When they reached their parked cars, Ella looked back at Violet's door. 'I can't believe we were sprung.'

'Do you mind that Violet knows?'

He didn't realise how much Ella's response mattered until she shook her head. 'What about you?'

He too shook his head. 'Noel knows as well.'

'I thought so. When I texted you, I saw him look across to where you checked your phone.' She squeezed his hand. 'So … your place or mine?'

'Yours. There's no guinea fowls.'

He silenced her soft and husky laughter with a kiss.

# CHAPTER
# 17

This would teach her to try and beat the Saturday lunchtime peak-hour traffic.

Ella sighed as she waited for a stream of cars to pass so she could turn onto the main street from the side road that ran in front of the vet clinic. She'd finished work and for a change was out the door before Penny. At Penny's surprised look she'd mumbled something about having a busy day. The truth was she couldn't wait to get home to Saul.

Her fingers tapped on the steering wheel as the cars and utes filed past. Between the farmers' markets and kids' sport events, half of the district seemed to be in town. The hay runner trucks had also passed through. A client who'd had a puppy with a grass seed in its ear had mentioned people were lined along the roadside with signs and flags to wish the truck convoy well.

Finally there was a break in the traffic and Ella joined the queue leaving town. Scattered across the bitumen were small pieces of straw that had blown off from the hay bales heading west. Even as she watched they were swept into the air by the wind accompanying the approaching cold front that would deliver everything but rain. She hoped Saul's neighbour had their new water tank tied down.

The green streetscape soon gave way to bare and parched hills dotted with galvanised iron sheep and cattle feeders. Stock tracks ran like veins through the dust towards near-empty dams. She glanced at a mob of sheep that were almost indistinguishable against their paddock backdrop. Their coats contained so much red dust she didn't envy the shearers when it came time for shearing. If it didn't rain Woodlea would soon be on the hay convoy's itinerary.

She turned onto the road that wouldn't only take her home but also to Saul. They had a whole one and a half days together and she had nothing organised. Once the thought of having no set plans, let alone unlimited time with Saul, would have knotted her stomach. Now, while they weren't a couple, it felt right to have him in her space and for her to spend time at his place. As much as she'd maintained she'd been happy on her own, she now realised how alone she'd felt.

She drove through her front gate and ignored the insistent voice that questioned her decision to keep a safe emotional distance between them. She couldn't change the status quo even if she wanted to, even if what Saul felt for her was half as strong as what she felt for him. Their friends-with-benefits label was the only thing making her feel as though everything was under control.

She parked in the carport. Now it was the weekend, Saul and Duke would be over later and she'd be extra glad of their company. As much as it saddened her, after lunch she'd heed Violet's request and start packing up her youngest daughter's room.

Even when the room no longer held Libby's possessions, the light and cosy bedroom would always be hers. Ella just had to think of a use that would be a fitting tribute. Daniel at the police station had passed on that at the time Libby's childhood friend Fee apparently hadn't known anything about Libby planning to leave. Ella didn't know if it was foolishness, or simply stubbornness, but until she talked to this Fee and there really was no more hope, she'd continue to leave the veranda light on. So far she'd discovered three possible Sydney matches for Libby's old friend in the online telephone directory.

As Ella left the driver's seat, a gust of wind blew her hair across her face. Once in the kitchen, she sat her bag on the bench and called Saul. She'd check that he'd had lunch in case he wanted to have some with her. When his phone went to voicemail, she left a brief message. He'd be busy fixing the roof on the cement water tank that had lost half of its tin.

She placed her mobile on the bench only to pick it up again as it rang. Except it wasn't Saul calling.

'Hi, Hewitt.'

'Hi, this will just be quick. Fliss is flat out as a road train has hit a car east of town but she's worried about Violet. There's a massive dust storm coming and the hospital at Trangie is already treating people for breathing problems.'

'I'll check on her.' Violet's asthma could render her vulnerable and while she'd be well supported in Woodlea Lodge her ingrained independence might make her slow to seek help. 'I haven't heard anything about a storm, though.'

'Pictures are just appearing on the net. I'd better get the horses in. I left a message for Saul, but it might be worth you following up.'

'Will do.'

She ended the call and scrolled through her social media feed. Images posted from friends further west showed a sky-high wall of red dust rolling in billowing waves eastwards. She dialled Saul's number as she raced to the front veranda. Whatever he was doing his phone mustn't be close by. She stepped outside and her hair again blew across her face. But while the tops of trees swayed and windows rattled, below the clouds the sky appeared its usual airbrushed blue.

When Saul's number went through to voicemail again she left another message. It was unusual but not a cause for concern that she couldn't reach him. When it came to farm safety and working with his bison he wasn't one to take risks. He'd be on the ladder, with both hands busy, fixing the tank roof.

After making sure Cinnamon and Nutmeg had food and water in their shed for when they sought shelter, she returned to prepare a sandwich. Before the wind became too fierce and made it nerve-racking to drive, she'd text Violet to see if she wanted company. When the wind gusts whistled beneath the roof eaves she abandoned her lunch to reach for the phone. As she sent Violet a text, she massaged her scar. She usually avoided being out in any type of storm.

While she waited for Violet's reply she messaged Claire who was the on-call weekend vet saying she was free if she needed any help. It wasn't just humans that could have respiratory difficulties from breathing in the fine dust particles. The extreme heat had already seen an increase of breathing problems in the short-nosed dog breeds. Once the dust storm hit there would be even more of a reason for local pugs and bulldogs to be kept inside.

Her phone chimed like the church bell tower on Cressy's wedding day as a flood of messages came in. Violet answered to say that she would be fine and to not come in. She'd sit her asthma puffer within reach beside her chair. Claire's message said she'd been busy and hadn't known about the incoming storm, and Cressy's told her to stay safe as her side of town would be hit first.

She replied to each and then, coming to her feet, grabbed her bag. If she left it too much longer to hear from Saul she wouldn't have the confidence to get behind the wheel to check on him. It wasn't just the tops of the trees now bending in the wind.

As she drove through her front gate there was no doubt about what would soon arrive. Her windscreen framed the western horizon, which was now a mass of billowing red clouds. She shuddered as twigs and leaves slapped against her side windows. The light had dimmed, reducing visibility, and she leaned forward to get a better look before she turned onto the road.

A cluster of leaves bounced off the windscreen and she wrapped her clammy hands tighter around the steering wheel. A dull ache throbbed behind her scar. She wasn't in England on a narrow lane lined with hedges. She wasn't in a snowstorm where the only thing she could see were heavy, blinding white flakes. She was fine.

The black metal fence flanking Saul's entryway loomed in the fading light and the four-wheel drive rattled as she crossed the cattle grid. Saul still hadn't called, or texted, and the feeling that something could be wrong lifted the hairs on her nape. Grey flashed to her right as Duke appeared and she released a sigh to dispel her tension. Saul had to be over in the sheds. Maybe his phone was flat.

She followed Duke as he raced past the bison handling yards and the stables where Cisco and Amber were inside and protected. In the paddocks to her left bison appeared as dark, solid shapes as they waited for the dust storm to reach them. Unlike cows that tended to drift with the wind, bison turned towards a storm and walked through it.

Beyond the stables stood the concrete water tank, except there was no gator parked at its base or any sign of Saul. By now the wind gusts had the power to rock the four-wheel drive and an orange haze had replaced the waning daylight. Cockatoos screeched as they fought the wind to land on the solid cream bough of a gum tree. A flock of crested pigeons took flight and flew in the direction of the open-bay hayshed. She clenched her teeth against the need to also seek shelter and kept following Duke.

He led her to a small shed tucked away beyond the other farm improvements. With its rusted iron and irregular shape, it would have been an original farm shed. The sight of a gator out the front ushered in a rush of relief. After fixing the tank roof Saul must have gone to work on the shed, which looked as though iron was missing from a side wall. Except as she drove closer she realised that two-thirds of the wall had collapsed. The roar of the wind faded. Her heart beat in her ears. Iron and timber weren't the only things lying on the ground.

She came to an abrupt stop. Uncaring that the storm tore at her clothes and whipped tears into her eyes, she left her four-wheel drive and ran over to where Saul lay on his back. Duke now sat beside him. The toppled ladder, the phone that lay a distance away and the bloodied handprints on the corrugated iron told their own story. The unstable wall had given way in the wind. Saul must have been conscious enough to drag himself out from under the wreckage.

Her fingers found his pulse as she bent over his mouth to check his breathing. Beside her, Duke's whine thinned as it was swept away. At the strong pound of Saul's pulse and the regular undulations of his chest, she assessed him further. A gash on his hand appeared to be the main source of blood. The dark stain at the top of his left arm and the unnatural angle suggested a compound fracture and his unresponsiveness a head injury.

Keeping a hand on his chest to reassure herself that he was alive, she pulled her phone free from her shirt pocket. Between the storm and the road-train accident they could be waiting a while for an ambulance. In the meantime she had a blanket in the car to keep Saul warm and a first-aid kit. She glanced around. If she moved her four-wheel drive it would also block the main force of the storm. Once the dust hit she'd just have to improvise with a tarp to provide them with as much coverage as possible. If Duke would leave Saul, he could shelter in the four-wheel drive.

She went to dial triple zero when Saul's hand stilled her fingers. Her attention flew to his face and his dark eyes met hers. Talking was impossible. The wind stole her words even as she opened her mouth, so she pressed a kiss to his forehead before pointing to his arm. His hand briefly left hers to gesture towards her four-wheel drive. She shook her head. She wasn't moving him. She lifted her phone to call an ambulance and this time his hand covered her phone. The strength of his grip reassured her he was fully conscious.

Sand and a fine, stinging grit peppered her face. Saul's gaze didn't leave hers. His message was obvious. He wanted her to take him to hospital and not the ambulance. She frowned as she made a gesture of a sling. Now wasn't time for a battle of wills over how badly he was injured. To her relief his hand dropped away from her phone in a silent agreement he did need his arm stabilised.

She raced to retrieve her first-aid kit. When she returned Saul had manoeuvred himself into a sitting position. White beneath his tan, he didn't grimace or move as she applied pressure with a clean bandage and then used a sling to immobilise his arm.

He again pointed to her car and this time she nodded. He wasn't showing any further signs of injury and she needed to get him to help as well as out of the storm. She assisted him to his feet and then into the passenger seat. Moving as fast as she could, she opened the back seat door for Duke to jump inside and went to collect Saul's smashed phone.

As she slid into her seat, she dialled the hospital. After a quick call to say what had happened and that she was bringing Saul in, she glanced at him. Her mouth dried. His head was tipped back, eyes closed and his good hand lay lax against his thigh. He'd again passed out.

The storm lashed at the glass and steel sheltering them as if determined to gain entry, but she couldn't take hold of the steering wheel. Her leg burned from where long ago metal had ripped through the flesh. She was again trapped in a car. She again had a man appear lifeless beside her. Things again were beyond her control.

A wet doggy nose brushed her cheek. The touch jarred her out of the past and into the present. She shivered and forced herself to focus. 'You're right. We need to get going.'

She started the engine and swallowed down her terror at having to drive when she could barely see and sat straighter in her seat. Unlike on that narrow and icy English country lane, she knew the road well. Unlike last time, the road had two lanes and there wouldn't be a tractor coming head-on.

With every blurred landmark that passed they were that little bit closer to the hospital. But with every anxious sideways glance at Saul and every touch to his motionless arm, her emotions unravelled until there was nothing inside but a familiar hollow and numb void.

From day one she'd known she needed to stay away from him, and she hadn't. Saul made her feel more than anyone else ever had.

But with love came great highs as well as lows. With hope came intense happiness and also fear. She'd never felt such disarray or vulnerability. She couldn't take away Saul's pain, let alone make his eyes open.

She needed certainty. She needed to feel empowered. It was the only way she'd survived the loss of her brother and the disintegration of her family. The only way she'd physically healed and made a new life for herself after leaving England. The only way she knew how to cope.

Throat tight with unshed tears, she glanced at Saul who still hadn't regained consciousness. Love wasn't enough. A friends-with-benefits label wouldn't protect her. The only thing that would was being alone.

Saul knew he was in hospital. There was no mistaking the sterile smell, the muted sounds and the sense of confinement. Tape was strapped to his hand, which meant he had a drip. He must have had surgery again.

His eyelids refused to lift. He just didn't know what hospital, what town or what lapse in judgement he'd made this time to be thrown from a bull. His head pounded as though it would implode. His left arm felt leaden and there were other aching parts of his body that reminded him he wasn't getting any younger.

A memory of wide brown eyes and a beautiful but pale face had his eyelids almost open. Snippets of a conversation returned. In a moment of awareness he'd told the solemn female doctor that he wasn't staying a week in her emergency department. He also thought he'd been in an ambulance.

'Saul.'

A man's voice said his name and he forced his eyelids to lift. Denham was with him and would get him out of there. He dreaded the time when they'd both come off second best against a rodeo bull and neither would be in a state to get the other home.

Denham touched his hand and he fought to think clearly through the confusion and disorientation dulling his brain.

'Welcome back.'

Saul went to nod and then spoke instead. 'Thanks.'

His voice was a harsh croak. Memories crashed over him. He knew exactly where he was and what had happened. The shed wall had given way when he'd been securing a piece of tin. He'd managed to get the heavy weight off him but couldn't make it over to where his phone had fallen. What he didn't know was why he felt an acute sense of uneasiness that far outweighed any reaction he'd had to any other anaesthetic. The image of Ella's face again appeared. She hadn't only looked worried; there'd been a bleakness in her gaze he hadn't seen before.

He went to say her name.

Denham spoke quietly. 'There's been a dust storm ... Ella's in Woodlea helping. We're in Dubbo Hospital because your arm needed a plate.'

'How long?'

'You'll have to stay here tonight but Fliss's working on getting you back to Woodlea so you can have your IV antibiotics there.'

He frowned.

'I'm sorry, mate. If I could I'd break you out but Fliss made me promise I wouldn't. She said you'd also need a couple of days in Woodlea Hospital. Duke's with Ella and Tanner's feeding those bison of yours, which all weathered the storm fine. I also spoke to Nathan and he said he'd call tomorrow.'

Saul closed his eyes as lethargy dragged at him. He vaguely remembered wind tugging at his clothes and the scent of blood and dust. When his thoughts formed coherent sentences he'd use Denham's phone to call Ella. He had no idea where his was.

When he resurfaced the lights were dim and a nurse was checking on him. Denham was asleep in a nearby chair. The rattle of a food trolley and the aroma of coffee were the next things he registered. This time when he opened his eyes a mental fog no longer filled his head. Natural light brightened the room and from over in the chair Denham drank from a takeaway mug.

'Morning,' Denham said, his greeting cheerful despite his glazed gaze.

Saul swallowed past his dry throat. 'Morning. Sorry you had to do another all-nighter.'

'That makes us even. I still owed you one.' He rolled his shoulders. 'Besides, it's getting me ready for when baby Rigby arrives. Babies can't be delivered in Woodlea, so even though Cressy has booked a Dubbo apartment, I'm sure I'll be spending a night or two in a chair just like this one.'

'I'm looking forward to meeting baby Rigby.'

'Cressy has already bought the cutest little pair of cowgirl boots.'

Saul glanced at Denham's phone that lay with his wallet beside his chair.

Denham bent down to reach for his mobile. 'Before you call Ella, you should know Fliss said she looked quite shaken when she brought you in. Cressy's also worried about her.'

The memory of Ella's ashen face and haunted expression returned. He too was concerned. 'I'll keep it brief.'

Denham pressed some buttons before handing him the phone. 'She's probably not had much sleep. Stock have run through fences and she's posted a list on social media of lost and found animals so she'd have a few strays at the clinic.'

Saul touched the screen to call.

The phone rang and just when he thought she wouldn't pick up, her voice answered. 'Hey, Denham.'

She sounded exhausted but the lacklustre edge to her voice was what troubled him the most. 'Hi, it's me.'

He didn't imagine her sharp intake of breath. 'Saul … you're awake.'

'Yes, and ready to come home.'

Her brief laugh emerged as hollow. 'I bet you are. Fliss said you should be back here by mid-afternoon.'

'Ella … thank you.'

She didn't immediately reply. 'Duke was the one who led me to you. It might also be an idea while Denham's in Dubbo that he pick you up a new phone. Your other one's in pieces.'

Saul didn't miss the practical way in which she spoke. Her emotions were tightly locked down. He glanced at Denham who watched him, face serious. 'I'm sure Denham would love to go shopping for me.'

'I'm sure he will too.'

Her tone was devoid of amusement and caution had slowed her reply. His grip on the phone tightened. Her wariness had returned.

He cleared his throat. 'Duke okay?'

'He's missing you but otherwise fine.'

He silenced the words he wanted to say. He needed to end the call before he caused her any more stress and before she heard in his voice that of all his pain it was his heart that hurt the most.

'Hope your day isn't too out of control and you can catch up on some sleep.'

'Thanks. You too.'

He lowered the phone and stared at the screen. There'd been no mention of coming to see him in hospital when he returned to Woodlea.

Denham shook his head. 'Don't even think about it.'

Saul held his stare.

Denham sighed. 'Maybe … before I drop you at the hospital we could swing by the vet clinic on the off-chance Ella's there. It is Sunday you know, and Fliss will smell a rat if we're late.'

The trolley clattered outside his door as Saul's breakfast arrived. He handed Denham his phone. 'We'll just have to leave earlier.'

Despite his desperate need to see Ella and to leave Dubbo Hospital, it wasn't until after lunch that he was cleared to go. Denham not only had time to show him the photos of Hewitt's irrigation pivot that had flipped over in the storm and buy Saul a new phone and clean clothes, he'd also completed two jobs for Cressy.

'Okay?' Denham asked as he clipped in Saul's seatbelt.

Even though he was supposed to have travelled to the Woodlea Hospital in a patient transport vehicle, Fliss had pulled strings so Denham could take him. Weak and frustrated, he managed a nod. On the short walk through the car park he'd savoured the fresh air that washed over his face and the warmth of the sun on his shoulders. Soon he'd be back in hospital with the PICC line in his good arm hooked up to intravenous antibiotics and yet more people intruding into his personal space.

He hadn't realised he'd sighed until Denham's voice said quietly, 'Hang in there, mate.'

For most of the drive he slept. But as yarn-bombed windmills signalled they were nearing Woodlea he forced himself to stay awake. He had to be clear-headed if Ella was at the vet surgery. He'd use the excuse of needing his sim card from his damaged phone to see her. Until they met face to face he wouldn't have a chance of finding out what was going on between them.

Denham glanced at him as they entered the town limits. 'You sure you're right to do this?'

He ignored the hammering in his head and the throbbing in his arm. 'I am.'

Denham stopped in front of the vet clinic. The closed sign on the front door was to be expected but Saul had been hoping to see lights on inside. Denham drove around to the back. There were no cars parked near the stables, not even the vet ute.

'Sorry, mate,' Denham said as they returned to the main street.

Saul was saved a reply as Denham's phone rang. He answered using the buttons on the dashboard.

Fliss's voice sounded. 'Hi, guys, just checking in to see how far away you are?'

Denham swapped a look with Saul before he answered. 'Not far.'

'Great. Just in case you were thinking of making a detour, Ella's dropped Saul's old phone here.'

'Detour?' Denham said with a laugh. 'I don't know what you're talking about.'

'I'm sure you don't. See you soon.' She paused. 'You also might want to check your rear-view mirror.' She ended the call.

Saul made no effort to check the side mirror.

Denham groaned. 'Just as well you can't turn around. Edna's cheery wave isn't always something you want to see.'

For once Edna was the least of his concerns. He closed his eyes, bracing himself for when he arrived at the hospital. Fliss would be all business and he wouldn't be able to get away with saying that he was fine and right to go home.

He'd been injured enough times to know the drill. His head injury meant he needed to take it easy for at least the next two weeks while his broken arm could take eight weeks to heal. Denham might know of a young local keen on farming who could help out for the next month or two. With there still being no rain he wouldn't be putting in any winter oats.

As Denham parked outside the red brick hospital building, Saul paid no attention to the panoramic view. He'd be counting down the hours until he was back amongst the rolling golden landscape with Duke and his bison and not looking at it from behind glass. Pain that had nothing to do with his head or arm tightened his chest. Up until yesterday Ella would have been at the top of that list. Now the feeling grew that he had no right to include her.

Senses dulled, and sleep tugging at his eyelids, he answered all of Fliss's questions with no more than a one-word answer before lying back in his hospital bed to let his IV antibiotics do their work.

He wasn't sure how long he'd slept when an excited child's voice questioned outside his doorway, 'Is it this one?'

He came fully awake as Rosie burst into his room.

Her brilliant smile didn't waver when she saw him hooked up to a drip. She'd spent so long in such a world that it didn't bother her. She stopped to turn and wave to someone beyond the door. 'Come on, Dad. Hurry up.'

Not waiting for Nathan, she sped over to the bed and, careful not to bump Saul, stood on tiptoes and kissed his cheek. 'Surprise, Uncle Saully.'

He was glad he had an excuse for not sounding normal. Even if he had been fit and healthy, the love in Rosie's large blue eyes would have still hit him right in the chest. 'Hello, Rosie Posie. This is a surprise.'

His brother walked through the doorway, his pace slow as a grey orthopaedic boot made movement cumbersome. Behind Nathan, Hewitt gave him a wave before leaving to allow Saul to spend time with his family. Hewitt would have made the trek to Dubbo to collect Nathan and Rosie from the airport.

'A great useless pair we are.' Nathan's smile turned into a grimace as he lowered himself into the nearest chair. 'Mum would have read us the riot act for not taking more care.'

Saul shifted his legs so Rosie could climb up onto the bed. She carefully tucked herself against his good side. Her dark hair tickled his chin and smelt of vanilla.

Nathan lifted his phone to snap a picture of the two of them. 'Amy sends her love.'

'Thanks.'

Rosie remained silent while she examined his padded and bandaged arm. 'Do you really have screws in there?'

'I do.' He glanced at Nathan. 'My spare key's in the tackle box in the garage and there's plenty of food in the fridge and freezer.'

'Thanks. We're having dinner at Fliss's tonight and then are on the late flight home tomorrow.'

Rosie's animated chatter and endless questions cocooned him while Nathan swapped the contents of his old phone to his new one. All too soon a dinner tray arrived and it was time for Rosie and Nathan to leave.

Rosie patted his good hand. 'I'll bring my tablet tomorrow and we can watch that snowman movie. I don't want you to get bored.'

'I'd like that.'

'When can I see Ella and Duke?'

'I'll text her.'

Rosie's smile shone sunflower bright as she again kissed his cheek. 'Love you, Uncle Saully.'

'Love you too, Rosie Posie.'

Nathan gave him a smile and a nod before he followed Rosie out the door. The small hospital room suddenly felt too large and empty without Rosie's bubbly presence.

Taking his time to type using one hand, he messaged Ella.

*Thanks for the phone. New one is up and running. Nathan and Rosie are staying at mine. She'd love to meet you and Duke.*

He didn't have to wait long for a reply. Instead of the usual simple chime of his old phone, Rosie had chosen a dramatic ringtone.

*Of course, I'll pop over. How are you feeling?*

*I'll be better when I'm out of here.*

He didn't add that he'd also be better when he saw her.

This time it took several minutes for her response, which consisted of a smiling emoji and a single word: *Night*.

His earlier unrest returned, followed by a deep-seated dread. He stared at the drip attached to his arm and resisted the urge to flick back the bed covers, disconnect himself and walk through the door.

He'd lost more than consciousness when the shed wall collapsed on him. The certainty grew that he'd also lost the woman he loved.

# CHAPTER
## 18

'It's a new day.' Ella repeated the affirmation she said every morning when she woke.

Except today it failed to lift her spirits or usher in a sense of peace. She wasn't just numb, she was broken. It had been three days since she'd found Saul lying on the ground as though dead. The wonder of being with him had given way to a loss so consuming she'd taken time off work.

She closed her eyes and made no move to leave her bed. She stretched her hand to her side to feel the empty space beside her. The chill of cold cotton had her retract her hand.

Fliss had let her know that Saul was leaving hospital yesterday afternoon. So she'd left another carrot cake and a lasagne with Rosie and Nathan, who also had Duke with them so he would be there to welcome Saul home.

Now he was out of hospital she couldn't avoid him. Over the past few days, as well as being incapable of seeing him, she'd tried to keep things uncomplicated between them. He needed to focus on getting better. As for how she would explain why she couldn't be with him, even as a friend with benefits, she had no idea what she'd say. She only hoped that by this afternoon she'd have a clear path forward. She'd given herself until then to formulate a plan as Saul would have to know something had changed between them.

She opened her eyes and headed for the shower. As for finding a way to carve out her own space to learn how to live without him, she also had a plan. The strategy she'd adopted when he'd first arrived to simply stay away was no longer tenable. She'd rarely taken holidays and now that the loose ends involving Charles were neatly tied off, she felt able to return to England.

Taylor wouldn't hesitate to come with her to see her Irish boyfriend. She just hadn't spoken to her about it yet. Her emotions remained too volatile. She wouldn't be able to justify her last-minute decision to take a holiday without Taylor sensing something was amiss let alone not dissolving into tears. As for what she'd tell Fliss and Cressy …

Ella pulled on short black leggings and an old Sydney University T-shirt before heading to the kitchen. Another thing she couldn't do was pack up Libby's room. It reminded her too much of putting away her brother's belongings. She hadn't had a chance to call the Sydney numbers to see if one of the three Fees was Libby's childhood friend. Perhaps by the end of the week she'd be in a better place to do both.

The sound of a car driving on the gravel driveway had her stiffen until logic told her that Saul wouldn't be capable of getting behind the wheel yet. Heart aching, she walked through the silent cottage.

If Duke had been there he would have barked to let her know she had a visitor and already have raced to the back door.

As she opened the screen door, Cressy greeted her with a cheery smile. 'I hope you haven't eaten breakfast yet.'

'No, not yet.'

'Wonderful. I went a little overboard cooking bacon and egg muffins and was coming to town so thought you might like some.'

The aroma of bacon and eggs reminded her how many meals she'd forgotten to eat over the past few days.

She led the way into the kitchen that she'd stayed up late giving another spring clean. She made them both a cup of tea before they sat at the small table. Cressy had wrapped the basket of muffins in a blue-and-white striped tea towel and when she placed a muffin on Ella's plate, it was still oven warm. At the rumble in Ella's stomach they both laughed.

While they ate their muffin, Cressy went through what changes she'd made to her nursery plans. She'd now decided on an animal theme and had found prints of a local artist that would be perfect. She showed Ella the designs of a foal, calf, lamb and duckling that she had on her phone.

After she returned her phone to her handbag, she gave Ella one of her no-nonsense looks. 'Ella … we're all worried about you.'

'I'm … fine.' She chewed slowly, stalling for more time to allow the swell of emotion to subside. 'I had a busy weekend.'

'You did but that's not why you've lost weight, haven't slept and have that look of fragility you had when you arrived.' Cressy paused. 'As for you taking time off work …'

Ella remained silent as she assembled her words. Cressy needed to know why she'd been struggling since her wedding and why she now appeared such a wreck. All her friends did. She couldn't let her past control her anymore even if her future felt so uncertain.

She let out a deep breath and wrapped her hands around the warmth of her mug. 'Seeing Saul lying there … I've lost people I've cared about before.'

'Oh, Ella.' Cressy touched her arm.

As Ella filled Cressy in on the gaps in her life, tears welled in her friend's eyes.

'I had no idea you had a brother. I thought you were an only child.'

Her own eyes teary, she went to collect her phone from next to the microwave. She opened a folder that contained much-loved images.

Cressy scrolled through the photographs. 'Aiden looked so much like you and you both take after your mum.' She held up a photo of Aiden dressed in skydiving gear. 'He was a bit of a thrillseeker, I think.'

The picture was one of Ella's favourites. 'He was my complete opposite. He thrived on unpredictability and adrenaline. His favourite saying was "just go for it".'

'Sounds like Fliss and me.' When Cressy came to the end of the photos, she handed the phone back to Ella with a wry grin. 'I'm not going to ask to see any of Charles.'

'Just as well, because I don't have any. I deleted them as they reminded me of the perfect man I thought I'd lost. Now they'd have been deleted because they'd have shown me what a young fool I'd been.'

'I'm glad things didn't work out as then you never would have come to Woodlea. Speaking of perfect men … you and Saul only had eyes for each other the night of Edna's party.'

Ella tried and failed to stop herself from tensing. 'You know, I actually convinced myself no one would notice and that we could keep things a secret.'

'That's an all too familiar blissful bubble, but when reality intrudes, it doesn't have to burst.'

Ella swallowed past the emotion lodged in her throat. 'It was a bubble I shouldn't have been in.'

'Why? Didn't you want to be in there?'

'I did and still do … more than anything I've ever wanted … but it's just not an easy place to be.' As her voice cracked, she took a sip of tea.

'Ella, you deserve to be happy and so does Saul. What you have is real. That's all there is to it, no matter what that clever brain of yours keeps saying.'

Ella didn't reply, just stared at a blemish in the wood of the table.

Cressy rubbed her arm. 'You're sleep deprived, in shock and need time to process things. You've done the right thing taking time off. What are you doing today?'

This was a question Ella could answer. 'Reading and taking Cinnamon and Nutmeg to the river before it gets too hot.'

'Perfect. If you want some company later, I'll be doing bookwork and needing a distraction.'

Ella gave her a brief smile. She knew how much Cressy hated being inside and not out in the paddocks that she loved. 'I will. Thank you.'

They each ate another muffin as talk turned to the aftermath of the storm.

When they both stood, Cressy gave her a hug. 'Everything will fall into place. I mightn't know when it will rain but I do know you and Saul belong together.'

Even though Ella nodded, after she'd walked Cressy out and the driveway dust had settled behind her silver ute, she let her pretence slip. There was no way forward with Saul that didn't require risk.

And as much as she wished she could handle such uncertainty, the truth was she simply couldn't.

Once inside she filled a water bottle before fitting her beach towel into a small backpack. With her Woodlea vet cap pulled low, she headed out to open the gate to Cinnamon and Nutmeg's paddock.

With Cinnamon ambling beside her, and Nutmeg jumping off anything above knee-height, they made their way along the track to the river. Despite the fresh blue of the sky and the serenity around her, the sun failed to thaw the chill inside and the warble of a magpie didn't make her smile like it usually did. She kept her eyes on the path in front of her and away from the nearby boundary fence. She needed to clear her thoughts so she could finally think of what to say to Saul when she went to see him that afternoon. This would be one time when it would be essential to have a plan.

At their usual place by the river, where the bank gently sloped to the shallows, Ella spread out her towel in a patch of cool shade. She lay on her stomach. Cinnamon and Nutmeg grazed close by. Exhaustion caused her eyelids to grow heavy. She fought to keep her thoughts clear. But between the gentle rush of running water and the lilting notes of birdsong, her eyes closed and she rested her head on her arm.

Her respite was short-lived. Nutmeg bleated her strangled cry before a wriggling mass of soft Australian shepherd burrowed in beside her, trying to lick her face.

Despite driving the gator at low speed and avoiding as much of the rough patches of road as possible, the trip to the river seemed to shake every bone Saul had. His arm ached and the bruises along his hip that were now more yellow than blue weren't impressed he'd left the house. Fliss might have specified no driving but he'd made the executive decision that steering a gator didn't count.

Duke had disappeared over the riverbank and there was no point whistling him back. He hadn't come to surprise Ella or to catch her off guard. Duke would have found her and his presence would give her the heads-up he'd soon be along too.

Since Duke's snake bite he and Ella had barely been apart. Now he hadn't seen her for four days. To anybody else the cake and dinner she'd delivered, along with her note saying she hoped he was feeling better, would have appeared warm and caring. It's just that after the intimacy and closeness they'd shared over the past week, it was a no-brainer something was seriously wrong.

Nathan hadn't said anything but he'd given him a long look when he'd mentioned meeting Ella. As for Rosie, she was already besotted with her. She'd said Ella was as beautiful as a real-life princess and that he should get her to help them build the hay bale castle he'd promised to make the next time she visited. Saul only hoped his expression hadn't been as desolate as how he'd felt on the inside.

He'd gone to call Ella twice last night but hadn't pressed the dial button. He needed to be patient. He'd be a fool to rush in when seeing her in person was the only way to talk through whatever had caused her to pull away. When he'd caught a glimpse of two brown-and-white goats walking along the boundary fence in the direction of the river, resolve filled him. He wasn't waiting any longer to go after the woman he loved, even if Dr Fliss took him to task for driving.

The gator engine chugged as it negotiated the rise over which Duke had disappeared. Ella had walked with the goats to the same spot where he'd seen her while in the tinny with Tanner. As the slope below came into view, he saw her come to her feet before turning to look at him. His jaw locked and tension set his shoulders like granite. She didn't wave.

He parked, then made his careful way out of his seat. By the time he stood clear of the gator, Ella had reached him. She stopped a body length away. Their eyes met. He again saw the bleak despair that had caused his deep uneasiness in the hospital. Her skin was far too pale and smudges of exhaustion shadowed her face. As the silence lengthened she wrapped her arms around her chest.

He spoke before he could reach out and touch her. 'Hi.'

'Hi.'

Her reply was so quiet he barely caught it.

Duke sat between the two of them, looking from one to the other.

He swayed as he calculated how many steps were needed to make it over to the fallen tree that would give him a place to sit. His knees would just have to support him until he got there.

Ella's eyes widened before she closed the distance between them to slip an arm around his waist. Without speaking, he put his arm around her shoulders. He didn't need her help, but this might be his last chance to feel her warmth against him. As he eased himself onto the tree trunk, he had to force his arm to drop from around her.

She sat a careful distance away before facing him. Her features had settled into the expressionless mask he knew so well from the night they'd met.

Her chin lifted. 'I was planning to see you this afternoon. I still can if it would be better to talk somewhere more comfortable.'

He shook his head. Even the drilling against his temples wasn't going to stop them from having the conversation they needed to have right now. 'Here's fine.'

'Are you sure?' A fleeting smile shaped her lips. 'If you pass out and I have to call Fliss, we'll both be in trouble.'

'I'm sure.'

'Saul ... I'm so sorry I never came to see you. I couldn't.' She paused as her fingers twisted together. 'I've been trying to think of the right way to say this but I just need to come out and say it. I can't do friends with benefits. I can't do anything. I know it's a cliché ... but it's me not you.'

'I understand. Something about what happened has thrown you.'

For a long second he thought she wouldn't speak, then when she did the sheen of distress darkened her eyes. 'Seeing you on the ground and unconscious in the car ... I thought I'd lost you.'

He reached for her hand. She didn't curl her fingers around his. 'You're not going to lose me.'

She remained motionless and stared over his shoulder.

He caressed her cheek to try and bring her back to him. 'Ella, talk to me.'

'If I could, I would.'

'You can. The words are there. You don't need to think of the perfect way to say things or to plan every step. It's okay to not always be in control. It's okay to feel like the world's spinning. I've been there. The sun will still come up tomorrow.'

The gold in her eyes shimmered with unshed tears. 'You sound like my brother.'

He nodded, giving her the space for her emotions to settle. She broke eye contact and rubbed at her scar. As if suddenly conscious of what she was doing, she glanced at her hand before slowly lifting her arm.

This time when she spoke her voice sounded steady. 'My scar reminds me every day what happens when I lose control. Charles had asked me to marry him and I'd said no. I wasn't ready and yet he made me feel guilty and selfish. The weekend of our accident it was snowing and I was behind the wheel. When he said he had something important to ask me I thought he was going to propose again. Distracted and upset he hadn't listened to me the last time, I wasn't concentrating. Then, this tractor flew around the corner …'

This time when Saul took her hand, her fingers linked with his. 'It was an accident. Charles said so in his letter. What happened had nothing to do with you being out of control.'

When his words didn't ease the tension stiffening her hand, he spoke again. 'You've had more loss and uncertainty in your life than anyone should bear, but you also cope with unpredictability far better than you think. Look at the work you do. Sometimes the outcome is simply beyond anyone's control.'

When she didn't reply, he thought he still hadn't reached her. Then her grip on his hand strengthened. 'I'm scared.'

'I am too, not about what lies ahead but of not having you in my life.'

'If I lost you, I'd fall apart.'

'You can't lose me if I'm not going anywhere. I'm here to stay.' He lifted their joined hands and pressed a kiss across her knuckles. 'I love you, Ella.'

She remained still, then she touched his jaw. 'You love me?'

'More than I can say. I never truly loved Trish; if I had, I would have fought for her and Caleb instead of walking away.' He paused as his throat tightened and words thickened. 'I will always fight for you. We don't need a plan, just each other.'

His gaze held hers. Whatever she saw in his expression caused her fingers to tremble in his.

'My fears have controlled me long enough. All we do need is each other.' She stopped to smile her beautiful smile. 'I love you too, Saul, and I'm also not going anywhere.'

Incapable of words, he slid his hands into her hair and kissed her.

Breathless minutes later, they drew apart just enough so they could look deep into each other's eyes. Even then he found there was too much distance between them.

He brushed his mouth over hers. 'For the record, jet lag isn't the reason I look so dazed in the wedding photographs, and also friends with benefits doesn't cover staying over at each other's places.'

Her lips curved against his. 'You have no idea how many red heart emojis I've had to delete from my texts. Now I'm taking you home before Fliss calls to check on you.' She stole a quick kiss before pulling him to his feet. 'I've also got the whole week off so no more sneaky driving for you.'

Her arm around his waist, and his encircling her shoulders, they walked towards the gator. Except their progress was halting, not because of his injuries but because he had to keep kissing her to prove to himself that he hadn't lost her. When they finally reached the gator, Cinnamon and Nutmeg lifted their heads from where they grazed before wandering along the track that would lead them home. Splashing sounded as Duke left the river. When he drew near, he shook himself so water droplets flicked all over them.

Ella's soft laughter contained a joy that made his heart whole. He again sought her mouth. His dreams of finding someone to love and to raise a family with, dreams he'd thought were nothing but dust, had been fulfilled.

# CHAPTER
# 19

'I think my workaholic days are over,' Ella said with a smile as she settled onto Saul's lap where he sat at her kitchen table finishing his breakfast coffee. 'Who knew having time off could be so relaxing.'

The long T-shirt she'd worn as a nightshirt rode up high on her right thigh but she made no move to tug the hem lower to cover her scar. The days of hiding herself were over.

Saul wrapped his good arm around her. 'Speak for yourself about having time off. I've got a full day ahead.'

Ella ran her fingers along the stubbled line of his jaw. 'Since when? Fliss hasn't given you the all-clear?'

'Since Denham heard Edna say she'd be dropping round today.'

Ella masked a smile. 'I thought you were fine with Edna?'

'I am when I know I can make a quick getaway.' He frowned at the sling securing his arm. 'I can't quite move as fast as I used to.'

'Don't forget we're visiting Violet so that will at least have your morning covered.' Every day they'd talked about going to Woodlea but so far they hadn't left Ella's cottage. Content with their own company, they'd made up for the time apart when Saul had been in hospital.

She dropped a kiss on the top of his head as she came to her feet. 'This afternoon then I'm sure I can think of something to keep you busy.'

His grin made her wish that they could have another day to themselves but Gemma had driven ten hours with her father and had asked that Saul, Ella and Fliss meet them at Violet's mid-morning. Ella bent to pat Duke who'd claimed the spot beneath the air-conditioning before heading off to finish packing another box from Annette's room. So far she'd phoned one of the Sydney numbers for Libby's friend Fee and it hadn't been her. She'd call the final two possibilities when back from Violet's later on today.

The pipes in the old cottage creaked as Saul took a shower. Ella smiled as she sorted through the bottom drawer in Annette's cupboard. Saul had walked through the doorway at Cressy's wedding and her world had never been the same. But just like Saul had said, every day the sun came up and every day she opened her eyes to see him beside her.

She hoped Aiden would be proud. She'd thrown her fears into the wind and just like he'd always encouraged, she'd gone for it. As difficult as it had been to take that final step into the unknown, she finally had. With Saul she now knew without a doubt she'd be safe. She no longer needed a plan, or to be in control, to feel comfortable or at peace.

She'd also taken two smaller steps and called her parents to tell them about Saul. Since then her mother had rung twice, once on her tablet so she could chat to Saul face to face, and her father had invited the two of them for a weekend in Adelaide.

When the cardboard box at her feet was full, she closed the lid and gazed around Annette's empty room. Even though Gemma hadn't said anything, since Simon was making the long trip with her Ella guessed they'd made the decision to tell Violet who Gemma's real father was. She also suspected Fliss was invited, not only because she was involved in looking for Libby, but if the news about who Gemma's real father was upset Violet then medical help would be at hand.

Bare feet sounded on the hallway floorboards before Saul came up behind her smelling of fresh soap and sundried cotton. He brushed back the hair on her nape to kiss her neck. 'Everything okay?'

'I hope so.' She turned to slip her arms around his waist. 'I'm worried about Gemma and Simon's visit.'

He nodded. 'My creaky old bull-rider bones tell me it's either going to rain or today's going to be difficult for Violet. If it is, she's surrounded by people who love her and will help her through.'

Violet wasn't the only one surrounded and supported by love. She leaned into Saul's warmth and strength. She still couldn't believe he was part of her life. A thorough kiss made her forget all about the time until his good arm lowered from around her.

'You'd better get dressed or we'll be late,' he said, voice husky.

She snuck a final kiss before she moved away. While she still liked to be on time, being late didn't fill her with the same dread it used to.

They arrived at Violet's just as Fliss left her four-wheel drive. She gave them a wave as she walked over to open Saul's passenger side door.

'How's my model patient?' she said, looking into the F-truck with a smile.

Ella lifted a brow. 'Are we talking about the same patient I've been trying to keep still for the past two days?'

'Of course. Saul was so well behaved in hospital that I wish all my patients were like him.'

Saul grinned. 'Make sure you tell that to Denham.'

'I will.'

Ella shook her head as she left the F-truck to collect the chocolate slice she'd brought for morning tea from off the back seat. Before they'd left Saul had been sitting in the driver's seat determined to drive.

As they walked along the path to Violet's front door, Fliss tucked her arm in Ella's and said quietly, 'I'm so happy for you. Cressy and Denham's wedding wasn't just a day of new beginnings for them. But please … keep Saul out of my emergency department. Having him there with no shirt on was far too disruptive.'

Ella was still smiling when Violet opened the door.

'Hello, there.' Violet looked between them. Today her cheeks had a tint of colour and her gaze was clear behind her thick glasses. 'Saul, what am I going to do with you?' She focused on his broken arm. 'You scared me half to death.'

Saul's grin turned sheepish. 'Sorry.'

She beckoned them to come inside. 'I'll put the kettle on.'

After Ella arranged the chocolate slice on a plate and placed it on the table, she sat between Saul and Fliss on the lounge. Violet had already shooed the two of them out of the kitchen.

A knock sounded. Violet's smile softened her face, making the years melt away. She shuffled over to open the door.

Gemma and Simon entered. Ella could now see where Gemma had inherited her height from. As well as being tall, her biological father had a kind face, blue eyes and salt-and-pepper hair. But otherwise Gemma very much resembled her mother.

When introductions had been made and hugs exchanged, everyone settled around the small living room. Gemma sat with her father at the table with Violet. While Violet poured everyone's tea, Ella offered around the chocolate slice. Gemma's serious gaze met hers and Ella gave a nod at the unspoken message this wasn't just a social call.

Ella returned to her seat. Gemma glanced at the clock on the wall before reaching across the table to take Violet's hand. 'Oma, Dad and I have something to tell you.'

Simon cleared his throat. The concern tensing his mouth reassured Ella that he was a man who cared deeply about the impact of what he was about to say. 'Violet ... I don't want you to think any less of Annette ... but there's something you should know. Unlike Jeb I never had the confidence to act on my feelings for Annette until they were on a break ...'

Violet's brow furrowed. 'Break?'

Gemma replied. 'Yes, it was around Libby's sixteenth birthday. Mum had had enough of Jeb's drinking and partying.'

Simon's attention never left Violet. 'We were only together for one night and I thought I made sure there wouldn't be any consequences.'

Violet's hand went to her chest and her breathing quickened. 'Gemma?'

Both Gemma and Simon nodded. Fliss went into the kitchen and returned with Violet's asthma puffer, which she placed near her.

Violet's hand lowered but she didn't reach for her inhaler. Instead her fingers grasped Simon's arm. 'You're Gemma's real father?'

'I am.'

'You have no idea how happy that makes me.'

Gemma blinked. 'You're not upset?'

Violet patted Simon's arm before letting him go. 'I'm just relieved Annette had been coming to her senses where Jeb was concerned. Lloyd and I always liked you. Are you sure?'

'There's no doubt,' Gemma answered.

Ella studied Gemma's face. They'd revealed the truth to Violet but there remained an underlying tension that kept Gemma sitting on the edge of her seat.

Gemma briefly checked her phone before sharing a look with her father. She took hold of Violet's hand again. 'Oma, there's more.'

'More?'

Gemma took a moment to answer. 'Yes. After we realised Aunt Libby may have had a child, I put my DNA on a larger database. Three days ago I received an email about a match.'

Ella heard Fliss's sharp intake of breath but she didn't dare glance at her. She couldn't look away from the shock, and then the hope, that swept across Violet's face.

The solemn cast of Gemma's expression didn't change. 'Oma, we found Libby but she isn't who she used to be.'

Violet's trembling hand reached for her puffer. Fliss moved to sit in the empty chair beside her.

Violet's mouth moved but no sound emerged. She tried again. 'She's alive?'

Still Gemma didn't smile. 'She is. But there was an accident and she suffered a brain injury.' Gemma came to her feet. 'It also isn't my story to tell. It's her daughter's.'

Gemma walked to open the door.

Simon's quiet voice sounded as shock sabotaged everyone's words. 'Her name's Thea and she's been searching for you for years.'

Ella couldn't remember breathing. All she knew was that as a figure stepped inside she could have sworn her heart stopped. Dressed in a simple white sundress, Thea was petite and shared Jeb's symmetrical features. But the shade of her long brown hair and her heart-shaped face were an exact replica of Libby's.

Thea gave everyone an uncertain smile but when her gaze found Violet her nerves appeared to ease. She went straight towards the chair Gemma had left. When Violet moved her shaking hand towards Thea, she clasped it within both of hers. Neither spoke.

Ella wiped the corner of her eyes and leaned against Saul as he put his arm around her. He kissed her temple as if understanding it was as though she were again hearing the news that Aiden had been found.

Fliss returned to the lounge to allow Gemma to sit next to her grandmother.

Violet broke the silence, her words faint. 'You look so much like my Libby.'

'I do … except the mum I know is called Lilibet.'

Violet's lips trembled. 'That's what I called her when she was little.'

The two women smiled at each other.

'I'm not sure how to begin,' Thea said, glancing around at everyone. 'It's all a bit overwhelming.'

Violet squeezed her hand. 'Just start where you're comfortable, dear.'

Thea glanced at Gemma, who gave her a smile, before she again focused on Violet. 'Gemma and I should be about the same age but I was born early so am a month older.'

Fliss caught Ella's eye. Between Libby using a different name and Thea not being a full-term baby, it was no wonder they couldn't find any birth record. Both looked back at Thea as she continued to speak.

'I grew up on an orchard three hours south of here. To help pick their fruit my grandparents employed backpackers as well as casual workers. It was apple season and one day my mother turned up. She'd walked from town. It soon became obvious she was a runaway and also pregnant. My grandparents never had children and they took her in with the intention of keeping her safe and helping her return to her family. But I turned out to be a high-risk pregnancy, so Mum wasn't well, and then I arrived before anyone expected.'

Sadness clouded Thea's expression. 'I was three weeks old when mum went to town. Because she didn't have a driver's licence she rode her bike everywhere. On the trip home she was hit by a car.' Thea paused while Violet closed her eyes. 'But she was a fighter and defied the odds, even if now she isn't quite the Libby you remember. Granny and Grandpa looked after her, plus me, for as long as they could. Then Grandpa became sick and Mum had to go and live in a nursing home in town. I'm at university in Canberra but I visit her every fortnight.'

Violet's eyes didn't open, even when tears slid down her cheeks. Gemma moved to wipe them. 'Oma?'

'Libby's alive and I have a granddaughter called Thea. This is more than I could ever have hoped for.'

When Violet again opened her eyes, Thea rubbed her hand. 'I'd love to take you to see Mum. I understand if it's too much or too soon.'

Violet sat taller in her chair. 'I'm not doing anything this afternoon and neither are Gemma and Simon.' She looked over at Ella, Saul and Fliss.

Ella spoke even though her voice would be husky. 'We're not, either.'

Fliss sighed. 'As much as I'd love to come too, I'm on call.'

Violet slipped her hand from Thea's and grasped her walking stick. She pushed herself to her feet. 'Now, young lady, how do you take your tea?'

Over an early lunch travel plans were made, a bed and breakfast at Grenfell booked and cherished memories shared. Thea called her grandmother who invited Violet for dinner that night. Thea had explained her mother was always better in the morning so tomorrow after breakfast they would visit the nursing home.

Thea touched a photo of Libby riding a grey pony in the photo album open in front of her. A tan kelpie ran beside the pony. 'Mum looks so happy.'

'She was.' Sadness lingered in Violet's voice. 'I just don't know why she felt she could never tell us about you. We would have been shocked but would have supported her just like we did Annette.'

'Mum's never been able to talk to me about why she left but Granny put everything together. Mum was besotted with her older sister's boyfriend and one night when he was drunk he mistook her for her sister. Mum didn't correct him. When she realised she was pregnant, she also knew her older sister was as well. She said to Granny she couldn't bring even more shame upon her family let alone be a burden. She'd planned to find work and to have me. She just didn't know what she'd do after that, only that she wanted to finish school.' Thea looked back at the picture of a young Libby. 'She also wanted to come home.'

Ella collected the empty plates to take into the kitchen. Any more heartbreaking emotion and she'd be shedding more tears, both happy and sad. For Violet, the news that had finally brought her closure had also delivered a new granddaughter to love.

Saul followed her into the small kitchen and tugged her close. They did the washing up while Violet remained distracted.

The afternoon drive south took longer than three hours. Between stops to make sure Violet had a break and a laughter-filled stop at a coffee shop in Eugowra, they arrived at Grenfell as evening shadows dusted the main street. By now Violet's energy was flagging and Saul too appeared weary. Even though he'd slept for much of the way while Ella drove, fatigue added a grey hue to his tan.

While he rested on the four-poster bed in the historic bed and breakfast, Ella snuck out to let everyone know they'd have a quiet night in while the others went to have dinner with Thea's granny. When Ella returned Saul was already asleep.

At breakfast the next day in the quaint dining room where they enjoyed a cooked breakfast, a new peace had settled over Violet. After meeting the woman who had raised Thea and taken Libby in and cared for her as if she were her own daughter, the decades of fear that had gripped Violet appeared to have fallen away. The two women, now both on their own, had promised to see each other again soon.

When it came time to travel into Young to see Libby, Violet was the first one waiting in the hallway by the heavy wooden door.

Ella gave her a hug. 'We'll see Libby soon.'

'Thank you.' Violet looked at Saul. 'Both of you. This day would never have come without you.'

Saul bent to kiss Violet's cheek. 'Or you.'

Gemma and Simon joined them and their two-car convoy left to meet Thea in town. She was waiting for them outside the entrance of a red-brick set of buildings surrounded by neat lawns and established trees.

Ella waited with Saul to allow Violet, Gemma and Simon to walk ahead. Saul entwined his fingers with hers as they followed. After a word with Violet, Thea disappeared inside while Gemma helped Violet over to a shaded bench beside a footpath.

When Thea pushed a wheelchair through the door, everyone turned.

Ella's breath caught. Libby was easily recognisable as the fresh-faced girl that had graced the hay bale challenge banners. Her brown hair fell thick and glossy around her shoulders and her heart-shaped face possessed a peaceful repose. As they moved closer Libby's expression didn't change. Ella's hold on Saul's hand firmed. Libby's eyes were vacant.

Gemma and Simon came over to stand beside Ella and Saul so as not to overwhelm Libby. Violet slowly came to her feet as Thea wheeled Libby closer. Ella almost couldn't watch. She thought her heart would burst. The love and desperation in Violet's expression was an image that would forever stay with her.

Thea bent and touched her mother's cheek and murmured something to her. Still, she didn't react. Libby looked at Thea, at Violet and then back at her daughter. Ella pressed her lips together to silence her anguish. Thea had prepared them for the reality that Libby mightn't recognise Violet. But seeing Libby's gaze slide over Violet, without pausing, was almost her undoing. The warm weight of Saul's arm settled around her waist.

Violet remained unmoving. Her grip on her walking stick was now white-knuckled. She spoke softly, 'I've got so much to tell you, my beautiful little Lilibet.'

Libby didn't react, she just stared straight ahead. Then she slowly looked at Violet, her expression still unchanging.

Ella wasn't sure why Thea's hand flew to cover her mouth.

Then she saw why.

A single tear slid down Libby's pale cheek. Followed by another. And another.

Violet shuffled forwards to give Libby a hug. Eyes closed, and her own tears falling, Violet held her daughter like she'd never let her go.

No longer would the veranda light need to be left on.

Libby was finally home.

# EPILOGUE

What a difference a decent fall of rain made.

Ella steered Saul's F-truck around a muddy pot hole in the dirt road that would take them up the hill, through Fliss and Hewitt's farm and towards the river. Leaves glistened and dust no longer rose in choking red plumes. The scent of rain-soaked soil filtered in through the air conditioner vents. It wouldn't be long before a fresh green tinge carpeted the paddocks.

Tyre marks imprinted the dark wet earth. They weren't the first to arrive at Fliss's paddock picnic. Instead of a regular weekend barbeque Fliss had invited everyone for a low-key Sunday lunch. Even though in true Fliss style the picnic was highly organised, complete with emailed invitations.

Saul grinned across at Ella. 'Who knew that Fliss having a picnic was what it took to make it rain?'

'I know. There's more storms predicted next week.'

'Which means there'll be plenty of tractors working to put in winter crops.'

The eagerness in Saul's voice made her smile. He'd spent the morning making sure his air seeder would be right to go. His arm might still be in a sling but pain no longer stopped him from doing the bulk of what he needed to do. He'd also found a young farmhand to help out and would be keeping on once he had the green light from Fliss to drive.

Saul's clothes now filled her wardrobe. While they still divided their time between their two farmhouses, they were spending more nights at Ambleside. Within the warmth of the sandstone walls they felt truly at home. Thea had been to visit and had helped Ella to pack up Libby's room. She'd taken some items to decorate Libby's nursing home room and to keep as her own mementos.

Ella had also called the remaining two numbers and had tracked down the right Fee. Libby's childhood friend had driven from Sydney to Young to see Libby. As it turned out Fee too hadn't known anything about Libby's pregnancy so would have been another dead end.

Ella had also worked out a special use for Libby's old room. One day it would make the perfect nursery. When she'd mentioned this to Violet, her smile had been joyful and content, and when she'd talked about it with Saul the love in his eyes was another image she'd remember forever.

She cast him a quick sideways look. Instead of looking through the windscreen, he gazed at her. 'Have I told you how much I like that dress?'

She laughed, her heart full. Saul had already told her how much he liked her floral wrap dress. The trouble was it then hadn't stayed on long and was the reason why they were now running late.

Saul wore a crisp blue button-up chambray shirt with wheat-coloured chinos. His wide-brimmed hat sat on the back seat. Fliss had given the picnic a frock and fedora theme. For any males who wouldn't be caught dead wearing a fedora hat, which was basically all of them, a felt hat had been deemed as acceptable by Fliss.

Ella looked back at the road as they topped the hill, only to suddenly brake.

The warmth of Saul's hand cupped her shoulder. 'Ella?'

'What is *that*?'

Saul too stared at the small white wooden building that had appeared. 'A ... shed?'

'No way. Even Fliss couldn't have ...'

'Done what?'

Ella turned to him. 'That building wasn't there last visit, and it isn't a shed. It's a church.'

Saul gave a low whistle.

She looked at her dress. 'This isn't a frock and fedora picnic, this is a *wedding*.'

She checked her rear-view mirror and when she saw no one behind her, she scrambled through her bag for her phone. But there were no new messages. Edna's surprise party wasn't the only recent celebration to be planned in secret.

Mud splattered the underside of the F-truck as she descended the hill. Cars were parked in neat rows and she pulled alongside Tanner's blue ute. A boy raced in front of the chapel and Ella recognised Hewitt's freckle-faced nephew, Quinn. She glimpsed a tall man who had to be Hewitt's father and a well-dressed lady beside him before the couple entered the church.

Above the doorway glass glinted from small diamond-shaped panes that formed a round feature window. Beside the entrance two pedestal pots contained blooming white roses. A new tin roof shone in the sun and along the side she glimpsed three windows. Surrounding the church was a post and rail fence with fresh dirt at the base of the solid posts.

Saul shook his head. 'No wonder whenever I saw Hewitt in town he had wood in the back of his ute. They must have had the church moved here by truck and then done it up.'

'It's just so gorgeous.'

As she left the F-truck she saw a small white marquee and caterer's coolroom behind the church. A young girl with bouncing auburn curls skipped over. She wore a pretty floating cream dress that fell past her knees. In her hands she held a cream satin-lined box.

'Hi, Ella.'

Ella bent to give Hewitt's niece a hug. 'Hi, Lizzie. Is this what I think it is?'

Lizzie's smile widened. 'Uncle Hewitt and Fliss are getting married.' She held out the box. 'My job is to collect everyone's phones. Mum says Quinn's to stay out of the mud.'

Saul laughed while she smiled. Fliss was leaving nothing to chance about her surprise being spoiled. Saul placed his phone in the box and then she added her own.

'Thank you,' Lizzie said, beaming.

Then, walking very carefully, Lizzie carried their phones over to where Ella could see a table with an assortment of mobiles laid out in tidy rows.

Saul offered her his good arm and together they headed towards the church. They stepped inside and took a seat in the white chairs midway along the aisle. More white roses were draped across the pulpit and spilled from huge vases placed on either side. Their perfume drifted through the small wooden building.

Ella waved to Tanner and Neve who sat further inside with Bethany, Mac and Finn. Freya and Drew were beside them and next to them Hugh, Sibylla and young Riley. Sue sat in the row behind alongside Meredith and Phil. There was no sign of Taylor and Ella guessed she was helping Fliss get ready.

Cressy and Denham stood up near the pulpit as maid of honour and best man. A celebrant spoke quietly with Hewitt, who wore a dark suit and boots. Ella had never seen the quiet pickup rider smile so much.

When Cressy turned and saw Ella, she walked down the aisle towards them. Cressy's hair had been styled in a messy bun and a bouquet of pale roses filled her hands. Her cream high-waisted dress concealed her baby bump and the long hem swirled around a handstitched pair of cream cowgirl boots.

She gave Saul a kiss and then Ella a hug.

'You knew?' Ella asked as she returned to her seat.

'I found out *yesterday*. Needless to say, Fliss had a dress that fit me and a suit Denham for once didn't have to try on beforehand.' She rubbed her stomach as baby Rigby kicked. 'Only Taylor was in on it but even she only found out last week when Fliss asked her to keep this morning free.'

Ella gazed around the picture-perfect chapel. 'This will be a hard surprise to ever beat.'

Cressy smiled. 'It will be. The wedding really was going to be in the summer but Fliss said they couldn't wait that long. She also wanted everything in place …' Cressy again placed a hand on her stomach. 'For when her very active godchild has a naming ceremony.'

'That's so Fliss.'

The soft strains of classical music filtered into the church and Cressy returned to the front. Ella laced her fingers with Saul's before turning to see Edna and Noel take a seat a few chairs behind them. From the smugness of Edna's smile at least one person had worked out why Hewitt had made more frequent visits to the hardware store than usual.

A hush sounded as Lizzie walked down the aisle, her expression serious and eyes sparkling as she tossed white rose petals. Quinn walked beside her, a small green-and-yellow toy tractor clasped in his hand.

Then Fliss appeared. Her coffee-brown hair hung in loose and soft waves with not a trace of Taylor's trademark hairspray. An elegant, fitted strapless dress was matched with a waist-length veil. In her steady hands was a large bouquet of roses. Ella blew Fliss a kiss as she glided by. She'd never looked more stunning.

While Fliss took her place beside Hewitt, Saul turned to look at Ella, his brows raised in an unspoken question. Vision blurred, she nodded. Her plans for a return trip to England were still going ahead. Except it would be Saul, not Taylor, travelling with her and they'd be staying in honeymoon suites. They'd been talking about a small, intimate wedding and his unspoken question had been to ask if she too thought this chapel ticked all the boxes. She rested her head on his shoulder.

The freshly painted walls surrounding them wouldn't just bear witness to today's wedding and baby Rigby's winter naming ceremony. This little country church, which had been given a second lease on life, would echo with a new generation of laughter and dreams. But most of all it would celebrate everything that made small town Woodlea a town not only of windmills and yarn-bombing, but of belonging and, most of all, love.

# ACKNOWLEDGEMENTS

It's been such a joy to be back in small town Woodlea and to give Ella the happily-ever-after she deserves.

Thanks so much to HarperCollins and the ever wonderful Rachael Donovan, Julia Knapman and Annabel Adair. Your wisdom and attention to detail is very much appreciated. Many thanks also to the talented design team who created yet another fabulous cover.

Huge thanks to my lovely writing partners in crime who are always at the end of an email.

Special thanks to my children, Angus, Bryana, Adeline and Callum, who remain a constant source of inspiration. As always, thanks to Luke, my rock, for his unconditional support.

Finally, thank you to my readers. Woodlea, the tiny town of windmills and yarn-bombing, came to life because of you and I am so very grateful. Hope you enjoy Ella and Saul's story.

# Other books by

# ALISSA CALLEN

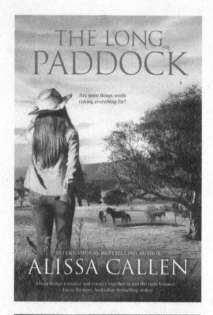

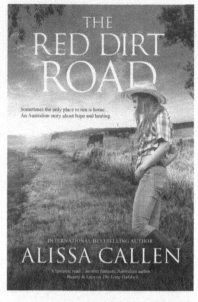

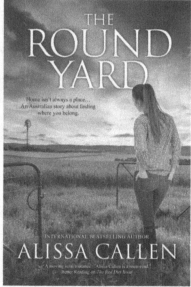

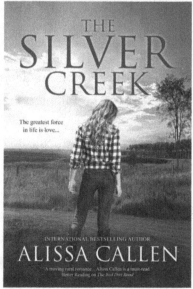